Endless Travels

Reincarnation and Memories

Paul D. Escudero

WORKBOOK PRESS LLC
187 E Warm Springs Rd,
Suite B285, Las Vegas, NV 89119, USA

Website: https://workbookpress.com/
Hotline: 1-888-818-4856
Email: admin@workbookpress.com

Ordering Information:
Quantity sales. Special discounts are available on quantity purchases by corporations, associations, and others.
For details, contact the publisher at the address above.

Library of Congress Control Number:

ISBN-13:   000-0-000000-00-0 (Paperback Version)
                000-0-000000-00-0 (Digital Version)

REV. DATE: 22/07/2022

ENDLESS TRAVELS REINCARNATION AND MEMORIES

BY PAUL D. ESCUDERO

Table of Contents

Chapter One
First Life

Harkey didn't seem to have many memories before the age of three. Perhaps that's because he spent some time in the hospital with pneumonia and that's because the primative technology of the Chevolite Sect nuns put him into scaling water as a last-ditch effort to save his life. He was being scalded, but the Chevolite Nuns had this technique down to a science through trial and error. If they left him in the tub for of extremely hot water for an additional ten seconds it would have killed him, but he was in long enough to do enough damage to the bacteria in his lungs to where his immune system had a fighting chance.

Harkey was an odd duck. He had siblings who kept his mother quite busy all the time. He was young enough to be ignored as the elder children in the family drew all the interest through his life. His most remarkable memory of his childhood and young adult years was the total lack of interest from his parents who focused on the other children. Even though it might seem to incite loneliness, there was a wonderful result. They didn't interfere with his inquisitiveness.

From early childhood looking at books with pictures of angels and demons and the artwork of the heavens gave Harkey a lot of motivation to think and explore and even though he was educated like all the other children in his community, those numerous hours of neglect by Harkey's parents provided a unique mold. His thoughts and ideas were not polluted by myth and society's indoctrinations that many were built on falsehoods by purveyors of mind control and standardization of society as the way they thought it should be. And it was all manifested on that great and seamless element of *Faith*.

In the early days of society, due to isolation and the lack of transportation, there was very little intercourse between far flung regions. There were Chevolite's in this hemisphere of the planet Ergzlt, and there were Atheists in the other hemisphere, which always created a witch's brew of conflict that seemed to last endlessly. But as the Chevolite's ventured out into space and colonized other worlds in other solar systems it was only a matter of time before they run into another civilization that created huge problems that dwarfed the local issues. Intergalactic warfare now existed at the frontiers in the early stages of conflict.

Harkey's father was spared spending time with the Chevolite's military because he was too young for the first war and too old by the time the next one began.

Harkey's grandfather wasn't quite so lucky as he found his way into the primative front lines and trenches where men savagely killed each other to gain a foot a day. The slaughter was immense, and the memories spawned the next generation of fighting as soon as everyone licked their wounds and was ready to try proving it wasn't insanity all over again.

Perhaps it was a lack of interaction between Harkey's father and his grandfather may have been why there was such little interaction between Harkey and his father.

Harkey grew up with little adult guidance. Perhaps that's what made him different. He dabbled in sports, music, history, math, drafting, and woodworking. As a teenager his homelife was so boring he got a part time job and actually made a decent income.

Then disaster struck most of his siblings grew up and moved on. Suddenly, he was a target. His parents woke up one morning and discovered they had a son who could conceivably get in trouble either by criminal activity or unprotected sex resulting in an unexpected pregnancy that might complicate his life. The sudden undue interest and control his parents attempted, made life unbearable. The logical conclusion was to find a way to leave home and get as much distance between him and his parents as possible.

Harkey's sister was the only person to wish him off, neither mother nor father showed any sort of interest their son was leaving for the rest of his life. In later years his sister recapitulated that final moment.

The transporter stopped in the town to pick up passengers. Harkey hugged his sister and stepped aboard the transporter and was essentially gone forever.

Harkcy arrived at the provincial city of Darvner. He checked into a hotel as directed and would be notified when to proceed to his appointment.

By evening it was a foregone conclusion Harkey's interview would not start until in the morning. After a movie he went back to his hotel room and relaxed and before he fell asleep received a text message on his communicator to proceed to a building at a specific address for an appointment at mid-morning.

Evening turned into morning and after a good sleep Harkey dressed, took his few meager items with him, and went to the building he was directed for his appointment. Harkey soon met people who took him through an elaborate series of tests and examinations and fed the results into a computer that classified him as ideal for a purpose they had in mind.

Harkey had no idea he was flagged as one of the golden

wave boys, meaning he had mental and physical conditions that placed him in a psychological and physical zone that fit into a mold individuals imbedded at the processing center sought for the Special Force's Directorate.

At the completion of the three days, Harkey was put in a transportation vehicle with 30 other recruits and taken to the space port.

The twin engine space craft looked utterly terrifying to the young lad, Harkey but he surmised *the handlers must know what they are doing.*

Had Harkey not wanted to get away from his over-bearing parents, its unlikely he would ever get a chance to ride on an inter-stellar transport. This was not a Graviton ship like special forces used, it was old school conventional engines with the ability to take off and land on standard runways, where atmospheric craft operated.

This journey was one of those red eye flights where they would land in the morning at their destination, on the planet Beckcen. In the next few days, Harkey would learn the irritants of his parents didn't come close to comparing to the discomfort he was now going to start experiencing. It was a colossal screwup in his lifetime. But Harkey was an honorable and respectable person who knew he signed on the dotted line, and for a few years the devil himself would own him (as the recruits named their new masters).

The first few days were mild as the paperwork and physical exams and delousing took place. Three days later when all the recruits were skinheads, they were starting to realize their recruiters misled them. It wasn't the exciting and cool journey they thought they were embarked upon.

Harkey thought he was going to be trained to fly Graviton Ships. But he now discovered the unbridled truth, he first had to achieve the insignia of special forces troops before he would ever stop foot in a Graviton craft of any sort. Another thing he would learn the hard way as his training developed, he would have to go out on special forces missions with the grunts and get the true taste of combat before he would ever be allowed to step foot in the cockpit of a Graviton Craft.

Harkey's masters figured it out a long time ago. They didn't want cowards in the cockpit. They wanted someone reliable who would not abandon the troops and take a missile up the ass if necessary to demonstrate they would answer to a higher calling because the missions these special forces endured were full of unpleasantries.

On day four, the paperwork, haircuts, physicals, and all other extraneous BS was out of the way. It was now time to envelop the training and slowly evolve into the fighting force expected out of them. It would not be a shame if they flunked out as 50% or more did. The trainers systematically cut the dead weight fast and only advanced those who they would want to be with in a fire fight.

In fact, the instructors were rotated after a period of time to give them a rest period training the recruits back into combat status. They all knew the rules and regulations. They would be united with some of their students on purpose. The idea is: *If you do not train them well you get to die with them.*

In some cases, instructors moving on to a very special elite group could cherry pick their students. These instructors knew once they got their new orders, they would face challenges unlike any of the other instructors would ever endure. Part of the price of being part of a Special Projects Force, meant you would endure the most pain and have the least number of odds in your favor.

When a student gets tagged by an instructor who was getting orders to a Space Squadron Service, he was notified approximately three months prior to the departure date. There were written and unwritten rules, especially for the Special Projects Force. Since the Space Squadron Service knew these brave men would be facing the toughest challenges in their lives, they had private meetings and were given a system to employ.

Computer records would be tampered with, and even though regular administrative personnel made the assignments these recruits would go off and do, as soon as the instructor gave his list to his special handler, the computer files would be altered and the normal administration people who had closed the books and detailed these young men to their next assignments would not know they got switched around after the fact.

With the large throughput of personnel, nobody would ever know. It was assumed based on grades and evaluations each person would transfer to his squadron trainers if they were to be pilots based on their overall scores which were highly compartmentalized. They had no way of knowing they had been duped by this clandestine feature the Spec Op boys developed over time.

Of course, regular Army and Air Corps were always suspicious of how the Spec Op boys always seemed to end up with the cream of the crop. There was never any admin forensics because the admin folks knew they were perfect, and their assignments were spot on. So, it would be impossible for any mistakes.

During those grueling days where it would be easy to quit and simply get transferred to a homogenous regular duty corps, the candidates were exercised and motivated by the best psychoanalysts on the planet. Some of these professionals knew what they were doing was immoral by enhancing their exercised and learning regiments by constant doping. Their food was laced with mental and physical enhancers.

So even though 50% quit, they did have massive amounts of preparation. The demand and risk grew high. There was no other way to feed the cannon fodder of the Special Force's Directorate. Simply put by simple statistics alone, the number of boots on the ground mattered, as long as they achieved the high standard of training.

Every single one of the instructors was battle hardened. They had been to hell and back and knew what these neophytes would be soon facing. So, they poured on the coals in the training regiment. The physical training was exhaustive, and the mental training was three shades beyond cruelty. But this was all necessary to supply fresh meat to battle weary battalions in desperate need of competent reserves.

Swimming, running, parachuting, rock climbing, rowing, and marching with 100-pound load on their backs took its toll on the non-hackers.

Harkey screwed up on a couple of minor training measures. Unfortunately for him the way it worked, the instructors had to make examples out of people and his company commander sent Harkey over to the discipline squadron where he would virtually get the shit kicked out of him for a couple weeks and it would also mean his pilot's training would be canceled and he would be a ground pounder with no future career and possible death from combat with nothing to show for it.

Harkey wasn't the least bit happy that his company commander chose him to be the "example." Strange things happened during the interview process. The company commander and the interviewers had no idea the Special Force's Directorate had already tagged Harkey hence he was under a lot more surveillance than they realized. In fact, every day a board of a half dozen spooks would get together and do a critique on their candidate. The fact he screwed up on a couple minor inspection items was trivial BS and they didn't like the way the company commander decided he would make an example out of their candidate who had already gone past the point of no return of being detailed to the spooks.

Training had four phases and the big screening process happened in phase one. The phase three instructor who was a prick and singled Harkey out with no knowledge of the level of surveillance on him would have derailed any other candidate. But the spooks all knew by the time they went into phase three training, their trajectory had already been charted.

The Company Commander was all smiles thinking that in a couple weeks when Harkey came back and rejoined the platoon and described to his buddies the ass kicking's he got, that would keep these others in line. Lead by example!

Just as one of the chief psychologists was getting ready call Harkey in for his interview that was already rubber stamped, he was going to a disciplinary company, a much more senior officer came in and sat down next to the Major who knew who this guy was. They dealt with them several times a year.

"What can I do for you?"

"Let me see Harkey's evaluation page."

The interviewer handed Harkey's evaluation sheet to the Major knowing damn well he didn't want to piss this spook off or he could be instantly sent to the ice planet for calibration and retribution.

The prefilled-out sheet the interviewer to the Major that had already signed off that Harkey was going to the punishment even before there was an interview.

"You know this is fucking bullshit. You can't do this to people. You haven't even interviewed him. How the hell can you have this already filled out?"

"His company commander had strong words in his report."

"Yea that dickhead is fucking idiot too. He doesn't have a clue what the fuck he's doing. The Major then pulled out a sheet already filled out and said, "This is your evaluation you will submit."

This is crap, you can't force this evaluation on me."

"Do you like cold planets?"

The interviewer took a deep breath and started thinking, *do I want to go to a cold planet just because some company commander is a prick and selected Harkey to be his example boy?*

The interviewer took the sheet and then walked over to a copier, but the master copy into the file and took the copy, stamped it and put it into a sealed envelope and waited for Harkey to enter the office for the interviewer. The major sat there with a stern look on his face that sent the chilling message, *if you know what is good for you, keep your hands off Harkey.*

A minute later Harkey was called into the office and handed a piece of paper and said, "Take this back and hand it to your company commander."

Harkey had no idea what was in the envelope and took it back and the company commander was quite surprised to see him come back so quickly.

"The interviewer asked me to give this to you."

The company commander had only once before seen one of these quick round trips. Fear now gripped him as he realized he just stepped on some tows by picking the wrong recruit to make an example out of.

After he opened the sealed envelope and read the contents, he quickly said, "Go out to the exercise court with the rest of the company, we'll be going on a march in a few minutes."

"Yes Sir!"

"Harkey turned around and walked out the door. When he arrived out at the exercise court where everyone was putting on their 100-pound back packs he got a lot of stares. Nobody expected Harkey back today, and rumors were floating he was already getting his ass kicked by the *black anguletes* who wore a *black uniform shoulder cord* whose main purpose in life was to calibrate screwups company commanders didn't have adaquate time to deal with.

But because of the corrupt system, a lot of company commanders schooled by their mentors were trained to pick on one of the recruits, send them to the correction *black anguletes* to kick their asses for a few weeks and when they returned and told their buddies the horrors they went through, it would have an effect on the rest of them so the lazy company commander could glide along and not have to put great efforts into molding his troops.

This particular company commander had now received his second warning. The paperwork indicated that by direct observation of evaluation staff, the company commander could not justify the adverse action and that going forward, he and the recruit would be on administrative observation to determine if the company commander was following rules and regulations properly in the training regimen. Also, his supervisor was notified, and he was scheduled for a critique. The message was clear, hands off this recruit. He had no idea what was so special about this recruit, but he also now knew he was forbidden fruit and to stay the hell away from him!

Actually, there was nothing wrong with this recruit, the company commander knew he simply has screwed up and tagged the wrong person to be used as a scapegoat to influence the others. He also knew he was in a lot more trouble than the recruit could ever imagine, and he was on shaky ground.

Harkey knew what as in store for him. He felt exhilarated he wasn't going to go through two weeks of ass kicking. More than ever he now regretted being in this situation and knew there was no way he could get out of it.

Eventually Harkey finished phase four training and went on to a technology training where he would be prepared for combat duty which he had to complete prior to acceptance to any flight school. During this technology training he purposely attempted to flunk out. Unfortunately, the instructors already knew him too well and during his disciplinary critique, the senior instructor asked, "Do you honestly think you are the first person to ever try to flunk out of here?"

Harkey sat their and remained silent, then he was given the ultimatum.

"We already know you can pass this course. The weeks you already completed are far more difficult than what you are now learning. In fact, this week is one of the easiest weeks of the course and we know you purposely chose the wrong answers to avoid the extra time you are committed for later after flight school."

Harkey knew they were on too him and sat there quietly.

"When we discover someone like you who's capable of passing intentionally fails a test like this, we have a policy. You will stay in this school for however long it takes to pass the course. If you want, we'll set you back two weeks and you will be in the class behind you. Your other choice is I will give you a new test right now to take and if you pass you will continue as if nothing happened."

Harkey knew they were on to him, there was no use in fighting the system, so he said, "I would like to take a test again."

"I figured you would. Here's the test. You got thirty minutes to finish."

Harkey filled in the multiple-choice questions and received a 95% score.

The head instructor then said, "We know what's going on in your mind now. We can't outright accuse you of dereliction of duty without causing you very serious consequences, so the only way forward is for us to evaluate you had a poor week of study and will be on academic probation for thirty days to ensure you have no further weakness in exams."

Harkey nodded his head.

"Do you understand what you have to do now?"

"Yes, I do."

"Very well return to your class, I will brief your instructor during your next break."

With a heavy heart Harkey stood up and walked out of the instructor's office and went back to the classroom and got a lot of stares by the other students.

It could be worse. Some of those who attempted to pass but didn't have the academic capability found themselves in mortal combat and perished on the battlefield with the rest of the grunts.

The instructors of this fine institution were given reports on the deaths of former students and posted them on the wall of fame at the entrance of the building and all new classes that started, were briefed on the hall of fame to act as a motivation to pass their course. The instructors also knew there were a few like Harkey willing to take their chances on the battlefields to avoid the extra time required for pilots training and subsequent service.

Time passed and Harkey graduated and was sent to a battalion where he would get his baptism in fire and experience live combat to instill into him the psychological indoctrination of direct ground support. He would soon be on the receiving end of how important those pilots supporting the missions and sometimes providing direct ground support understood the importance of their mission. They would thus be bonded through combat with the troops they would support in the future.

When troops graduated from their training which Harkey just completed, families usually showed up to show their support to their loved ones, especially knowing what the young men faced. A lot of them would be killed in this cruel war. Even so, many families didn't bother taking the effort to go and be there during this special event in the young man's life.

Harkey's parents had more important things to do. His graduation was thus private and alone, like many of them. That situation was not going to change for the rest of his life. Harkey simply flushed it out of his mind. Later Harkey was the only sibling that did not live near the family located in one central area. Since Harkey had been away from home for over a year, he earned time off and went home. He flew to a nearby airport and spent a couple days simply resting and waiting for his report date and time that was soon happening.

There really wasn't much to do at his parent's home, they had their own lives and their own challenges. He visited with some of his siblings the rest were off somewhere getting an education and he would not meet up with them at this time.

Growing up as a teenager Harkey worked, made good money, and bought his first vehicle. It was used but excellent condition and low miles. The upholstery and carpet were pristine. When he visited, he discovered his brother had rolled it in a drunk driving accident and destroyed it. He loaned money to some of his siblings and his mother, none of which attempted to repay him back and conveniently forgot about it was in this backdrop of why he never wanted to visit home. Harkey decided he would move away a far distance and see them once in a blue moon. The way things shaped up, Harkey didn't feel obligated to visit too often and took solace in the fact by not visiting he could avoid hearing about their problems, trials, and tribulations. They could screw up well enough on their own, they didn't need his help!

At the end of this short vacation Harkey flew to a destination he would embark with his new battalion. He had his standard issue required and all the remainder of his personal items were put in storage to be returned to him if he survived or given to his relatives if he didn't. As part of his pre-deployment, he was required to do a will and power of attorney then sign a bunch of none-disclosure forms for the mission he was going on.

Then he boarded the special craft, and they were on their way. In the span of about a week after dodging a few meteorites and dealing with a few space pirates who didn't realize at long range they were approaching military craft until it was too late, Harkey got some minor baptism of fire. The Battalion used the space pirate ships as training opportunities to see how well the men would conduct themselves. The battalion was fifty percent experienced warriors, the rest were neophyte's strait out of training. It was a good mix to have proficiency and young guys who felt invincible who had never experienced carnage before.

The Battalion Officers had no empathy towards the space pirates who frequently boarded civilian transports and robbed them, often taking terrorized female passengers off to be used as sex slaves. If there were women on these Pirate ships, they were immediately considered victims even though many of them had already been impregnated by the horrible excuses of human flesh that made vast profits in human trafficking. If they were lucky enough, they would rescue some recently acquired victims.

The Pirates had substantial weapons but once surrounded by a Battalion, there wasn't much they could do, and they were warned if they attempted any evasive maneuvers or launched weapons their craft would be destroyed.

Often women and children were used as human shields but far out in space the one hundred-million-mile rule applied, and the Battalion Commander responded to the threats by the pirates, "Nobody will know we killed all those women and children with you. Unless you do exactly what we direct you to do, you all will die today.

Usually, the Space Pirates traveled in packs and thanks to the great scanning ability of the Battalion escort frigates, they knew which ships contained most of the civilian hostages and demonstrated their ability to destroy the ships on the others they knew based on scanner probes were not crowded with hostages. Usually after the second of third pirate ship destroyed, the rest then followed instructions. Once the civilians were in protective custody and Pirates arrested, they used neurological probes to quickly vet the horror stories that women and children stated. Pirates that molested children were quickly turned into Eunuchs.

Some pirates had fast ships but at the present time, none of them could outrun a Frigate. The pirates that tried to run away even spouting they had human shields onboard, were warned the Frigate had the legal authority under the one hundred-million-mile rule to destroy the ship and not waste precious time chasing them. The current policy for Space Command is to destroy every Pirate ship even if it took a few civilians with them. After careful analysis Space Command determined even if they killed a half dozen civilians in the process, the 5,000 civilians they would prevent taken into slave sex trade would be worth it. Liberals of course were working hard to overturn the policy because they flunked math. Sex slaves usually had very little desire to keep living after a while and often diseases killed them after a few months of sex slavery.

Harkey a certified weapons operator destroyed one of the Pirate ships they chased down, and soon got to meet some of the sex slave victims he helped rescue. From that day forward Harkey had no love for Pirates or the Sex Slave Trafficking Cartels. Even though Harkey was a junior guy often called a Nub (Non-qualified useless bubba), he was monitored very closely by his superiors who constantly evaluated him as to determine what types of missions he could support based on his personal initiatives, proficiency, professionalism, and conduct.

Harkey was a loner. He really didn't have a best friend growing up. He had a few causal friends, but nothing enduring. He was somewhat introvert and people barely noticed him on the spacecraft. He was more or less just part of the fixtures. He was always reading and studying because he needed qualifications to advance to higher responsibilities. Accepting those responsibilities and doing what it took to complete those qualifications is how he would advance. Nobody schooled him on that, he inherently knew what he had to do as he listened to the conversations of a lot of senior people. He already knew what went on was not always fair based on his two training incidents and that not everyone is on your side.

Harkey was often passed over by others due to social engineering, bias, and preconceived notions. Those scenarios ultimately benefitted him because it taught him, he simply had to work hard and accept terrible assignments to advance. Some people would advance because of patronage or political influence. Harkey only had one thing in focus. Get qualifications and valor completed to ensure his seat in a pilots training course. Nothing else mattered and if he got killed along the way, that was alright because at least there would be no further suffering of psychological damage.

The fleet always carried excess number of Frigates with them traveling to the war zone because they expected to run into pirates or have skirmishes that resulted in injuries and the Frigates were the fastest spaceships to get people back to better medical treatments. By the time they arrived in the War Zone, all the Victims from pirates were on their way back to Empire worlds to get treatments and make their cases against the Pirates who kidnapped them and forced them into the sex slave business.

Because some of the pirates were willing to sign confessions and rat out the others to prevent them from also becoming Eunuchs, the convictions were almost assured, and the Pirates then discovered the harsh realities of enslaving people for sex slavery. Half were led before laser firing squads and put out of their misery, while the others were castrated and wished they were dead in the sterile confines of a formidable prison and God help them if they were also pedophiles.

As they got in vicinity of the warzone, it was battle stations and nothing mattered but the upcoming combat.

The space trenches had been here for many years. Two Empires each thinking they could win a war of attrition. Both were wrong and they kept down that path of insanity.

The day of destiny was finally upon Harkey as he soon found himself on a landing craft coming down from space join the foray on the front lines on the planet Arkadanstra, one of the adjacent planets being contested as it was a key location for surface to space (S/S) weapons operations.

The main purpose of Harkey's Tiger Team Battalion participating in this skirmish on Arkadanstra was to give all the new guys some battlefield experience. What doesn't kill you makes you better.

Chevolite forces on Arkadanstra were holding their own. The Tiger Team Battalion would do a three-day turnover with the Cactus Battalion they would relieve. The Cactus Battalion was war weary and in need of a rest period and reconstitution of replacement warriors since they were now down to 50% fighting strength. The enemy also knew this sector was in the hurt locker and had every intention to probe it a few days but were unaware the Cactus Battalion troops were withdrawn past the escarpment that provided them structural security and would be very difficult for Spetznar troops to do a head on attack.

It would be foolish for Spetznar troops to attack within the next three days because the troop strength for the sector would temporarily exceed 150% and only one third of the total amount were tired and war weary. The rest were fresh meat ready to be butchered and could fight back.

The Tiger Team chain of command hoped an attack would unfold before the turnover was complete knowing the effective troop strength would exceed Enemy awareness by a large factor.

Unfortunately for the Tiger Team, the Spetznar troops were presently licking their wounds and would not recommence the attack until several days after the Cactus Battalion was back in a reserve force going through training and reconstitution.

The basic training where they were conditioned to carry 100 pounds in special backpacks now became apparent why. The forward observers and command posts received all their supplies hand delivered via trenches and tunnels. Wounded were carried out in gurneys. To maintain health and sanitation at the front lines, forward observers, and command posts, ammunition boxes once emptied were filled full of sacks of solid waste carried on a pole by two grunts. And they would make as many trips as required because maintaining health and minimizing filth on the front lines enhanced recovery from wounds.

Not all battles were fought in this insane war of attrition. Some were based on maneuver, element of surprise, and combined three-dimensional warfare including tunneling operations.

The Chevolite Tiger Team Battalion was not going to be dumped on the front lines and kept here as an integral part of a standing army stuck in a set piece battle. They would hold this position and fight for a few weeks while the Cactus Battalion licked their wounds and trained replacements. Eventually the Cactus Battalion would come back, and the Tiger Team would leave and go prepare for the real reason they were sent to this sector. An assault on enemy stronghold Praximus Gartuka a nearby planet that was the main powerful enemy Spetznar Garrison for this area. The fighting there would be fierce as there was much, they could lose. Very few Chevolite forces that landed on Praximus Gartuka ever made it off the planet alive.

The Chevolite Tiger Team Battalion's assignment to Praximus Gartaku was a closely guarded secret and only the Commanding Officer and his Executive Officer knew the plan existed and only because they had to be informed why their troops would be exercised in this battle to give them good combat experience and develop proficiency as a killing machine. They would have reserves such as the Cactus Battalion to bolster them if they had significant difficulties, but the Commanding Officer knew there would be no reserves to bail them out when the fighting got ugly on Praximus Gartuka.

Since Harkey was one of the NFG (new effing guys) or often referred to as a NUB, he was paired up with his *Sea Daddy* a term left over from their amphibious assault days. His instructions were simple: "Do whatever the heck I tell you to do, and you might just stay alive."

Harkey and his *Sea Daddy* were part of the support squad positioned around the forward observers to protect them. It was crucial in the battle the forward observers remained at their post until all was lost and the ability to hold the position was determined not to be possible. One of the criteria for permission to bug out included the loss of all the support troops around them requiring them to fight all the way back to major portions of their front lines.

The battle usually had drones, drone zappers, lasers, mortars, ballistic and kinetic weapons. Exoskeletons fitted with all the heavy weapons proceeded with infantry support hammering their way in trying to create a breach that could be exploited. Defenses in depth usually made the breaches untenable so the current tactics since maneuver was not possible did nothing more than grind up men and machine in a war of attrition that nobody was going to win any time soon.

Success in this battle led through the strong hold of Praximus Gartuka. If Praximus Gartuka could be knocked out the Spetznar troops on Arkadanstra would lose the support, they needed to protect their front lines. A new dynamic would then form, and this sector of space could be neutralized allowing the war to move into a more decisive state and creating a pathway to ending it.

One of the critical tasks in warfare is for INTEL to figure out the disposition of the enemy. Discovering a fresh battalion facing your force on the front likes is critical information. It means the front lines are now crowded with NFG's (Nubs), possibly triggering an offensive to hit this sector hard to create a breach and possible advantage to exploit. Such a demonstration of tactics would cause far more casualties than planners wanted.

The Chevolite Task Force Commander wanted the Tiger Team to get actual live fire combat training but not at the expense of collateral damage to the point they would not be quickly deployable afterwards to Praximus Gartuka. Hence the Tiger Team vanished All their insignias were replaced with Cactus Battalion markings. All their communications and forward observer reporting copied Cactus methods identically. To help promote the ruse, some of the forward observers were left in place so that communications to the command posts had the familiar voices and led the enemy to believe they were facing the Cactus Battalion that had been blooded.

After licking their wounds for a few days, it was now time for Spetznar Enemy troops to go back on the offensive before the Cactus Battalion attacked. Two nights after the turnover, the stage was set to recommence hostilities across the broad area where these powerful forces faced off.

The good news for the Chevolite's is the forward observers had become quite experienced at detecting a real attack verses a faint. Even though it would be the Tiger Team doing the fighting, the Cactus forward observers had to make the reports as to not give away who they really were.

Spetznar commanders knew the Cactus Battalion has been weakened and troop strength was down to approximately fifty percent combat ready, the rest being casualties at aid stations recovering from projectile and laser wounds. Hence the Spetznar troops were led to believe they would not receive substantial punishment from the weakened enemy and pressed their advance forward almost with *caution thrown to the wind.*

The forward observers saw the movements coming forward in well concealed and camouflaged components. They had the uncanny ability to predict when the exoskeleton mortar barrages would do the initial bombardment before the concentrated attack. At H-hour when it appeared those exoskeletons were moved in place to start shooting mortar barrages, the forward observers gave a code word to the support troops around them to get under the portashields that would do about a ninety percent success at protecting them from the mortar carpet bombing. Anyone in a standard foxhole would be killed.

Well camouflaged portashields dotted the landscape. Also, portashields decoys were used to cause the enemy to expend large amounts of ordinance.

As expected, it felt like an earthquake with all the rumbling and explosions going on all around the forward observer station. This was one of the prime targets to deny the enemy with a set of eyes and ears that could give coordinates for counter fire.

Flexible hoses that went out steel pipe from the forward observer stations protected by the portashields acted as a telescope and a laser designator which highlighted counter fire targets. Shortly after firing the first salvo towards the Cactus Battalion, the Spetznar exoskeletons started receiving deadly counter fire. As expected, the multi-legged that were not destroyed quickly crawled back in their portatubes that acted as portashields and would stay parked there until battlefield management artificial intelligence directed them back out into the open allowing them to fire the next salvo.

Enemy Infantry would never know the efficacy of the preparation bombardment when they attacked. They could only hope enough damage was done to allow them to not get slaughtered. Some of the Spetznar Shock Troops were designated to take out the forward observers to deny the enemy a set of eyes and ears. Hence the forward observers always got pounded the hardest and took a much higher number of casualties in a battle.

Harkey was in the middle of the fray. His *Sea Daddy* was having him reload his shoulder launched missiles he continued to fire until a sniperbot took him out and Harkey had to do it all by himself. Harkey and a lot of the troops were under surveillance, not so much for battle information, but to provide superiors in depth knowledge of how these Tiger Team guys would hold up against a tough enemy. This was one of the most ferocious areas on the front lines that often drew the most casualties. Hence it was a good test and evaluation to determine if they would be ready for prime time on Praximus Gartuka. No battle had had this amount of video and sensor recording before and probably afterwards. This was all about the after-action report and discover if their training had been adaquate as well as their screening process to cherry pick the right men for the Battalion.

Since Harkey's *Sea Daddy* was currently incapacitated and probably dead, he doubled up his efforts to attempt achieving a rate of fire they provided before the casualty.

Harkey also utilized some of his recent training and knew better that to keep firing from one location like his *Sea Daddy* did that drew the fire upon himself. It took slightly longer to get off the rounds, but Harkey made sure he was a moving target.

Harkey was in essence improvised Infantry Artillery. His missiles had dual roles: take out heavy armored battle craft or use the rounds as artillery on infantry targets. The proximity fuses did a great job of exploding the ordinance where it mattered.

The Tiger team was not the under-strength Cactus Battalion

the Spetznar Enemy troops thought they were attacking. In the minds of the Spetznar soldier, the enemy shooting at them was weak, demoralized and just one shade away from collapsing. As their superiors had brain washed them for this battle, all they had to do against this weak sector was to push extra hard and they would achieve the breach, hold it and send reserves pouring through to get in the rears and the Spetznar would tear them up in a great victory.

The Spetznar didn't know they were facing a full-strength brigade with one hundred percent effectives, that were better trained than those troops they faced up until today. These were consummate special forces troops that were not going to cower and would stand and fight a slugfest. All the logistics people in the Cactus and Tiger Team Battalions were able to keep providing ample ammunition and replacement missiles to front line troops. Having such a robust resupply capability throughout the battle proved to have serious consequences. There was no rationing of fire, the lead kept pouring down on the enemy with frightening results.

The very strong Spetznar formation hitting the Chevolite forward observer post started out with a great deal of arrogance knowing they had extras to make sure they took this command post and blinded the enemy.

The withering fire coming from the Tiger Team around the forward observer post was unlike anything they ever experienced before. These enemy were fighting like crazy; it was an incredible display of valor and something they were not accustomed to. The closest any of the Spetznar troops got to the forward observers was 50 yards.

The Tiger Team troops around the forward observer post slowly withered away as they were systematically being killed and wounded. Even wounded Tiger Team troops continued fighting away. Harkey received three wounds but none of them were life threatening as he applied the battle-magic patches that had terrific adhesives and had chemicals that helped stop bleeding. Harkey had a lot of pain, but he knew he was not going to bleed to death, which gave him more resolve to continue firing those shoulder launched missiles as long as his logistics train was able to keep feeding him more weapons.

All throughout the battle the well concealed video and sound sensors recorded every one of Harkey's actions. After action reports on this outstanding performance would be viewed by the Commanding Officer and the Executive Officer as they endorsed the report and forwarded it to headquarters. Harkey's extreme valor was a footnote in the report. High up the chain of command one of the reviewers who looked at the service contract Harkey served under noted he was destined to pilot's training and added a comment, *based on his valor on the battlefield if this warrior completes flight training, I would assume he would also show this level of effort in the skies in close air support.*

Harkey's destiny was now charted, but he wasn't done quite yet with his experience with the infantry. His biggest exposure to ground warfare would be on Praximus Gartuka where one of the most important battles of the war was just about to happen.

The Spetznar commanders were utterly shocked they received such a terrible beating. The deciding factor to call off the attack was based on the strange phenomenon; they could not take out that forward observer posts even when putting in double the normal number of assault troops. Spetznar commanders knew they had killed a lot of Chevolite forces, but they continued fighting with tenacity, unlike anything they had experienced before. With great reluctance Spetznar commanders called off the attack to regroup and let INTEL explain to them what went wrong. The Spetznar battalion had so many casualties, they had to go back in bivouac and lick their wounds and wait for significant number of replacements and reinforcements. By the time they were ready to attack again, the Cactus Battalion was back in position, fully reconstituted, trained and in great shape to repeal any further attacks.

One of the Spetznar after action reports up their chain of commands indicated the Chevolite could have exploited their defeat but never left their trenches. This was one of the big mysteries of the war they never did figure out. The truth was simple, the Praximus Gartuka attack was the major goal and the Chevolite's could not risk having Tiger Team members captured by the Spetznar. Hence the Spetznar were unaware the Tiger Team was ever there in the first place.

When the enemy retreated a great distance from the front line, the Chevolite's sent in medical teams to rescue all the casualties and reserves were sent in to replace all the wounded. The first aide providers saw the blood-soaked clothes of Harkey who was now starting to have issues with pain associated with his wounds and wasn't sure he could walk so he was carried away in a gurney and put on a robotic exoskeleton that transported him back to an underground shelter set up as a triage site for casualties. After doctors assessed his wounds and knew he had lost a lot of blood had him quickly start receiving transfusions and pain medications. Harkey went unconscious and eventually made it into surgery where his three wounds were repaired and almost twenty-four hours later came out of the drug induced fog and discovered he was in a clean hospital.

Soon doctors came by and checked up on Harkey and gave him a quick report on his injuries and informed him he would be discharged from the hospital in about three days to go rejoin his unit. He was also given some good news the person in the next bed was his *Sea Daddy* who lived and was expected to be back on his feat in a few more weeks as well.

Six hours later Harkey's *Sea Daddy* woke up and found himself next to his NFG and smiled. "You are the last person I would expect to wake up next to in a hospital."

"Well, if it had to be anyone, I'm glad it's you."

"How did the battle end?"

"The enemy retreated. They were not able to take out the forward observers."

"That's good. Did we have a lot of casualties?"

"I don't know for sure, but I think when the enemy retreated there were only five of us still standing, but we all had wounds."

"Did you get a chance to shoot some rockets?"

"Oh yes, shot quite a few, with double the logistics thanks to the Cactus guys supporting, we had a constant flow of ammo. We never ran out."

"That's amazing."

Shortly afterwards a meal was served and both men were hungry since neither had eaten in approximately 36 hours.

Soon after the orderlies took away all the serving trays, dishes and eating utensils there was some noise down at the end of the ward. As Harkey looked on, he noticed a dozen men with combat gear on walking down through the ward talking to the troops. They were older men some with grey hair and insignias on them that indicated they were superior officers.

In the middle of the group was the Battalion Commander and his Executive Officer. The older grey-haired men with them, were their bosses including their commanding officer out to see the troops and shower them with accolades.

One of the persons with the group was a Yeoman carrying an electronic tablet that had the bios on each of the men they stopped at. They didn't stop at all beds as some men wounded were simple casualties that had no bearing on the outcome of the battle and had not recorded valor. Each bed had a number, and the tablet had a spreadsheet that had the details of each bed number occupant.

As the group of senior officers got closer Harkey could hear some of the conversations. These men did some amazing acts of courage. They were all hero's and gave much of themselves in the battle. Hearing their stories made Harkey feel proud to be around them. Eventually they came to Harkey's bed. The Executive Officer introduced the Commanding Officer. "Sir this is Sargent Harkey. His conduct during the battle was exemplary and despite receiving three serious painful wounds that required eighteen hours of surgery after the battle, he kept firing shoulder launched missiles until the enemy retreated."

Harkey felt embarrassed but said, "Sir, I'm just a corporal."

"Sargent Harkey, what you don't know is you got a battlefield promotion. Well done."

The commanding officer walked up to the bed and held out his hand and shook Harkey's hand and said, "I got to see some of the video of you in action. I'm very proud to have someone like you in my battalion."

"Thank you, sir."

The commanding officer stepped aside and one of the grey-haired men stepped up and said, "Sargent Harkey, I'm General Crispar. I too saw some of the video showing you in action. I endorsed your battlefield promotion. Well done soldier."

General Crispar held out his hand and shook Harkey's hand.

"Thank you, sir."

The men then continued down the ward and made a dozen other stops. As General Crispar informed the Battalion Commander earlier, "The training and the planning for this event proved what we intended to do was achievable. I have confidence the next phase of our plan will work. I've ordered Cactus to start swapping out your guys in a week as I expect they will be fully reconstituted by then. You will then proceed to the training facility and prepare for the mission at that time."

"We'll be ready sir."

"I have faith you will. Hopefully most of these wounded guys will be healed up in time to participate."

"At least half of them will be, the others have substantial wounds, and the doctors give a prognosis of about three months of recovery."

"These are real leaders. If we get half of them back it will be hugely beneficial."

"I agree sir."

In three days, Harkey was discharged from the hospital and sent to rejoin up with his battalion bivouacked off to the distance from the front lines and were slowly coming back from the front lines ass the Cactus Battalion was now starting to slowly swap out personnel as to not alert the enemy of the ruse.

Some of the old salts didn't like the idea they had this young punk sergent that got a battlefield promotion. In cohesive units like these special forces, there is great visibility to the officers and a lot more surveillance than they ever dreamed of.

One day later as one of the old salts was giving Harkey some harassment and threatening to kick his ass, the old salt was suddenly taken away for a critique and a private meeting. The commanding officer chaired the critique!

"Sargent Chuk, I have direct evidence of you hazing Sargent Harkey. We can't allow that kind of behavior in this unit. I know that you are upset that such a young man has achieved such a high rank in a rather short period of time. The fact you don't like it questions my ability as a commanding officer to reward for valor, isn't that, right?"

"Sir, have no questions about your ability."

"Sargent Chuk, I'm the person that awarded this battlefield promotion to Sargent Harkey and if you don't like it, that means you are questioning my abilities."

"Sir, I would never question your abilities."

"Sargent Chuk, I'm questioning your ability now as a leader and I have something we are going to look at together and when we get done watching this, I expect you to give me two explanations, one why you questioned my abilities because of that battlefield promotion and explain to me your own actions."

The Commanding Officer turned toward the Executive Officer and said, "Play Sargent Harkey's video first. He then turned toward Sargent Chuk and said, "I'm now tasking you to count the number of missiles and the number of wounds Harkey received and when."

The video started playing. In the early portion of the battle Harkey was handing missiles to his *Sea Daddy* doing the shooting until he was wounded. Harkey took over with no help getting the missiles, but his rate of fire was rather spectacular. Then he got wounded, put on his battle dressings so he wouldn't bleed to death and started firing again. Sargent Chuk could see the blood coming out of the wounds that appeared painful while the battle dressings were going on.

When the video ended, the Commanding Officer looked at Sargent Chuk and asked, "What did you see?"

"He had three serious wounds and fired 37 missiles."

"Your count was off by one, he fired 38 missiles."

"Alright sir, I made a mistake."

"Play the next video XO."

Soon the video was of Sargent Chuk who was further back and in a much safer area with less targeting around his position. His performance was dismal, and he cowered behind the portashield for half the battle and only managed to get away six missiles.

Now it was time for Sargent Chuk to receive his down dressing.

"It's a good thing we have people like Sargent Harkey in our Battalion because in this battle you proved to me, I can't count on your when I need you."

"I'm sorry sir."

"Next time you or your buddies think you are going to badmouth Sargent Harkey, you know I got videos of you as well as them too."

"Understand sir."

"You all need to improve the way you fight because in future battles we may get defeated if you only get away six missiles."

The CO who was mildly distressed that his senior enlisted would conduct themselves in the manner they did and after a pause said, "We will be getting some special training real soon and now you know you are under a lot of visibility, plus you now have my personal interest. Do I make myself clear?"

"Yes sir."

"You know what I expect out of you, and I caution you not to let me down."

"I promise to not let you down."

"Very well, you are dismissed."

Sargent Chuk left the room in the most humiliated manner he ever felt. But he also knows some vital intel. They are all under scrutiny and the Commanding Officer is gunning for him.

In a weeks' time, Harkey's *Sea Daddy* returned and was fit for duty. He had a lot of surgery and thanks to their advanced battlefield surgical techniques, his wounds had healed considerably.

They were doing modest training and the troops wondered why they were taking it so easy. Soon they would find out.

Unexpectedly a few days later, transports came to the planet delivering more troops. Enemy Intel thought they were bringing in more troops to set up an offensive. The truth was by bringing in more troops the enemy could not see them removing all the Tiger Team Battalion. In fact, they never knew the Tiger Team was ever here, one of the greatest secrets in military history.

The Tiger Team made their way to interplanetary transports and were soon heading far away from the battlefield to a lesser-known planet referred to as planet-X for security reasons. Its sole purpose in life was it had similar topology and geography that exists on Praximus Gartuka. There was a unique escarpment on this planet that was identical to where they would land on Praximus Gartuka. By landing on the top of the escarpment would make it difficult for the Spetznar Enemy troops to dislodge them.

The main purpose for the Tiger Team in this battle was to create a target and a serious threat that would force the Spetznar to divide their troops on Praximus Gartuka and while they were concentrating on the Tiger Team, other Battalions would land elsewhere and hopefully take out the command center to make this area of space untenable for them, which would also quickly end the fighting on nearby Arkadanstra and insure Arkadanstra would become a secure Chevolite garrison to support systematic expansion into other contested solar systems.

It took a week for the intergalactic transports to deliver the Battalion to its new operating base. The shuttlecraft poured out of the transports and came down and landed at the escarpment base that was laid out exactly how they would do it on Praximus Gartuka. The combat engineers and all the logistics personnel studied the plans for this planet-X facility carefully as they were duplicate it at some point on Praximus Gartuka. Escarpments that were tall enough acted just like a river crossing for a natural barrier making it difficult for another Army to easily penetrate. Because the way the facility was spread out with flanking protection, they only had to worry about defending one direction: one hundred and eighty degrees relative the front lines.

Tunnels and trenches were designed. Engineering marvels called *Spatializers* that applied frequencies to the tunneling equipment to make the rock have lower mechanical impedance sped up digging process enormously. This escarpment was honeycombed with tunnels the combat engineers had produced very quickly just like they would at Praximus Gartuka.

Because of their heavy weight and design, portashields

would be deployed in a re-entry space craft that after passing through the ozone layer would launch these shields like flying saucers that would spin and fly down to their destination burrowing into the soil and be positioned to go in place where needed quite abruptly where the Tiger Team planned on landing on the escarpment which was notably far away from Spetznar troops.

The D-Day planners figured it would take the Spetznar troops three days to get in place for a counterattack. By then, thanks to the *tunneling Spatializers*, the tunnels and trenches could be built and the portashields in place where they needed them very promptly. The *tunneling Spatializers* put out very strong frequencies that changed the mechanical impedance of the rock and mantle the Combat Engineers had to drill through making the drill heads nine hundred percent more efficient allowing drilling to proceed at a very high rate.

Just like in the air, where drones were used to test missiles and aircraft, on the ground there were exoskeleton drones used to attack the escarpment fortifications. Infantrymen were directed to take cover under the portashields while the land based robotic drones shot salvos of mortars, missiles, projectiles, and kinetic warheads.

The infantry using improvised shoulder fired artillery and missiles systematically took out the exoskeleton drones and the robot infantry sent along to simulate an actual attack. These were live fire training scenarios and even with all the protection and procedures, only a few men managed to get injuries. Because of the timing, they would be nursing their wounds in an infirmary long after the Tiger Team Battalion was on its way to that identical escarpment on the enemy stronghold of Praximus Gartuka where Spetznar troops would love nothing more than destroying their fair share of Chevolite forces just like they did on Arkadanstra.

The week of training helped to knock the cobwebs off all the old timers who didn't get a lot of action in the skirmishes on Arkadanstra. Harkey was once again teamed up with his *Sea Daddy*. Sargent Chuk was moved to a different platoon far away from Harkey as to prevent any possible fragging incidents. Sargent Chuk lived with the humiliation he experienced. He was glad that none of his peers were privy to the videos that didn't shine him in a good light.

At the start of the training Harkey and *Sea Daddy* were still suffering a lot of pain, but thanks to the pain killers and combat dressings of their wounds with special substances that promote healing internal and outside, by the end of the training period, most of the pain and misery was gone. They were ready to experience hot combat again.

Each platoon loaded up into their own shuttle craft and flew out into space and mated up with their transport that would take them to their designated location on Praximus Gartuka.

Harkey got to see what his future would be like as a pilot when suddenly, he was called to the Commanding Officers Space Cabin.

"Reporting as ordered sir."

"Sargent Harkey, I've gleaned some information out of your personnel folder and know you will be leaving us after this battle to attend flight school."

"Yes sir, I'm looking forward to it."

"The reason why I asked you to come here is to allow you to observe a portion of the space battle that will occur as our Space Force helps us force our way in down on the planet."

"Thank you for the opportunity to watch this."

"You earned the opportunity by fighting so courageously

back at Arkadanstra. My video review of the battle shows no other person who sacrificed as much as you did and continued fighting even after receiving three very painful injuries."

"Sir, I knew how important it was to protect that forward observation post."

"How did you come to that conclusion?"

"My *Sea Daddy* explained it to me. I understood right away what he meant by telling me it was crucial for the mission to protect those guys in there so they could call in the artillery and report what the enemy was up to."

"I'm glad you took your *Sea Daddy's* instruction so well, because what you did was exactly what your *Sea Daddy* knew you had to do, or it might have turned into a very bloody battle with far more casualties."

"Thank you, sir."

"Okay us watch the display screens, its about ready to start happening."

"Yes sir, I'm watching."

The Executive Officer with the Commanding Officer knew this was a special gift to Sargent Harkey because he displayed uncommon valor during their big test on Arkadanstra. The Executive Officer also knew Harkey would be going to flight school after the next battle if he survived and this would be a rare opportunity for Harkey to see exactly what the Space Force did during planetary invasions.

The Transports could not disgorge the Tiger Team until an area of space and aerial supremacy was set in the area above their landing zones on the escarpment area.

Moments after the Commanding Officer said it would begin, it started. Two massive Air and Space Forces met head on.

The fighting was immense. Spacecraft were blowing up one right after the other as the laser and beam light show lit up the space in front of them.

Fighter Bombers and Anti-Air suppression craft and drones went about their deadly chores of neutralizing the enemy. Drones went in first forcing the Anti-Air sites to expose their positions by lighting up the drones and firing on them. It would be utterly impossible for this landing force to neutralize the entire planet and that would be an extreme waste of resources. All they had to do was pave the way to the landing zone and keep enough enemy fighter bombers away from the fleet to allow the transports to unload their precious cargoes of warriors and weapons.

The Commanding Officer didn't want to talk because he didn't want to distract Harkey who was watching this all unfold. Harkey was given a catbirds seat to watch how the integrated Space Forces performed their elaborate maneuvers and attacks to achieve their results.

Part of the plan was deception. Through the use of double spies and disinformation, the Spetznar Forces thought Arkadanstra was the target for this massive force and thus reinforced Arkadanstra with scarce resources, leaving them out of position to repel the real threat on the actual target. With the Spetznar Space Forces divided, it gave the Chevolite Fighter Bombers a much higher ratio of attacker's verses defenders.

By the time the Spetznar Forces discovered the error in their ways, the transports had a clean path to send down their forces including a few transports that had to land on the planet to deposit critical machinery such as the *tunneling Spatializers* that would be immediately camouflaged and put to work.

Air Defense Forces were some of the early arrivals to set up and increase the fire power of the Chevolite Space Defense that would make it very difficult for Spetznar fighter bombers to get near the Tiger Team troops.

Combat Engineers and their security force were early groups to deploy because they were needed to operate the *tunneling Spatializers* to create enough protective structures to minimize risk to the Infantry personnel defending them.

The withering fire from Chevolite Space Force assets slowly eroded the combat capabilities of the Spetznar Space and Air Forces in this region of the Hemisphere almost on the opposite side of the planet from the main Praximus Gartuka Garrison.

Part of the plan was to suck away Praximus Gartuka Garrison defenders using the Tiger Team as bait, so that the next invasion force would go for the Garrison's Juglar veins and snuff it out forcing the Spetznar to abandon the planet and no longer be in a position to support Arkadanstra with reserves and supplies, that meant eventually they would die at the vine running out of food, water, and ammunition with no way to effectively get evacuated. If this battle succeeded, it would eliminate a very long stalemate and allow an eventual conclusion to the fighting ushering in an armistice and a period of peaceful coexistence.

Thanks to Chevolite Space Forces achieving air superiority in a remarkably quick manner, just as the planners figured it would take at least three days for the Spetznar Forces to travel across land to take on the Chevolite's.

About the time the air battle appeared to die down on the video, the Tiger Team Commanding Officer said, "Harkey, I hope that by watching the air battle you just witnessed, it will instill in you the seriousness of our pilots and how they were crucial to this operation. Without them, we could never have contemplated this action."

"Yes sir, I understand it quite well and I appreciate you

giving me the opportunity to observe this."

"We will be deploying your unit in a short while. Report back to your unit and please do not discuss what all happened here to anyone. All this space battle video is classified much higher than all their security clearances."

"Understand sir."

"Very well go rejoin your unit and good luck on the planet."

"I will do my best, sir."

"I know you will."

Harkey stood up and walked out of the Commanding Officers Space Cabin and went back to his unit. As soon as he arrived, *Sea Daddy* said, "We are just about ready to deploy. Get all your equipment and follow me."

"Understand. I'll be ready in a moment."

As soon as Harkey was ready, *Sea Daddy* led him to the landing craft where they got on board. In the bowls of this assault transport were forty such landing craft that would be launched out of the atmosphere and come down as gliders to the escarpment destination. Even though they could fly off the planet with half a load of troops back out into space, the rocket thrusters would not put out much power on the way towards the planet and were used only for vectorized landing patterns and if necessary, avoid space mines or potential missiles that managed to break through the safety corridor.

The platoon had all their battle gear and Harkey's job was a mule carrying the backpack weighing exactly one hundred pounds full of reloads for the shoulder fired missile launcher that could take out armored vehicles or exoskeletons on the ground or switched in situ simply by voice command to anti-aircraft mode. If the laser designator was pointing and aircraft at time of fire, the voice command was redundant, but a lot of old crusty sergeants liked that feature as it gave them a more sense of confidence on the mode shift. The missile guidance system algorithms would be looking for an air-based target vice ground based and more likelihood of achieving hitting the target.

Any of the forty platoon members in that landing craft that were not scared were probably pathological liars because their trek down to the planet was extremely dangerous as none of them knew the efficacy of the anti-air suppression that was ongoing. They would only know the success of anti-air suppression when they landed and quickly climbed out of the lander down the ramp. The guys in the lead were trained, *get your asses flying down that ramp because there are a bunch of scared men with heavy backpacks behind us and you don't want to be ran over by the stampede.*

In their training they also knew to get out of that transport as quickly as possible because they were sitting ducks. If they were lucky enough to land next to a recently prepared position the combat engineers created with the *tunneling Spatializers* that were also excellent trenching machines and portashields laid sectionally over the tops of trenches with several ramps down into the trench allowing quick egress. Otherwise, they would be caught out in the open with the only hope of finding boulders or debris to crouch behind. The problem was quite complex in that none of them knew which direction the enemy were currently.

INTEL reports were obsolete in thirty minutes due to a constant dynamic, so they were trained, *don't assume you know which direction the enemy will attack you from. Be prepared to face them in any direction.*

Another factor they all wished was they were positioned close to drone killer squads and anti-armor platoons to give them an added layer of safety.

To Harkey's delight and sudden surprise, his platoon landed adjacent to prepared positions that had been completed only a few minutes ago during their travel down to the planet surface.

Thanks to the element of surprise, disinformation campaign, and effective employment of forces to create a robust safety corridor, the landing force was arriving mostly unopposed. The enemy got caught flat footed and was now scrambling to make up for their biggest screwup yet, since their arrival and turning this Chevolite world into a Spetznar Garrison to support the offensive now ongoing on a dozen nearby worlds in five different solar systems.

Those portashields were highly important because just about the only ordinance they could not stop would be projectiles, kinetic weapons, and ballistic missiles. Around this time over half the troops had portashields in their sectors and if the expected ballistic missile strike occurred the rest of them could crowd in that safety zone during the blasts. Meanwhile the combat engineers operating the *tunneling Spatializers* were building more trenches, caves, and moving portashields by cranes on top of the trenches to give an element of overhead protection from sudden drone or cruise missiles saturating the area with bomblets that are deadly in uncovered trenches.

If the cranes got knocked out, working parties of twenty men could slide the portashields over the top of planks above the trenches. At this point in the battle the cranes had done an effective job and well over a half of all portashields were in place for this set piece battle where height mattered. At the very top of the escarpment, the Tiger Team lookouts using high quality photonics could see for many miles, including partially over the horizon in daylight as well as at night with infrared an stealth penetrating radars. The electronic battlefield was apparent on the ground as well as in the task force commander's ship in a geostationary orbit over the planet.

The Tiger Team Commander and his Executive Officer were now on the ground inside the well protected command center in one of the first caves drilled with the *tunneling Spatializers*. Combat Engineers installed tubing with immense strength in the wake of the *tunneling Spatializers* that would prevent cave-ins if the enemy got lucky and placed a burrowing depth charge nearby. With the specialized flooring installed the construction technique produced a relatively clean environment and ample storage was provided below removeable floor plates. Folding tables, chairs and shock protected portable command consoles were rapidly installed and hooked up to flat antenna's pointing out into space that could easily be changed out in a few moments if the enemy got lucky and damaged it with shrapnel or direct hits. Everything present was designed with sheer ruggedness in mind. If it couldn't take a beating and keep operating, they would not use it and carry it all the way to the front lines.

The combat in the skies continued through daylight hours and into darkness. Infantrymen standing sentry watches looking to the stars were given a light show all night long. It was impossible to know whose ships were being destroyed and they wouldn't know unless the space fighting suddenly ended and they started taking a pounding, *meaning our side just lost.*

The Spetznar Enemy troops were the consummate professional Army. They came here ready to do business. They knew theses kinds of operations happened and expected it. Unfortunately, they got snookered into thinking the target was Arkadanstra, divided their forces and were not in position to repel the invasion, they only thing they could do now is defeat the Tiger Team on the ground and force them to evacuate the planet.

The Spetznar immediately put together a rapid deployment force Combat Team A and Combat Team B And sent them into battle facing the Tiger team. They knew based on early satellite imagery before the Chevolite's destroyed them, this invasion piece started landing at the obscure escarpment. They were not an immediate threat to Garrison bases, but if they were allowed to get a lot off facility construction done, they would have a base to launch strikes from, then it would get dicey.

Based on the last satellite imagery, Spetznar Combat Team A was sent down Praximus Gartuka road structures East of the escarpment, and Spetznar Combat Team B was sent over the higher altitude planes West of the escarpment that would allow simultaneous attack from two directions.

Meanwhile Spetznar Space Force was sent to Arkadanstra to facilitate repatriating as many ground forces as possible back to Praximus Gartuka to help improve the odds of this upcoming decisive battle as they saw it.

Chevolite Space Force predicted their move and hence *the Great Air Battle of Arkadanstra* started. This was an air battle in size and scope that dwarfed all the major campaigns taught at the military schools.

The Chevolite Space Force understood vividly that by preventing the repatriation of those forces, it would have a huge material impact on the Praximus Gartuka. Normally fighter pilot jockeys loved mixing it up with enemy fighter bombers, but their special instructions with emphasis directed their attention to the transports to make sure very few troops made it off the planet. Because they were not going after the Spetznar fighter bombers, the air war took it toll on Chevolite Space Force, but that too was anticipated and the Chevolite fleet engaged in the air battle had been augmented by forces taken off a dozen other planets.

This gut-wrenching air battle lasted a full forty-eight hours with high attrition on both sides. When it became apparent the Chevolite forces were making good progress at destroying the transports, Spetznar commanders decided to spare the remaining transports and get them away from the war zone, otherwise they would not have the means to evacuate their own staffs if the battle of Praximus Gartuka became a misfortunate event for them.

Spetznar Combat Team A and Combat Team B were expecting numerous reserves pulled from Arkadanstra. Hence in the early part of the battle, they spared no troops and drove that sledgehammer home, killing many of them in the process. About forty-eight hours into the fighting as they neared the Tiger Team Battalion, they had to slow down because reserves they were pleading for were not showing up and headquarters kept saying the same lies, they will eventually get there when in fact they knew they were not on the way.

Since the Spetznar Combat Team commanders had served at headquarters staff they knew the reluctance of pulling garrison troops to bolster the combat teams because they were cowards and wanted to protect their own rears!

Based on INTEL and intercepts the Spetznar underestimated the size and scale of the force they faced.

Going up against the escarpment was an extremely tough passage as they had no choice but to scout out ravines and work their way up from there.

Coming in from the other direction was not difficult other than operating out in the open and thus were compelled to attack at night. Any attempts during daylight hours would cause excessive number of casualties and deplete strength to the point no power projection could be done.

Using combined planning, the Spetznar Combat Team A laid out their attack routes to Combat Team B that would attack the same exact area simultaneously to weaken the defenses and give the group attempting to scale the escarpment support to allow penetration followed by exploitation of panicked troops.

Sargent Harkey and his Sea Daddy were positioned in a double portashield position they knew would get pounded during the preparations of the enemy. Timing was easy as they had no reason to come out from under the protection of the portashields until the Spetznar Infantry supported by weaponized exoskeletons were climbing up the ravine. Exoskeleton gunships were in the lead with the Infantry closing in behind hoping the exoskeletons would draw most of the fire and spare them. Four ravines were scaled in parallel and the penetration in any of them would permit an exploitation area for the Spetznar troops.

Sargent Harkey and Sea Daddy had their ear plugs and acoustic dampening headphones on when the pounding began. It was like living in a major earthquake as the place rumbled as the weapons struck the double portashields hastily bolted together. As long as the dozen bolts held the double portashields would remain in place depressed down into the trench preventing them from being flung out of the way, with weights of numerous filled sandbags acting as anchors.

In their headphones they would have spy drones giving them a battlefield report. Their ravine was called '*Blue*'. Adjacent *Red, Yellow,* and *Green Ravines* were similarly noted. All they had to do was pay attention to *Blue* reports from drones and communications. They each knew the obvious about the time the pounding ended would coincide with reports of enemy coming up the ravine with their exoskeletons they knew were on the way.

Today was different than the previous battle *Sea Daddy* and Harkey each had shoulder fired rocket launchers and each one had their own reload assistant That would open the breach and stuff in another rocket and shut it and tap Harkey on the shoulder meaning, "ready to launch." That was a backup in that eyesight's gave missile ready status.

As soon as the drone spotters said enemy at 100 yards, Harkey nodded to Sea Daddy and they walked over to the launching position, flipped the portashield hatch out of the way stepped on the platform, pointed the launcher at the target and fired the weapon. His assistant then grabbed the lanyard pulling the portashield cover back down and loaded the next round. Both missiles from Harkey and Sea Daddy hit the leading exoskeleton, not putting it completely out of commission as it still had weapons ability, but its propulsion mechanism was damaged, and it was now a fixed launch site with the driver seriously scared the next round would get him and the exoskeleton would no longer be functioning.

Just like teamwork, Harkey, and Sea Daddy, prepared and fired the next rounds. One missile hit the cab of the exoskeleton and penetrated the bullet proof glass canopy instantly killing the driver who lost control and his final movement caused the exoskeleton to fall over sideways partially blocking the path making it difficult for other exoskeletons and Infantry to get past. This was a major break for Harkey and Sea Daddy as it delayed the enemy long enough to allow them to feed quite a few more missiles down on the enemy.

Thanks to the lucky shots, they could now interchange between exoskeleton killer rounds and anti-personnel rounds. The anti-personnel rounds exploded overhead based on ranging coefficients calculated upon launch using photonics. This round would not necessarily kill a lot of enemy troops, but they would all receive shrapnel wounds and death by 1000 cuts. They were painful injuries and quickly eroded the *esprit de corps* in the attackers. After about another dozen missile launches, the attackers retreated to rethink their game plan.

Meanwhile the poorly timed attack from the other direction materialized. Had this force had better leadership and attacked exactly when directed, the combined effort would most likely have taken out Harkey's position and the plan would have worked. Unfortunately, the battlefield management of Spetznar Combat Team B was over evaluating instead of simply following the attack orders.

The Spetznar Combat Team B leadership might have thought they were doing their soldiers a favor sparing lives by dotting their I's and crossing their T's and verifying all the INTEL before they initiated the attack. But dillydallying around cost Combat Team B big the element of surprise and because by the time they got into the fray, the escarpment attack had already failed and now they were on their own. Instead of receiving only half of the firepower directed, Spetznar Combat Team B now received the full punishment, and out in the open even at night they were sitting ducks thanks to infrared and nanometer radar illumination.

Harkey was now fully entranced in the battle and when he got into position fired the missile, directed his helper to reload immediately in this position and kept firing away. His rate of fire was impressive and was quickly noted by the integrated battle management software showing the continuous rapid fire from this sector that quickly had a material affect on the attackers. When an Infantry observes those in front of them getting cut down in ferocious attacks, it quickly dampens their enthusiasm. The psychological impact cannot be overstated.

Sea Daddy was operating per training, firing ducking, reloading, and firing. He knew based on Harkey's posture it was only a matter of time before he would get wounded, and it didn't take long. A location where most of the damage is coming from always gets the attention of the enemy and they responded and a few minutes later, Harkey was down under the portashield suffering from a very painful injury. His assistant was great at getting on the battle dressing preventing him from bleeding to death. Harkey was in a lot of pain that truly made him angry. The best way for him to deal with the pain was to release death and destruction upon the enemy so he gathered his strength climbed up on the short platform, flew open the portashield hatch and launched his next round.

The enemy was now concentrating its attacks on all the missile launchers that started out piece meal but motivated by the way they saw Harkey's position flinging missiles at great frequencies, the enemy rate of fire improved appreciably. Once again Harkey stood in the open hatch directing his helper to keep reloading him and just when the leading elements of the enemy spear was getting close enough to do damage Harkey's rate of fire decimated them and caused panic among their ranks and a temporary retreat. It was only thirty minutes before early morning twilight that would terribly expose the enemy, therefore they had no option but to go back replan and critique the battle and figure out what went wrong. Just before they cleared out, Harkey received his next serious wounds. When daylight returned, the carnage that laid on the battlefield was quite impressive.

The Commanding Officer knew he had accomplished his mission. He too received wounds and, in a while, he was airlifted back up to the command ship with the other seriously wounded soldiers. After the Commanding Officer's surgery, he ended up in the infirmary with this first group of casualties and soon visited by the Task Force Commander, General Crispar. He was in bed number seven, and next to him in bed number eight with Harkey still unconscious with IV's stuck in his arm.

Meanwhile the rest of the plan was unfolding. The main garrison on Praximus Gartuka was being hit hard by another Chevolite Force that came in unexpectedly. The Tiger Team thus was just the diversion, to weaken the garrison and make it an easier target. In another three days the Combat Teams were recalled back to the Garrison to help in the siege, but by then it was too late, the damage was done, and the Tiger Team had completed their mission in one of the most spectacular land battles in recent history.

The war was a long way from being over, but it was now clear the garrison at Praximus Gartuka was no longer tenable and after a few more days, during the cover of night, the remains of the Garrison was removed and sent back to their nearest strongholds. With Praximus Gartuka Garrison gone, the situation on Arkadanstra was bleak and the enemy evacuated all they could, leaving behind many POW's to be traded sometime in the future which was the only way the Chevolite's ever hoped to get their own POW's back.

Harkey finally became conscious and was surprised to discover he was in a bed next to his Commanding Officer.

"I see you made it back alive."

"I'm glad to be back, but something tells me after the pain killers wear off, I'll feel some pain."

"I just finished reading the battle report. The Executive Officer who's acting Commanding Officer of the Tiger Team left a few minutes ago after briefing me. I'm pleased to inform you Sargent Harkey a couple things are going to happen with you now."

"What is that sir?"

"First thing is your infantry days are over. You are going

to the combined base at Cronstine to complete your medical recouperation. Then you will be put in a holding company awaiting the next flight school to start."

"I thought I had at least six more months of deployment."

"The main reason for your participation in these Infantry events was to give you battlefield experience to prepare you for the days you'll spend in the cockpit of a fighter/bomber. Higher ups decided you had already proved your ability in live combat and because you fought so hard, because that's your nature, they needed to pull you out of combat before you got killed and they lost an excellent pilot candidate."

"I don't mind training for flying now but at the same time I feel like I'm abandoning my friends I served with."

"Speaking of friends, you have a couple coming here to visit you in a while."

"How did I get so lucky?"

"These other two individuals had to be pulled out of the line to be presented to the Task Force Commander, General Crispar who is rewarding them today with battlefield promotions for their distinct display of personal sacrifice in the face of overwhelming enemy attacks."

"May I ask who's coming?"

"Your friends Sea Daddy and Sargent Chuk."

Shortly their meals were served, and the conversations died down. Harkey had missed out on food for almost 48 hours he was very hungry and almost felt like requesting additional servings. But they soon found out the orderlies had to quickly clean up because dignitaries would soon be coming in.

Fifteen minutes later there was commotion at the end of the hallway and in came the brass and several enlisted in dress uniforms along with a few photographers.

They stopped at the bed side of four or five other wounded soldiers including a couple pilots.

Harkey could hear their presentations and some of these guys did the utter impossible. Sadly, some were missing arms or legs. One guy was missing an eye, he would never fly again.

They eventually made their way to bed number seven the Commanding Officer. The Tiger Team Executive Officer was with the Task Force Commander, General Crispar who said, "Colonel Kollins, based on your injuries and the time you will be in recuperation, I'm sending you to Cronstine where you will attend Staff and Command School then be reassigned. I think if you do a good showing at the Staff and Command School, you have a shot at a Task Force Commander slot."

"I'm not a pilot, how could I possibly get such an assignment."

"We understand that and as such you will also be attending flight training with Sargent Harkey where the two of you will earn your wings together."

Colonel Kollins looked over at Harkey and smiled.

"What about the Tiger Team?"

"We are getting ready to redeploy them off Praximus Gartuka and send them to Arkadanstra for the mop up operation under the leadership of your Executive Officer who has been promoted to Commanding Officer and after they finish that mission, they will be sent to Cronstine where they will begin training for their next future operation."

"They will be in good hands with my Executive Officer," Colonel Kollins noted.

"I learned a lot from you sir," the Executive Officer said looking directly into Colonel Kollins who also had some significant valor in the battle that resulted in his wounds. The Executive Officer saw Colonel Kollins get cut down just as he was firing his laser pistol into the breach where Spetznar special forces troops came very close to taking out the command post. He saved all their lives and at first, they thought he was dead, but a very caring medic, put forth a vital effort to safe his life so he could come back and fight another day.

"Colonel, your performance was utterly impressive, I've stated so in your service record, and I've highly recommended you for promotion. We'll have talks in the future before you leave the ship and head for Cronstine, but I need to have a little talk now with Sargent Harkey."

"Thank you General, and yes Harkey has more than earned your comments."

"Colonel, its your kind of leadership that inspires young men like Harkey. He is a product of your effort and you training. You all did well."

"Thank you General."

General Crispar took a few steps towards bed number eight and looked down at Sargent Harkey with a big smile and lots of warmth and appreciation.

"Sargent Harkey, why is it I keep running into you in hospital beds?"

"I'm not sure sir, perhaps I just had bad luck."

"Sargent Harkey, the battle was well recorded. We know all the important events that occurred during the battle. Individual sacrifices are a force multiplier. According to the doctors who patched you up, you ended up with three serious wounds in this battle and you had three bad wounds in the previous battle you fought in. I can't tell you how critical it was that your own efforts delayed the enemy attempting to make their way up that ravine to scale the escarpment."

"Thank you, sir for the praise."

"Sargent Harkey, your actions were so decisive and quick that you stalled the Spetznar Combat Team quickly before they could receive support from another major attack from the opposite direction. We had a lot of issues elsewhere on the battlefield, but because of your actions it gave us breathing room and the time to deal with those other exigencies."

"I tried my best sir."

"Sargent Harkey, I saw everything you did on video and I'm very proud of you. In every major battle we get one or two men like you who make a significant difference. A lot of people owe their lives to you, and I have a big surprise for you. Two senior enlisted requested permission to leave the planet and come up here and have a few words with you."

General Crispar turned towards the acting Commanding Officer and said, "Could you please bring in the two men."

"Yes, sir."

The acting commanding officer went down to the end of the hallway and opened the door and said, "Would you guys please come in now."

With slight pain, Harkey set up in his bed and here they came, *Sea Daddy* and Sargent Chuk. Why Sargent Chuk a man who used to haze his ass all the time was here seemed like a big mystery.

The men approached bed side all smiles and *Sea Daddy* started first.

"Harkey, I'm glad you survived. I didn't think you would make it; you really made the difference, and I learned a lot from you during the battle. Being a senior enlisted, I thought

I knew everything. I was your *Sea Daddy* and treated you like a NFG and a NUB. Buy you proved to me in live combat you were never a NFG or a NUB."

"You gave me a lot of inspiration, *Sea Daddy*."

"Harkey, I look at you as my equal. I'm very proud to have served with you. He then held out his hand and Harkey took it and shook it feeling the strong handshake that conveyed how sincere *Sea Daddy* was. When you go to hell together and come back alive, the bonding is strong.

Sea Daddy stood back and now it was Sargent Chuk's time.

"Harkey, I know I rode your ass relentlessly. I though I was doing the right thing to instill fighting spirit in you. What I didn't know at the time I misjudged you and learned through a couple battles you had more fighting spirit in you than I did. I will admit in the first battle I sucked. I'm actually ashamed of my performance. But after I watched the video of how you handled yourself you inspired me so in the second battle, I decided I would give it all I got in honor of you."

"Thank you, Sargent Chuk."

"Harkey, everything I did in that second battle I did so in the back of my mind I was ashamed of my previous actions, and I wanted to demonstrate what I could do to get up to your level. I did my best and I fought like crazy, unfortunately you got wounded and I got lucky that's how wars are."

"Understand."

"I want you to know the decorations I now carry are due to the inspiration that you gave me. I seriously doubt I would ever have put forth that effort had you and I not met up and I got schooled by you. All my awards are because of you. I hope that in the future we can be friends and keep in touch. And I do wish you the best."

"I would like that too."

Sargent Chuk held out his hand and Harkey shook it. This meant a lot to the two senior officers present. It was a phenomenal display of courage that seldom happens. It was moments like this that made it all worthwhile for those senior officer's present to feel like what they were doing mattered. It also would add to their own inspiration and help them during tough times they knew they would meet in the future.

CHAPTER TWO
FLIGHT SCHOOL

When Harkey showed up for flight school, he was in a class of college graduates with no military combat experience. These were pipeline cadets that would be flying transport craft and a lot of other things and not necessarily combat equipment. Most were egotistical and of a social stratum that would easily look condescendingly down on Sargent Harkey who was entitled to wear all his decorations on his dress uniforms required to be worn in the classrooms.

All the cadets were proud of their uniforms and knew that in a matter of time they would be going on the biggest adventures in their lifetimes. All had passed strenuous psychological tests. There were no panzies in the group. And most of them were boisterous and loud.

Harkey was naturally quiet and had to get a waiver for his medical condition from the six wounds he obtained. His pain was almost over but there were some lingering pains that came and went with weather conditions.

What astonished the cadets was they had a full bird Colonel in their class which of course caused the instructors a little stress, because they never knew for sure if he was evaluating them. Sargent Harkey and Colonel Kollins tended to sit at the back of the class and kept quiet. After a few class sessions the first instructor a guy by the name of Major Adams, went to his superior Lieutenant Colonel Webb and explained, "I feel a little stress with the two unusual students in the class. Is this some kind of setup?"

Lieutenant Colonel Webb invited Major Adams into his office where they could have a private discussion.

"Major Adams, I'm going to give you a special briefing. What I tell you in this office is not to leave this office, do you understand?"

"Yes sir. I will not divulge it to anyone."

"Colonel Kollins is probably going to be promoted to a Task Force Commander, but he's not a qualified pilot which is one of the requirements. He will earn his pilot qualifications here and get as much time in aircraft as we can arrange and after he finishes his other training will be reassigned to a task force most likely as commander or executive officer, and then promoted to Task Force Commander after a period of time."

"That's understandable."

"Colonel Kollins is a great guy. Don't worry about him. Its all your other students you need to worry about."

"What about Sargent Harkey. He's very quiet and seems to be a friend of Colonel Kollins?"

"Sargent Harkey received his battlefield promotions twice from Colonel Kollins. In two major battles he received major wounds and had to receive a waiver to be allowed to take this course."

"So, they know each other?"

"Yes, in fact they were in hospital beds next to each other for almost two weeks after the last battle where each received some substantial wounds. Colonel Kollins also had to receive a waiver to attend this school because of age and those wounds that are still healing."

"So, Sargent Harkey is the real deal?"

"Yes, he's one of the highest decorated Sargent's in the special forces."

"What kind of aircraft will he be flying?"

"The reason why he was put in those combat missions was to give him a taste of live combat and develop a perspective towards close ground support. His pilot's training was delayed until he completed those assignments."

"That makes me feel a lot better about the situation."

"I can't share with you his service record, but I was required to read portions of it so that I would understand he's slated for close ground support aircraft and what they did to prepare him for that assignment. But I will tell you the endorsements by the Task Force Commander were rather substantial. He is a must pass student at any cost. He's earned this opportunity many times over and I don't care how long it takes for him to get his wings, he will even if I must personally take him up in the trainer aircraft."

"Not to worry sir, I will make sure he learns how to fly."

"Major Adams, that's not good enough. You need to work with him to get him to the level he needs to be to fly close in ground support. I know from your personal history you are a great pilot and can fly any type of mission so be sure and keep in mind the kind of missions he's going to fly and impart with him some of that great knowledge you have from many hours in the cockpit with all your broad spectrum of assignments."

"Knowing where Sargent Harkey is going to go, I will do my best and help him be able to carry out those missions."

"He has an incredible history and proved in combat he's a

brave warrior, all we need to do is help him master close in support aircraft because I know he's the kind of person that will put forth the maximum effort."

"I'll work with him sir."

"How's his test scores?"

"He's doing as well as anyone in the classroom. His academics are quite acceptable and based on test results he catches on to the subject matter quite well and I have no concern about his academic ability."

"Good. If any issues develop, come see me right away."

"I will."

"I know you have an unusual class. You probably will not experience this again, but one thing I want you to remember is Colonel Kollins is a great guy and a superb tactical commander. Feel honored to have him in your class. In due time I'm sure you will take a liking to him."

"Anything else sir?"

"You know what you need to do Major Adams. I have faith in you."

"Thank you, sir."

That little pep talk helped Major Adams quite a bit. During the next classroom session there was less tension in the air and Major Adams felt more comfortable on the podium.

During training the curriculum allowed for instructors to populate their training materials with some anecdotal information that pertained to the subject matter such as aerial maneuvers and how certain battles transpired.

One of the students asked a question about the training materials they were discussing and if it pertained to recent combat at Praximus Gartuka that was in the news since it was liberated, and holographic news agencies were having big discussions about it and requesting the government release some of the video so that they could share it with the public. Thus far the government had censored the video *not for release* and was reluctant to do so because much fighting was left to do in this war that had gone on far too long:

"Major Adams, during the invasion of Praximus Gartuka, what was the air war like?"

"Cadet Zdzislak, I wasn't there for that battle, but we have two people in the classroom that were. Colonel Kollins, do you have any comments?"

"Major Adams, I watched the initial Space Battle in my space cabin, and I invited Sargent Harkey to observe it with me because we had about an hour before we would be boarding our landing craft. The reason why he was in my cabin was to reward him for his valor in combat where he was severely wounded and kept fighting. I would also like to add the video of his fighting are now being showed at infantry officer training courses. If you don't mind, I would like Sargent Harkey to explain what he saw."

"Sargent Harkins, your comments please," Major Adams requested.

"Harkins stood up and began his comments: First off, I would say the air and space battle inspired me. Those pilots flying combat missions were giving it all. We were landing on the dark side of the planet in a night mission arrival and were able to see the explosions a lot better because of no sunlight. It was an incredible vision to me and there were a lot of explosions."

"Do you know what kind of weapons caused the explosions?" a student asked.

"There was a mixture of weapons used from beam weapons to lasers, to kinetic weapons and missiles. It was an incredible light show of lasers and beams and missile exhausts. I've never seen such a massive attack before in my lifetime including movies or old war film clips."

One of the students asked, "What was the enemy like in those battles?"

The enemy was fighting just as ferociously as our guys and to be honest I wasn't sure we would be alive before we got down onto the surface of the planet."

"Did we lose a lot of transports?"

"Our air support and space defense did a superb job in protecting us. The safety corridor they provided allowed most of us to get to the planet in good shape."

"Did the ground forces start fighting as soon as you landed?" A student asked.

"We were all situated in secure defensive positions before the enemy attacked."

"How did our forces manage that?" One of the students asked.

"Since the combat engineers were able to get down to the planet surface with their *tunneling Spatializers*, they were able to build us trenches and tunnels providing us safety in case the enemy pounced on us right away."

"Any lessons learned?" Major Adams asked.

"My takeaway from the battle was our pilots were courageous and it helped inspire me to fight as hard as I could."

Harkey sat down with the class focusing in on him, but the chest full of ribbons he wore spoke volumes about he had been to hell and back.

"Any other comments Sargent Harkey?"

"That about sums it up for me."

"Colonel Kollins?"

Colonel Kollins stood up and said, "What Sargent Harkey said pretty much sums it up. It was a massive air battle and we do have a lot of gun camera video from the surviving craft as well as photonics from my ship and others. I hope that after the war, the defense department releases the videos because the men who participated in it deserve some recognition, especially those who did not make it back with us."

Colonel Kollins then looked around the classroom at the somber cadets who were in awe of these two and felt he needed to say something: "All you cadets, do the best you can and remember a lot of men paid for this victory with their lives. The reason why we were so successful in space and on the ground later was our space and air forces protected us. You all have a critical function, especially if you get in the role of supporting future task forces. Try your best and do your best in this school. None of you would be in this class if you had not already proven something to someone. Keep up the effort and hopefully one day you will join Sargent Harkey and I on a mission of equal importance."

Colonel Kollins then sat down, and Major Adams then looked out into the class and knew this was going to be a special class because Colonel Kollins and Sargent Harkey's personas were rubbing off onto the students who were super motivated and ready to jump to the next level and demonstrate their commitment.

The class had an element of Physical training in it. They sometimes put on tee shirts shorts and running shoes and went out to the track and made laps. Occasionally they went to the swimming pool and swam laps because they needed to be strong swimmers, especially if they had to ditch their aircraft at sea.

The first time they saw Sargent Harkey in his swim trunks getting ready to dive into the pool to swim laps with them, they saw all the scars. To some extent it seemed frightening. With his clothes off Sargent Harkey was a walking Frankenstein. Colonel Kollins was no exception, he had to run and swim with the boys, which he didn't mind. He also had some genuinely terrible scars from his wounds.

Somehow those scars drew the cadets closer to these two guys and by the time they finished phase one of training which was mostly ground school, technology and a few extras, every single student in the class was doing quite well and the class grade point average was way above normal that caused a critique.

There was disbelief by a lot of instructors, so Lieutenant Colonel Webb personally proctored the next examination which the class did very well on and then he took all the instructors that were making unwarranted comments into a private meeting and explained the facts of life to them.

The Phase Two instructors were more than ready for this class because this was when they would first start flying in simulators and trainer aircraft.

In phase two, they all flew the same trainer aircraft and spent time in the simulators of the same type of aircraft.

The simulators could run sixteen simultaneous scenarios for sixteen pilots if necessary.

Luckily due to class size, the entire class was in the simulators at the same time.

During phase two they were just learning how to fly and

navigate. In case the NAVAIDS got destroyed they had to know how to fly as a conventional pilot.

The simulators were outstanding and had all the features of the real aircraft. Sitting in the simulator, you felt as if you were in the real aircraft except feeling the G forces.

The learning modes of the simulators were quite ingenious, and the artificial intelligence gave many measurements. It was no longer instructor subjective call. It was artificial intelligence measuring the student compared to many other and the relative strength index was the measure. Students could look at their relative strength index across the board and quickly determine which areas they needed to improve the most.

It was almost like biofeedback as the evaluations gradually improved the pilot and by the time they finished with Phase Two, they were well charted on their progress. This class somewhat motivated by Colonel Kollins and the Sargent Harkey seemed to score higher than all other classes previously. There definitely was a strange influence that benefitted them all.

In the second half of Phase Two, they flew actual trainer aircraft. One day while flying around, Harkey asked, "Why is the student in the front and the instructor in the rear seat?"

"That's so we can beat the student over the head when he makes mistakes."

"What if it's a female pilot?"

"We have some tough bitches for instructors. We'd put a female instructor with a female student with issues and she would beat her over the head."

"How tough are the female pilots?"

"When they have 8,000 hours in the cockpit they usually are

as good as anyone else."

"How did they do in our recent space battles?"

"The number of casualties were about the same. It really mattered which target you had to attack. Some are more deadly than others."

Part of the course grade was derived from the number of hours a student spent in the cockpit flying an aircraft. To get students to spend more time in the flight simulators, the policy was after their records indicated they completed three hours of flying in the simulator, they were allowed one hour flying time in a real aircraft. During weekends when they could be off enjoying themselves many were in the simulators flying to earn the hours in the cockpit. Saturday and Sunday turned into a full workday for most of the class. Every single student was eager to earn their wings.

Harkey wanted to get Phase Two over with so he could start flying tactical aircraft in the simulators instead of the trainer two-seater aircraft. During the final week of phase two training, the students thinned out on Sunday afternoon, but Harkey was there, and Major Adams was supervising the trainers that could actually simulate most aircraft types. At the completion of one of the scenarios, Major Adams impressed with Harkey's dedication thought it would be a waste of his time to spend another couple hours flying a trainer aircraft and he initiated a conversation.

"What type of Aircraft to you plan on specializing in?"

"I'm slated for direct ground support role aircraft."

"Everyone else is gone for the day. You are the last student here. How would you like to fly an Albatross Varco?"

"I would love to fly one, but I'm not familiar with all the flight controls since I've never studied the aircraft."

"I teach Albatross Varco tactics for phase four students. If you want, I'll change the simulator over to an Albatross Varco and talk you through the controls until you get the hang of it."

"Sure, I would love to do that."

Major Adams reconfigured the simulator that took a few minutes and they were ready.

"I've initiated a simple training scenario we take pilots through for knobology and flight controls proficiency. The Albatross Varco as you can see is now at the end of the runway ready to take off."

"Alright I'm all set."

"Go ahead and advance the throttles and start the roll."

Harkey advanced the throttles, and the simulator imagery gave the three-dimensional appearance they were rolling down the runway.

"Flaps are prepositioned, and the aircraft trimmed for takeoff."

"So far so good."

"When you hit one hundred fifty knots start the rotate and at one hundred feet, retract the landing gear." Major Adams pointed to the landing gear controls.

In a moment when the speed was ideal, Harkey said, "Rotation."

"Keep an angle on the aircraft to keep the speed above one hundred fifty knots and begin landing gear retraction at 100 feet.

"At 100 hundred feet, retracting the landing gear," Harkey stated when the simulator indicated the Albatross Varco was at 100 feet.

"At 500 feet reposition the flaps to zero degrees."

Moments later, "At 500 hundred feet, resetting flaps to zero degrees."

Level the aircraft and trim the aircraft to cruise orientation.

Harkey saw the trim tabs and indication for cruise and adjusted to match.

"What now?"

"Climb up to twenty thousand feet on a heading of 090 degrees."

Ten minutes later Harkey reported, "We are at twenty thousand feet on a course of 090."

"The autopilot controls on the Albatross Varco work the same way they do on the aircraft trainers you flew. Go ahead and enter course 090 and altitude of 20,000 feet into the autopilot controls."

"Autopilot set for 20,000 feet and a course of 090."

"We are going to fly a box pattern for a few minutes. In five minutes, change course to 000 degrees and altitude to 15,000 feet on the autopilot."

"Roger that."

The next auto pilot changes went to 270 degrees heading at 10,000 feet and finally 180 degrees at 5,000 feet. After five minutes heading at 180, Major Adams said, "Take it out of Autopilot and go back to 20,000 feet heading 090 and repeat this box pattern in manual flying."

"Understand all."

While they were flying, Major Adams went over all the knobology and instruments. In two hours', time, Harkey was feeling good about flying the Albatross Varco. He wasn't looking at the clock, nor was Major Adams who had great appreciation for this man who made tremendous sacrifices in live combat to prove his Metal.

After flying the box in manual control, Major Adams said, "It's time to do some touch and goes. Now that we are on the final leg of that box, when we steady up at 090, change altitude to 800 feet maintaining 200 knots, and two miles from the runway deploy the flaps to the landing position and slow to 150 knots then lower the landing gear."

"Understand all."

In a few minutes Harkey announced, "We are at 800 feet doing 200 knots, deploying the flaps now and slowing to 150 knots."

"Good."

Moments later, "We are lined up nicely on the runway at 150 knots, lowering the landing gear."

"After you land on the runway and get the aircraft stable, take off again."

"Understand, take off again after landing."

The aircraft came down and Harkey seemed to have the handle on it and hit the runway as soft as a feather and when all the wheels were down solid on the runway and the aircraft was slowing, he advanced the throttles and momentarily said, "Rotation."

"Good. Fly the box again but only go to 1000 feet with five minutes on each leg and come back and land exactly like you just did."

After about 10 touch and goes, Major Adams said, "I think you got the hang of it. You spent enough time in the trainer today to earn two hours of flying time in an Albatross Varco.

"I thought I would not get to fly that plane until phase four."

"Since you will be flying close in ground support missions, as your instructor I can advance you in aircraft types. All I must do is send a justification memorandum up to Lieutenant Colonel Webb for approval."

"Do you think there is a good chance he'll approve it?"

"I'm sure he will, because us face it, you are not likely to spend a lot of time in multi-engine cargo aircraft or space fighters with your slated combat support roles for task forces."

"I appreciate that."

"But let me make one thing clear, you will still have to fly all the aircraft types in phase three and phase four training. In order to get the extra time in an Albatross Varco, you will have to spend a lot of time in trainers and simulators."

"That's alright by me if it means I'll get extra training in the Albatross Varco."

"I think you know by now; you and you alone control how much time you spend in a simulator. You have already seen where the extra time has paid off because you already have earned two hours flying time for an Albatross Varco."

By the end of phase two every single student in the class successfully soloed cross country and obtained a flying license. Based on their contracts the were all now promoted to second lieutenants including Harkey. Since they had to show up in their classrooms wearing their dress uniforms, Harkey got a lot of stares from a lot of people, because it was extremely rare to see a second lieutenant with as many decorations on their uniforms as Harkey. The one decoration he loved the most on the uniform was the pair of wings.

Some of the students in the class came from well to do families and others came from families with military history, either fathers or grandfathers. Once or twice a week those well-connected families who knew Colonel Kollins and contacted him. The discussions were usually the same.

"Colonel Kollins, I heard you are in the same pilot training class as my son Jeremy."

"Yes, Walt that's correct."

"How's he doing?"

"He's doing great. Really nice person and I expect him to do well in life."

"Do you think he will pass the course?"

"He just finished phase two and now has a pilot's license. Yes, I believe he'll make it."

"I really thank you for giving me the insights how he's doing."

"Walt, he may not appreciate me talking to you about him, so us keep this conversation between just you and I."

"No problem I do understand the sensitivity in all this, and I do appreciate your candor."

"You know me from the past, I'm not politically correct and I take pride in making sure men under my jurisdiction are well cared for and given the pathway to success."

"Your secrets are safe with me and thank you for your observations. I feel a lot better now about all this."

"Not a problem. Have faith in our son, he's a good guy."

"Coming from you makes me proud of him."

"You should be."

"Thanks. I'll talk to you again one of these days. Us don't be strangers."

"Of course not."

CHAPTER THREE
ADVANCED FLIGHT TRAINING

Harkey was now where he wanted to be and had given so much of himself to be here including getting severely wounded. Few if no second lieutenants had two decorations for receiving serious wounds in battle. Harkey also had a very unusual decoration, the medal of valor which is the second highest award given to any Chevolite military person. The supreme medal of valor was given only to those killed in the line of duty that exhibited incredible valor like Harkey but died from their wounds as a result. Many men and women who deserved the Supreme Medal of Valor never received it because their circumstance could not be officially reported due to issues like a ship exploding in space with them aboard or all eyewitnesses wiped out which often occurred in hellish battles.

Colonel Kollins was pleased to see Harkey as a second lieutenant wearing a pair of wings. He even got more enthused about the young man when a few days later they were going out to the flight line to get on aircraft to fly. Harkey walked up to his plane first which surprised Colonel Kollins the young man was going to fly an Albatross Varco.

"You are going to fly this thing?"

"Yes, I've earned now four hours of flight time thanks to my time in the flight simulator."

"How did you get to this assignment?"

"Major Adams sent the recommendation to Lt. Col. Webb who approved it."

"Are you going to fly the other aircraft designated for phase three?"

"Yes, I will fly all of phase III and phase IV aircraft, but since I earned the extra time in the Albatross Varco, Major Adams arranged for me to fly it today."

"Good luck on your flight." Colonel Kollins expressed his firm wishes for the young man he admired and knew there were not many like him.

"Thank you, sir, the same for you and the cargo plane."

"I'd much rather fly Cargo planes than the Albatross Varco."

"Well sir, if I'm going to fly close ground support and help all my buddies on the ground in a battle like we experienced at Praximus Gartuka. I expect it will be like Praximus Gartuka."

"All those ground pounders are lucky to have someone like you that wants to assist them."

"Well sir you know because you were there, they earned my respect, and they sacrificed a lot."

"You got that right and I'm glad you feel that way."

"I'm proud to be wearing a combat badge."

"As you should be."

"Thank you,"

"See you when you get back. Maybe one of these days you

can take me out on an Albatross Varco."

"Sir as soon as I finish my qualifications in this Albatross Varco Trainer, you would be the first person I would want to fly with. I'll even let you sit in the front seat and fly the plane."

"I'll take you up on it when we are ready. See you in a while."

The Colonel continued down the flight line while Harkey climbed up into the front seat of the Albatross Varco. To his surprise, Major Adams was in the back seat smiling.

It was rather interesting that today, they flew the same geometries they did in the simulator. Harkey felt very confident because it was just like flying the simulator except, they got to feal real G forces.

As part of pilot training, all takeoffs and landings are video recorded. The process was automated so after four hours of continuous flying, including touch and goes and cross-country navigation exercises, Harkey landed the Albatross Varco and pulled it up to its tie-down zone and shut the engines down and did the post flight checkoff. Major Adams waited until he completed all those actions then stepped out of the rear seat of the fighter bomber onto the portable stairs and glided down to the tarmac and turned around waiting for Harkey to exit the craft.

Moments later Harkey was down to the Tarmac standing next to Major Adams who said, "Alright us go over to the debriefing room and see how you did today."

Harkey knew there was always room for improvement but felt he did a good job flying today. Major Adams simply gave him the geometries to perform and directed him to perform the touch and goes. Other than that, there wasn't much conversation going on in the Airplane as Harkey was paying attention to everything going on around him in the aircraft as well as visual flight rules efforts to detect any other aircraft in the vicinity.

The evaluators looked at the score sheet and were amazed that after 16 hours in the simulator and 4 hours flying the trainer, a student would do so well.

Every one of Major Adams actions in the rear cockpit were automatically recorded. If Major Adams had to adjust any control or give instructions, that would be logged and evaluated as points against Harkey. The system worked on a 5.0 top score and went down from there based on any mistakes made or any corrections the instructor had to do to the flight controls to conform with requirements.

A magnified aircraft orientation was replayed. Normally a pilot may not see or see the subtle aircraft movements, but with the magnification, any slight changes were somewhat exaggerated mainly so the student could see the attitude of the aircraft during the debrief and critique.

The debriefing was quick because there wasn't a lot of criticism to go over. Flight instructor comments were now examined and when it was all said and done, they were ready to post his score.

"Second Lieutenant Harkey, your score is 4.87. This sets the record for first flight of a student in a new type of aircraft. It appears you made good use of you time in the simulators. Your takeoffs and landings met or exceeded pilots with over 1000 hours of flight time in this plane."

"I owe a lot to Major Adams for preparing me for the flight."

"You were a good student, Harkey. If all our pilots applied themselves the way you do, our class grade point averages would be a lot higher."

"I know I need to apply myself because I've got to see firsthand what aerial combat can be like. Every pilot needs every edge they can get, and some of that is in the preparation."

"You are absolutely right on that, and we feel students underplay the importance of the simulators."

"The simulators make me feel a lot safer when I get to the plane."

"That's what we hope."

The debrief ended and Harkey went to his living quarters where he showered then changed into civilian clothes because the class was going out in town tonight celebrating earning their wings and their promotions. Harkey got the largest promotion going from a Sargent to Second Lieutenant.

They all met outside the bachelor officers' quarters at the prescribed time and managed to fit in a couple taxi-limousines that could pick them up on the base and take them out on the town.

Eventually they made it to a swank bar with live entertainment full of pretty ladies wanting to latch onto a flyboy. Half of the class came from well to do families and their parents had already selected them a future bride. Not necessarily someone they wanted, but it was all part of the game of quid pro quo and blending wealthy families together. The marriages acted as a treaty document that bound the two families together. This was one of the methods of them protecting their wealth and multiplying it.

Once in a blue moon disaster struck as young military men from such families married a woman who was the daughter of a business rival. Then it really got complicated.

Harkey was an outsider. He wasn't a big booze drinker and really didn't like alcohol, so he was very gentle on the drinks while the rest of them proceeded to get *shit-faced*. Harkey's physical conditioning and self defense training he received as a ground pounder would go a long way to protect him and looks were deceiving. Since he was with the group of flyboys, some of the rascals at the bar that wanted to beat the snot out of the flyboys' assumed Harkey was a pussy like the rest of them. After the flyboys got inebriated and boisterous, the troublemakers decided to make their move since they were also chemically altered and feeling invincible.

Harkey had just met a female Lindy Foster; that was gravitating to his quiet nature. The conversation lasted fifteen minutes then the fireworks started when a couple of the bruisers decided they would punch out a few of the scrawny pilots now juiced up and not all there.

Harkey sitting on the sidelines saw two of the bruisers grabbed young Jeremy and one was beating the crap out of him while the other was holding Jeremy.

Harkey quickly stood up and said, "Take your hands off my friend."

"Who the fuck are you, wise guy?"

"Listen, I don't want to have to hurt you."

"You want some of me, do you?"

"Like I said, I don't want to hurt you, but since there is a bunch of you in here, I'll have to hurt you really bad, I might even accidentally kill you."

"Okay fucker, us see what you got." The bruiser turned towards battle hardened Harkey who had lots of hand-to-hand combat training and even with the injuries outclassed the idiot by several stratums.

Harkey let the monkey throw a punch and grabbed his hand in flight and squeezed it hard so he could not shake it and with Harkey's other hand pumped four fast hard punches into the rib cage breaking one of the ribs in the process.

When the guy bent over sucking for air, Harkey's knee hit him in the head and knocked him out. He then walked towards the guy holding Jeremy who was bleeding very badly and reached over Jeremy and punched him hard in the face which dazzled him with a star field, and he immediately released Jeremy.

About that time four other bruisers came at Harkey who knew he would have to get very dangerous now to save his own life, side stepped one, banged another, and grabbed a third and threw him into two others real hard which knocked them over giving him the opportunity to kick one nice and hard in the testicles and that idiot started shaking like a leave.

Two other local boys now came flying at Harkey a former football player used to stiff arming and getting rid of defenders, but now he had combat training to save his own life. He took one hard punch from one of them giving him a bloody nose before Harkey knocked him out.

Harkey had motivated his classmates. They didn't know *anything* about fighting but they wanted to jump in there and the combination of Harkey's real combat techniques and these airmen doing the best they could in another few minutes ended it.

Harkey could see Jeremy was beat up terribly bad, so he said, "Guys we need to get Jeremy to the infirmary he's in bad shape."

Luckily this upscale club had several taxi's outside, and they carried Jeremy to one of them and Harkey got in with him and they drove directly to the on base hospital and took Jeremy into the emergency room.

Shortly after they were gone the police showed up and were utterly shocked these troublemakers who they had run ins in the past were devastatingly beat up bad requiring a police investigation, especially since one of them lost a testicle.

Thanks to video recording Harkey and Jeremy were flagged by the police and even though Jeremy wasn't in any shape to fly the next day, he at least made it to class.

Halfway through the morning Harkey and Jeremy were led out of the classroom by military police and soon in the local civilian county jail cell together.

Thanks to Colonel Kollins being in the classroom, he called Jeremy's father Walt Pazar and explained how Jeremy was in serious legal trouble and what happened.

Walt hopped on an intergalactic transport with several lawyers from one of the capital's prestigious law firms. Normally Harkey would have been screwed especially bad and tossed out of flight school for this incident. After Jeremy explained what happened and how Harkey had saved his life, Walt Pazar decided to go to bat for Harkey with a law firm made available for Harkey.

A few days later the Kangaroo court in town started and the district attorney and the judge and the Kangaroo jurors were all present some of which were almost wanting to giggle because they thought they were going to get the rich kid and the other person that injured some of the towns people's children.

When the judge discovered the law team, she was facing she knew this was going to get some serious investigation by higher authorities and the sparks started flying when the lead attorney asked the simple question, "Your honor, the two men listed as victims first grabbed Jeremy and started beating him up, why is it they have not been charged with an assault and battery?"

"The police didn't charge them."

"They don't have any choice. As a member of the court, I've already filed a brief in Federal Court, and I've been informed the Feds have looked at the video and are sending agents here to arrest them in a few hours. Because of the terrible beating they gave Jeremy they will likely spend 20 years in prison. Also, Federal Agents I've discussed the case with, and my charges say all the other towns people involved in that altercation will also be arrested today and are looking at 5 to 10 years in Federal Prison."

"Will the defense and the prosecution please approach the bench," The judge said now knowing this case was out of control.

When they were in the huddle, the Judge asked the lead attorney, what do you expect to get out of this display you just did."

"Your honor, we are in the process of petitioning the appeals court to move this case to a new venue because Jeremy and Harkey cannot get a fair treatment in this town, especially when the Feds haul off their eight relatives. Also, we will be vetting the jury to insure none of them are related to the eight men."

The judge knew the town was trapped. It would hurt the town severely if those eight young men were hauled away so she knew there was always a settlement. She looked at the prosecutor and said, "I'm sorry Prosecution, but if you do not settle the case now, I will toss it out because the police screwed up the investigation.

"I'm not going to agree to a settlement," the prosecutor said.

I can do a summary judgement now and declare the two accused soldiers are not guilty."

"I'm not going to agree to a settlement, I'll recharge them with other crimes." the prosecutor said.

"Very well gentlemen, take your seats."

After the attorneys sat down the judge said, "I could toss out the case, but the problem is the prosecution could file another case and place the two accused in double jeopardy. Its clear that what went on in that bar is nothing like reported in court filings by the prosecutor. I'm considering charging the prosecutor with misconduct, but in the end that will not serve much purpose. As a judge I have the legal authority to make a summary judgement when I find the conditions of the case are so seriously flawed the defendants cannot get a fair trial because the warrant is tainted and stinks."

The prosecutor attempted to start saying an objection but was quickly overruled and then the Judge did as she had indicated during their short conference.

"I hereby find the two defendants NOT GUILTY. Case is closed." The judges hammer came down in a shocking moment.

Soon as the crowd was filing out of the court room the head defense attorney approached the prosecutor and said:

"I just want you to know Mr. Prosecutor, if you take any further legal action against these two young men, we will file suit against you in Federal Court for misconduct. I also want you to know the funds required to litigate you indefinitely are available and will be used."

The prosecutor was feeling scorched and reacted, "I do not like the way the judge handled this case, I still might press new charges."

Don't even try that BS with these fine young men. What you did to them is despicable. I don't know how you can sleep at night. As a criminal prosecutor you have the moral obligation to serve justice even if it goes against your town's will."

The prosecutor realized this case was now over. Nothing would be gained by him attempting any further actions and simply departed the courtroom feeling humiliated and resentful.

Harkey and Jeremy were led out of the courtroom by the military police to a van that was going to return the *not guilty airmen* back to the base as Jeremy's father approached them and said, "Sir may I have a few minutes with these two young men."

"Sure, not a problem." The Military Police said since they would be going back to base quite early and the two men and been vindicated.

"Looks like you guys are going to be okay," Walt Pazar said looking appreciatively at Harkey.

Harkey knew one thing for sure, had Jeremy's dad not protected him, he would have been ruined by those criminals. He then spoke, "Mr. Pazar, I appreciate what you did for me. Without your legal help my days in the service would probably be over."

"Call me Walt."

"Sure, and thank you Walt."

"Harkey, my lawyers have exceptionally good investigators, and we have copies of the video from that bar. Its clear to me they might have killed Jeremy had you not jumped in and saved his life at a critical moment. My legal team also got released to us the medical treatment Jeremy received after you rushed him to the hospital. He had a serious concussion and medical experts I hired said had he received a couple more blows to the head, it could have easily killed him since he already had that serious head wound. I also know that for quite a bit of the fight you held off eight guys by yourself. It was an incredible act of bravery, and I am in debt to you for saving my son's life."

"I did what I felt I needed to do to protect my classmate."

"In case you don't know it, Colonel Kollins and I are good friends. I've known him most of his life as we grew up together and our families were close friends. I gave him all the information our investigators discovered and he's aware that all you did was to try to save my son's life. He informed me he will be your advocate in case the military decides to discipline you in any manner. He's pretty sure none of this will be permanent in your record as it shouldn't be. He has already taken this matter to the General who has since directed personnel department to be sure and leave your record untainted."

"I really appreciate that. It means a lot to me."

"I'm very proud to know my son has a friend such as you. Its rare when we go through life that we meet people of exemplary manner."

"Thank you."

Walt turned to Jeremy and said, "Colonel Kollins is a great man. He's led a lot of men in combat including Harkey. He's a good judge of character. He's said some good things about you. I'm proud of you. Keep up your good efforts. I'm sure you will be a great pilot."

"I'll do my best dad."

"I'll come back and visit you guys when your class graduates. I wish you the best."

Walt tapped his son on the shoulder then he turned and held out his hand and shook Harkey's and said, "I wish you luck and hope you stay safe."

"Thank you."

Walt turned around and walked to one of a couple Limo's the legal team soon departed in.

As soon as the Military Police Van returned to base they went immediately to the base commander's office. This would be the next hurdle they would have to get over to become pilots.

Harkey assumed he would probably get an ass chewing and possibly even tossed out of flight school.

They were ushered into the Base Commander's Office and there he was with a couple more visitors. Captain Kollins and the Task Force Commander for the Praximus Gartuka operation. The three had received the word from court monitors sent there the fast end to the farce and the *Not Guilty Verdict*.

Harkey and Jeremy were standing at attention in front of the Base Commanding Officer who then said, "You guys stand at ease. In fact, please have a seat as he gestured to two chairs in the middle of the room obviously brought in for their use.

The Base Commanding Officer then explained what was happening.

"It looks like the planets aligned for you two pilots. Because of your not-guilty verdict and the Feds involvement there will be no disciplinary action taken against you. The video tapes show that Jeremy was the Victim of an unprovoked attack. Lt. Harkey, based on reports I've read from the doctors, you probably saved Jeremy's life. I wish the rest of the class had jumped in sooner to beat those goons off but its moments like this we freeze in shock. The good news is they eventually came to and realized they needed to protect their buddies and that may have saved the both of you."

Harkey looked at the Base Commanding Officer wondering

what was going to happen next. He was feeling better with the the sentiment he received, buy knew there was more in store for them.

"You two guys are now high profile. We cannot afford to have you go back out in town again before you graduate, do you understand?"

"I understand sir," Harkey quickly responded.

Jeremy nodded and didn't have much else to offer.

"I want you to promise me you will stay on base until after you graduate. What I'm going to now tell you does not leave this office do you understand?"

"Yes sir."

Colonel Kollins has been selected for promotion. He's taking additional training here at the staff and command school and as soon as he finishes, he will relieve the Task Force Commander who is here to see the two of you. The Task Force Commander will then be reassigned to war planning at Headquarters. He has specifically requested the two of you be sent to his task force right after graduation. The Task Force has left Praximus Gartuka and is in route to a different sector of space where the fleet will go through a maintenance period and bring on replacement crews and conduct training. We expect you to graduate just in time to participate in the training."

"Thank you, sir," Harkey said, and Jeremy nodded in unison.

"In case you don't know it, Harkey you will be detailed to fly with an Albatross Varco squadron."

"Thank you, sir, that's what I want to fly."

"Jeremy, you have shown exceptional flight skills and will transition into a space fighter squadron."

"Thank you, sir, I always dreamed of being in a space fighter."

"Normally we do not inform pilots of their destinations until they finish phase four training, but we know the two of you will do well in the remainder of your training. Since you will not be going out in town until you graduate, you should have plenty of time in the simulators to improve and advance your skills.

"I will work hard at it," Harkey responded.

"I will also," Jeremy added.

"Another thing I want to point out and the reason why you are not permitted to discuss anything said in this office today. You don't know this, but some important people went to bat for you. It wasn't the lawyers that got the Feds interested in your case, it was other people up high."

"I appreciate that, sir," Harkey responded.

"Jeremy's father's legal team helped with the investigation, but it was very powerful people that stood by you and would not have permitted bad things to happen to you."

"I appreciate it sir."

"Harkey you might as well know it, you earned that protection because of the tremendous sacrifice you made at Arkadanstra and again at Praximus Gartuka. We know that as a close in support pilot you will face a lot of hazards, and your next time may not be so lucky. In essence you paid in advance."

Harkey stood there feeling a lot of emotion and had to fight hard to not allow tears to form. It was one of the most difficult moments in his life as his emotions were now elevated to a breaking point.

"I also know a lot about you, and I know you will not let us down. Its not every day I get a student like you Harkey or a new pilot like Colonel Kollins. It's very strange to say the least."

The task force commander approached Harkey and said, "The last couple of times I saw you were in a hospital bed after almost getting killed in the line of duty. Now I get to see you after a Kangaroo Court. This has been an interesting experience for me. But I'm proud to have served with you."

"Thank you, sir."

"Alright gentlemen you are dismissed and since you missed out on a lot of flying time sitting in that local jail, I've given directions to your instructors to take you flying today. Go get changed in you flight suits."

"Right away sir."

"Harkey you will of course be flying an Albatross Varco with Major Adams who volunteered to fly with you."

"I appreciate what Major Adams has done to help me."

"Jeremy, you will be jumping up to phase four curriculum and get a four-hour indoctrination ride in a space fighter."

Jeremy asked, "Will I fly the space fighter around the base?"

The Base Commanding Officer said, "I don't want this to go to your head, but the task force commander's Space Carrier is in Geosynchronous Orbit directly over us and you will take a shuttle flight up to the carrier and deploy from there just like you would in real combat."

"In a 2-seater?"

"Yes of course until you get certified in the craft."

Jeremy was all smiles because he didn't think he would

make it to that upper crust of pilots where only the top twenty percent got to fly space fighters.

In a short period, they were dismissed and changed into their flight suits and ready to start training.

The two men stayed on base like they promised and spent most of their spare time in simulators and trainers. Since the instructors understood these two were ear marked for the types of aircraft, they were flying they were dismissed out of flying the other types which placed them into phase four training that was meant to give them the combat skills they needed to survive. In an accelerated fashion because of all their flying time, they soloed and were now able to fly single seaters and chart their own destiny.

~~~

The Space Force had to bring in a carrier for phase four training providing space carrier operations for the students and the crew didn't mind because they got extra liberty calls down to the planet. Jeremy's days were longer because he had to fly up to the carrier on a shuttle flight and then deploy from one of the individualized hangers that held a single space fighter. The Space Carrier had one hundred of these individual hangers that allowed them to launch vast numbers very quickly should such a battle like on Praximus Gartuka happen.

The other flyboys went out in town and during one of these visits, the nice-looking lady, Lindy Foster approached them and asked, "Are you friends with Harkey?"

"Yes, we are his classmates."

"Could I give you something to give to him for me?"

"Sure."
~~~

She handed one of the nice and polite young men an envelop with the word Harkey on the front of it. The pilot took the small envelope and put it in his pocket.

Lindy then left the restaurant-bar a short time later. She was hoping they would give the envelop to Harkey because she wanted to see him again.

Harkey had another tough day with Major Adams who taught combat maneuvers. Phase four was the toughest phase of the course because that's where they learned real combat flying. The instructors couldn't shoot at the plane flying in air, but they could shoot at Harkey's aircraft using the simulator.

The mental exhaustion from the simulator was staggering to say the least. Harkey was thinking had he not had the privilege of flying the *Albatross Varco* during phase three, he wasn't sure he could have survived phase four. Major Adams was doing Harkey a favor. The simulators have twenty levels of expertise and difficulty. Levels fifteen through twenty were tough on anyone, including fleet returnees. Normally phase four started a pilot at level one and slowly worked their way up to level twenty which was paramount and difficult for all pilots.

Based on Harkey's experience level in combat on the ground as well as his significantly increased hours of flying time, Major Adams started Harkey at level ten. The pace of the course moved up levels in just a couple days. So instead of getting a forty plus day of the normal progress students experienced, Harkey did it in ten days. He didn't know he was being pushed extra hard, he had self-doubt that he just wasn't as good as he should be. He also thought it was rather odd that Major Adams didn't hammer him on some of his screwups in the simulator.

Major Adams played coy and knew he was busting Harkey's balls, pushing him harder than any student before. But he was doing it for his own good because he could end up in combat a lot sooner than he realized, and he had to be ready. Decoys, egress techniques, and emergency procedures were every day and at increasingly difficult training levels.

Soon after he showered there was a knock at the door, and it was already getting late. One of the classmates was there and said, "A lady named Lindy Foster asked me to give this to you."

"Thanks."

The man turned and left, and Harkey went inside and shut the door to his quarters and walked over to a chair and sat down and opened the envelope.

It contained a small picture of Lindy and a note with her communicator number on a business card she included.

Harkey's time at the Cronstine Base and Flight School was getting close to the end. It was a shame he didn't meet her several months back and got to know her, but now it was quickly becoming too late.

Lindy Foster had never got tangled with any of the flyboys because she realized they lived a dangerous life, and she didn't care to be around the military. It was way out of character for her to even give a hint to a service member she had any slight interests. But there was something about this Harkey person that intreagued her.

Harkey was very soft spoken and didn't drink too much and almost an introvert. After fifteen minutes of casual conversation where he didn't probe or exemplified himself in any manner, the altercation started and POW! He was a man of action.

Harkey was so worried about his friend's injuries; he didn't even stop to say goodbye and hustled his wounded friend out of the bar-restaurant as quickly as he could. And then he disappeared until she started reading about his criminal trial that really upset her. But she was very happy the way the judge ruled in the case. Harkey didn't even know she was in the court room taking it all in. But it was crowded as it was a sensational case.

Harkey would probably not have picked Lindy Foster out in the crowd because she had on a business suit as she was a corporate executive. She was a couple years older than Harkey, but she didn't care as long as he didn't care.

Lindy Foster wrote to Harkey:

> Harkey,
>
> I really enjoyed meeting you and I was sad that our wonderful evening had to be ruined by those jerks that beat up your friend. I would like to see you again. If possible, would you mind giving me a call, anytime during the day or in evening would be fine too.
>
> With warmest regards,
>
> Lindy

Harkey looked at his wrist band chronometer saw it was already 9:00 P.M. and wondered if it were to late to call Lindy. In some ways he regretted calling her, but she was very nice to him, and he liked her, so he said to himself, *the hell with it.* Then he called Lindy Foster.

Lindy being someone important in the corporate world and had to protect herself and had powerful caller identification. There were numerous calls she would never answer. She saw Harkey's name associated with the caller I.D. and her heart went pitter pat and she immediately answered.

"Hello." Harkey heard the nice voice

"Hi. This is Harkey I received your card."

"Where have you been? Am I that ugly?"

"No, nothing like that at all. Because of the altercation in the bar restaurant, Jeremy and I have been restricted to the base."

"That's terrible I was hoping to see you and continue our conversation."

"I'm sorry that's how things are."

"Is there anyway we could get together."

"If you can take a limo-taxi to the base, I can meet you at the front gate and escort you in. I can take you to the officer's club. They have a nice restaurant there and tomorrow night they will have a pianist performing on a grand piano during dinner time."

"I would love to."

"Would Seven O'clock be, ok?"

"Yes, that would work out just fine."

"Alright I'll see you at seven."

"Thank you for calling me."

"My pleasure."

"Good night, Harkey."

"Good night, Lindy."

That phone call meant a lot to Harkey. His life journey had been a lonely one. It would be nice to be friends with such a wonderful lady.

The next morning Harkey was back at the meat grinder. Major Adams put him through a grueling session and knew by Five P.M. Harkey had done more than his fair share and needed some unwind time least they end up in a training accident.

"Harkey, we are done for the day. You did a really good job today."

"I thought I wasn't doing too well. I don't know why but it seemed like it felt very difficult. I must not have been up on my game plan today."

"Harkey, you had some exceptionally hard training scenarios today. You actually did quite well. You need to understand, sometimes its not how good a pilot you are, there are other things that come into play such as luck and opportunity. What you experienced today is very close to the real battlefield that's why it felt so hard because it really is. The reason why we teach those extremely painful egress techniques is one day you may need to do it to save your life. Go home and take a shower and relax. This was a good training day for you."

"Alright, see you tomorrow."

Harkey did not seem as negative as he could have been. Major Adams knew that he had made several very mature and capable pilots just about cry with the scenarios ran today. Major Adams was quite surprised that after getting his ass kicked so hard in the trainers today that Harkey would leave on such a positive manner. Little did he know Harkey suddenly had Lindy Foster on his mind.

Harkey didn't come from a rich family and didn't have a large wardrobe because he figured he probably didn't need one knowing where he was going.

He had at least a couple good change of clothes and after a nice hot shower with that wonderful tea-tree based shampoo, his body was feeling great. A quick blow dry of the hair and a little deodorant and cologne and Harkey was ready to put on his clothes and go meet Lindy at the front gate that was not too bad a walk from the BOQ (bachelors officers' quarters).

Harkey didn't have any personal transportation and he wasn't going to wait around for the scheduled base bus to come by, so he headed out on foot.

It took him about five minutes to walk to the gate and nobody was coming and going, and the gate guard came out and asked, "Are you waiting for someone sir?"

"Yes, a lady friend is coming probably in a Limo anytime soon."

"What is your rank sir?"

"I'm a second Lieutenant."

"A student pilot?"

"Yes, I got my wings and am training in the Albatross Varco."

"Awesome Aircraft."

"I agree, though today, I found it rather challenging."

"Why's that?"

"My instructor gave me some hard ass scenarios. It was the hardest I've ever had to do before."

"What doesn't kill us makes us better."

"You can say that again."

Suddenly headlights were coming towards the gate. It was a Limo. When the guard stopped the Limo, he asked, are you here to pick up this gentleman?"

Lindy overheard the conversation and said, "Yes that's him."

"Are you going on base?"

After Lindy explained to the driver, the driver repeated the information to the gate guard, "I'm taking them to the Officers Club for Dinner."

The guard walked around to the passenger side door and opened it and said, "Hop in sir."

The guard took the opportunity to see what kind of eye candy was inside. He wasn't disappointed. He then walked up and asked the driver, "Will you be leaving and coming back to pick up the lady after their dinner?"

"Yes, that is what I assumed."

"I'll be on watch here when you come back so you will not have any hassles."

"Thank you I appreciate that."

"Take good care of that pilot that's in your Limo. He's one of the good guys."

"It will be my pleasure."

"Do you know where the officers club is?"

"Yes, I've driven Officers there many times before."

"Have a nice evening, you may proceed on base."

"Thank you."

"You are most welcome."

Harkey looked and Lindy and smiled. She definitely looked exotic tonight. In fact, Harkey had never been with such a beautiful and well-dressed woman before in his lifetime. He was suddenly happy he made that phone call.

Upon reaching the officers club, the Limo Driver opened the passenger door and the two got out and the Limo driver knew Lindy would call him when she was ready to leave. She was one of his regular clients and a great tipper, so he was happy to provide her transportation for the night.

The two went into the formal dining hall where the Maitra d' was there to seat them. Do you have a reservation sir?

"Yes, under the name of Harkey."

The Maitra d' crossed Harkey's name off the reserve list and asked, "Would sitting near the piano be, okay?"

"Sure, why not."

The Maitra d' let the couple over to their table. The pianist was already performing a lovely soft dinner music that set the ambience but didn't sound so loud to distract people from their numerous conversations.

Unfortunately for Harkey their table also put them in the limelight and people often glance over at the pianist now and then, especially with the lovely female performer who looked utterly seductive with her fantastic looks and features. There was no doubt *why* this lovely woman was performing. The pianist provided the eye candy for the many single pilots having dinner there tonight.

After getting their drinks ordered the waitress went away for a while to give them a chance to look over the menu. Lindy wasn't interested in food at the present time, she was more interested in learning about Harkey and his life's journey.

"Tell me Harkey, where did you come from?"

"I grew up on the planet Ergzlt in a somewhat small down far from any large cities."

"What did you do for fun?"

"Sports, reading, music."

"Do you have a girlfriend back at Ergzlt?"

"No, I was spared that trouble by working part time and doing sports all year round."

"That's probably a good thing, otherwise you would not be training as a pilot now."

"Yes, but I took the tough way to get here. There could have been an easier route."

"Sometimes our lives are planned out for and there's nothing we can do about it."

"Tell me about yourself Lindy."

"I grew up as the typical girl, then went to school for quite a few years and after I finished my education, I got hired as an intern and slowly rose the corporate ladder and now I'm an executive."

"What type of company?"

"It's a tech company and we provide software and hardware innovative products."

"This isn't a large city, why are you here?"

"I'm an executive in the IT department. Our work force is spread all over, so I really do not need to be located anywhere particular. My parents live here so I decided I would move here to be with them to help them if I could. Once or twice a month I hop on a transporter and go somewhere and deal with company requirements, then fly home and work remotely from my home.

Harkey looked out around the restaurant taking it all in and noticed he got a lot of looks from a lot of individuals. *Perhaps it's because Lindy is dressed up so nicely?*

It wasn't long before Harkey discovered in the mix of onlookers was no other than Colonel Kollins. *Colonel Kollins seems like he has a Cheshire cat smile,* Harkey thought.

Like many stories he heard while in training many of them would make the wrong assumption of this woman. *But if that's what they want to think, then I'll just let them dream it's true.*

Eventually they looked at the menu's and ordered some food. World class chefs keeping the pilots happy was necessary.

The food was soon served as the lovely piano music continued. After forty-five minutes the pianist took a break and left the dining room and walked across the hallway to a bar and nightclub set up for the officers. On weekends it got rowdy in there. The class would have had a much better party had they had it there and avoided the issues out in town.

Harkey enjoyed his time with Lindy Foster, but realized it was a terrible shame that such a gorgeous creature was so far away from him, and he may not survive the war. If he did survive and came back alive, he would no doubt seek her. *But would she wait for me?*

The dinner passed by too quickly, but the piano player was back working the keyboard with dynamic objectivity as she interpreted the music her way and added a slightly different rendition of the original compositions.

The officers club had a patio bar that overlooked a beach

area that seemed to draw couples to. The bar inside the officer's club was full of hot steamy women trying to coerce the highest-ranking dudes into their personal honey trap and lifelong agony if the suckers fell for it. But there were also some very intelligent and well-meaning women in the fray who were praying they would not get stuck with a loser. It was the superb chess match, and nobody could really predict the future or how many of these pilots would actually be alive in a years' time.

The night was still early, but unfortunately being stuck on the base didn't offer Harkey many options to make his date elevate the status.

After paying for the meal, Harkey looking out the large picture glass window towards the patio bar suggested, "Would you like to continue our conversation out on the Patio. We could find a nice cozy place to enjoy our conversations."

"I would be delighted to," Lindy responded.

The couple walked out to the patio. Colonel Kollins noted the barracuda leading young Harkey by the nose was well dressed about ten levels higher than Harkey, but she seemed enthused, and her body language showed great interest in the young man. She might have already developed an attraction to him.

The two were enjoying another drink in the patio bar area and had been withering in their conversation. They didn't have a lot in common, just a physical attraction and Harkey was such a pleasant man, not making any suggestions or hints he would want to capitalize on the night's events with some premeditated unrequited gratification like a lot of young men were guilty of.

Lindy could sense Harkey wasn't very experienced. She would have to help the process along if they were ever to get somewhere.

As it was nearing nine o'clock, Harkey realizing he was going to get another dose of supreme fatigue in the simulators or up in one of the training aircraft in the morning said, "Lindy, I've really enjoyed my time with you tonight and want to see you again. But I have a very tough day ahead of me tomorrow, so I think I need to be getting some sleep soon. I'm afraid we must end this early, but if you're available on the weekend, I would give you all the time possible."

"That's very nice of you to explain that and make such an offer. Of course, I would like to see you on the weekend."

"All right I will stay in touch with you, and we will figure things out."

"I'll be ready Harkey; I enjoy being with you."

"Thank you I enjoy being with you as well."

"Should we walk to the front entrance, and I'll call the Limo?"

"Sure."

Just as they stood up and were about to head out, Colonel Kollins approached the couple and said, "Good evening, Harkey, I was wondering when you were going to introduce me to this nice lady."

"Colonel Kollins, this is my friend Lindy Foster."

"Pleased to meet you, Colonel Kollins."

"Likewise, Lindy."

"I'm sorry Colonel, we were just about to leave, I have a big day ahead of me tomorrow, so I had to call it an early night."

"That you do. And so do I, but I'm sure your day will be

tougher than me in that souped up transport plane."

"It's all teamwork and it all matters, Colonel."

"Not many young men know that like you do Harkey."

"Chalk it up to experience."

"I'm not sure I know anyone your age with those number of experiences."

"Well, what doesn't kill you makes you better, right?"

"You have certainly proved that to me several times. Also, I must compliment you on your taste of women. You are going high places one of these days. A good spouse is always a career booster for an officer."

"I agree totally and that will be my focus, find a good one and keep her."

"That's the best way to proceed."

"I must say good night, Colonel, and hopefully we can meet up after you finish your flights."

"Stay safe Harkey, you would be very hard to replace, not only for the service but also for her."

"Thank you."

"Mam." Colonel Kollins bowed and turned around and walked away and headed for the inside bar where he was going to have a drink with his general friend and get some idea when he thought his new posting as Task Force Commander would occur.

When they arrived at the front of the Officers Club, Lindy called the Limo. They stood there holding hands just talking about irrelevant things then the Limo pulled up.

"Can I give you arride to your Officer Quarters?"

"It's not that far I can walk it pretty quickly."

"Actually, I would like to give you a ride so I can tell you something in private."

"Alright then."

The two got into the Limo and after asking Harkey what his building number was, Lindy directed the Limo Driver, "Take us to building 140 where his quarters are, I'm dropping him off there."

"Yes mam."

As they were heading to building 140 that would take a maximum of five minutes, Harkey asked, "What did you want to tell me in private?"

"This." Lindy threw her arms around Harkey and kissed him. Harkey responded and the affection was genuine and before the kiss was finished, they pulled up in front of Harkey's quarters.

"Thank you for a lovely night, Harkey."

"Thank you for giving me a lot of happiness tonight."

"I want to give you more happiness, please call me."

"I will, and I want to."

"Thank you for being such a nice gentleman."

"I like you. There are some things I want to tell you in the future."

"I'm expecting that."

"Alright, I will try to give you a nice weekend."

"It's mutual Harkey."

"Good night, Lindy."

"Good night, Harkey."

Harkey didn't know what caused his irrational act, but Harkey grabbed Lindy and kissed her one more time. She was grateful because Harkey initiated it on his own. She knew now he had some emotion for her, and her intuition gauged it was especially strong. She would explore it further this weekend.

She would then try to discover as much about Harkey as she could. She would treat this no different than a corporate exercise was staying ahead of the competition sometimes requires extraordinary efforts. Her guess was Harkey's friends would show up at the watering hole she seen them at several times, and she knew the old age adage, "loose lips sink ships." She knew how to losen a few lips and she would bring along a couple of her girlfriends to act as eye candy to help corral some of Harkey's associates.

Harkey knew he had a couple more days of ball busting training then there would be the weekend where they would not schedule, and trainer aircraft and the simulators would be voluntary only. Harkey figured Major Adams would like the weekend off so he would let him know his plans on Friday morning, so he didn't spend a lot of extra time in the simulators on his behalf.

The next night Lindy had her two barracuda friends with her who loved to sink their fangs into these young pilots who were young, dumb, and full of cum. She would be the designated driver so there would be no issues with alcohol impairment.

The local troublemakers that got their asses totally beat by Harkey were politely informed by bar management to stay the hell out of there and their presence was not desired nor required. So, it was a much tamer crowd on this night.

The women were set up on a table that could easily squeeze in another four chairs and after several men made advances the squad turned them away as they were only interested in meeting up with Harkey's buddies. In due time they showed up some looking for a piece of ass, others just a good time. And as soon as Lindy invited the nice guy who gave Harkey her letter, to the table, there was quickly three other horny pilots moving in sights on their targets, all buddies of Harkey.

Lindy instructed the waiter to put all their drinks on her tab and keep their glasses filled, which the waitress was very happy because the airmen kept on paying for the drinks which she thought was odd and tried to give the money back one time and about that time Lindy pulled her aside and said, "You and I know I'm picking up the tab. You just collect the money for you tips and keep the other assholes away from us, do we have a deal?"

"Oh, hell yes." And the two women giggled.

After about the second or third drink Lindy started in and asked the guy, who delivered the letter, "Tell me what you know about Harkey, he seems like a nice guy."

"He's more than just a nice guy."

"What do you mean by that?"

"He came into the service under a very strange program. He was recruited by special projects to eventually become a close support pilot. But to weed out chickenshits, they send them to the infantry for a while and let them do some ground pounder battles to make sure they can hack it and are reliable."

"So, Harkey fought in the land battles?"

"Oh man did he. If you see him with his clothes off, you will see all the bullet holes scars where he was wounded six times in a couple battles. He has a lot of prestigious awards."

"Tell me, how does he know Colonel Kollins?"

"Colonel Kollins was his Commanding Officer during two of the biggest ground battles we had in a long-long time. He visited him after one of the battles to give him his awards, and the second time they were both wounded and in hospital beds next to each other."

"So, Harkey's the real deal?"

"Yes, we are proud to be their classmates."

"What do you mean by "their?"

"Colonel Kollins was sent to flight school to become a pilot which is a requirement to be a task force commander. He's one of the students in our class."

"That's kind of an interesting coincidence."

"It sure is and had Harkey not been here a while back that one dude would have killed Jeremy."

"How's Jeremy doing? He looked beat up bad."

"He's doing fine. He's restricted to the base just like Harkey is because their worried about reprisals."

"Interesting."

It all started to make sense now to Lindy. Harkey turned out to be much more than he seemed. But she liked that. He truly was an extraordinary man, one of which she wanted now more than ever.

The two barracudas were not in the mood for any boom-boom with these guys, as they seemed a little too young for their taste and Lindy could tell by their body language it was time to depart.

"All right girls, I'm ready to go where we planned tonight."

Lindy signaled to the waitress who came over immediately and she said, "We are leaving now, could you settle my tab?"

"Yes, you will get your receipt sent to your communicator in a couple minutes."

"Thank you."

The flyboys were a little sad the women were suddenly leaving, but they had to go back to the base in a while anyway, so it really didn't matter.

Lindy drove her friends home knowing they just wanted to call it a night since Lindy already bought them dinner at another nice restaurant as they planned this mission.

The next day after Harkey finished four hours of flying, he ran into Colonel Kollins who had also just finished flying for the day.

"Nice looking woman you were with."

"Yea, I like Lindy."

"What does she do for a living."

"She's an executive in a technology company."

"Nice."

"I'm planning on spending the weekend with her, but I'm stuck on base."

"Consider this a down payment because I know you will be flying for my task force soon enough. I will go talk to the Base Commanding Officer to get the restrictions lifted for you. But under no circumstances are you to hang around the town.

You have too much at stake. The city is only an hour away, go with her there, plenty of things to do."

"How soon will you know?"

"Meet me over at the Officers Club for Dinner, I'll have the details for you then."

"Colonel, I really appreciate what you are doing for me, I really like that woman."

"Harkey I could tell by her dress and her demeaner she's a quality person. You are very lucky to have met her. Its probably a chance of a lifetime. Few people know what you have already given of yourself in two major battles. I'm privileged to have you as a friend. You will be flying the Albatross Varco soon supporting my troops in another operation. I know what you are going through in training and what you will go through in actual combat. This is the least I could do for you."

"Thank you, Colonel."

"Harkey, when we are in privacy, call me by my first name Jeff."

"All right Jeff. My first name is Douglas. I never tell anyone that because I do not like the name." Okay Harkey, I will not call you Douglas and I understand."

"Thank you, Jeff."

"After you get cleaned up meet me at the Officers Club around seven O'clock at the bar next to the dining room."

"Sure."

Harkey went back to his BOQ room all jazzed up thinking he could get off base and go into the city with Lindy. Right after he showered and changed his clothes, he called Lindy.

"Hello."

"Lindy how are you doing?"

"Harkey, I'm doing fine thank you and thank you for calling me."

"Say, this weekend I might be able to go to the city with you. They will not let me stop in the town outside the base, but I figure that's okay."

"That's more than okay, when will you know?"

"I'm having dinner with Colonel Kollins tonight; he will affirm my change in restrictions to the base posture."

"Good, I have a lot of connections in the city, we can have a fun time."

"That sounds great, I'm sure I am willing to do anything you want."

"Be careful with making those kinds of statements, I might want more than you can imagine."

"I trust you. I know you would be safe for me."

"That I will, always."

"Alright after dinner I will call you and let you know."

"Thank you, Harkey this means a lot to me. You just made my evening."

"It made my evening too."

"All right call me when you get back, I may want to tell you some lovely things."

"I will."

"Bye."

"Bye."

Harkey made his way to the Officer Club and met Colonel Kollins with his General friend.

Harkey had never met this General before, he looked a lot older with grey hair. Colonel Kollins worked for this General many times in the past. There was definitely huge mutual respect.

"This is Second Lieutenant Harkey, General Seslame"

"It's a privilege to meet you General."

"Tell me Harkey, I've always wanted to know how men like you found the courage to conduct yourselves in the manner you did."

"General Seslame, it was kind of strange, I didn't feel fear. But I did have some other feelings that prompted me to do what I did."

"What were those feelings, Harkey."

"Sir I hope I'm not out of line for saying this, but the enemy made me angry. I knew based on my military training they were trying to kill me and all our troops. The anger in me drove me to do what I did. Then I was wounded, and they upset me even more. I wanted to do more damage to them even if it killed me."

"Harkey, it almost did, from what I read."

"General, would you like to inform Harkey what you decided on his weekend adventure?"

"Sure. Harkey you can go into the city with your new girlfriend, but you must stay out of that town."

"Understand I will bypass the town."

"Shall we order gentlemen?"

"Absolutely."

It was a good dinner with a couple drinks and Harkey said, "General, I'm pleased to have met you, but I have some serious flying to do tomorrow, I need to get a good night sleep."

"Alright Harkey, in case I don't see you again, good luck in your romance and stay safe when you go flying."

"I'll try my best sir."

"I know you will."

Harkey walked back to his BOQ room and soon called Lindy.

"Good news, they will let me go to the city this weekend."

"Great. I got a good idea. I'll come to the main gate and pick you up in my car."

"I'll be ready, what time do you want to meet?"

"How about Eight O'clock?"

"Works for me."

"Thanks for calling me back, I can make reservations in the morning."

"All right, see you in a couple days."

"I'm looking forward to it.

The next day was the final ball buster that Major Adams did to Harkey. After four hours in the simulator and four hours in the 2 seater Albatross Varco trainer, Harkey was exhausted. He had no strength left in him. The final act was the critique. Major Adams said, we have a visitor for the Critique. Moments later Colonel Kollins arrived and took a seat at the table, and they went over it detail by detail.

Harkey wasn't sure he had flunked. He really had an

extremely tough time.

"Tell us Harkey, how did you feel about it today."

"I'm not sure how well I did. I just knew it was one of the toughest battles I've ever experienced."

"Harkey, you effectively graduated today. You just completed all Twenty Levels of the training modules for phase four. We make level 20 particularly hard to impart with you how tough it can really get out there and why not to let your guard down."

"We are only halfway through phase four time wise, what does that mean for me going forward?" Harkey asked

"We certainly are not going to graduate you ahead of your class, that's not possible because of our rules and regulations. But you have completed all academic as well as practical exams for the course even though it's only been half the time allotted to phase four. You will still have to attend training for the remainder of the course, and we'll make some proposals to you as to how to best utilize the time left."

"What do you have in mind?"

"I know you may not like the idea, but if you do as I'm recommending now, you will be glad you did later, because it will greatly increase your flying time."

"I'm all ears."

Our policy of simulator time to earn flying time will be greatly shifted for you. We also do not want you to reveal this to other students as it could cause us some difficulties."

"I promise not to reveal it. What is the change in policy?"

"We have done this before with accelerated students. We had one student who was a qualified pilot with a lot of flying time who finished the course in four weeks. His friend who came here with him finished it in five weeks. What we will offer you is one hour of flying time in trainers for each hour you put in the simulators."

"That's very generous of you."

"This is only possible because you put forth a supreme effort that is very rare. Most students do not put in half the time in the simulators that you did. Your success in the trainers and the combat training, we instructors believe is directly proportional to your time you spent in the simulators. Your actions in the simulators were clearly demonstrating you viewed it as a training opportunity, and you had something to learn by it. Your attitude is why a lot of instructors put forth extra effort in the simulators. The bottom line is you were exposed to far more than we could hope for any particular student."

"I appreciate the help they gave me."

"The net effect of all the additional simulator and trainer time is you will leave this school as if you had a lot more hours in combat. Your survival in future air combat is greatly enhanced because all those extra hours. The only thing you lack is luck on your side. In combat, there is an element of luck as well as timing which you will never be able to control. It's simply the circumstances that you fly into."

"Yea I realize that."

"This final scenario twenty you just finished is exactly what happens when your luck and timing do not work out for you. All you have left then is your own personal actions. But sometimes even if you do everything perfect, you will not be able to overcome if the enemy gets lucky."

"Yes, I understand that."

"You have had a very stressful week. Few pilots have gone though this much in a week in this school. Take the weekend off, enjoy yourself, then on Monday morning we can get together and work out a timeline for you on how best to utilize the time you have remaining before your class graduates."

"How's it looking for the class?"

"Your class overall has been motivated and excelled. All your classmates have done exceedingly well, and I have no doubt they will all graduate phase four and go on to be great pilots."

"That's good to know."

"Enjoy your weekend and see you on Monday."

"Thanks."

Harkey departed the school and walked back to his BOQ room exhausted and felt like he had just been reamed, and he had been. The school knew they had pushed him harder than any student before. But they also understood that with pending fleet action, the Albatross Varco would be a deadly machine to be flying in the next major operation against the Spetznar.

It was Friday afternoon and Harkey was exhausted. He took a nice long Hollywood shower and after an energy drink started to feel alive again. He then decided to call Lindy Foster.

"Hello"

"Lindy?"

"Yes Harkey, its nice to hear your voice."

"I'm officially done now for the weekend. No simulators or trainers until Monday."

"What are you doing this evening?"

"I really didn't plan anything since we'll be going into the city tomorrow."

"I know time is precious for you, I have a really good idea."

"What's your idea?"

"I could swing by this evening and pick you up, we could go to the city tonight and be ready first thing in the morning to take in all the sights since we would not have to travel."

"I suppose that would work."

"How soon can you be ready?"

"You know me, I'm just a pilot without much. I'm already dressed. I could leave anytime."

"All right I'll come over there and pick you up. Worst case you may have to walk down to the front gate."

"I do not mind that at all."

"I'll call you from the main gate when I get there."

"All right, I'll be waiting for your call."

Harkey wondered what he should take with him. He didn't need much. He had plenty of money since he had not spent any of the combat pay, he earned over a long period as well as his salary. He could just buy new clothes if he needed them. He threw the bare essentials into his grip and then waited for the phone call."

Lindy had worked that day and had some video telecoms, so she had to have on her makeup and nice dress to impress her superiors. She didn't need to change her clothes and had just showered a few hours before. The video telecom only lasted an hour, and she was still fresh and thus ready to go.

As a world traveler with short notices, Lindy always had

one bag packed for emergency trips. She meticulous packed her fly away suitcase number one (as well as three others) and was ready to go for any situation and she had everything she needed for up to almost two weeks.

Lindy grabbed the suitcase on rollers and pulled it along out to her souped-up vehicle that would impress most people. Thanks to her corporate footprint all she had to do was tell the artificial intelligence in her vehicle, "Book me a room at the Swiftshire Hotel in Bazanga Metropolis for two nights this evening."

The artificial intelligence immediately responded, "Do you want a class 1, 2, or 3 room."

"I want a Class-1 room with an excellent view."

"Do you want to charge it to your corporate account?"

"No, charge it to my personal account."

A moment later the Artificial Intelligence reported, "Lindy you have confirmed reservations. Your confirmation has been sent to your communicator."

"Thank you."

"My pleasure madam."

Lindy was a safe driver and covered the distance to the base in a reasonable amount of time. When she pulled up to the main gate, the nice guard that was there a few nights prior was at the post again."

"Hello Mam, what can I do for you."

"I've come to pick up Harkey who lives in BOQ building 140."

"Alright, I need to contact him to verify he is sponsoring you driving on base."

"No problem."

"Do you by any chance have his number so that I do not have to look it up?"

"Yes, here it is," Lindy responded then pulled up her communicator with the number to speed dial and the guard immediately called it.

Harkey answered the phone right away.

"Hello."

Lt. Harkey, this is the main gate, we have a woman here named Lindy Foster who says she is coming by to pick you up. Can you confirm that?"

"Yes, I'm at BOQ building 140. Can you please give her directions, so she knows how to get here?"

"Not a problem sir and enjoy your evening."

"Thank you very much."

Lindy really didn't need the directions but took them out of respect and then continued her way to building 140 and outside was Harkey with a small handbag.

Harkey easily recognized Lindy and waved to her, and she waved back, and he walked abruptly to the passenger car door and opened it.

Harkey didn't know it but a half block away Colonel Kollins in his sweat suit was jogging along and saw Harkey get into the nice car and as it curbed out of the pickup zone back to the main road, he observed the nice lady Lindy driving and was happy and hoped Harkey would get lucky tonight as his future was filled in high risk being one of the pilots that would have to do decisive ground support in an upcoming battle in order to dislodge the Spetznar from one of their major strongholds on the planet Kattnoggar.

When Lindy's car passed by the main gate now having low traffic, Lindy waved to the guard who waved back and saw Lieutenant Harkey in the passenger seat. He hoped they had a lovely evening.

Harkey didn't know what to expect. He figured they would check into a decent hotel with two rooms. He didn't know he was going to the best in the city. Lindy looking at Harkey knew he wasn't dressed for success, but she knew the Hotel could take care of that easily with their staff of fashion designers who could dress him up nicely. In fact, she would have them dress them both up tonight so when they went out on the town, it would be with sheer elegance. With Lindy's seven-digit income and her vast gains in securities as she understood how to play the stock market, she could spoil Harkey very easily with all the cash she had available.

In the past year alone, Lindy paid of her parents' home and paid cash for her own. She would have invited Harkey over but didn't want to scare him. It would be best they consummated their friendship before Harkey discovered he had a woman with means offering herself to him. She was only a couple years older than Harkey but didn't look it. But her business and financial prowess came about at an early age thanks to finishing high school and college four years ahead of her peers including graduating the top of her class with full honors.

If it wasn't for the fact Lindy wanted a man in her life, she could easily proceed up the corporate ladder to the next level as she knew she could beat the performance of most of the male peers that were executives where she worked. The President of the Company knew that as well, she was a very smart cookie.

"How are you doing today?'

"If I didn't confess, I was a little stressed out from activities this week I would be lying."

"Why was it so tough?"

"As you know I was restricted to base for a long while over that incident in the bar. I had nothing better to do than spend a lot of time in simulators and the trainers. I advanced a lot quicker because of that. At some point in time leadership at the school decided to spoon feed me as much training as I could take. I'm halfway through phase four training. Even though I already have my wings and am a licensed pilot, phase four is designed to teach us combat skills in the types of aircraft we'll be assigned in the future. It was really tough, and I was worried I wasn't doing too well until today when my instructor informed me what went on."

"And what was that, Harkey."

"I didn't understand why this week was so particularly hard until this afternoon when we were wrapping it up for the day. That's when they notified me this week was the twentieth element in my phase four training. I'm officially done with all phase four requirements."

"What does mean for you now? Will they be transferring you somewhere?" Lindy asked with an element of worry, the man of her dreams would slip away just about the time she was going to hook him.

"Please keep this confidential between us."

"Sure, I will not discuss you with anyone unless you tell me what I can say and to whom."

"I appreciate that."

"Will you be leaving soon?" Lindy asked emphasizing her desire to know what Harkey's fate was.

"My lead instructor informed me that because of the nature of my training which I'm not allowed to disclose to the other students, I will have to remain here and be part of their normal graduating class."

"If you got all your training done does that mean you can take more time off?" Lindy asked in a hopeful manner.

"I'll still have to show up for school just like everyone else and go into the simulators and trainers like everyone does. But since I no longer have any training requirements, they will simply take the time to get me additional flying time."

"Is that good for you?"

"Definitely. Every Commanding Officer of a squadron takes notice of how many flying hours a pilot has in his particular aircraft because it gives some gauge as to proficiency."

"That sounds logical."

"But since I did so well, they are going to reward me with a new policy for me only."

"What's that?"

"Normally for every three hours in the flight simulator they give us one hour of flight time in an actual aircraft-trainer."

"Okay, and?"

"For each hour I put in the simulator they will give me one hour flying time in an actual aircraft."

"Sounds like you will end up with a lot more hours in the aircraft."

"Exactly."

"Will you have your evenings off?"

"Yes, but I can't go into the town at any business locations due to my restrictions."

"You could always come to my home and hide out."

"I think I might like that."

The travel into the Bazanga Metropolis was interesting and Harkey got a lot of sight seeing in. It felt refreshing to be away from the base and back into society again.

As they got closer to the center of the city the buildings appeared much more immense. Bazanga was truly an impressive and clean city. You can tell how successful a mayor is by the conditions of the roads and the cleanliness of a city. It was apparent that Bazanga Mayor was exemplary.

Around this point in time Lindy said to her artificial intelligence, "Please navigate me to the Swiftshire Hotel in Bazanga Metropolis."

"Madam do you wish hands off driving?"

"Yes, please."

"Autopilot is now in control of the vehicle in accordance with safest practices. Your personal control is no longer necessary, but if you chose to take control of steering, breaking and acceleration, you will be permitted."

"Also navigate us to Valet Parking at the hotel."

"Madam, I understand you want me to navigate you to Valet Parking at the Swiftshire Hotel in Bazanga Metropolis."

"That's correct."

"Next stop will be Valet Parking at the Swiftshire Hotel in Bazanga Metropolis."

"Thank you."

The vehicle glided along seemingly gleefully through the city and eventually slowed down and turned into a driveway that led up to the front entrance of the Swiftshire Hotel. Harkey knew this was going to be expensive, but he didn't care. In six months, he could be dead. After his experience with the Infantry, he knew to live for today. And here he was with such a beautiful woman, and he would enjoy her this weekend and money was not something to deter him. He was ready for what bestowed upon him, though he did feel physically tired.

After the car stopped, the Hotel security opened the driver and passenger doors simultaneously so the passengers could get out. The hotel employee asked, "Do you have reservations, Madam."

"Yes, my name is Lindy Foster."

The hotel employee had artificial intelligence assistance and an ear bud and was immediately informed, "Lindy Foster's room number 4141 is ready. Have the Bellhop take all their luggage up to the room immediately and have Valet parking take her car to designated parking spot. Her Valet Parking receipt has been sent to her communicator."

"Madam, your room 4141 is ready. The Bellhop will take your luggage up to your room and Valet Parking will take you car to designated parking. Your receipt for valet parking has been sent to your communicator."

"Thank you."

"You are most welcome."

The Bellhop asked Harkey, "Sir would you like me to take your handbag up to the room with Ms. Lindy Foster?"

"Sure."

Artificial Intelligence determined Harkey was a companion of the guest Lindy Foster and had him co-registered. The Hotel didn't know the guest's name but would soon find out.

By the time they got up to room 4141 it was not too far off from dinner time. Lindy who had stayed in this luxury hotel a few times to be with exclusive business clients and cut deals had utilized their fashion designer services and suggested:

"Listen Harkey, we kind of rushed getting up here and didn't spend too much time planning. This hotel has one of the most exclusive restaurants in the city. But they have a dress code. We can't get in there looking like this. They have good fashion designers here to dress up hotel guests. If I call them now, they can be up here shortly and dress us for dinner. It's all on me doesn't cost you anything."

"Sure, if that's what you want."

"All right, I'll call guest services right away."

In a way, Harkey was happy that was happening because he felt too exhausted to endeavor in horizontal tango now and preferred a good night sleep before delving deep into romantic proclivity.

In a brief period, the fashion designer and her staff were in the room preparing them. Makeup artists, hair designers, the whole works was duly engaged. They assumed this was a couple and had seen their bodies before. Lindy was not the least bit bashful because she planned to show it all real soon any way. They were stripped down because designer clothes required bare skin almost for perfect fitting clothes.

Harkey was being a gentleman and not looking at Lindy. But Lindy on the otherhand was seriously checking Harkey out to corroborate the story one of the flyboys told her about this combat hero. She was then astonished when she discovered how poor Harkey's body had been raged by enemy gunners.

He was damn lucky to be alive and only because he was lucky to be treated by some of the best doctors in the Chevolite's military, he lived to fight another day. Partly because Harkey's valor became known to the doctors after the first incident, when Colonel Kollins his benefactor asked the chief surgeon to give this particular soldier special attention and explained why. The surgeon was thus motivated to not only save his life but also attempt to restore all his motor functions so that he would be able to continue in life normally. Many combat troops were not so lucky and ended up paralyzed for the rest of their lives.

In the second go around just before Colonel Kollins was given anesthesia, he again informed the chief surgeon that was the young man he once glued back together in the previous battle and in this fight, he showed extreme bravery and may have single handedly stopped the enemy attack and to please do everything he could. As Colonel Kollins was going under the fog of anesthesia, he did so with the good feeling the chief surgeon promised him he would put forth maximum effort to save the boy's life.

When Colonel Collins woke up in the infirmary laying in the bed next to Harkey, he was quite pleased the surgeon lived up to his promises.

There were many unspoken things about Harkey's life, but Lindy Foster saw it all herself now. She almost wanted to cry but knew that would spoil everything, so she put forth her maximum effort to remain calm and composed. Thankfully Harkey had his clothes on soon and spared Lindy further undue stress looking on the ravages of war.

The fashion designer had a brother seriously injured in the war. The scars of those wounds gave her vivid memories of her brother. She knew this young man had suffered gravely. The designer was going to do a simple class A fashion design make over for the couple, but after looking at those scars on Harkey she decided they would get an AAA makeover at no additional cost.

The fashion designer looked at Harkey and said, "I'm sorry but I do not like the way that suit looks on you, I need to step outside with my assistant so I can give her some directions of what we want to do with you."

"Okay."

The two went outside and one of the most prestigious fashion designers in all Bazanga Metropolis informed her assistant, "Did you see those scars on his body?"

"Yes, I did, I almost wanted to cry."

"He's paid the price. I want to do something special for him. We'll do a class AAA tonight on the couple."

"Understand and I will be most happy to assist."

"Thank you, go get another wardrobe. And for the lady I want her fitted with my latest design we just finished a short while ago."

"I'll get those items and be right back."

"Thank you for understanding and helping out."

"No problem, I want to help too."

The fashion designer went back into the hotel room and said, "Lindy, I'm going to have you showcase my most recent design. Nobody has seen it before. There will be huge bids for the garment after tonight."

"That sounds fun."

"Lindy, when we do these special events, since it helps me a lot, we are going to loan you some expensive diamond jewelry.

Hotel security will be bringing the jewelry up in a bit and you will have security near you for the rest of the night, but we cannot allow you to leave the hotel with the diamonds."

"Not a problem, I think we'll remain in the hotel tonight."

"When you come back up to your room later, hotel security will be here to take care of the diamonds and return them to our secure storage."

"Sure, not a problem. I don't mind looking good tonight."

It took an extra half hour to get the couple ready, but when they stepped out of their hotel room heading for the glitzy restaurant, they looked spectacular. The makeup on Harkey altered his image slightly and his hair design created an utter spell binding image that would impress every woman in the restaurant. Everyone left the hotel room together as the fashion designer team was like an Indy racer pit crew who were extremely efficient in all their actions.

The fashion designers went down the freight elevator, while Harkey, Lindy and two bodyguards went down the elevator together.

The bodyguards didn't know who the male was because the room was reserved in Lindy's name. One of them asked Harkey:

"Sir, may I ask you what your name is?"

"Call me Harkey."

"What do you do for a living Harkey?"

"I'm a pilot in the Air and Space Force."

"Really, what do you fly?"

"I'm qualified on a number of planes, but I'm primarily an Albatross Varco pilot."

"Wow that's amazing."

"Were you ever in the service?" Harkey asked the security man.

"Yes. I was an aircraft maintenance technician. I'm well acquainted with the Albatross Varco. Only special forces fly that aircraft."

That man now looked at Harkey in a new light. He definitely was a special dude and here he is with a glamourous woman with millions in credits worth of diamonds they were protecting. This made the evening even better knowing he was protecting a good guy and not just some Mr. Money Bags with a hot girlfriend."

The Maitra d' observed the couple and the security men approaching. When the Maitra d' saw the two hotel bodyguards and the woman with all the diamonds she knew this was the couple.

"Are you Lindy Foster?"

"Yes."

"Let me escort you to your table."

Soon they were seated at a table with a great view of the city and the performers on the stage. The fashion designer had her special arrangements with the hotel manager and alerted them that Ms. Lindy Foster with her companion Harkey would be showcasing her latest design and to have them seated appropriately.

This reservation was made a good thirty minutes before they arrived, and the table had been cleaned off and tablecloth changed from the previous guest who had departed with reserve signs with their name on it.

This reserve table had a great view to all the other restaurant guests who wasted no time in discovering the lovely Lindy.

As soon as they were seated their waiter took their drink requests and handed them napkins.

This table had a very nice candle arrangement. It was developed to accentuate the diamonds that in turn provided the glitter for the guest. The lovely music, the sparkling reflections from the jewelry and the elaborate fashion design created an image that Harkey would never forget. The couple had been warned a photographer might come in and take their picture so they would have a way to remember this evening. Just as a choreographed activity seemed to be planned at the perfect time, the photographer arrived before the table was cluttered with drinks and meal components.

"Sir, we would like to take your picture for the fashion designer, and we'll leave copies in your room."

"Sure, why not."

The photographer was world class and by the time they arrived back at their room they had several framed pictures with a lovely note from the fashion designer, "These pictures are compliments of the hotel for having two incredibly attractive guests to help improve the image. We are so happy that you allowed us to work with you tonight and provide the luster for other guests to enjoy."

The piano, singer, and other members of the music group created lovely music that made the experience even better. The singer focused on Harkey as if she were singing her love songs to him exalting *Demonic Propensities*.

In a way she was because he truly moved her, and she knew nothing about him.

Lindy was also moved especially now that she knew how well Harkey could look if properly dressed. And she had the financial power to keep him well dressed despite his meager military pay.

Slowly feeling at ease with the nice alcohol enriched drink Harkey was feeling slight exhilaration looking at the beautiful woman, Lindy, in front him. As the candlelight flickering created millions of reflections on the jewelry that added tremendously to the luster, the emotions were elevated. *Was it post-traumatic stress driving my thinking*? Harkey wondered.

They had a lovely dinner; the food was exceptionally good. The chef was alerted table 15 had VIP's and to take extra care of them and he did.

After the meal was finished a couple waiters assisting cleaned the table off, removing all the dishes and changed the tablecloth in a minute and a half in a remarkable display of efficiency for these VIP's.

Their drinks were also removed even though only half finished and replaced with new drinks.

Harkey was just sitting back enjoying the music. This was actually only his second down time since he left combat. The first ended in the bar fight that created his legal problems. He needed this down time and realized he needed to unwind. He appreciated Lindy more than she would ever know.

The performers took a break, and the singer approached the table and said to Lindy, "I really love your dress. You look so beautiful."

"I did it for him." Lindy smiled and nodded at Harkey who was feeling quite emotionally from Lindy's comment, but he was a gentleman and asked, "Would you like to join us for a drink?"

"I would love to."

Harkey gestured to the chair between he and Lindy, and the singer sat down.

"My name is Lexi Marceau."

"I'm Harkey, and this is my lovely friend Lindy Foster."

Lindy took notice of how Harkey introduced her. It made her feel warm inside. She was already emotionally attached to Harkey and when she saw all those scars on his body, she was almost overwhelmed. She now felt good she figured out how to control herself and not break down. But she knew one day they would likely have a conversation about it, which was a day she was not looking forward to because she wasn't sure she could handle it.

"Nice music tonight."

"Thank you."

Sitting in his BOQ room relaxing in the evenings watching a little entertainment and listening to music, there was a popular song that had been playing for a while that kind of influenced Harkey, so he asked, "Lexi, do you sing any requests from the audience?"

"If we know the song, sure."

"Does your band perform the recent hit, "How to Keep Smiling When the Sun Isn't Shining?"

"Actually, we have practiced that a few times and performed it a couple times but not in a few days."

"Would it be possible to attempt it tonight?"

"I would be most happy to attempt it. After the break I'll talk to the band and put in your request."

"Thank you I appreciate it."

"Tell me Harkey, what do you do for a living?"

"I'm a Space and Air Force Pilot."

"Really? You fly military jets?"

"I sure do."

"What kind of planes do you fly?"

"I'm proficient in a number of types of Jets, but I've been specially trained in flying the Albatross Varco."

"Is that a major combat jet?"

"Yes, it is."

Lexi didn't want Lindy to think she was trying to steal her boyfriend, even though she wouldn't mind, turned to her, and asked, "Lindy, what do you do if you don't mind?"

"I'm a corporate exec. I'm in charge of the IT for a tech company."

"Wow, that must be exciting."

"It is but it doesn't quite give me the excitement that Harkey does."

Lexi took that as a woman-to-woman message, *hands off my boyfriend.*

Harkey was naive and had no idea how powerful women operated. He would be learning soon.

They chatted for another few minutes then the band members were going back to their short stage and Lexi said, "I really enjoyed talking with you, and thank you for the drink."

"Our pleasure Harkey said and smiled."

"Lexi went up to the band and they had a huddle. They

normally would not have inserted that song in their performance tonight until Lexi notified them, he flies combat jets the least we could do is play one song for him. That did the trick and the band immediately agreed and soon when they started the song, Lexi announced at the beginning, "This song is for the lovely couple in front, Lindy, and Harkey. Thank you for being here tonight."

The crowd was now focused on who Lexi was referring to and the woman with all the diamonds in front quickly gave them clues.

Lexi sometimes walked out among the crowd and sang. Tonight, she slowly approached Harkey and Lindy's table then sang for them leaving no doubt in the minds of all the guests who Harkey and Lindy were.

Lindy knew this was the song Harkey requested. She also knew another thing. Lexi was singing it for Harkey! She wished they could get the hell out of here fast!

After the song Lexi Marceau went back up on the stage with the other musicians as they performed their next piece. Harkey was fully satisfied but he was now tail dragging (pilots' term).

"Lindy, I'm terribly sorry, but I'm very tired. Could we go back to the room now?"

Lindy was feeling instant relief and said, "I would love to."

Harkey signaled to the waitress who came up quickly and asked, "Can we have our check please."

"Sir its all been taken care of. You do not have a check." The beautiful waitress smiled knowing the deep secret she could not reveal. And she looked very fondly at Harkey because the fashion designer's associate who set this all up gave her a little INTEL on the couple. The waitress felt so moved by the man. He was an incredible example of the best of the best and she felt privileged just to have served him knowing what he and endured.

"Thank you." Harkey said wondering why the special treatment, then assumed it was a form of a bribe from the fashion designer to show off her fashion ware to the numerous wealthy clients in the restaurant then.

The couple stood up and as they were leaving Harkey gave a short wave to Lexi Marceau, a beautiful singer with an incredible voice that resonated the song he requested in his memories. Some of the clientele observing the couple leave also noticed the well-dressed security men tailing behind which left them wondering *who are they?*

They went up to their room and the security men went in the room with them and as Lindy undid the borrowed diamonds, they put them in a small carrying case that fit inside the coat jacket of one of the men. Harkey noticed as they left there were two other men with them to take the diamonds down to a secure holding place where hotel guests could also park expensive jewelry for the night.

Once inside the room alone Lindy quickly undressed herself and walked over and crawled in bed waiting for Harkey to undress and join her. Soon he was almost bare except for one piece of under garment and climbed in bed and turned out the last light. They kissed and Harkey held Lindy and made no movement towards a sexual activity and soon he was sound asleep.

Lindy knew Harkey had been through a lot lately and was no doubt exhausted and gave him his peace. She felt good just being in his arms. She too went to sleep. In about four hours Harkey suddenly became awake and assessed his situation around him and the smell of Lindy's perfume quickly helped to his arousal. He was suddenly feeling invigorated. He reached down into her panties and felt her moistness which further intensified his sexual interest then moved over on top of her and slid her panties of and soon joined her into the perfect coitus. The love making was quite sensational especially since Harkey had not had sex in several years, and when he did it was a lackluster performance with someone not special to him.

Lindy felt special to him. This was an emotional covalence that created their combined orbit into the celestial feast that exploded their passions resulting in that powerful release of gratification. Afterwards they laid there holding each other in a loving fashion. They both felt love and the song Lexi Marceau sang was replaying in Harkey's memories as this would be an indelible memory about really the first woman he ever fell in love with. He didn't know what love was until tonight. He was spell bound and full of emotion. In a while the succumbed to post love making sleep and became incoherent until several hours later when the sun was shining, and it was a new day forming.

Harkey felt fresh and happy that he had two full days of totally unwinding with the help of this lovely woman.

Lindy was a beautiful an vibrant woman. She knew the obvious and the intangibles. Harkey didn't have a lot of time before he had to get back to that training regiment and it was up to her to make sure he got to see and enjoy as much of the city as possible in a brief period.

Having seen a lot of the city, Lindy knew where most of the things were that Harkey would enjoy seeing or experiencing and thus led him on a two-day wonderful journey through this wonderful metropolis. They saw some art studios, parks, went up to observation lounges in tall buildings that had telescopes to look at the city. The view was inspiring. The experienced some nice restaurants and some daytime shows. The two days were full of adventure and surprises.

The next night the couple was again dressed up as VIP's again because the fashion designer had already sold the dress Lindy was wearing the night before to an exclusive client for top dollar. Every nickel she invested in their dinner and the rental on the clothes paid her back one hundred-fold. The fashion designer in essence was using a beautiful fashion model for free.

Lindy didn't mind getting dressed up so provocatively as she knew it would help Harkey develop some motivations for later in the night. And now that he had a good night sleep and low stress, he might be able to perform before he fell asleep. She of course would help the process along as she was well read and always wanted to perform fellatio on her male lover but had never had one yet.

Tonight, Lindy was dressed even better and sexier than the night before. Lindy couldn't believe the fashion designer could out-do herself. It turns out the fashion designer was saving this new design for a special event. With the feedback and the emotions, the designer developed with Harkey, she was going to make a fashion statement tonight. Harkey was along for the ride in ways she hoped he would benefit and something in her female intuition told her Lindy would make that happen.

Once again, they received preferential treatment in their reserved table. The presence of the lovely couple seemed to stimulate some of the regular customers who drug their friends along for the festivities.

The beautiful singer Lexi Marceau figured the lovely couple would be back tonight. She would like to see Harkey again, and if she could ever entice him, she would show him *love making on a theme from Paganini.*

Lexi Marceau had a few extremely sexy outfits she wore especially when recording execs were coming to see her and the group perform. Her manager was already working on crafting a recording contract. In a few weeks she would know the results of those negotiations.

Lexi Marceau had on one of those outfits that made a couple recording execs salivate that put her in the real possibility of making it big. And she did it all for flyboy that she would love to sink her fangs into.

Tonight, was almost a repeat performance. The main difference was during her break, Lexi Marceau wasted no time to get to the couple's table and with her sexy and alluring attire, had no problem of shifting the eyes of every male in the restaurant towards her and onto the table with the fabulously sexy dressed woman sat with that super hunk of a well-built man. Harkey was built well for one major reason. He was physically conditioned to participate with the special forces in epic battles he managed to live through despite incredible trauma.

Lindy had felt Harkey's muscles and his thrusts when he was at the pinnacle of his release of quintessential gratification. Harkey had put a love spell on Lindy that could never be broken. She would work vigorously to protect her lover and keep the venomous barracudas' away from him.

After watching Lexi Marceau do everything in her power to seduce Harkey, Lindy was more than happy when Harkey suggested they go back to the room. Unlike the previous night Harkey didn't need a four-hour break to get his body in a condition to perform. He was ready at the starting line and was getting all set to perform his magic when Lindy said, "I want you to lay back and relax. I want to do something to please you, and then you can take care of business after that. She then dove below the sheets and showed Harkey she knew a thing or two and got him into a mental state that when she climbed on top of him and made love to him, Harkey quickly exploded in a phenomenal release of splendid euphoria from his wonderful intense steaming gratification.

This night it seemed like there was more visibility on the couple and there was. Monday morning, the corporation that Lindy worked for started making inquiries about this fantastic looking man she was with in some pictures high profile individuals took silently in the restaurant that made their way in the hands of her superiors. Corporations are of course concerned about high profile employees and when she was on a video telecom with a few select senior executives getting a grilling they forced her to disclose who Harkey was. They were utterly stunned when they discovered he was a high-profile military pilot with a chest full of ribbons and awards.

One of the corporate executives who had interesting connections to the military scored privileged information about Harkey and quickly discovered he was profoundly a national hero. The company was stunned. And now this friend of Lindy's was a pilot. THIS GUY HAD DONE EVERYTHING.

Lindy was pulled one more step up the corporate ladder because of her involvement with Harkey. She quickly determined the company was very proud that she would somehow become a person of interest to this pilot. It clearly showed a side of Lindy they never saw before. She truly was an enigma, but a very pleasant person that everyone loved to work with.

Chapter Four
Training Ends and the fun Begins

Time passes too quickly when you are in love. The more pleasant life seems causes time to warp. Misery helps time linger. Harkey continued training but with far more satisfaction since he spent more time in the cockpit due to this new arrangement. His new squadron commander would call into question about the hours Harkey claimed even when the school sent his records and statistics to his next duty station.

One could say the squadron commander, Lieutenant Colonel Baxel almost had it in for Harkey over his claim of flying hours.

"There is no way a student pilot comes to this squadron with that many flying hours. Do you think I'm really that dumb!"

Harkey didn't like the down dressing but refused to give in.

Lieutenant Colonel Baxel refused to grant Harkey leave requests for a couple weeks to go visit Lindy. Nevertheless, Harkey continued corresponding with Lindy and giving her updates as to why they couldn't be together. It was getting critical because if he didn't see her soon, his Assault ship would be leaving the solar system and going on deployment where they might see a lot of action.

The showdown finally happened on the same day the new

Task Force Commander showed up.

Harkey was written up for insubordination because he refused to bow into the squadron commanders demand to retract the flying hours or else.

A general court martial was convened and the old Task Force Commander was now gone and suddenly recently promoted General Kollins arrived taking over all administrative and legal control on the Assault ship and the task force. It was provincial General Kollins was on the same ship as Harkey.

General Kollins could not believe the crap when he was given a briefing by his executive officer about the court martial that was about to convene.

General Kollins read the charges and looked up to his executive officer and said, "Get Lieutenant Colonel Baxel's ass in here now, I want a piece of it."

When Lieutenant Colonel Baxel arrived at the XO's stateroom all smug because he was going to make an example out of Harkey, the XO said, "Do you know how bad you are screwed?"

"What are you talking about?"

"One of Harkey's classmates just arrived and verified his flying hours are correct and the Task Force Commander had determined you took illegal and immoral actions against Harkey."

"Well, who the hell is the student, I'll make an example out of his ass too."

"General Kollins."

"You got to be shitting me?"

"I think you will be transferred to the training command this afternoon. I'm taking you up to see the boss now. You should feel lucky he didn't toss your ass out of the military."

The two men went up to the Boss stateroom and Lieutenant Colonel Baxel wasn't feeling so froggy now.

The XO knocked on the door and the General responded, "Come on in."

"Have a seat Lieutenant Colonel Baxel."

"XO you can leave, this will be a private discussion."

"Yes sir."

"What do you want to talk to me about sir?"

"I just tossed your stupid court martial out and sent a message to the legal staff that you misrepresented the truth. Not only did I vouch for Major Harkey, so did the school which you ignored."

"There is no way a student came her with that many flying hours."

"One of the reasons why you are being transferred to that school is so they can train you to the same schedule Harkey did. That's your punishment. If you refuse, then you might be the person with a general court martial."

"General, this is bullshit, and you know it."

"Colonel, I really do not like your attitude, and I do not like the way you are addressing me."

Lieutenant Colonel Baxel suddenly realized he was in serious trouble and his career was now in jeopardy and decided to start listening instead of running his mouth.

"I'm sorry sir."

"Did you ever see Harkey with all his clothes off?"

"No why?"

"You would be surprised at how many scars he has on his body from battles he served under me. He's very lucky to be alive."

The Lieutenant Colonel sat there taking it all in.

"I was in Harkey's Class, and I witnessed him flying all those hours. Whether you refuse to believe it or not, he did it. Harkey's records and his claims are all true. There is absolutely nothing incorrect in his records."

Lieutenant Colonel Baxel started to feel the burn and it was only getting worse.

My boss suggested I toss your ass out of the service for this behavior, but I'm willing to give a person a second chance. The instructors have a complete record of every simulator, and every trainer Harkey flew. They have video recordings of every take off and landing he did in the trainers, and you being the *dumb son of a bitch* that you are, totally disregarded all that information and laid it into Harkey, and you also disapproved his many leave requests.

"I'm sorry sir," Lieutenant Colonel Baxel responded but quickly realized he had badly burned his bridges.

You are disgusting to me but I'm going to fix you. Harkey is hereby transferred to another squadron. Because of your blatant illegal actions against him, you are forbidden to be in his chain of command. Any discipline or other actions you took have been removed because you didn't know what hell you were doing, and I do not ever want you to be a squadron commander in my task force.

"Yes sir."

My superiors have agreed to your punishment if you agree to do it. If you refuse, then my only other recourse is to toss your ass out of the military now. What do you want to do?

"You really do not give me much choice. I have to go to that training command."

"The commanding officer of the training command will arrange for you to have a supervised review of all of Harkey's take off and landings, his trainer records, and his certified simulator sessions.

"Okay."

"Then you will be required do all that he did, and we'll see if you are man enough to get it done at the pace he did.

"Understand sir."

"Because of your actions I must delay transit to our deployment area because I must personally take you and Harkey down on the planet so he can do two days of leave he requested a long time ago and I want to make sure the Commanding Officer at the school understands what you agreed too. Here's the paperwork sign it."

"Yes sir."

The former squadron commander knew he had to sign it, or his career was finished. Something told him if he went along with the punishment, he would get a chance to redeem himself.

~~~

Harkey had two quality days with Lindy including visiting her parents and they immediately liked Harkey.

The day General Kollins had to take himself and Harkey back to the assault ship, the President of Lindy's company
~~~

arrived as he wanted to personally meet Harkey. It was truly an interesting situation where one of his best executives somehow became so close to a national hero.

Just before they were saying their goodbyes for a while, the company President got to also meet General Kollins which gave him a personal thrill, as well as the interesting conversation he had with Harkey.

During small talk that lasted for a few minutes before they departed. The company president said, "I'm very happy that one of my top executives is close to such an outstanding pilot."

General Kollins lit up the President when he stated, "Harkey was with me during two major task force operations, and I had the privilege of attending flight school with Harkey where I was qualified as pilot and earned my wings. He was the top student in my class. He is no doubt one of the best pilots in my task force. That's why I'm happy to personally come here to take him back to my command ship.

General, that is really good to hear, and I admire what you guys do to protect us. My thoughts and prayers will go out to you during your deployment.

"Thank you I appreciate that."

By then Harkey's former squadron commander was really upset with himself for his conduct. After the instructors schooled him on what all Harkey did, he was sick to his stomach at his own personal behavior. He almost wanted to cry for what he did for to that excellent pilot. All his claims were true. Though semi-unbelievable.

The former squadron commander went to the School's Commanding Officer and asked him to send General Kollins a communique on his behalf. In that communique he said after fact finding at the school, I discovered all of Harkey's claims were true and I was a total idiot for my behavior. I will do my best to complete the training, but I want to apologize to Harkey because I was so terribly wrong. When General Kollins was back on his assault ship, he received the correspondence from the school commanding officer, his good friend.

General Kollins personally witnessed how Sargent Chuk had changed when he discovered the truth about Harkey and decided perhaps the Squadron Commander had learned so much so quickly, maybe it would be better to take him with him and sent an immediate message back to the School Commanding Officer directing him, "Send Lieutenant Colonel Baxel to my command ship immediately. I thank you for training him so well so quickly. I want to take him with me to the warzone."

The school's commanding officer chuckled and yelled at his administrative aide, "Get Lieutenant Colonel Baxel in my office immediately, there has been a change of plans!"

As the task force was about ready to launch into high speed to transit to their next assignment, the shuttle craft landed delivering Lieutenant Colonel Baxel who was immediately escorted to General Kollins Office. As soon as he arrived, General Kollins said, "You got smart fast. I read your confession and decided the best way to give you a second chance is to bring you with me and let you prove your worth in live combat."

"I will do my best sir."

"Good, I have someone to see you now."

General Kollins walked over to the door and looked out to his yeoman and asked, "Is he here now?"

"Yes sir, should I send him in?"

"Please."

Harkey was brought in. General Kollins had informed him someone wanted to apologize in a previous discussion. He walked in and Lieutenant Colonel Baxel almost felt like he saw a ghost. The emotions were quite intense.

General Kollins being a very smart social engineer said, "I think you guys need a few minutes to talk privately. I'll be outside. Come on out when you are ready."

General Kollins knew Lieutenant Colonel Baxel had to eat a lot of crow now. This was probably the most humiliating thing he ever had to do in his lifetime, but when you are wrong you are wrong, especially when the boss knows it.

Harkey never held a grudge and never discussed it with anyone. Lieutenant Colonel Baxel now knew this was an extraordinary pilot and had General Kollins not intervened, he would have destroyed a very good pilot. He was ashamed of himself, but he knew what he had to do in the future. Do a better job of investigating things before he made bad decisions and possibly ruining someone's life.

Chapter Five
Kattnoggar and Remembrance

Curse the wind

Curse the sea

Curse the individual

That must flee

Ski Beach May 2022

It was now time to head near Spetznar stronghold area of Planet Kattnoggar. Due to the element of surprise and the secrecy of the mission, training was on the way. It would take two weeks to get in position to attack. However halfway there the fleet would stop and go through all the assault practice. There was an inhabited planet in route that was relatively reasonable representation of Kattnoggar. This offered an excellent opportunity to exercise all elements of the invasion. To General Kollins extreme delight, the Tiger Team was embarked on the transports. The day before the kickoff of the practice sessions, while the wardrooms were going over all the planning details, General Kollins saw it fit to take Harkey with him over to one of the transports that had most of the Tiger team aboard.

As expected, when word was passed, Sea Daddy and Sargent Chuk were there to meet the two distinguished guests. The reunion was quite a happy event and General Kollins insisted having a meal with the troops and Harkey.

This was the first time the men saw General Kollins and Harkey wearing their wings. General Kollins was fully certified in transports, but he was also certified as a Space Fighter pilot mainly to allow him to fly space fighters from one spaceship to another, especially in the heat of the battle if he needed. A Space Fighter Craft was far more able to protect itself than any other form of aircraft, though they were most likely to get destroyed by the nature of the action in an all-out battle.

For the next few days, the men worked hard to practice all the necessary actions they needed to take.

Even the Albatross Varco close ground support space-aircraft made simulated runs on enemy strongholds to support the invasion force.

What made the Albatross Varco such a splendid weapon system is it could deploy out of a space transport outside the atmosphere of a planet and proceed down near the surface of the planet as a fighter-bomber providing close ground support to the special forces on the ground who usually landed in deadly highly contested landing zones.

Harkey flew twenty sorties over the next few days and now felt very pleased the instructors had worked hard with him so well and helped him get ready for all that was to unfold. But he also knew there was a big difference between simulated fighting and the real deal when the enemy was trying to kill you.

General Kollins carefully observed the training and reviewed a lot of video and communications stream to get a complete assessment of how things were going. He was working 20 out of 24 hours, but he knew that as soon as they went back to transit speeds heading for the point Q where the fleet would deploy the forces, he could catch up on his sleep and be rather recovered from sleep deprivation by then. However, he knew once the fighting started there would be several sleepless days as this major battle manifested.

At the end of the transit, they all rendezvoused at point Q to ensure the element of surprise and avoid the enemy from detecting and tracking a large formation. Spreading out the ships for the transit avoided large ion wakes and X-ray emissions usually associated with task force transits.

H-hour began, and the fighter bombers and arsenal space barges flew to the planet and began their softening up and clearing a space column to allow the landing craft to get to the planet without sustaining a lot of damage.

This was a hard-fought battle and in the span of a day Harkey flew a dozen sorties, coming back, getting rearmed and refueled.

Squadron commander, Lieutenant Colonel Baxel observed the conduct of all the space and air forces and could hear through the chatter many things Harkey was doing. He was proud of Harkey for his efforts as well as he never carried a grudge and just before they left the General's quarters on the assault ship, Harkey offered the best way out for both of them.

"Us just forget all of this happened. You have an important job to do and so do I. I want you to be successful because we have tough days ahead of us and we all need each other."

Squadron Commander, Lieutenant Colonel Baxel would never forget Harkey's words. He quickly took a strong liking to the pilot because he had done an incredible feat at school logging more flying hours than any previous student by a large margin. It really was truly a remarkable record and the Squadron Commander loved remarkable records.

This was one of those battles the Spetznar could ill afford to lose. They put forth the maximum effort. It was a slug fest. Suddenly the Tiger Team was bleeding. They were taking a lot of casualties. Those were Harkey's brothers down there dying. Each time he came back for reloads and fuel, he was animated and dedicated to the cause.

Harkey's Albatross Varco devastated a lot of the enemy. He was giving the Tiger Team some breathing room which they appreciated, and they somehow knew it had to be him. Nobody else was pressing home the attack so fiercely.

Time after time those passes Harkey's Albatross Varco made were shifting the balance in the favor of the Chevolite forces.

General Kollins watched all this unfold. He prayed for Harkey's safety. He knew Harkey was giving it all he got and at that critical moment when they had to take out that cluster of exoskeletons or the Tiger Team would be done in, Harkey made the supreme sacrifice. He came down and laid his eggs on over half of the exoskeletons that really put a major halt to the Spetznar counterattack. No previous attack was so devastating. It made a massive difference. But one exoskeleton got a lucky shot and Harkey's Albatross Varco which went down in a ball of flames. His telemetry ended and he was most likely dead.

Thanks' too Harkey's actions the battle shifted and a couple days later the Spetznar stronghold surrendered. The Tiger Team licked their wounds and proudly marched in as the occupying force with hundreds of thousands of Spetznar enemy POW's.

General Kollins walked into the squadron's ready room and saw squadron commander, Lieutenant Colonel Baxel sobbing. He wanted confirmation Harkey was gone. He knew this man had been touched by Harkey like no other because of the situation they had a while back. He got his answers with the tears. The entire squadron was sad, especially since several of them came from Harkey's class in flight training.

General Kollins knew Jeremy Pazar was a close friend of Harkey and said, "Jeremy, I plan on visiting Lindy Foster when we go back. I would like you to go with me."

"General, I would be very proud to go with you."

Squadron commander, Lieutenant Colonel Baxel then chimed in and said, "General I would like to go with you to pay my respects."

"It would be really good to have a squadron commander there representing Harkey, I would like you to go with us."

"Thank you, sir."

The Task Force Commander must go visit the troops, especially after a decisive victory and flew down to planet Kattnoggar and visited the Tiger Team Commanding Officer and requested Sea Daddy and Sargent Chuck to give them the news.

"We'll have to go to the infirmary; they were both severely wounded in the battle."

"Us go right away."

Sargent Chuk and Sea Daddy were feeling a lot better as the treatments for their wounds were slowly improving the situation. Of course, they were deeply saddened to hear about the loss of Harkey.

Chapter Six
Sudden Awareness

Bradly was watching TV with his father. There was a scene in the movie where fighters were dive bombing the enemy. Bradly felt a strange sensation like he had experienced that before. He of course had no idea how. But he knew he had dive bombed. From time-to-time Bradly dreamed about flying and even though he was still a kid he dreamed about a lovely woman. It was almost as if he had a previous relationship with her. But he was a kid how could that be?

Bradly lived with his parents in a modest home tucked neatly in the farming belt and in a town that could not be misconstrued as a city. There was a downtown area, two banks, a restaurant, news paper company on its last and dying leg, a couple hardware stores, and a couple grocery stores, one on the edge of the downtown area and another along the two main Hiways that intersected the town, one going East to West, the other North to South.

It was a great place to grow up in. Community Swimming pool time in the summer was mandatory. Sports year round was also a priority. And then of course the farming in the area created the economy to keep the town alive.

The town of Nazara was located a good distance from the dormant volcano Avon Mons that had a snow and ice crust on it ten months out of the year. Only did late summer reveal the rocky volcanic outcroppings that led to a lot of rock-climbing enthusiasts.

Bradly's education was lackluster, but he excelled in music, history, and sports. In his freshman year he dreaded the Algebra teacher who he learned was a disgruntled college professor and took it out on his high school students by teaching them at the college level. Luck was on his side. After a brutal first quarter where he barely clung to a C average, the math teacher was suddenly on a leave of absence due to personal problems. A substitute teacher, Mr. Grady came in who was far laxer and had a policy if you participated in sports, you automatically got a B as a minimum score in his class because he knew athletic practice had a negative impact on study time. He also knew the value of sports training for young men and how it would help mold their lives.

In short order, Mr. Grady gave the class a test that probably the previous Math teacher had developed and planned on giving to the class.

Bradly's technique was not to be the best score in the class, his motivation was to be the first person to hand in the test regardless of the test score.

True to his form, Bradly handed the filled in test which had multiple choice answers and the great wisdom Bradly received from his lackluster friend Darrell: *"If in doubt, pick C."*

Darrell also helped Bradly out good the following year in Trig with the fundamental understanding of the memorization for Trigonometry functions:

Salley Can Tell Oscar Has A Hard On Always which was the code for Sine equals Opposite divided by the Hypotenuse, Cosine equals Adjacent side divided by Hypotenuse, and Tangent equals Opposite divided by the Adjacent side.

Darrell who wasn't the smartest guy in school was a year older than people in their class and owned the first automobile of any student in the class. It was a fixer upper that had electrical problems from time to time. Darrell who worked at a service station had a lot of older buddies who liked him because he fixed their cars quite often and helped soup them up and make them sound better with highly illegal exhaust systems. Hence Darrell was always well equipped with alcoholic beverages and Bradly enjoyed drinking with him as the drove around town while listening to those ancient forms of tape recorders that allowed selection of 8 different tunes without rewinding the tape.

When Bradly handed in his math test, Mr. Grady looked up and said, "Bradly, I would like to talk to you after class."

Bradly was a little apprehensive because he sat between two brainiacs and feared he might be accused of cheating. Of course, he never cheated he never had to because his buddy Darrell's advice *if in doubt pick C* always accelerated test completion time.

This was the last class of the day, soon the bell rang, and all the other students left the classroom. Bradly was fearful Mr. Grady would lower the boom on him shortly.

"Bradly, what do you have planned this weekend?"

"Not much Mr. Grady. It's break time between sports, and I will not be practicing for another few weeks."

"If you are not busy this weekend, would you like to come out to my farm and help me haul hay?"

Bradly was one of the biggest boys in the class and he excelled in sports, so Mr. Grady knew he was in great physical condition."

"I suppose I could."

Bradly's grandparents were ranchers, and it was assumed that people in the community should help out when they could because there were not enough laborers because most young people left home, went to college, and never came back. He had seen a lot of people helping his grand parents in the past, and they usually had a feast afterwards because his grandmother was a phenomenal cook.

"Good, how about after class on Friday, you ride the school bus home with my daughter Rachel, spend the night with us work Saturday and Sunday, and I'll drive you home Sunday evening?"

"That sounds okay," Bradly said as he realized this would get him out of going to church which he hated.

Bradly's three older sisters hogged the bathroom on Sunday morning spending countless hours on their makeup and fighting over bathroom access, thus the family always showed up to church late and had to sit up front which Bradly hated as everyone would watch him sing when they sang hymns as part of the church service. Bradly couldn't stand it so he would walk to church but that didn't work either because his father would come tap him on the shoulder and make him sit next to his loser sisters. Thinking this would get him out of church instantly made it worthwhile.

Bradly's parents did not like the idea of their kid's drinking soda pop all the time, so they served milk, orange juice or water with meals. And there was always plenty of milk.

Bradly didn't know what to expect, but he figured the meals would have to as good as the slop his mother made, including disgusting breakfasts where he was forced to eat cereals he could not stand.

Bradly walked up to the bus Mr. Grady's daughter Rachel was waiting to board on Friday afternoon. Mr. Grady had informed Rachel to make sure she took Bradly to the right bus to avoid that 15-mile drive from town.

As soon as they arrived at the farm, they were all set to start working. Because of the early fall, there was still enough time in the afternoon to work for several hours and they did.

Mr. Grady's farm hand who complained about a bad back drove the truck, and young buck Bradly took the bales of hay off the conveyer and stacked them onto the truck until they had a load then they disconnected the conveyor machine and drove a few miles to the farm where they started building a haystack. Bradly could see there was a large field with a lot of hay and knew there was no way they could get much of it completed the weekend, but he worked hard, nevertheless.

That evening to wash down the farm fresh steaks William Grady's wife, Darlene cooked to perfection was copious amounts of soda pop. The one meal alone was worth coming out for the weekend. And the delightful notion of missing church added the exclamation point to it.

After dinner it was TV time. The farmhouse had a very large living room where Darlene and Rachel watched evening cabaret type shows, while in Mr. Grady's (aka Bill Grady) den was another TV and had a baseball game on. This was the perfect setup as it was major league baseball playoffs.

After the game and as it was approaching 9:00 P.M. which was mandatory bedtime for all, Darlene showed Bradly to his room down in the basement and a shower where he could clean up. Noticing the poor kid didn't bring anything with him, Darlene noting Bradly was about the size of her husband also issued him some sleeping garments he could change into after his shower. She directed Bradly to leave his dirty clothes in the shower room where in the morning he discovered Mrs. Grady laundered for him the night before, so he had fresh clean clothes to put on in the morning plus Mr. Grady gave him a nice denim jacket to wear since it was chili and it protected him from the bales of hay better.

The room even though down in the basement was still better than sharing a room with his brother. Plus, it got nice and dark after the lights were turned out.

With the nice calories of the dinner that included some apple pie with vanilla ice cream, Bradly was sound asleep but had no problems waking up in the morning for two reasons: chickens crowing in the chicken pen not far from the farmhouse and the lovely smell of bacon cooking.

After a fortifying breakfast with bacon, eggs, toast with farm fresh butter and jams, another big plus up was Bradly was offered coffee! Talk about getting a grand slam home run, it was too good to be true. His parents would frown at him drinking a lot of soda pop and coffee, so Bradly made it a point to paint a picture that resembled what to expect at home. His parents never did catch on.

Away they went to the field and hauled hay until lunch time and soon Bradly was enthralled with a Sunday like meal on a Saturday: Country fresh fried chicken with copious amounts of soda to wash it all down.

It was a very productive day, but Bill had so many bales of hay to haul, they didn't even seem like they made a dent in it.

The next day was almost too good to be true. He was out hauling hay and skipping church. And to think he was going to get a B in math class made it all very good to be alive back in an era when kids could live and enjoy life without the fear of Armageddon hanging over them. It was hard work, but Sunday lunch was exemplary, and that's when Bradly realized what an outstanding cook Darlene was.

At sundown on Sunday evening, Bill drove Bradly back to town. Bradly assumed he was just *helping*. The fact he got great meals and soda pop all week end long and was able to skip church made it all worthwhile. And just as he was getting out of Bill's vehicle in front of his parent's home, Bill said, "Wait a second, I got something for you. Bradly thought it was kind of odd Bill handing him a piece of paper folded in half and he opened it out of curiosity and saw it was a private bank draft check with lots of credits on it made Bradly's eyes just about poke out of his head. Bradly was astonished. He had never seen this amount of money before in his lifetime and that's when Bill asked, "Do you think you can come out next weekend and help haul hay?"

"I would be very happy to help you haul hay."

"Alright, ride the bus home on Friday like you did this time."

"Definitely, see you then."

Bradly closed the passenger side door and Bill drove off. Bradly put the check in his billfold that didn't have much in it and did not reveal it to his father for fear of confiscation. It was tough getting to the bank to deposit it because they closed at 3:00 about the same time school ended. But this week they ended up with a short day for teacher conferences and school was let out at 2:00 and Bradly made a bee line to the bank and deposited his check from working. He currently had twenty credits from mowing lawns and doing odd jobs and could never find enough work and was getting to the age where kids wanted nice clothes to keep up their image. His father always bought him a new pair of "clod hoppers" twice a year and what he was wearing looked disgusting. Thanks to the bank he now had blank checks to write to purchase things. Automation and personal communicators were decades away. The following week, he was in one of the very few retail stores in town and purchased himself a couple new pairs of denim jeans, tee-shirts, and new type of boots that made a dude look cool.

Six months after starting to haul hay they finally cleared the last bale of hay out of the very large field and had built two ginormous haystacks on the two farm properties Bill owned. Bill had since let his bad back farm hand go because he was incapable of doing basic work and always complained about his back. Bill informed Darlene, "I don't need the farm hand because I think Bradly can do all his work."

As soon as they deposited the last of the hay on one of the stacks they had built, Bradly was sad because he realized his vast earnings were quickly coming to and end and it was only Saturday around an hour before lunch time.

Bill said, "Come with me."

Bradly thought he was going to take him to town and drop him off. Instead, he walked over to a tractor and said, "Hop on."

Bill drove the tractor from the farmhouse area out down the nearby pasture and then to a field that looked like it was full of weeds that had been a crop the year before. There was a large plow parked on the side of the field. Bill backed the tractor up to it and hooked up and pulled it out onto the field and then dropped the blades down with a manual control. He got back on the tractor and made a couple laps around the field plowing it real nice. After a couple laps of explaining how to operate the tractor and the plow, Bill asked, "Do you think you can do this?"

"Sure."

At the southern end of the field Bill stopped the tractor and took it out of gear. He then said, "Keep plowing I'll be back in a while to pick you up for lunch."

True to his word, Bill showed up in about an hour in a pickup truck that had fuel tank on it and signaled to Bradly to stop. After Bradly stopped, Bill climbed up on the tractor and said,

"We are going to fuel up the tractor then we'll go to lunch."

The process was relatively simple, take the cover off the fuel tank, put the hose fixture on the tank and walk over to the pickup and start manually pumping the fuel. There were other times with another truck they simple poured the fuel through a nozzle down into the tractor's fuel tank using five-gallon fuel cans.

It was about this springtime the days started getting longer quicker and soon they could work until 7:30 in the evening or even later. Bill asked Bradly if he could plow after school, and he would give him a ride home. Now Bradly's bank account started growing a lot faster and his shoes and clothes were improving all the time to the point some girls in school who would not give him the time of day were starting to be a lot more friendly, though Bradly avoided the pitfalls of teenage relationships which he was grateful because other boys in the town were always ending up at shot gun weddings with a knocked up bride.

For almost four years, Bradly was Bill's personal ranch hand. He didn't realize it until later that Rachel's parents were trying to set him up to be permanent through her. However, Rachel was a wild girl and rumors floating around would not please her parents.

In the meantime, Bradly met another girl, was falling in love but then jolted as her father flatly rejected him and informed his daughter to stop seeing Bradly or else! Perhaps therefore he never connected with a woman from his community.

Bradly didn't believe in UFO's or Aliens even though there had been several television shows about them. He also didn't subscribe to the notion that all you needed was faith for religion to work for you.

One year near the time Bradly would leave behind the town

forever, there was back-to-back rainstorms around planting time. Bradly a conscientious person suggested to Bill that he plow the field after dark using the tractor lights to give, he sunlight a few days to kill the weeds as the weatherman forecasted rain in about four days and it was getting late in the planting season.

Bradly didn't know why but he suddenly felt kind of strange right after sundown. He didn't know why he did it, but he stopped the tractor which had a nice cab on it and opened the rear door to the tractor's cab and looked to the horizon in the direction where the sun had just gone down, and the azure sky was turning slowly purple before nighttime.

Bradly noticed a large object probably a thousand feet away. It was a black triangle UFO silent and just sitting there, huge, and probably five football fields in length. That triangular shaped object scared Bradly quite severely. He was not too far from the pickup truck, so he turned off the tractor and ran to the pickup truck and drove back to the farmhouse. He was almost done plowing the field so he could easily finish it first thing in the morning.

Bradly never did confide that information to anyone for fear of being called crazy. The country sheriff two days later announced a cattle mutilation about two miles from Bill's farm.

~~~

Up in that triangular shaped UFO was a Colonel Jeremy Pazar of the Chevolite scientific foundation expedition. This was Jeremy's last mission before he retired after forty years of service.

Jeremy had pursued Lindy Foster and didn't mind she had an illegitimate son from her deceased lover, Harkey, but she refused to date or marry. She loved Harkey to her dying days
~~~

which occurred recently in the past, and she was happy to go, hoping in some way she might meet Harkey again in another life in another time and place.

One of the pilots aboard the research craft hovering above Bradly's tractor was Harkey's son, Edgar, fresh out of flight training and very similar to his father in many ways. Jeremy had pulled strings to get Edgar assigned to his defense squadron because he didn't want him killed like his father, especially since the war was winding down and in a few more months there would not be any more combat deaths. By the time they arrived at their base at the Chevolite planet Beckcen, they expected the peace treaty to be signed and this war that had drug on far too long would finally be over.

Jeremy looked at the photonics recordings of the young man running from the tractor towards the pickup truck. He said to himself, that person sure looks like Harkey. *Was it an image he wanted to see or was it really what it seemed?*

After their last animal samples to determine if the DNA would be suitable for future introduction into their agricultural database and potential future exploitation, the Chevolite research vessel went back out into space and landed in a converted assault ship that had once been the home to the illustrious Chevolite Tiger Team. The ship then made way towards a distant solar system and the Chevolite planet Beckcen where all the scientific data collected would be systematically brought down to the elite Chevolite Scientific Foundation where scientists would study these samples for many years to the future.

Chapter Seven
Following the Near Star

Bradly left home at an early age. Perhaps his time as a rancher helped mature him years above his peers, he was given great responsibility at an early age. Thanks to his second year in high school where he had this wonderful old man named Shively as a math teacher in Trig class that had mostly seniors who needed it to graduate and a low student count, Bradly did well.

Between Pathageryns theory that Mr. Shively taught so well and Darrell's secret formula (Salley Can Tell), Bradly tested high enough in his military entrance exams to be selected for a nuclear weapons program. And just when he was finally out of school and sick of school, there he was back in the classroom in one of the most intensive math and electronics courses administered out of the Marstich Institute of Technology (MIT). In eight weeks', time, Bradly learned more new mathematics than he did the entire time in high school. Without Mr. Shively and Darrell's great innovative mathematical learning processes, Bradly would have performed terribly on Limit theory, Tangent Functions, and differential and integral calculous that began after eight weeks. The school was intensive and had a sixty percent drop out rate. Looking back on it, Bradly couldn't believe he got past it and was eventually helping make the nuclear weapons program successful as men like him maintained the weapons successfully preventing malfunctions and improper maintenance actions that could create serious maintenance related failures.

Darrell who enjoyed a career at a fuel station doing oil changes and being a grease monkey, didn't have to waste his time in school. During his sophomore year, he co-cocked the science teacher with a stapler and was expelled out of school.

Bradly didn't see Darrell much after he left home.

Bradly found himself on Pasagralgian Space Force *Ballistic Missile Spacecraft* (referred to as boomers) making space patrols. The government refused to disclose Aliens existed but the Armaments they carried could possibly be used to defend the planet, even though were for use on the planet in the event of a major war erupted with their arch enemies, the Collectivist Confederacy Peoples (CCP).

Bradly didn't want to waste his time being a glorified hydraulic oil mess cleaning technician that missile techs really were, so he was selected among many of his peers to transfer to a group that was critically short of personnel, hence became a sensors technician.

Sensor equipment at the time was blossoming in massive expansion of technology. The sensors room on Pasagralgian space-boomers was slowly getting really crowded with new equipment.

Devices such as Tachyon Differentiators to Neutrino Spatial Pinger's along with their wide spectrum Chirp Convoluters, therefore were so many things to monitor, that sensor operators had a very short life span before they either went nuts or were hired by the Intergalactic Business Machines that built a lot of newer systems that were now in initial production that would integrate all the sensors and utilize a combination of artificial intelligence and fractal display technology to reduce the strain on sensor operators.

As it turned out, spiral developments made it even more complicated since the ranges to detections quadrupled and thus, they had far more targets to track such as space cargo ships and a greater number of military space craft. It also made it increasingly harder for the government to hide the presence of aliens because people like Bradly were watching them coming in from deep space routinely at the time.

Bradly's first space patrol on the bomber was exhaustive and draining. Being a NFG (new effing guy), he knew he would take a lot of crap from the senior guys and gals that had been around a while. It was all professional space force with zero conscripts. Everyone was a volunteer.

There were exciting moments especially when the Pasagralgian Space Force sent up a group of Chakravotry Class Fast Attack Space Warship to comb the area to make sure they were not being followed by a Collectivist Confederacy Peoples (CCP) Near Star Anti-Space Warfare (ASW) boomer killer.

Those dozen Pasagralgian Chakravotry Class Fast Attack Space Warship added enormously to Bradley's detection and tracking efforts. Every single piece of equipment was in full use and the watch section was indeed overwhelmed. Bradly could now imagine what it would be like in mortal combat when that many craft would be shooting at them and they would be taking evasive maneuvers which they practiced now and then during their In-Service shakedown tests where the craft was put through its paces just like it would in wartime. Those were some of the most unhappy moments for the crew as they were pushed to the breaking point. When it was all over everyone was happy, but they also realized they would get to do it again in a year, a depressive thought.

This was the mid-point in their patrol and some officers did not like the Chakravotry Class Fast Attack Space Warship sweeps because they feared they merely led the enemy to them they would have to contend with after the Chakravotry Class Fast Attack Space Warships all went back to the orbiting space station.

Even though the Pasagralgian Chakravotry Class Fast Attack Space Warship were leaving the patrol area, Bradly's efforts didn't lessen up for a while because the fear of dragging along a bogy to their patrol zone was indeed a real fear as it would not be the first time. The enemy appreciated the fact that incompetent Pasagralgian leaders and planners didn't see the errors in their ways and anytime a group of Chakravotry Class Fast Attack Space Warship flew out into space, the Collectivist Confederacy Peoples *Near Star* Anti-Space Warfare (ASW) boomer killers were sent out to scout the area as the policy was, they would be leading them to a prize kill, a boomer should a time of war start.

The only reason why *Near Star* Anti-Space Warfare (ASW) boomer killers were held back sometimes is the Collectivist Confederacy Peoples Space Force smelled a decoy to be used to fish them into revealing sensitive means and abilities. The boomer in question then turned out to be a Q ship with comprehensive Bogy Killer weapons that had it been in wartime would not ended well for the *Near Stars*. Sometimes the Collectivist Confederacy Peoples Space Force had heads up and warnings about such a ruse because spies were imbedded within Pasagralgian Defense Directorate.

Bradly remained poised after the Chakravotry Class Fast Attack Space Warships left the patrol area. He had some friction with his supervisor for some unknown reasons.

During the workup and training for this mission Bradly had attended sensor intel training and was quite competent in his assessments of sensor readings. If there was a point of compromise it was now and based on Bradly's training, he knew the fallacy of delousing by Chakravotry Class Fast Attack Space Warships, which turned out usually to be counter productive if not downright dumb.

A couple days later sensor readings indicated a *Near Star* at long range. Bradly reported it and his supervisor got bent out of shape and without spending much effort into vetting the report simply said *it was a long-range space freighter and don't get the control room all worked up about such nonsense.*

Little did Bradly know a day later Pasagralgian INTEL sent the Space Boomer's CO an *eye's only* message warning of a possible *Near Star* class space warship in the area.

There were a few more delousing's during the Space Patrol and within a couple days of that activity, the same dynamic occurred, up to the point the supervisor threatened to relieve Bradly and reassign him to Deck Division, a group that did all the dreadful tasks on the boomer, like cleaning up hydraulic oil leaks in the missile compartment.

On the 6th such event, the Commanding Officer followed Bradly's supervisor into the sensor room where they were isolated from the rest of the crew for security reasons as well as preventing them from panicking the crew in scary scenarios. The supervisor lit into Bradly like nobody had ever seen before, cussing him out and demeaning him. He was unaware the Commanding Officer was right behind him.

One of the senior guys cleared his throat loudly and wiggled his head in a way to cause the supervisor to stop and look behind and discovered the Commanding Officer was there and had overheard the entire incident. The door to the room was closed, they had perfect confidentiality.

Since the supervisor was cleared at the most secret level, he had privy to all the INTEL reports.

The Commanding Officer then started schooling Bradly's supervisor:

"Why is it you never correlated his previous five reports to the Operational Immediate warnings we got from INTEL?"

The supervisor remained quiet and knew this was turning out not to be such a great situation.

The Commanding Officer who had pioneered the use of Tachyon Differentiators and wide spectrum Chirp Convoluters, while serving aboard a Chakravotry Class Fast Attack Space Warship, asked, "Bradly, what do you think you got?"

"Sir I have a spatial ensemble tracker on contact C109 which I believe is a Near Star class space warship."

"Let me take a look."

The Commanding Officer played around with the settings to make the algorithms work more efficiently because the supervisor did not employ it correctly thus cut down significantly on detection ranges.

Within a short moment the Commanding Officer stated, "Bradly I concur this is a *Near Star* class space warship."

The Commanding Officer then turned toward Bradly's supervisor and said, "I'm pretty sure on the previous five reports Bradly was correct in his evaluations and you were wrong. From now on I will personally vet all his reports if you have a disagreement and if I find you continually make mistakes in your assessments, I may have to relieve you until you go back to the schoolhouse and get retraining."

The commanding officer then grabbed the microphone used

to make reports to the control room and said, "Control, this is the Captain Speaking. I will be conning the ship from sensors room. Change course to 287-190-025 and bring propulsion to all stop after the course change."

The space bomber then turned and pointed the *Near Star* class space warship that was definitely in a search pattern and with a low-level Neutrino Spatial Pings the Commanding Officer watched the scatter plot of the returns slowly build up three-dimensional time history of the Near Star. The fractal imaging software created a trace that looked like vapor trails coming off an aircraft high in the sky. At the head of the vapor trail like image was the latest return off the Neutrino Spatial Ping.

After the *Near Star* completed ten legs on its search pattern it maneuvered on a course leaving the area.

Normally when Space Boomers came across a *Near Star* they changed to an opening course to evade and disappear. The Commanding Officer then said, "It's not our job to track *Near Star* class space warships." He then directed the control room through the intercommunications reporting microphone, "Control come to all ahead one third and after obtaining speed, reverse course."

The control room helmsman repeated back the order and they slowly put the enemy *Near Star* class space warship behind them. This was final confirmation to the Commanding Officer that Bradly's supervisor was incompetent and like the other Commanding Officers stated, they didn't like delousing because it really created relousing. He would definitely transit and perform contact avoidance procedures from now on after every delousing since he was convinced the serious negative consequences of the ill-defined methods used that put them at risk.

Finally, the patrol was over, and Bradly's Space Boomer

pulled into a space Tender for turnover and refit. The space Tender was attached to a sprawling space station that had a lot of facilities, most importantly clubs where crew members could go unwind, get chemically intoxicated awaiting their transportation back to the planet for their off-crew time. There were two crews to a space boomer, the blue and the gold. After the turnover, Bradly's Blue Crew would descend to the planet for approximately four months, going through retraining and some rest and relaxation periods.

While parked next to the space tender prior to relief and transit back to the planet the crew made their way to the various clubs and facilities on the space station that had artificial gravity and was large enough to give a person they were simply inside a domed city, which there were a few on the planet.

Bradly met a female cryptographic technician during the turnover and subsequently remained her friend up until his last patrol before going back for more schooling at a nice semi-tropical base at *Lugar Perfecto Bajo El Sol*, before returning to the fleet with some advanced training and skills.

Bradly was a perfect gentleman with the Cryptologist and didn't try to have sex with her because he was playing for keeps and was attempting to go through the normal method of confidence building for a long-term permanent relationship. Unfortunately, the Cryptologist about then started having an affair during that period with her supervisor a Lieutenant until the Lieutenant broke her heart when he started banging the next gullible young sweetheart that showed up. Rumors started flying and the young lady was emotionally crushed and attempted suicide. To avoid a scandal the military offered the Cryptologist an immediate discharge which she wanted and also gave her a medical discharge based on her bad back. The Lieutenant was transferred out of that post and sent to one of those horrible assignments in a cold and frozen part of the world for punishment with warnings not to fraternize with junior ranks again.

Did she get the back injury doing the horizontal tango? Bradly always wondered.

At *Lugar Perfecto Bajo El Sol,* Bradly met another woman, Sandra Lane, but having been wounded twice by two previous females, he had a lot of reluctance to give his heart to Sandra. But the sudden attraction and desire for sexual activity since he was reaching the prime of life let his little head outthink his large head and he slowly became enamored with the transcendental effects of orgasmic gratification.

Bradly's training lasted six months at *Lugar Perfecto Bajo El Sol,* but reality struck home and he was once again heading back to the fleet. He kept in contact with Sandra Lane, but his new role would consume a lot of his time and efforts.

Bradly felt he was wasting his time serving on a Pasagralgian boomer and ended up as the only student in his class to get assigned to a Chakravotry Class Fast Attack Space Warship. Instead of operating with two crews from a Tender, the Chakravotry Class Fast Attack Space Warship launched from the planet with a minimum crew and no provisions, water, spare parts, or anything not required to get into orbit. Everything not onboard was brought up in shuttles or cargo space craft and delivered piggyback. Thanks to the design, there was a large cargo hatch that mated the space fighter with the cargo space craft where provisions, water, spare parts, lubricants, and anything else they needed delivered. Halfway through the cargo delivery, crew members were brought up to the Chakravotry Class Fast Attack Space Warship in small numbers repeatedly as they staffed the spacecraft. Those brought up first were the maintenance technicians and the logisticians require to help prepare the craft for deployment.

In due time the crew got everything prepared and the Space

Fighter went out for a month to do training and certification of the ship and crew for deployment. During this at-space period, they did lots of scenarios with their trainers and transited high speed out to an empty part of space a very long distance away from the planet to allow them to conduct maneuvers without prying eyes.

One such maneuver was the Capmoc-Drysvinskle that achieves two objectives: emergency weapon avoidance, especially if a kinetic weapon was fired at them, the second was an immediate fire control solution to a hostile threat.

The combination of Mass-Differentiator readings spliced overlaid on Neutrino Spatial Pings provided correlation in the algorithms to achieve the instantaneous solutions required to avoid extremely high-speed weaponry such as the kinetic weapons.

Time on Target for laser systems could be greatly reduced turning a kill shot into a minor wound.

It was assumed that Chakravotry Class Fast Attack Space Warship would be missile magnets for Pasagralgian boomers in a real shooting war, and if weapons launch authorization to the boomer had been received, the Chakravotry Class Fast Attack Space Warship had to position themselves in position of the likely track of the weapons to ensure the boomer had sufficient time to get off its salvo. The truth of the matter was nobody ever expected something like that to happen.

Half of the thirty-day mini-patrol time was consumed traveling to and from the operational area on the far side of a planet obstructing view to prevent enemy Near *Star* class space warships from observing the critical maneuvers and practice. Often three Chakravotry Class Fast Attack Space Warship were sent out for the training, as one simulated the boomer while one of the other's simulated the enemy Orange Force attacking. Sometimes they got followed as the enemy thought they were going out to delouse a boomer. As such a training day was always lost simply by searching their operational area to make sure there were no intruders. And if there were, they ultimately played "Chicken of the Space" routines that got rough and eventually the smart ones left the area. The dumb ones ended up being nothing more than training opportunity for the Chakravotry Class Fast Attack Space Warship crews. Some Commanding Officers who were involved in such incursions thought the realistic training provided by the real enemy turned out to be more valuable than the simulated scenarios they would otherwise perform.

The nice thing about having two other Chakravotry Class Fast Attack Space Warship it allowed Bradly to spend a lot of time gaining proficiency in the manipulating all his equipment. His former supervisor was not on this boat and the one he had was far more flexible in changing equipment lineups to maximize the performance.

Bradly knew of a few instances where supervisors got punched out when passions rose due to disagreements. He in fact knew a couple of those guys.

Finally, after thirty days the fun and games were over. Bradly's Chakravotry Class Fast Attack Space Warship would now pull into a space station where the Tender was parked. One of the benefits of not being a boomer crew member is they could leave their space craft and embark directly into the bowels of the space station through an air lock and not have to pass through the Tender, where the security people can be a real PITA.

The first person off the Space Fighter was the Commanding Officer. The next two was Bradly and his colleague Dongar. Dongar had been associated with this particular Space Fighter four years and had not rose in rank. He was a party animal and planned on becoming a civilian again as soon as this deployment was finished, so he didn't even bother taking the advancement tests. His only concern for the moment was to go find an establishment that served quintessential elixirs that helped to create a metastable mental condition and if possible, find a female that loved sex and had living quarters on the space station.

Bradly didn't expect to find any such persons and even though he wasn't yet committed to Sandra, at least held her in a respectful acquiescence that could possibly develop into a more significant relationship in the future. But he knew the spark like he felt from his high school girlfriend just wasn't there for Sandra. It might never get there with any woman. *Did my high school girl friend ruin me for life?*

Dongar knew where to go. He had this space station fully mapped out from his previous ventures including while he was a non-rated nub on a boomer with the nick name Teacup. The two entered Madam Ayumi's bar where they were quickly seated at a table in a prime location to see all the nice-looking women arriving.

Since there were a minimum number of boomers tied up and only one Chakravotry Class Fast Attack Space Warship, the number of females in the bar were a great percentage higher than the males.

Dongar had educated Bradly while they were on patrol standing sensors watch talking during no or low contact periods. Based on Dongar's indoctrination, Bradly was predisposed to believe most of the women present were there for the pickings (aka low hanging fruit).

Bradly was thinking he should indulge in the mannerisms Dongar had suggested as to when himself away from Sandra before that relationship went to far and he painted himself into a corner. He knew Sandra was all but ready to tie the knot and even consider pregnancy sometimes in the near future.

He didn't want to do a hit and run, but he felt like running!

Perhaps it was time to blow out Sandra's candle?

A group of women came in that were travel assistants who lived and worked on the space station. They had on their sexy blue uniforms and evoked transcendence in all their demure. Dongar had commented on these ladies. He said in essence they were hungry and wouldn't mind having a reason to get off the space station permanently. Finding the right mate would do the trick.

Bradly took all of Dangar's comments with a degree of skepticism, but nevertheless it did cross his mind as to how he might interact with one of these travel specialists.

In the middle of the group of women, Bradly noticed one nice looking lady in particular. For some very strange reason he felt like he knew her. He didn't know from where, but down deep inside his heart she was someone in his past. But the number of women Bradly had any slight romantic activity would be counted on one hand and just a couple fingers, so it didn't make sense how he could possibly know her. It almost spooked him. The woman caught Bradly staring at her.

In a situation like in a place such as Madam Ayumi's bar any woman catching a stare like Bradly's could easily surmise, this stranger was just another horn dog looking for a *biatche* to hump.

Amber Godot could easily be a top fashion model. She had incredible looks. Amber's eyebrows were complete and styled in the most evocative manner to showcase her beautiful eyes, her pearl white teeth, exquisite lips, and a nose with the perfect geometry. Her skin was amazingly beautiful. She didn't need makeup, even though she wore it just like a Knight wears his armor. From lackluster beginnings to advancement to a profession that put her in the top ten percent money earners for women, wasn't a bad step up the ladder.

Amber was self-sufficient, not vain and didn't waste her savings on frivolous matters. She invested half of her income and had a growing portfolio that would make any husband delighted he picked her.

Amber did not mind the concentrated stare from the space warrior wearing his working uniform that had an element of elegance to it. Such working uniforms created a respectful backdrop to the person wearing it. There was something about this young man that triggered her fancy. She didn't know why but she knew she had an attraction to him. Horndog Dongar went to bat and started swinging at any balls, he was ready for action and was willing to *go ugly early* as he liked to say. Dongar was sitting closest to the women, and he immediately struck up a conversation to the lady nearest to him that looked like she was long overdue for some quality horizontal tango time.

Dongar poured on the charm. Bradly was sitting at the table opposite to Dongar watching the connoisseur go to town laying on the charm to the lady sitting near him. There was another woman between Bradly and Amber, so she was somewhat in the way to prevent a conversation to develop. It was as if the planets were aligning and the woman in the way received a phone call on her communicator from some guy she liked and excused herself so she could go outside Madam Ayumi's bar and have a private sweet conversation with her new beau.

Somehow Bradly knew this was the do or die time with this woman he was increasingly wanting to get to know because she spooked him in a way because he knew that he knew her! But from where?

"Hello, how are you doing today?"

"I'm fine thank you."

"What's your name?"

"I'm Amber, how about you?"

"I'm Bradly."

"Nice to meet you, Bradly."

"Thank you, Amber.

"I see you are part of the military."

"Yes I am."

"What do you do in the military?"

"I'm a sensors operator on a Chakravotry Class Fast Attack Space Warship."

"Are you going to make a career of the military?" Amber asked because there was no way she wanted to be long term *Spacepac Widow* in case they developed a relationship.

"Space War is quite hazardous and its not conducive to family life, so as soon as my contract is up, I'm going to become a civilian and do something else."

"What do you think you want to do?"

"One thing all the training I received for me did was it demonstrated I could take on about any challenge in any career field. I will probably go back to school and become an engineer or a scientist."

"How soon will that be?"

"Within two years."

"No chance of changing your mind?"

"No, my mind is pretty made up. This is not my cup of tea,

but I'm an honorable person and I signed the contract, so I will finish it and leave."

"Without any regrets?"

"I made my contribution. They already got their money's worth out of me for my training. Plus, if I become an engineer or a scientist, I have a lot of unique experience that will help me deal with applications and technology in how best to design reliable systems."

As Amber looked upon Bradly, she felt strongly they had met once before. She didn't know how or why or when; she just knew it.

"Bradly, I don't want to offend you, but are you sure we haven't met before?"

"Amber, actually I wish we had. But now that I met you, I would like to see more of you."

"I would like that too."

Amber pulled out one of her business cards and said, "Here's my business card. Call me anytime, I would like to see you again."

"I will."

About that time the woman who had left arrived back and the women had finished their drink and decided they wanted to leave.

As they all got up and left, Amber smiled at Bradly in a way that sent a chill down his spine. She got to him, and he didn't know why.

Dongar struck out and knew where to go next, it was time to *get ugly early*. Then he informed Bradly his modus of operendus: SDHNC. They soon left Madam Ayumi's Bar.

The space station was very large as it provided housing and commercial space that gravity free space construction sites in a cluster a short distance away provided manufacturing materials and equipment for the planet that could only be built in space and drove very lucrative businesses.

The space station in orbit 25,000 miles above the planet allowed artificial gravity to not be affected by the moon and planet's gravity and was anchored in a spot in space that never deviated from its position from the planet in a perfect orbit that seemed to never move even while the planet spun on its axis. This space station was owned and operated by the Pasagralgian government and was one of those items constantly under risk if war started with the Collectivist Confederacy Peoples. Because the space station was so huge, it had its own internal transportation system based on monorails.

Dongar led Bradly to the monorail station nearby and they hopped aboard. The monorail was free, the government paid for it. This was one of the many perks to entice people to move up and live on the space station.

After the monorail made a dozen stops, Dongar said, "We get off here."

All Bradly had to remember was his Chakravotry Class Fast Attack Space Warship was parked at pier 60 and the monorail that made complete loops around the space station announced the pier they were approaching.

Dongar led Bradly into Anastasia's Artists, a bar that catered to Cougars wanting young dudes. There was nothing wrong with the Plethora of women present, they were just slightly too old for Bradly's taste. But in the spirit of Dangar's methods and adventures, Bradly simply went along for some alcohol intake and watch Dongar create an Oasis for a much older woman in his quest to *go ugly early*. No sooner than they sat down Dongar was hit on and Bradly wasn't too far behind.

After enjoying a lot of quintessential celestial recreation with Sandra Lane, Bradly wasn't interested in getting it on with a Cougar old enough to be Sandra's mother. He would abstain.

Dongar went *ugly early* and was soon heading out of the club with a cougar that would make Bradly want to stick his finger down his throat and puke. With Dongar gone there was no need to hang out at Anastasia's Artists, so he departed and headed over to the monorail and hopped on a train going in the clockwise direction on the double track mainline back to pier 60 because it was next to the hotel rooms the crew enjoyed in port since there were no Barracks on a Space Station. The bomber guys got to sleep on their space craft or on the Tender. But they were down on the planet half the time living in normal homes, so it probably didn't matter to most of them.

Bradly went up to his assigned room a place to take a nice Hollywood shower and rest or watch some videos. After a nice long shower, he sat down on the small sofa and started thinking about today's event and the extraordinary feelings he had for that woman he met, Amber. Bradly pulled out Amber's business card out of his billfold and stared at it for a while. *Should I do this*? Bradly asked himself.

He probably would not have called Amber had it been for the strange feelings that he had. Bradly wanted to be with her again and discover what it was. It seemed even more spooky that Amber was sure she had met Bradly once before. At the risk of humiliation and rejection he pulled out his communicator and clicked on the business card with the contract information encoded on a nice three-dimensional barograph and clicked on the call button that immediately placed the call. Since it was a local call on the space station it was automatic and quick. Calling down to the planet wasn't so seamless.

Amber heard the alarm on her communicator and looked at the display screen and saw not only the caller I.D. but callers had the option of showing the image the communicator cameras took of the caller to provide to the receiver.

"Hello Bradly," Amber quickly said as she clicked on the accept icon.

"Hi Amber, sorry if I'm disturbing you."

"Oh no, no problem at all. Thank you for calling me."

"I just wanted to let you know I enjoyed our conversation tonight."

"So did I."

Bradly didn't know where to take the conversation. He was trained in scientific and military matters and not social engineering skills. Amber on the otherhand was extensively trained in social engineering and knew there was an element of shyness with Bradly so if she wanted to get somewhere with Bradly, she would have to be the conductor of this train to romance.

"Say Bradly, I don't know what you had planned for this evening, but I'm getting kind of hungry and was just about to go out and get something to eat, would you like to join me?"

"Yes, I would like that very much."

"Where about is your spaceship parked?"

"We are at pier 60 but I'm in the hotel next to pier 60 where they put us up when we visit the space station."

"I know exactly where you are at. I tell you what, meet me at the front entrance of your hotel in about ten minutes and I'll take you some place where I know we can have food you would enjoy."

"Sure, I'll be there waiting for you."

Bradly had a change of clothes with him so he could enjoy his time not appearing as a space warrior and be able to interact with the public without them knowing who he really was as part of the processes they were used to so that spies would not attempt to approach them as they would be easy targets wearing uniforms.

Bradly's change of clothes were the latest fashions since he came from the planet a little over a month ago and purchased this outfit just before he left for that very purpose. After changing his clothes and putting on some expensive cologne that was advertised as laced with male pheromones to make the women horny, he was ready to go meet this mysterious woman who affected him in ways he didn't understand.

Ten minutes on the dot there was Amber wearing a nice dress that in no way appeared like her uniform she wore when they first met. In the uniform she looked cute, but in this dress with her shoes and hair made up and flowing down one side gave Amber a surreal imagery that easily could make Bradly hunger for love. She too was perfumed up nicely with female bearing pheromone perfume that by itself created a quintessential effect.

Bradly was now certainly happy he didn't follow in Dongar's footsteps and feel dreadful now getting ready to do some disgusting things with a Cougar.

As she promised, Amber led them to a nearby restaurant that had one other significant attribute. It had a tower that went above the space station allowing an incredible view of the surrounding area. All the lights and fixtures around the space station presented an incredible inspiring sight. And to add to the ambience here was Bradly with this gorgeous woman who knew how to be the consummate conductor and glide them into a new adventure they both would enjoy if there was some commitment at the end of the rainbow.

There of course were musicians, a singer and swank all around décor. The place felt certainly good and would just about be the very best place to start a romance. Bradly knew he was captivated by Amber Godot, a living princess and with her lovely dress, she certainly affected his valence of emotions now orbiting her. The Hedonic Tone that Amber Godot seemed to manifest had a stirring effect on Bradly.

Clear over on the other side of the restaurant was Bradly's commanding officer with just as delicious looking female. He was still single but thinking about changing that as his time left in the Space Force was coming to an end because he felt there could not be anything he could be assigned to nearly as exciting as commanding a Chakravotry Class Fast Attack Space Warship. An admin job at headquarters just didn't excite him. Plus becoming a civilian would allow him to further pursue this woman he was with and eventually settle down and have children. His retirement would take care of them, but if his spouse wanted to work that was fine by him as he would be more than happy to be Mr. Mom and take up all those domestic engineer duties required to keep a family healthy and happy.

As the Commanding Officer soon spotted Bradly and saw the woman he was with, his evaluation of him just took several more steps up the stratum as he knew, women like that could select the best of the best and here she was with Bradly and smiling most affectionately. The Commanding Officer was a social engineer. He had to be to oversee a lot of men with type A personalities, like Bradly's former supervisor who was calibrated by his Commander of the space bomber he was on. That Commander was his personal friend and when he heard Bradly transferred to his ship, he explained the altercation. He also stated off the record to trust Bradly because he's not going to let you down. He took a lot of personal abuse and in wartime would have saved all their lives despite an incompetent supervisor.

Bradly and Amber quickly transcended to a very friendly conversation. It was refreshing and somewhat insightful for Amber as she started probing.

Amber was a city slicker all her life until she moved up to the space station, so she enjoyed the farm stories Bradly revealed.

"What was the best part of staying and working on the farm?"

"To be honest, missing out on Church."

"Why was that?"

"Can you imagine showing up to church late every Sunday because my three older sisters fought over the bathroom to spend an hour each putting on their makeup?"

"I can relate to that actually."

Some of the other tangibles were discussed such as soda pop and coffee!

Amber rarely had sex she could count the times on one hand and wasn't likely to do it again without a real companion she would bond with. But tonight, there was that nagging question: Why did she know Bradly. She knew it. He was in her dreams somehow. His face, his voice, everything about him, she had seen before, but could not recollect *When* and *Where*.

The music, the entertainment, the view, it all added to the experience. The conversation propelled them closer together, but Amber knew one thing vividly, the restaurant was done with them and wanted them to leave so they could accommodate other diners since there was a line outside waiting for one of the best meals that could be purchased anywhere on the space station. The Chef was incredible, so she knew what to do.

Say listen, Bradly, I'm not a bad girl and I do not sleep around. I like to get to know my partner really well and only want to do it if I know we are in love. We need to leave because the waiters are giving us an evil eye, we could go up to my apartment and listen to music or watch a movie together."

"Sure, let me get the check."

Bradly signaled for the waiter that was so happy to get rid of them, he virtually flew over to their table.

"Yes, sir what can I get for you?"

"Just our check."

About that time, Amber said, sir, "Please take my business card and scan it and charge it."

Before Bradly could get out any words, the waiter took off with her card, and it was customary to return with a receipt and the card since the card was of no value to the waiter.

"I'm paying for the meal because I get some company perks for staying on the space station. I get a dozen meals a month for free and usually I have left over credits because I don't feel like going without someone."

"Sure, no problem," Bradly said as he realized things like this happens all the time.

As soon as the waiter came back he handed the receipt and Amber's card back to her and the two got up and left.

The Commanding Officer observing from afar, saw the beautiful woman pay for the meal. He was impressed at what Bradly had accomplished. A lot of the knuckleheads on his Chakravotry Class Fast Attack Space Warship would never experience something like this.

The couple went to Amber's apparemment. It was located on one of the many spherical shaped housing nodules attached branches off the space station that were above and below the main circular loop that had support beams going into the inner sphere like spokes on a bicycle providing incredible strength as well as all the conduits for electricity, water, purified air, and many other services. Amber had one circular window allowing her to look out to the stars, but if she wanted to look at all the views all she had to do is turn on her video displays that were part of her entertainment system that showed hundreds of views in high fidelity including the planet's surface, the moon, the stars, and magnifications of other planets in the solar system.

Bradly was very comfortable, and Amber soon selected some soft music to play in the background and sat down on the medium size sofa next to Bradly. She wasn't going to telegraph her intentions, but she was just about ready for anything, and it had been a very long time since the last time she had one of her rare sexual encounters. She was just going to let it flow naturally knowing well her perfume was laced with pheromones and cost a lot of money because desperate women who wanted to get their husbands to engage with them romantically paid what ever it took to get it done.

"Why is it I feel so comfortable with you? Amber asked.

"I was thinking the same thing, actually," Bradly responded and smiled.

Bradly was feeling those pent-up emotions and knew he might be living on borrowed time. One of the things discussed in the fleet was that people serving on Chakravotry Class Fast Attack Space Warship sometimes turned into heathens because they were going on very dangerous missions all the time and when the game of *Chicken of Space* cat and mouse game was played it sometimes got rough. There had been a few occasions in recent years where they got fired on but barely escaped destruction through superhuman efforts. And knowing that Dongar was with a cougar he most likely would not be willing to take home to meet his mother was a good indication of what space service did to them.

People serving exclusively on boomers seemed to escape a lot of that but due to the needs of the space force if they needed a sensor operator for a highly classified and important mission, if necessary, they would jerk a sensor operator off a boomer and slap him on a Chakravotry Class Fast Attack Space Warship if such a case existed.

Bradly had no intention of using Amber as a sex object for his personal gratification, but the mutual attraction was quickly making him lose control. After a few more discussions about the farm and Green Acres, Bradly decided his mental condition was evolving and transcending into a set of *feelings absent of restraint*. He decided to not fight it any longer. He could have walked out of there the moment before and kept this as a friendship, but his next movements precluded that from happening as he chose another route that would irrevocably tie him to this woman. Sandra Lane now escaped his emotional sphere, and he was quickly floating towards Amber Godot as his body was moving with or without his control as he embraced Amber and kissed her.

The way a man grabs a woman quickly signals to her the mannerism as how he is proceeding. This was an emotional and physical transcendence that seemed to have some special effects to it as Amber felt she was kissing the man in her dreams that had came back to her from somewhere she didn't understand. She just knew it was genuine love.

Bradly held Amber and kissed her for a long time as if she was a long-lost lover he rediscovered. The electricity flowed through Bradly and Amber which caused her to finally lose control and start conducting their reorientation towards an even greater physical covalence.

Bradly who was rather naïve didn't really know much about sex or what a woman would do in Amber's condition. Amber was more than a *bitch in heat,* she wanted it now. Time for discussions had long past them and now it was time for a physical embrace and splendid euphoria after long lasting transcendental gratification.

When Amber started unbuttoning Bradly's shirt, he started realizing what was really going on, she wanted him like there may be *no-tomorrow.* Her actions were clumsy but effective and after she got his shirt unbuttoned, she threw the fabric open and went down and kissed his chest all over then on his lips again then her next move quantified the physical reality that now evolved spontaneously.

Amber knew there were a few logistical matters such as getting off his shoes so she could unbutton and pull off his slacks which she did in the span of about a minute, faster than Bradly could do on his own, especially in the mental state he was in dithering from shock and excitement Then she pulled off his undergarments and saw his little head had already started spewing some of its witches brew that young men do in pre-coitus as natures most elaborate lubrication system.

It didn't take long to step out of her dress and discharge her panties and climb aboard Bradly again kissing him profusely and then did a very shocking event. She took his manliness and guided it inside her and made love to him because she knew this was the man from her dreams. She had no idea where the hell they met up in the past all she knew is she was from his past as well and they were special lovers brought back together for reasons she had no answers too.

Laying there not having to work too much saved all of Bradly's energy. He expended very little if no energy at all and finally when Amber reached her plateau of her gratification her pelvic muscles and her vagina went into a spasmic series of contractions that grabbed Bradly's manliness like he never experienced before causing him to explode in pleasure. Bradly's splendid gratification and his sublime emotions were quite strained for reasons he couldn't come to grips with.

Bradly's attraction to this woman was the strangest feelings he ever felt in his lifetime. She then collapsed on his chest just laying there for the longest time embracing the moment and the realization she had somehow in the mystery of the universe encountered her former lover who had been taken away from her without his or her ability to stop it. When two lovers are ripped apart there can never be an equivalent pain and suffering.

When pure love is killed the angel's weep.

After they slowly drifted back to reality and normalcy, Bradly said, "Listen, you have given me a lot to think about tonight. I know you must work in the morning and so do I. I think it's best I go back to my hotel room and attempt to get some sleep. If I stay here neither one of us will sleep and tomorrow will be a terrible day. I'll meet up with you tomorrow and we can be fresh and better enjoy our limited time together."

"Are you sure that's why you want to leave now?"

"Yes, I feel emotions with you I've never felt before. We may not have known each other a long time but I now have some growing feelings for you. I want to sleep well tonight, and tomorrow I'll explain more to you."

"You are not going to run away from me?"

"No, I may suggest at a later time when I finish this contract that you relocate to the planet with me because I've already spent all the time I need in space."

"Are you sure about that."

"There is something about you I don't understand, but I know it's in my heart."

"I feel like I've known you before. I don't know how or why. But I know it's true."

"Were we close?"

"Very."

Chapter Eight
The Calm Before the Storm

Serving on a Chakravotry Class Fast Attack Space Warship that was about to embark upon a very dangerous special operation had lots of security attached to it. Crewmembers were watched and Officers who noticed interesting events with them such as a sensor operator in an exclusive restaurant being wined and dined by a gorgeous creature created what's called a *red flag*. The Commanding Officer had no option but to report it and let the spooks check it out. If the lovely woman turned out to be just a nice girl, there would not be a problem and Bradly would never know he was scrutinized.

After the private discussion via a classified link to the Special Investigative Service (SIS), Bradly was soon under a microscope. So was Amber Godot. Neither one of them had a clue anything like this was transpired which is a good thing, otherwise it's quite possible Amber would have freaked out and Bradly became despondent to the point of dis-volunteering. If he did so his final two years would be pure hell and the chances of seeing Amber quite rare because he couldn't afford the fare to get up to the space station too many times and Amber was not permitted to leave the space station until her leave period once a year.

As the investigation went on in the background the

couple were frequent couple all over the space station. The commanding officer saw them carrying on a few times and remained open minded there was no issues they would find.

One thing the Commanding Officer noticed from afar was this woman was very classy, dressed well and looked utterly fantastic, so it troubled him what she saw in a semi-nobody, sensor operator on his space craft. There were plenty of awesome officers available from great families with lots of money. It would really make him feel bad if the spooks discovered she was a spy.

Bradly was such a fine and capable young man with a great future in front of him. The Commanding Officer hoped she didn't turn out like he feared. Nothing else made sense.

Preliminary reports indicated she was just a nice lady and all her communications which the spooks could get out of the archives that were secretly stored by the military in violation of the law but necessary in wartime clearly indicated she was no threat, but because of the way they carried on and the way that Amber spoiled Bradly left them with no answers other than to keep searching and the more they searched the least they found. They came up empty handed and with the gigantic price of the investigation, it showed they left no stones unturned even to the point of bugging her residence with sound and video recorders.

Some of the creeps enjoyed looking at her naked body, but she really had nothing whatsoever to indicate she was involved in any nefarious activity and worked for a very respectable company that paid her a very large salary that allowed her to spend money on the finer things in life including preferential housing and spoiling her boyfriend.

They also knew based on their research she had gone a very long time since she had her last boyfriend, and he was interviewed, and she dumped him. He was heart broken and assured the investigators, she might be strange, but she indeed was fully legitimate.

Finally, just before they deployed the final report came in with no evidence of any sort of nefarious activity. The commanding officer wasn't criticized for initiating a wild goose chase because in the mission they were about to perform, it was best to air on the side of caution. Interestingly they did however accidentally uncover some negative situations with a couple other crew members who were removed from the ship and taken down to the planet to some undisclosed location where the experts could dig the truth out of them. Had they not investigated Bradly and Amber they never would have caught the other two. So, in the end initiating the investigation produced results even though that's not what the investigation was intended to uncover.

Surveillance space craft go out a long time and Bradly would be gone a long while.

Bradly warned Amber he would be gone a very long time, but because of the secrecy of the mission, he could not give her any information on coming and going. He did one thing that made Amber happy, he said, "I've not introduced you to my parents only because we didn't have the opportunity to go there. When I get back, I'll put in for some leave and take you down to the planet and introduce you."

Amber was very happy for a few minutes until Bradly did the next few things, then anxiety arose in a major way.

"Space Service is dangerous. There is always a possibility I may not come back alive. I just did my will and power of attorney and if something happens to me, they will notify you and my parents. This is my parents' contact information."

Their address and communicator information were printed on the document stapled to a document filled out exactly the way Bradly stated he pulled out of a nice folder.

"I promise you if I come back alive you will be the first person I see. After I complete my time in the service, I never want to be separated from you again."

Amber broke down and started crying. This was right out of her dreams! *How could this be?*

Bradly held her for the longest time as Amber wept. It was a bittersweet sojourn that Amber realized she brought on to herself by pursuing Bradly. She didn't quite know what she was getting into, but her dreams and her thoughts drove her in ways she was unaccustomed. None of her friends or family would believe what she had just done. They would had been in utter shock and the parents might have suggested psychological treatment.

But that was all too late now. They had gone past the point of no return.

The days were numbered and finally they were down to a few hours as dread was sitting in. Pier 60 was a short distance away. Bradly had checked out of his hotel. All his possessions were aboard the space craft, not that he needed many. The crew went down to Pier 60 entrance that was blocked off by their security and at this time close to departure nobody not part of the crew was allowed onboard. Dogs had been already aboard sniffing for bombs, narcotics and stow aways. Yes, they had them too. Except for a couple officers, the entire crew was shoved off the spacecraft while the security sweep was done and nothing illegal was found and they soon left, and the crew was invited aboard to take their maneuvering watch stations.

Amber was dressed to impress. She noticed all the female crew members were plane Janes and of no contest. All the crew saw Bradly with Amber and rumors were a flying because the two had been seen together often during the upkeep period. All of them from the Commanding Officer on down were greatly interested what kind of pickup line Bradly had because this was an exquisite woman who might be the most attractive woman on the entire space station. What they didn't know was Bradly's influence on her heart caused the inner glow and transcendence to radiant beauty.

Finally, "Station the Maneuvering Watch," was announced and Bradly had to say his final goodbye.

The heart-breaking moment for the two of them existed because they knew they were in love. Amber knew most vividly because his will and power of attorney singled her out. If he died in space, his final desire was to give his estate to her and as he penned on the document, "Amber, I love you with all my heart."

Stationing of the Maneuvering Watch did a couple things. After the last crewmember (Bradly) stepped through the access door the security personnel closed it and it locked just like you see at airports. All the personnel walked aboard the space craft via the airlock, and it shut after the last person was through. The access door to the space craft shut and locked and gave the pilot and copilot indications it was locked and would not permit any intruders who might otherwise attempt to get onboard. In communications with the Space Station the robotic arms that gripped the spacecraft released it from its grip and the access tube contracted leaving a large space between the spacecraft and the space station.

Auxiliary thrusters under full automation started movement of the space craft. The speed was very slow to prevent collisions. Sequential thrusts accelerated the movement. From an observation window Amber watched the awesome looking space craft slowly move away from the space station. In a matter of moments Amber could see the space craft speed up. There were more sequential thruster engagements maintaining a straight path for the space craft that slowly appeared to be clear of the Space Station and more thrusts were seen and the craft slowly disappeared as it shrank in size and soon all that could be seen was the incremental rocket exhausts until it was very far away. Then unexpectedly there was a total flash with a very long exhaust that gave the appearance the spacecraft was turning and heading out into deep space. After a one minute burn the rocket engine shut down and the craft disappeared.

Other than the Commanding Officer, Executive Officer, and the Navigator none of the rest of the crew knew where they were going or what they would be doing. Were they on their way to delouse a boomer or were they springing a trap for an enemy *Near Star* class space warship? And most importantly what was the state of affairs on the planet? Were they at the verge of war or was this just another exercise in futility to keep the enemy guessing?

Just like when the Pasagralgian go out and play war games, the Collectivist Confederacy Peoples (CCP) *Near Star* class space warships and CCP Boomers did similar training. They also had security patrols to keep away the intruders from gathering intelligence. The name of the cat and mouse game was to get as close as possible without getting detected and targeted. The CCP liked to do their war games on the far side of the planet Nartone to obscure observations from the planet they shared. Until now they felt they did a good job of preventing someone from shadowing their fleet.

These wargames usually lasted one to two months depending on how in-depth they wanted to train. Usually when things were looking bleak on the planet, they would continue the war games past two months sometimes leading up towards two and a half months including dropping a hydrogen bomb on the backside of Nartone so that crews could do a life fire exercise and the force validated all their equipment and controls. Permissions, passwords, and planning the 3P's of such a nuclear attack required a significant effort because all the above required significant efforts and validations.

The special cryptology used for permissions took a half day alone to descramble using their processes. When it came down to terrible consequences there could be no simple way to do it because so much destruction and devastation would result including wiping out most of the population on the planet with these powerful weapons.

As the Pasagralgians viewed it, the Collectivist Confederacy Peoples (CCP) viewed their political aimes more important than the survival of the planet. CCP on the otherhand felt Pasagralgian greed and apparent entitlement to hegemony driven by international bankers and wealthy individuals was the curse to mankind. Neither side would waver, the ultimate showdown was in the cards.

Where the Collectivist Confederacy Peoples (CCP) made their mistake was Pasagralgians did systematic surveillance. After a few excursions out into deep space in the same general vicinity, Pasagralgians would position Chakravotry Class Fast Attack Space Warship at a distance in advance of those deployments to be out in front of them.

Pasagralgians knew approximately the direction CCP craft were heading, and it would only take a couple instances of these war games before a Chakravotry Class Fast Attack Space Warship backfitted with special photonics to monitor from a safe distance. This might have been one of the reasons why the Commanding Officer had Bradly under such intensive surveillance and needed to find out if that lovely woman splurging on him wasn't some sort of honey pot traps the CCP was famous for, though they loved to spring a homosexual honeypot trap since it always worked profoundly better than a normal female spy. Eventually as religion died out and promiscuity raged and so many homosexuals surfaced in society, the homosexual honeypot trap decayed in value.

Bradly had basic training on the new photonics, but hand not been indoctrinated about the ancillary use until he was fully cleared. Because of the deep investigation into Amber Godot his clearance was accelerated as they had to do a complete background check over that matter and quickly determined his security posture was satisfactory. Coming from a small town helped out immensely as it narrowed down the number of leads, they had to find.

It did get a little murky when they found out about Sandra Lane. The investigators had all kinds of anecdotal information that Sandra Lane was Bradly's lover, but in due time communications records gave the appearance their relationship decayed. Sandra Lane eventually figured out something was going on when lover boy was no longer exhibiting transcendental emotions and his communications broke off completely.

Sandra Lane figured he was under the spell of another woman, and she was absolutely correct. The investigators secret surveillance saw for their own eyes real and concise evidence of a relationship that was strong and genuine. Sandra Lanes involvement with Bradly was seventy five percent hearsay and they had no video or sound to back up any assertions. Sandra Lane hence became a former lover of Bradly that would likely never see again.

The Commanding Officer could not reveal how the clearance was accelerated. When he was about to leave the space station, he had the grim possibility he would only have one space telescope operator cleared who could easily have a mental breakdown from all the pressure put on him being on call 7/24. And during peak sessions of the wargames the radioman could easily be tasked 24 hours a day if it were mission critical, with the help of the medic to give him drugs to keep him awake if necessary.

When the Commanding Officer called Bradly into his stateroom to inform him, he had been cleared and despite the risk to the ship, he and the radioman would go into the sensors room in a few minutes, and each get fully indoctrinated by a tech rep sent aboard for training and maintenance. The rub was the maintenance guy was not cleared to look at the images during the event and today would be his last day in the room until they pulled off station in case, they had to let him in again and they would be nowhere near Nartone.

Once they learned the bells and whistles of the space telescope, they would be in a curtained off area doing the photography where the other sensor operators would have no idea what they were doing as this equipment was super sensitive and a game changer.

The only people that would see the results of their work would be the Commanding Officer, Executive Officer, Navigator, and INTEL officer.

Bradly wished he would be operating the other equipment, but he soon discovered that his buddies would have to take care of that business because what he was doing would be vital for fleet INTEL.

Collectivist Confederacy Peoples (CCP) were arrogant and disbelieved Pasagralgian INTEL could ever come up with such gadgetry to fully expose every move they made.

In private meetings with the CO, XO, NAV, and INT, Bradly and the radioman were directed to send the photonic files only to INT, and he would parse them and advice CO, XO, NAV of anything they needed to know, otherwise it would be buttoned up and hand carried to headquarters where only upper echelon individuals were cleared to see the information.

The days ground forward, and the Collectivist Confederacy Peoples (CCP) fleet exercises continued as expected. They fired lasers, beam weapons, kinetic weapons, missiles, and projectiles at the drones. The projectiles all had proximity fuses and had more hits that kinetic weapons that were range limited due to enemy ship maneuvers. However, if a kinetic weapon struck a space craft, it would tear it apart a lot more destructively than most other weapon systems and due to excessive velocity, there were frequent times enemy spaceships would close ranges to make fire control solutions more accurate and kill shots more probable.

Collectivist Confederacy Peoples (CCP) war games had not been observed for many years because of their clandestine activity doing behind other planets to shield the activity, including the gas giants, but now that Pasagralgians were venturing deeper into space, they had to go al the way to Nartone.

Even though Nartone was a long distance away from their Chakravotry Class Fast Attack Space Warship, the quality of the photonics was incredible and the far side of Nartone was exposed from their angle. Towards the end of the Collectivist Confederacy Peoples (CCP) war games, the secret they didn't want observed was the launch of an extremely fast missile that demonstrated it could pass through the planet's ozone layer and incredible speed and detonate a large hydrogen bomb. This was a game changer.

This new weapon meant that Pasagralgian cities could be laid to waste with little or no warning. But there was good news in that weapon was deployed from a unique ship with a unique launcher system that was physically different than all the rest. INTEL quickly surmised only this class of CCP space warships could deploy such weapons and the space warship they observed was the only one ever seen before. It was almost as large as a boomer but had that strange bubble on its hull in front of the control room and bridge area of the craft.

The new Collectivist Confederacy Peoples (CCP) missile launcher boat was given the classification designator as *Sinrex*. The CCP *Sinrex* would now receive special attention and if it deployed in a threatening position over Pasagralgian areas, the orders would be to destroy it immediately and the Chakravotry Class Fast Attack Space Warship were getting upgrades with a Drakon Laser System that would devastate the CCP *Sinrex* if they got into a shooting match.

The Chakravotry Class Fast Attack Space Warship Bradly served on had the Drakon Laser System upgrade, but only a few people on board knew it and had some idea its capability. Since it was tied directly into the sensors, the fire control portion of the system was integrated and to minimize exposure it was compartmentalized and the same people just operating the space telescope were also the only ones besides the CO, XO, NAV, and INT who could access the system and operate it. It was another one of those behind the curtain deals.

Since there were not a lot of Chakravotry Class Fast Attack Space Warships backfit with the new Drakon Laser System, if war erupted anytime soon, it was a foregone conclusion Bradly's ship would be in the middle of it and if the Collectivist Confederacy Peoples (CCP) deployed the *Sinrex*, it would be placed in the order of battle one notch above a boomer since its weapons were so fast, that made them extremely lethal. Based on operational guidelines, they would shoot at and attempt to destroy a *Sinrex* and ignore the boomers until that destruction was confirmed.

The Collectivist Confederacy Peoples (CCP) Space Fleet slowly peeled away from Planet Nartone. The CCP *Sinrex* was nestled in the middle of the formation. It was more heavily escorted than CCP Space Carriers and boomers. That alone demonstrated their concern for its protection as it was considered by them to be their most important weapon now. That meant whoever was sent into destroy it would have to run the gauntlet and most like turn into a Kamikaze in the process. A Kamikaze is a military entity that makes an attack requiring suicide in order to achieve success of the attack. Should the unthinkable happen and irrational people take control of the Collectivist Confederacy Peoples (CCP) and they took the gamble and deployed the *Sinrex,* there would not be many options as timing was ultra-critical.

A Chakravotry Class Fast Attack Space Warship equipped with the Drakon Laser System upgrade would now be placed in constant readiness condition and most likely moored at pier 60 at the space station except when underway nearby for routing training. Even if they were not deployed, they still had to get underway for readiness training and escort boomers out into space and block trailers while the boomer went flank speed and shot out to far space to hide with pride.

Any Collectivist Confederacy Peoples (CCP) that was intercepted and refused to back off would immediately get engaged in a shooting match while the boomer launched its defensive probes that amounted to space mines with propulsion and sensors. A CCP craft would be dumb to keep chasing because the space mines would quickly latch on to it if it managed to get past the Chakravotry Class Fast Attack Space Warship escort.

This was a slated long patrol for Bradly's Chakravotry Class Fast Attack Space Warship. They were not due back to home port any time soon. The Commanding Officer was on standby for additional tasking whether it be escort, delousing, ISRP or other activities.

After sending a few quick look reports via Ultra

Chirp, the Commanding Officer received the additional tasking he expected. He would do ISRP on the receding Collectivist Confederacy Peoples (CCP) Fleet and do a thorough survey to make sure no CCP assets remained near the watery Planet Nartone and when he determined no other space craft was in the vicinity, go to the far side of Planet Nartone and do a bomb damage assessment. Even if the planet was uninhabited there had to be some element of damage inflicted such a creating a crater like a meteorite would. There would be a few craters on the back side of the planet, but none of them would have the residual heat signature from the explosion where the temperatures would remain elevated upwards to a month before it cooled down to background.

If the weapon deployed was a burrowing type, the bottom of the crater would be extremely hot compared to surrounding areas. There was no telling how deep such a crater could be, and if necessary, they would be required to send down a shuttle to get a closer look and better estimates.

Time was at the essence in that the sooner they got to Planet Nartone, the residual heat would be greater allowing them much easier identification.

Luck was on their side in that Collectivist Confederacy Peoples (CCP) were transiting at high speed to get back to celebrate the successful conclusion of their war games, but most importantly, to hide the CCP *Sinrex* from prying eyes of the Pasagralgian Defense Directorate INTEL.

That very same day the Collectivist Confederacy Peoples (CCP) Fleet past Closest Point of Approach (CPA) and was clearly planet bound with a tight formation easily computed and measured with their own electronic gadgets that made the formation look so magnificent. The CCP Air Boss was pleased at how well their station keeping was and flawless flight especially if they were being observed by friend or foe.

CPA plus 6 hours was the trip wire to head for Planet Nartone. The Commanding Officer who erred on the side of caution directed the Officer of the Deck currently in chart of all flight controls to perform a Capmoc-Drysvinskle maneuver to make absolutely sure they didn't have any trailers of their own. From his experience, a well performed Capmoc-Drysvinskle maneuver usually spoofed an enemy trailer which gave away their position by an immediate collision avoidance maneuver to verify no weapons had been launched at them. As soon as the maneuver was completed and no other spaceship was discovered in the vicinity, they sped up heading to Planet Nartone.

To avoid giving their position away during the transit, they limited speed to two thirds. Going faster risked leaving behind an ion trail, when coupled with X-ray emissions from the power plant was a warship identifier. But at the present speed they would arrive at Planet Nartone, still soon enough to see the residual heat from the nuclear explosion using their infrared.

As predicted upon arrival to the back side of Planet Nartone that rotated once every 923 hours, the infrared easily picked up the hot spot and they quickly got a computer fix on it thanks to several large dead volcano mountain tops that were calibrated references to the impact zone.

The Chakravotry Class Fast Attack Space Warship was taken as close to the ozone layer without getting into it to allow the best view of the crater and hopefully obtain a measurement to avoid sending a shuttle down for more accurate measurements.

"It looks like they created a good size crater," The Commanding Officer said in his stateroom with the door closed with the Executive Officer, NAV, and INT in attendance to their secure private meeting, observing the video Bradly was streaming to them live.

"It's a large crater but I do not think we can get its dimension from up here. We'll have to send the shuttle down with a portable scope," the Navigator said.

INT, the intel officer stated, Headquarters will want those exact dimensions to get an appraisal of the energy release and do an assessment of how badly our underground command posts might be affected if they used them on us."

"That crater looks big enough to me to think our underground facilities do not stand a chance," the Executive Officer noted.

"Alright XO, get together an away team. We need to have a photonics technician and a couple surveyors. This is important; I want you to go with them to make sure we get what we need to avoid communications and tip off the enemy what we are up to."

"Understand, radio silence," the Executive Officer responded.

The Commanding Officer was not going to risk the radioman on the shuttle mission, that left one photonics operator: Bradly.

In thirty minutes, they were suited up and heading to the shuttle. Fifteen minutes later the shuttle was on its way down to near the planet surface.

The pilot had map overlays on his navigation display that showed the precise location of the bomb crater. The closer they got the larger it seemed. Just in the past six hours the atmosphere had cleared from smoke and debris to actually be able to fly and observe the crater, otherwise it would be fly by wire and reliance on instruments to get them near the crater. It pleased all of them they could see because nothing sucks worse than flying to a lifeless planet on instruments in the dark.

The XO made a command decision and suggested to the

surveyors, "I think if we hover at 1000 feet above the edge of the crater, we should be able to get the dimensions."

"Sir with all due respect, we'll actually have to fly down into the crater unless you are willing to let us use our ranging tools that would violate Captains orders of radio silence."

"How far down do we need to go?"

"We do not need to land but if we get to about ten feet above the bottom of the crater which we can only be for a few minutes before we'll kick up a lot of dust, we should be able to get all the data we need."

"Alright I'll agree to 10 feet and immediate lift off."

"That works for me, the pilot said."

As soon as they got the initial survey done at 1000 feet, it was that come to Jesus' moment and fly into the crater. Just like they planned they came down to about 10 feet from the bottom and lifted back off vertically leaving behind a nice dust cloud.

"Did you get everything you needed?"

"Yes sir, the crater is 200 feet deep."

"Damn."

"It had to be a burrowing weapon due to the oval shape of the crater. If it were air detonated or impact on the ground detonated, the crater would be wider and much shallower."

"I agree, it had to be a burrowing weapon, us get back to the ship."

The shuttle made its way back to the Chakravotry Class Fast Attack Space Warship. After it landed and the CO took the away team to the wardroom and sealed it off to everyone else except the NAV and INT, they discussed their findings.

"Thanks for the good effort, guys. Nobody outside this room is to ever know about this. This information is sealed indefinitely. You can never talk about it for any reason unless the Defense Directorate calls you in for an interview. The codeword for this mission is *Emerald*, I'm naming it *Emerald* because of those green colored radioactive rocks you filmed going down into the crater. If the Defense Directorate says they must talk to you about *Emerald*, you will know its about this mission. However, I think it dies with us as they have enough information to make their decisions on what to do next."

The XO asked, "How are we going to send this *Emerald* data to the Defense Directorate?"

"Good thing you brought that up XO since the NAV is here. We have no choice but to return to the space station and you will accompany me down to the planet with a data package. INT will be delegated authority as CO while we are gone."

"When are we returning?" The NAV asked.

"Right now, but NAV do not make a bee line from here to the space station. Proceed back to point Q, then we'll head for the space station from Point Q to foil any possible detection from the CCP.

"Understand all captain I will set in the navigation coordinates, and we will travel to point Q at two thirds is my assumption you want, then from point Q back to the space station we can speed up."

"NAV that's exactly how I want to proceed."

"XO, you, Bradly, and the surveyors put together the package. Anything you do not think we need in the package is to be destroyed. When we leave the ship with the package, I do not want a trace of it left onboard."

"Understand all captain."

"Very well everyone you all know what you have to do."

The Commanding Officer stood up and walked back to his stateroom where he pondered what would soon happen.

The transit to point Q took a while but from point Q back to the Space Station was quick.

Bradly was very happy because he knew he was going to get to see Amber Godot very soon.

The Pasagralgian Defense Directorate assumed Chakravotry Class Fast Attack Space Warship would be on patrol for other tasking as it came up and some mission planners were perturbed when it returned to home port early. Nevertheless, their supervisors knew the Commanding Officer and knew he would not be returning unless it was something important and the mission planners were not privy to *Project Emerald*. When the Pasagralgian Defense Directorate was notified the Commanding Officer and Executive Officer were coming down to Headquarters in a priority shuttle flight, those very few *Project-Emerald* cleared officers knew they were probably hand carrying a dynamite package and when a few officers who had their feathers ruffled tried to turn them around, they were quickly informed to stand down. They became even more perturbed for not being allowed to attend the meeting.

The grim reality now struck home and as the Commanding Officer predicted, his patrol was canceled, and he was given *local operations* for training to do.

For guys who had girlfriends on the space station, local operations were fantastic. It meant out for a day or two at the most and return to port. There just wasn't enough Chakravotry Class Fast Attack Space Warship available that had been upgraded with the Drakon Laser System. Should the enemy leadership get stupid, their course was charted. Other Chakravotry Class Fast Attack Space Warship would be sent as well to attempt creating a path for Chakravotry Class Fast Attack Space Warship CSF-111, the hull number of Bradly's ship. CSF-111 wasn't painted on the hull, it was an electronic designation that was fed into IFF (Friend or Foe identification systems).

As soon as liberty was put down for everyone except the duty section same as before CO was the first off, the ship followed by Dongar and Bradly.

"Want to go to the club with me?" Dongar asked Bradly.

"Are you still trying to hook me up with the Cougar's friend?"

"Sure, why not? The cougar said if I didn't find her friend someone quick, I was going to be forced to take care of the two of them."

"I'll tell you what Don (aka Dongar), come with me over to the Madam Ayumi's Bar, and I'll let you meet my friend, and you'll know why I'm not interested in a cougar."

"Okay big boy, us see what you got."

Bradly knew it was about time Amber Godot would be there and he wanted to surprise her.

As they walked into Madam Ayumi's Bar that had an excellent happy hour, there Amber was with her work associates having a cool one just from work to wind down.

Bradly saw the other ladies were acting normal but for some reason Amber appeared down in the dumps. She wasn't expecting Bradly, took a sip of her drink, sat it down and stared out into space. Then as Bradly got closer to their table Amber lit up like a Christmas tree jumped up and ran to Bradly and threw her arms around him. She was so happy; she couldn't believe it!

"I didn't expect you back this soon. Is this your interpretation of long trip?"

"The Space Force is always subject to change. We finished and came home early."

"I'll take it anyway I can get it."

"Amber, you probably may not remember him but the night I met you I was with my shipmate Don (aka Dongar) here."

Don looked at Amber and his tongue was just about to drag on the floor.

"Yes, I remember him now. Nice to meet you."

The table next to them was open so Bradly said, "We'll sit down here."

Amber said, "Don, why don't you take my seat and I'll sit with Bradly."

"That works for me." Dongar responded suddenly feeling like a horn dog and realizing he may not have to *go ugly early.*

One of the work associates was Amber's close friend. And close friends do girl talk, and the most important question Amber's friend Risa-Ann wanted to know is: "Did you do the big A with him?"

That led to some embellishment that fed Risa-Ann's wildest imagination. She now wanted to experience a space boy and get the humping like Amber got. Tonight, was Don's lucky night. His *go ugly* early and *SDHNC* was shuttled to the side as he now was facing an inquisitive woman more his age and soon ready to suck him dry like the octopus, she turned out to be.

Amber knew what she wanted. Time alone with Bradly but knew he probably deserved a drink, and she would finish her drink and then she would be the train conductor again and send them down the right track that would get them into position to be *working on the railroad* in her bed.

In due time they were alone, and Bradly suggested he shower first to get the spaceship smell off him, but Amber insisted on joining him in the shower and soon they were happy and playing like kids.

After they finished making love, Amber thought now would be a good time to discuss something.

"Bradly, I have something I need to tell you."

"Are you pregnant?"

"No, but I wish."

"Listen, you filled out that will, and power of attorney and my contact information was on it but so were your parents. While you were gone, they contacted me."

"How did that go?"

"It went pretty well. They insisted I send them a picture, so I sent them one of us together and they were quite happy."

"I see."

"I don't want to put pressure on you, but your parents invited us to go visit them."

"I suppose that's okay."

"I told them I didn't knew what your schedule was, but when they give you some leave time, maybe we could go down and see them then?"

"That would be fun. I would like that."

"Alright when you think you could get your leave scheduled, let me know and I'll talk to my supervisor. I'm about ready for some earned time off and if I'm close one way or another they can shift my leave window around to accommodate a family event."

"What if they refused."

"I'd simply just get pregnant and then they would have to find my replacement!"

"Don't say that. Newlyweds are supposed to screw around like rabbits for a couple years before they start having kids."

"I'm sure they will accommodate me since I know my supervisor Gloria loves me to death and would do everything, she could do to help me."

"Alright, I'll check into when I can take leave and we'll schedule it."

For the next few months Bradly's request for leave was denied and they refused to say why. The truth of the matter is he was most likely needed to operate the Drakon Laser System if the big showdown happened, and they had to destroy that new CCP *Sinrex class* space warship.

Just when Bradly was about to give up hope and Amber was having very bad vibes, he got called into the Commanding Officer's stateroom for a private talk.

"Bradly, I know how depressed you are getting because your leave keeps getting denied. I want you to know how important you are to the ship and explain a few things to you, then I got some good news for you."

"Alright sir."

"We had to keep you here in case we had to emergency deploy to go deal with that Collectivist Confederacy Peoples

(CCP) *Sinrex* space warship. Thanks to our spy network, we discovered it was damaged in a collision with another one of their spacecrafts in an accident and is now being put in the space dock for repairs. The CCP space dock workers are not the most efficient workers on the planet and our INTEL estimates are it may take several months to make these repairs then they would have to send it out on voyage repairs recertification. I think we have enough time now in the schedule to permit you to take a couple weeks leave and go down to the planet."

"I appreciate that sir."

"I value everything you do Bradly for this spacecraft. Your former Commanding Officer on the Boomer you served on spoke highly of you."

"He is a good man and he stood up for me one time."

"He explained that situation to me. Unfortunately, we have a mixed bag of personnel in the service, and sometimes we learn the hard way the ones we put the most trust in are actually duds."

"Well, my commanding officer had faith in me, and I didn't let him down."

"You know since he's a boomer captain he could steal you from me as he has priority on crew selection. If it were not for our photonics and new Drakon Laser System, you would be back aboard that boomer now."

"I did my time on boomers. For me to really experience the thrill of a sensor operator, I must do it on a Chakravotry Class Fast Attack Space Warship."

"I do not disagree with you on that. But one more thing I need to tell you. Everything you have done since you have been here is highly classified information. The information about the enemy drydocking is very sensitive. You are not permitted to reveal any of this information to anyone under any circumstances."

"Sir, I will never discuss it."

"Good, go make your plans to take leave and travel down to the planet. If you run into any snags let me know so I can help if necessary."

"Thank you, sir."

"Bradly, I'll be seeing you in a couple weeks. Hopefully you will have a big smile on your face."

"You know I will sir."

Bradly left the stateroom and went to his supervisor who was all smiles and said, the captain signed your leave request. Go take care of your business and we'll see you in a couple weeks."

"Thanks for everything."

"No, thank you Bradly, you earned it. And if you make the Commanding Officer happy, which you have done, you definitely make me happy. Enjoy your time off."

"Thank you."

Bradly grabbed his grip, went back to his temporary hotel room, and called Amber.

"My leave has been approved we can go down to the planet together now."

"Great, I'll talk to Gloria and let her know. She somehow predicted and knew somehow this was coming about, so she already planned for it. We can leave tomorrow."

"Thanks, I'll tray to get us reservations."

Bradly was happy as can be until he called reservations and got a run around. The earliest he could leave was four and possibly even five days from now. He was almost heart broken, this would be a disaster going to the planet, spending a day or two then must come right back.

Bradly remembered the conversation with the Commanding Officer whom he thought might be able to help in some way.

Bradly swallowed his pride and proudly marched back to the Chakravotry Class Fast Attack Space Warship and in passing his supervisor spotted him and asked, "Why did you come back?"

"Transportation problems. I'm going to go see the Commanding Officer and see if he can help."

"Good idea."

Bradly knocked on the door, the Commanding Officer was in there with the Executive Officer obviously in a management meeting to go over some important aspects of their day-to-day routines. The Commanding Officer was surprised.

"Bradly why are you back?"

"Sir I got transportation problems."

"I see come on in here a minute."

The Commanding Officer said have a seat and pointed to one of six empty chairs there for department head discussions, then asked, "Can you tell me what's going on with your reservations."

As soon as Bradly let it all out, the Commanding Officer was pissed and said, "More God Damn Bureaucratic BS. XO do you know anyone over at transportation?"

"Yes, in fact the OIC was my classmate at the Academy."

"Good, can you get him on the phone for me?"

"Right away Captain."

The Commanding Officer knew poor Bradly had been ran through the ringer, not only on this boat but his boomer too. And if he could fix this SNAFU for him, he would give it his best shot.

A moment later the XO came back through the private hallway between their staterooms and said, "Captain I have Commander Frye on the phone and handed the cordless to him."

"Commander Frye how are you."

"Doing great Captain."

"Say Commander, we have a little issue here."

"I'm well aware of the issue, the XO has filled me in. I've scanned all the reservations and found there was some low priority transportation that could be done some time later and have booked two seats for your guy Bradly and one other. I need the name of the other person for the reservation."

"Okay, just one moment."

The captain said, "Bradly, we got you reservations for two, but we need the name of your friend for the booking."

"Her name is Amber Godot."

The captain and the XO had to play dumb because they knew damn well who Amber Godot was since she was the most investigated woman ever on the Space Station.

The captain repeated the name to the Commander who then replied, "Captain let Bradly know their flight is set at 10:00 A.M. tomorrow and it leaves from pier 59 right next to where you are parked."

"I appreciate your help, Commander Frye."

"Not a problem but I think you owe me a beer."

"I promise you it will be the best tasting beer you ever had."

"I'm looking forward to it."

The conversation soon ended, and the Commanding Officer was quite happy he was able to intervene for such a deserving person.

"Alright Bradly, it looks like you are on your way. Your fight leaves at 10:00 A.M. tomorrow."

"Thank you for helping me, Captain."

"You are welcome, Bradly."

Bradly stood up and held out his hand and shook the captain's hand with a huge amount of respect and admiration.

The captain knew one thing about Bradly. When the time came, he would follow him to hell and back and just like he proved on the boomer, he would not compromise himself even if his supervisor was an idiot.

When Bradly got back to his hotel room, he called Amber and gave her the flight information.

Amber being a smart traveler and a business orientated person suggested, "Bradly, why don't you check out of your hotel now and come over to my place. Anything you want to leave behind you can just leave it here."

"Great idea, I'll be over in a while."

The two lovebirds were again up in that club that night enjoying life and celebrating their journey coming up.

The Commanding Officer had the XO invite his buddy

Commander Frye to the restaurant so he could pay up that beer he owed him. As the three men were looking at the beautiful eye candy all dressed up, the captain said, "Commander Frye, see that couple over there the guy with the lady who has on the bright red dress?"

"Yes, she's eye candy for sure, bet she's great in the sack."

"You helped them today."

"How did I do that?"

"That's Bradly and Amber Godot."

"That's amazing. I'm glad I helped them."

"I'm glad you did to because Bradly is one of my best men."

"That makes this beer taste even better Captain."

CHAPTER NINE
LOVE AND
REMEMBRANCE

After dinner and a few drinks, the two lovers were heading for a rendezvous of passions. There was no doubt in their minds or the three senior officers of what likely was going to happen soon.

It gets lonely at the top. They must be extremely careful who they associated with and if they wanted promotions, they would have to take on a bride because single men were considered defective and potentially victims of honey pot schemes. And when they made that choice to get married, if they didn't have a childhood friend, they kept close, their superiors would often pick women for them, a friend or a relative or a friend or relative of a higher-ranking official that would set the stage for patronage.

Some of the most butt ugly women ended up with very distinguished looking and successful officers because her daddy wore 3 stars on his shoulders. They took solace in their kids were usually all worth it and eventually the men grew old and wrinkled so it really didn't matter. There was no doubt in the three officers who watched Bradly take his true love out of the club, they would prefer being stuck with her instead of *the women who had a genuinely good personality.*

After another session of horizontal tango, the couple nestled close together in the small bed hugging and loving. Amber wasn't nervous meeting the parents because when they called, they were mildly shocked a stranger was given the power of attorney over their son's estate. They were now equally shocked because the couple would be arriving tomorrow!

During the conversation Amber had with Bradly's parents, they were really nice down to earth people who missed their son. They were happy during the course of events; Bradly found a nice girl.

Had Bradly brought Sandra Lane home to meet them, they would be in even a much larger shock once they looked at a woman that left no mystery about her body as she showed her stuff. Lucky for Bradly, Sandra Lane found another guy who was local and not out chasing the stars and could be much easier domesticated. By the time Bradly made it back to the planet, Sandra Lane was already married to Joe Six Pack.

The two woke up in the morning, showered dressed, and were soon ready to leave. They didn't have a lot of luggage because weight was expensive, and they would save money buying clothes on the planet and discarding them when they came back. Bradly's mother would pack them away and make them available should they visit sometime soon.

Rumors on Bradly's ship about him going to the planet got a few of them interested especially since Don was running his mouth again and embellishing stories. Their shipmate's thought Don was FOS, but what they didn't know is Don's speculation and embellishment came close to the mark.

Don figured out the only ship leaving in the morning to the planet was on the very next pier, so he took a couple of his compadres to scope out Bradly and Amber Godot.

True to his expectations at boarding time 09:30 there the

couple was, and Amber Godot was dressed in a way to give them wild speculation on how hot she is.

Out of the corner of his eye Bradly spotted Don but gave him no notice as they were quickly getting on the transport and Don was out of range to say or do anything. Nevertheless, Don's buddies were amazed about the eye candy Bradly met.

Don was also starting to get in the good graces of a good-looking friend of Amber and the Cougars were suddenly in great need hoping Don would make it back. Had it not been for Bradly, Don would never have changed and would have spent the rest of his life in Cougar heaven.

The transport soon left the space station and made its way down to the planet, where Bradly and Amber had to get on domestic flights to a nearby city and rent a vehicle to drive to Bradly's parents' home.

The drive from the city to the countryside was wonderful and Amber enjoyed it immensely. After being couped up in a space station for a while makes you appreciate the finer things in life like this wide-open countryside. They saw some wild animals running off to the side of the road.

Bradly said, "Those animals are called Antelope."

"They look so fragile."

"Keep watching you will see them jump over that fence."

"Wow, that's amazing."

"I've almost ran into a herd of deer out here early one morning as I was driving to the airport."

"How did you avoid them?"

"I have no idea; it was as if someone was talking to me and told me to slow down. As I was coming down this hill towards a river and a bridge, a whole herd of deer passed right in front of my car."

"That voice saved me. Perhaps it was the deer god talking to me?"

They passed by farmers on tractors plowing their fields. Bradly said, "When I was a kid, I did that."

It all looked so surreal to Amber, and she was taking it all in and enjoying her time with Bradly because she had a strange feeling about him. He meant so much to her and she didn't understand why. All she knew was Bradly was the most important thing in her life and she knew she had known him in the past, even possibly in a prior life, if there was reincarnation.

Eventually Bradly saw the grain elevators up ahead and he knew he was close to home. He passed by some of those huge grain elevators and there was an entire grain train getting loaded.

"See that train there?"

"Yep."

"It's 100 plus cars and they all are carrying grain to a hub or market."

"Wow that's huge."

"They grow a lot of grain around here."

They soon pulled into the town and made their way to Bradly's parents' home. This home was fairly new, they purchased it new a few years ago. Outside it was a camper and a boat. Bradly had never traveled in them with his parents. That came along long after he left home.

As soon as the rental car pulled up in front of the home with plenty of parking space unlike a city, the door opened and there was Bradly's parents and a couple of his older sisters that were there to meet the girlfriend and do their assessments and chase her away if necessary.

But with just one look at this woman, Bradly's family knew Amber Godot exhibited high quality.

Bradly grabbed their luggage, and they all went inside. Since all the kids were grown and long gone, the four spare bedrooms were available. They actually thought the two would be staying in separate bedrooms until Bradly took all their belongings into one.

That was an eye opener to them!

Amber Godot was a city slicker and had never really saw the countryside before. It was like being on another planet. But Amber also knew another thing, Bradly flew out into space which was far more complicated than most of the things any city slicker ever did. It doesn't matter where he came from, what matters is where he was going.

Bradly had some incredible opportunities. Amber knew from her own little world that contractors on the space station would pay big bucks to recruit Bradly after his contract was up with the space forces. All she had to do is make an appointment with one of the service contractors for Bradly and she would receive 20,000 credits. She knew that's how much they were willing to pay for space force personnel nuclear qualified or involved in photonics or INTEL.

Amber knew that they all didn't work at the space station, they just got recruited there, and many of them were terrestrial dwellers from then on. She knew vividly with Bradly's earning potential he could provide for their family. She also knew that her savings alone would take care of them for the next twenty plus years, so getting hitched to Bradly was an easy decision.

She was ready and found him to be such a pleasant person. His valence around her created the quintessential satisfaction any time he was near. She didn't know why other than she knew her destiny was with Bradly.

Amber's family might not accept Bradly because he's a hick from the sticks, she didn't care. Her relationship with her parents was so plastic it was with no emotions or the slightest amount of humanity in her viewpoint. They were social climbers, and nothing else mattered to them. She could come visit when she wanted, but she knew the first time she brought Bradly there, her mother might make a remark like, next time you come home don't bring the chimp with you. Having known the inevitable, that was not part of her game plan. She would concoct some story and they would never meet Bradly and they never did.

The leisure days passed quickly but Bradly had something to do. He knew his role and what he would soon be doing and in worse case he would probably get killed. He wanted to make sure Amber's power of attorney was legally solid as he feared his parents would challenge her in court based on legal disputes they had with relatives over similar matters. People are all nice to your face until someone dies then greed sets in. His cousin had been thrown to the street on a similar matter.

After a week visiting home Bradly told his parents, "I'm taking Amber to the city to do some shopping, we didn't bring enough clothes with us."

His mother immediately volunteered to go along but Bradly didn't want her interference and feared she might pull some crap and said, "We'll be going to the city again in a few more days for some souvenirs for our friends, we'll take you then. We'd like some time by ourselves."

The mother dropped the subject and Bradly headed to the city with Amber.

Amber was upset with Bradly and started venting.

"That was no way to treat your mother."

"She has already interfered too often in my lifetime. This is important to me, so I didn't want her to screw it up."

Amber was a little perplexed on that statement and didn't know what to make of it.

When they made it to the city, Bradly drove to a jewelry store he had researched that had rings in his price range. He had saved up quite a money on boomer patrols and could afford jewelry in far greater prices than his friends from high school.

Amber was a little confused at first but was delighted Bradly was buying her a nice ring and figured out that's why he kept his mother out of the car.

Then he totally shocked Amber when he pulled up to the courthouse where they could be legally married and took her inside. She was lost for words and Bradly said, "Listen, I could die tomorrow, and I want to make sure the girl I love ends up with my estate and there are no court battles."

Amber cried in an emotional outpour. This is the last thing in the world she expected. As she and Bradly discussed it further, she realized his fears and her own as well. She finally concluded that since they were destined to be partners anyway, if it made Bradly more comfortable, then she would go along with it.

Thirty minutes later after filling out all the appropriate paperwork, they were married. Bradly said, "We will hide this but, in the future, we will have a real ceremony after I get out of the military service."

"What if I have a couple little Bradly's walking around by then?"

"That works for me, I don't care. All that matters now is if something happens to me now, nobody can take anything away from you."

After they did some shopping to make it all look feasible, they went back out to the sticks and Bradly's parents' home.

The following day Bradly informed his parents he was going to take Amber out to meet his old boss, Bill.

Bill's wife had passed away and the poor soul was by himself. But he had a couple granddaughters staying with him keeping him company.

Bill had aged. Oh, had the wonderful days had passed and the wonderful memories. His two kids were long gone, but they visited now and then, mainly when they needed more money.

Everything Bradly had mentioned to Amber came true to life, the Den, the basement, the Kitchen, and even a painting on their fireplace Bradly did when he was in high school that looked really nice.

As they were leaving Bradly looked at Bill who was always upset Bradly didn't marry his daughter Rachel and become a permanent Rancher, he could turn the farms over to, was the first-person Bradly informed.

"Bill, can you keep a secret?"

"Sure, what is it?"

"Amber and I are married. My parents do not know yet."

"Good luck son I wish you the best."

"Thank you. I always felt like your son."

"Bradly, I enjoyed every moment you were here. So did the family. We miss you and hope you come back and visit us."

"You know next time I'm back I'll visit you."

On the way home to Bradly's parents, Amber asked, "When are you going to tell your parents?"

"They didn't have much to do with raising me. Bill raised me from the age of fourteen. Prior to that I was just another mouth to feed because they were too dumb to use contraceptives."

Amber realized that was a touch subject and let it drop. Her own parents were assholes so she could equate.

Home on the range lasted a few days longer and soon time was running out.

Bradly's mother didn't push him for a ride to the city because she was so overwhelmed with some of the loser kids she had. The fact they didn't make it to the city was easily obscured with a few crazy kids she thought she was helping by her involvement in their lives. Little did she know she was just the enabler for most of their troubles. Had Bradly's siblings known the best course of action was to move as far away from mom as possible, the better their lives would have been.

Finally, the last day came, and they went to the regional airport to get them to the space port. Bradly's parents followed in their own car as he had a rental he had to drop off.

After checking their baggage, they all went to the airport lounge to have one final goodbye.

None of Bradly's siblings were there which was more evidence he didn't matter in their lives. The parents were only doing the basic decent thing, otherwise they would be looked down upon since they hadn't really spent much time with Bradly in his lifetime.

Just before they were scheduled to board their aircraft Bradly made the big announcement. "While we were here,

Amber and I got married. She's now my legal wife, so anyone who has any questions about the power of attorney, no longer need to think about it."

"You got married?" Bradly's mother asked in exasperation.

"Hey. don't worry about it. I know you were busy with my brothers and sisters. Good luck with them."

Bradly could see his mother was hurting. His father had no emotions or care, that was expected.

"Why did you do this?"

"I wanted to make sure Amber has no issues in the future."

"We should have talked about this and planned this and met her parents."

"Mom don't worry about it. You were not involved in my life since I was fourteen, there is no reason to think you need any involvement now. Plus, I think you have your hands full with the loser brother and sisters of mine."

"But…."

"There is no buts about it. I have my own life now and I will succeed in spite of you."

Bradly knew he had crushed his mother and Amber was tearing up feeling the emotion.

"I'm sorry but we need to board our flight. Maybe in a couple years we can come back and visit after I get out of the military."

Amber knew they were way early for the flight, but kept her mouth shut because she didn't know the background for what just happened.

Bradly stood up and started walking away. His parents

thought they deserved a hug or something. Later that night as they discussed this bizarre departure, Bradly's mother mentioned to his irate father, "When was the last time you had any involvement with him?"

There was no answer because there was none.

Bradly was glad because he accomplished two things, introduced his wife to his parents and secondly, made her legally the manager of his affairs if something happened to him.

Other women might have turned on Bradly for being such a dullard, but Amber had such nincompoop parents of her own, so she knew she had no right to criticize or make statements about this bizarre event. Bradly was very happy that Amber responded as it showed to him, she understood why he did this.

The flight to the space port was not very long. Soon they were aboard a shuttle going up to the space station and back to their circumstances, which was fine with Bradly, because if he remained in the space force, they would come and go to the space station which was really the only option for this Chakravotry Class Fast Attack Space Warship.

After they arrived, they went to Amber's apartment, and she notified the manager of the complex she was now legally married, and her husband Bradly was moving in with her.

The price of the rent was based on occupancy because two people used more water, air, sewage, and garbage services. The price hike was not significant to Amber, and it would not affect the way she lived in any manner. However, she did request a larger bed be installed which was scheduled for the next day while Bradly was at work.

Due to rules and regulations Bradly had to report his change in status since he was no longer single and even though his wife was living on the space station nearby, they had to pay him separation pay and various other allowances which increased the size of his paycheck significantly. He had a copy of his marriage documents with him when he reported to work the next day and the admin people scanned it and entered it into his electronic records which were mirrored on the planet at a secure location.

Bradly was in an inviable situation getting separation pay even though he went home to see his wife every evening while they at the space station. The rules didn't account for it since it would be extremely rare if not impossible for this situation to occur because most families had no desire to live on the space station and many had no desire to ever go into space due to the fear of the dangers associated with space travel.

The Commanding Officer had to endorse the change of status, which he gladly did, then he walked over to the sensors room where he knew Bradly was working.

"Bradly, can you please come to my stateroom for a minute."

"Yes sir." Bradly responded with some trepidation as he knew his actions may have caused some issue along the way.

They went into the stateroom and the Commanding Officer closed the door and said, "Have a seat."

Bradly sat down wondering just what was going to happen.

"The reason why I had you come here is I wanted to congratulate you personally about the girl you just married."

"Thank you, sir."

"I'll be frank with you because I like you and am pleased at your performance, there are sometimes events that happen that cause the security aspect of our job to investigate someone's background quite significantly. Because of the extreme secrecy of the equipment you operate, we must be cautious."

"I understand sir."

"Some time ago when you first met Amber Godot and you were seen in venues that are atypical of a space warrior, you set red flags. In fact, you soon hit a tripwire. When it was compelling that you were in a romantic involvement with Ms. Godot the military had no choice but to vet her. I'm sure you can appreciate; we have Collectivist Confederacy Peoples (CCP) spies here on the space station."

"I suppose I would not be surprised," Bradly said waiting for some very bad news he feared he would soon learn. It would of course break his heart if Amber turned out to be a spy, because that meant she was fake and was merely manipulating him in a complicated honeypot trap.

"There are a lot of things I can't tell you because you are not entitled to know about them, but all new spouses go through a thorough background check. We really must know if they are a potential source of compromise."

"I can see why," Bradly responded.

"Because of whom you are and what you know, we had to do a background investigation on Amber Godot even though she wasn't your spouse."

"Was there a problem determined?"

"None whatsoever. The two of you have been checked out rather thoroughly."

"So, what does that have to do with us now?"

"That investigation was along the lines of a criminal or espionage investigation. The results cannot be revealed, just a positive or negative outcome."

"That's good to know."

"Unfortunately, that investigation is wrapped up in super secrecy and cannot be used as part of the standard background check we have to do on your new wife. However, knowing the significant amount of discovery in the past investigation, I do not believe they will find anything negative, so there isn't anything you need to worry about."

"Alright, but why are you telling me all this?"

"You married a very nice girl. She comes from a good family. I think you got really lucky meeting this woman who has not socialized with a lot of men in the past. Perhaps that's why you got lucky, she was ready to meet someone, and you just happened to stumble into her life's travels. It's one of those mysteries of life we can never predict, plan, or even mitigate. If we could grade spouses, you managed to meet a four-point zero woman with a perfect scorecard. Feel lucky you met Amber."

"I do."

"She's a fine lady, I know a lot about her which I can't reveal, so be sure and treat her well, because you have married a very fine lady that a lot of men never get the chance to meet."

"I will treat her well."

"I'm the biggest fan of you as a couple. I'm very happy this worked out for you."

"I could not have done it without your help especially with the transportation problem."

"Bradly, you earned by assistance many times over, but also consider this a down payment for the future, because there will come a time when I will need you the most."

"I promise not to let you down sir."

"I know that Bradly, that's why I called you for this private meeting because I felt I owed it to you to explain a few things and also to let you know you got my support. Keep your bride happy and hopefully when this assignment is all done, the two of you can go off and live a normal life together."

"We will, thank you sir."

"I doubt the two of you will want to remain on the space station."

"I'm from the country with wide open spaces. That's where I want to be, and I think Amber will gladly go with me wherever I go."

"I know she will."

~~~

In the days and weeks to follow, Bradly was glad the Commanding Officer had that talk with him because in due time he started spotting the surveillance. But he already knew someone already knew the investigation would turn up positive and life would go on, now it was just a matter of finishing his contract and get out of the space force."
~~~

Chapter Ten
Sinrex Showdown

Time seemed to pass too fast and just when Bradly was starting to enjoy his space craft being a fixture at pier 60, new developments started. Collectivist Confederacy Peoples (CCP) *Sinrex* class Space Warship left the space-dock and was operational again. Tensions were mounting again and the mad CCP leader invaded a neutral country located very close to the Western Alliance.

Just when the world was enjoying peace and eager for freedom and prosperity, this egotistical madman advised by his INTEL apparatus it would be a cake walk, didn't count on the Western Alliance to back the poor helpless country invaded by the huge Army that was systematically destroying the country. Effective weapons were pouring in and the CCP was now bleeding and getting angrier by the day. Eventually it was at the breaking point and as soon as the CCP *Sinrex* class Space Warship suddenly deployed after a weapons load, tensions mounted even further when spies picked up some INTEL the madman planned to destroy the Pasagralgian Space Station.

The military could not evacuate all the civilians without potentially compromising their code breakers effectiveness. They would simply have to allow all those innocents to get slaughtered if they could not stop the CCP *Sinrex* class Space Warship, then they would unload, and the madman would at best have a Pyrrhic victory and most likely killed in the process.

The commanding officer informed the crew after muster in the morning they would be getting underway, and the brow (access tunnel) was secured and no entry to or from the ship would be allowed until further notice and to station the maneuvering watch.

Bradly had informed Amber, the day would come when he would not come home from work because his space warship could not reveal its departure under certain conditions, and not to ask question, but just understand that happens. She knew this so she didn't panic when Bradly didn't return that evening. She walked down to pier 60 and Bradly's Chakravotry Class Fast Attack Space Warship was gone just like he warned her it might one day. She went home not worrying because she knew Bradly was always spot on in about all regards. She was further happy she made him give her some horizontal tango that morning. She was still filled up with some of Bradly's magic juice that made her feel so gratified.

Bradly's Chakravotry Class Space Fast Attack with the Drakon Laser System soon arrived on station with several other Pasagralgian Fleet assets, but only one third of them had the upgrades. They were flying in a formation right along the electronic boundary that separated the space between the nations. Their twelve-mile limits rose radially out into space on an electronic mapping system. However, the enemy would fly up to the 12-mile limit, and there were numerous maneuvers that suggested an aggressive behavior on the part of the CCP forces. This could be the showdown. Bradly's heart was saddened because he knew if the shooting started, the CCP would target the space station and kill his beloved Amber.

The CCP nutjob eventually did the irrational. He ordered

attack and the Armageddon commenced.

The Commanding Officer knew he had to lay back and observe prelaunch actions of the *Sinrex*. His assignment wasn't to fight and take out enemy *Near Star* class space warships, there were plenty of other fighters there for that purpose and they were going at it and enemy *Near Star* class space warships were exploding in large numbers and the space fight was extremely lethal, they could not let any of them get near the space station which was a strategic asset.

Chakravotry Class Space Fast Attack Fighters were also exploding in the melee.

There were no prelaunch activities yet such as opening a missile silo hatch, so the Commanding Officer did a Capmoc-Drysvinskle maneuver to make it harder for him to be a target and get a good range on every enemy spaceship. Thanks to Pasagralgian cryptologists, the Commanding Officer also knew the CCP *Sinrex* had one mission in life: *destroy the space station.*

Bradly didn't like being behind the curtain and wanted to be operating all the sensors with his buddies, but he was a dedicated soul and just like the Commanding Officer said, he counted on Bradly during this urgent moment.

Finally, the prelaunch activity began. They knew they had less than five minutes to kill the CCP *Sinrex*, or the Space Station was toast.

The Commanding Officer did his tactical maneuver and, in the process, warned Bradly, "stand by to fire the Drakon Laser System on my orders."

The ship was moving at flank speed closing the gap quickly and violating the 12-mile limit, but in wartime those limits quickly end.

The captain knew he had about two and a half minutes or it would be too late but knew the longer he waited the more lethal the Drakon Laser System would be. Power in the laser worked in the reverse inverse square law. If he cut the range in half, he quadrupled the laser power.

With about a minute left before the expected enemy launch the captain said, "Commence Fire of the Drakon Laser System."

Bradly was fighting for his wife's life. Never in his lifetime had Bradly a more gallant reason to do the supreme sacrifice if necessary. Bradly was a great shooter and poured on the coals and the laser started chewing up the CCP *Sinrex*. He first achieved a major success in jamming the *Sirex* hatches preventing launch, but he didn't know that, as far as he was concerned until he killed the *Sinrex*, it might be able to kill the love of his life.

One of the downsides to the Drakon Laser System firing as aggressively as Bradly was doing, made his Chakravotry Class Fast Attack Space Fighter Warship a target and something to aim at.

The CCP knew how important the *Sinrex* was for this battle. It was their super-secret weapon that would take out the Space Station and win the war. The entire CCP fleet went to the *Sinrex* rescue. In just a few more moments of Bradly's aggressive firing of the Drakon Laser System, the Sinrex finally blew up. The Space Station was saved!

Unfortunately, with all the weapons aiming at Bradly's Chakravotry Class Fast Attack Space Warship, Bradly and the crew could not escape their own destruction and moments after rejoicing he saved Amber's life, his world exploded.

The CCP firing on Bradly's Chakravotry Class Fast Attack Space Warship were not taking prudent measures in protecting themselves and made themselves easy targets and soon many were destroyed soon causing panic in their fleet as they started scattering like scared pigeons flying away from a hawk.

A single Space Warship doesn't stand a chance when it has 3 or 4 enemy ships chasing it down. Had they received better leadership and ordered to close ranks and withdraw to come back and fight another day, all would not have been lost, but the scattered pigeons were easy to pick off one by one and in a short period of time there were no longer enough of them to constitute a CCP space force.

The Pasagralgian Defense Directorate then ordered the fleet to proceed to Collectivist Confederacy Peoples Capital and demand surrender personally by the madman or they would raise every city. Once you lose space superiority, you are at the mercy of the enemy. The madman's intelligence bureau gladly gave him up to spare their own skin, the war was finally over, and 200 years of surreal confrontation was finally ended.

The Pasagralgians only lost ten percent of their fleet thanks to Bradly's aggressive fire. As it turned out, they had no other option. The Commanding Officer knew in advance it might come down to this, and in his private meeting when he informed Bradly he earned his help as a down payment for the future, that really turned out to be the case.

Amber of course was heart broken and decided to return to the planet and be with her family to help her get over her tragic loss. When she finally felt psychologically able, she traveled and visited Bradly's family and gave them a lot of pictures and a lot of Bradly's personal items. She also set up a trust for them since she didn't need Bradly's inheritance and insurance since she was the heiress to her family's fortune.

Amber went out and visited William (aka Bill) Grady his former farm boss and was surprised she had the opportunity to meet Bill's daughter Rachel who was staying with him and assisting in his old age.

Amber had a long discussion with Rachel and of course she wondered if Bradly had ever tapped the farmers daughter. Rachel of course was heartbroken. She thought very highly of Bradly and cried like anyone would who lost someone close to them. Before Amber left the farm, Rachel showed the painting that Bradly had done that was still sitting on top the fireplace and asked Amber if she would like to take it with her.

"I'm sure Bradly would want you to keep it. You family was special in his life and his second family. He loved you as much as he did his own family and told me staying here was the happiest days of his life. He was also sad that he could not introduce me to your mother."

"My mother really liked Bradly. Its probably a good thing she's not here now because I know Bradly's death would have hit her hard."

"I'm leaving now and going home. I'm glad I stopped by because this puts closure in my life and I know I need to move ahead."

Bill and Rachel walked Amber out to her rental vehicle, and they were all crying. Bradly would be missed.

CHAPTER ELEVEN

TRAVELING THE HMY XĪWÀNG ZHĪXĪNG TO THE STARS

The decision was finally made as the pilot Canaris Bartrum flew His Majesty's Yānjoyduī (HMY) Xīwàng Zhīxīng the first Space Craft to leave the solar system. This would be a mission with predictable discovery as well as tremendous risk. The stage was finally set to find out more about the universe because the quantity of Alien visitors had finally reached a level where government coverup was no longer feasible. The public was in a sour mood as more whistleblowers came forward and named names. Members of the deep state that controlled information flow were exposed and their ability to hide the truth from the public eroded in each passing day.

There were now believed as many as 100 inhabited planets by intelligent beings within twenty light years from Canaris Bartrum's planet *Zharkon Xestra* the name for their esteem planet. The inhabitants of *Zharkon Xestra* didn't know the source of the name for their own planet as this was given by Aliens that lived in some of the civilizations within those planets that were becoming obviously determined inhabited by space telescope observations.

The latest space telescope sent a half a light year out of the solar system to get out of the near field brightness the sun created. Once deployed operating on a nuclear reactor with liquid sodium coolant, the artificial intelligence programmed to search the stars within the 20 light year range and automatically detect and track planets contained in the solar systems and take impressively high magnification pictures and transmit them back to the planet.

One of the easiest ways to detect intelligent life was to catch lighting on the dark side of planets. This could never have been done before because photonics required didn't exist. Thanks to the massive growth in technology photoreceptor camera lenses with vast ability came into being that now allowed this new generation of space telescopes to provide vivid detail like never before imagined.

Some conspiracy theorists claimed the space telescope lenses came about from dissecting a crashed alien ship that didn't disintegrate upon landing. In one case unknown to the public, an alien space craft crew was able to safely land, but due to the mechanical failure, their propulsion system was damaged beyond repair and after sending off distress signals to their home world that would take five years to arrive, they abandoned the spacecraft almost entirely intact to go find food, water, and achieve basic survival.

Eventually they obtained supplies and when they returned to their spacecraft, they found it was gone and they were now marooned on the planet! Their spacecraft had been tracked by the Yānjoyduī planetary security forces and landed a fact-finding team via military VTOL assault craft.

The aliens never believed such a scenario would ever occur because they assumed they would never land on the planet. Hence there were no locks to prevent intruders entering because there was no way to lock the spacecraft. They wanted to preserve battery life to allow future communications, so the ship was powered down. A breaker panel in the control room was easily found and the Yānjoyduī planetary security forces determined in the future they would be able to power up the system at a secure location.

Since the spaceship was abandoned, Yānjoyduī planetary security forces realized the best plan would be to relocate the space craft to one of their secure bases that experimental craft were tested and would be out of the public view. A VTOL Skycrane was flown there, and a hauling net was secured around the alien space craft about fifty feet in diameter, with three internal decks for all the equipment and storage for food and water required. Discarded empty food containers were scattered around the space craft crash site so they know the aliens had been here a while and most likely ran out of food.

Using hydraulic lifts, the space craft was lifted off the planet a few feet allowing the riggers to get the cargo net under it and was sit back down on the planet and a VTOL Skycrane placed a lifting bucket above the space craft where the technicians could combine the corners and side cables and attach them to the large hook on the VTOL Skycrane netting. In just the span of a few hours the sky crane was able to lift off and relocate the crashed space craft where further details would soon emerge.

There were two survivors remaining from the hard landing but since they did not experience one of those "unscheduled rapid disassembly's," they were able to simply walk away from the crash.

Government officials started a massive manhunt for survivors and set up surveillance on the crash site and as soon as the two marauding survivors arrived searching for their spacecraft their digital communications and emergency compass had maps and exact coordinates to lead them back to the crash site, they were dismayed and saw there were some tire tracks where their spacecraft had been and they assumed it was hauled away, but didn't know a super large VTOL craft flew it away.

The alien's had on their flight suits that were slightly soiled from scavenging the area for food and water, but they were clearly nothing earthlike so the investigators looking for them could easily determine from a distance who these people were walking to the crash site. No sooner than they shrugged their shoulders and contemplated their fate and proceeded to walk in a direction their sophisticated communicator and navigator arm bands provided to the nearest city. Then suddenly Yānjoyduī planetary security force investigators came out of their camouflaged hiding with weapons drawn circling the aliens.

The Aliens each had a laser blaster with them, but realized they were severely outnumbered and if they brandished their weapons, they would no doubt be killed. The Aliens meekly stood there awaiting their fate. Yānjoyduī planetary security forces soon had them on a VTOL transport hauling them to the base where their wrecked spacecraft now sat parked inside a building sitting on a portable double low boy truck transport. The hanger was just barely large enough to accommodate parking the spaceship in there.

The Aliens had studied Zharkon Xestra languages and had electronic translators built into their communicator/navigator wrist packs.

Conversations began and they informed their captors they needed to charge up their communicators on the spaceship or they would soon be out of power and not be able to communicate. Several of the Yānjoyduī planetary security agents took them up into the spacecraft and observed his actions including turning on a few switches that allowed him to hook the device up to a cord to start the charging process.

The Alien indicated, "This will take about ten minutes."

This alien was well indoctrinated on how to deal with the situation he was in. He was not required to undergo any torture because the ship was a standard scouting vessel that had crashed on numerous planets for a variety of reasons and their enemies already had operational models so there were no secrets to protect.

During the ten-minute communicator charge, the Alien was asked a variety of questions which he truthfully answered. That led to the Yānjoyduī planetary security forces discovering the space telescope that was nothing special in the Alien's home world area of the galaxy and their enemies had much better models.

Canaris Bartrum, the Xīwàng Zhīxīng pilot years later heading out to space had a re-engineered space telescope base on the Alien technology. With him was a highly developed Robot that in all practical purposes looked and acted real. Her name was Zainia, and she had all the features of a woman and if Canaris Bartrum ever got the notion to have sex with this female robot, she would inform him her highly developed sexual simulated hardware would seem so real to Canaris he would not be able to tell the difference. Plus, she had several containers loaded with pheromones in perfumes that pleasure women on the planet wore while they were making money pleasing men.

Zainia's programming centered around facilitating the maintenance of Canaris Bartrum's health. Lack of sexual intercourse was considered a health risk so, Zainia was fully equipped to deal with that matter if it came up.

Canaris Bartrum spent several years in simulators with Zainia and learned to interact with the Robot. At some point Zainia started feeling as if she was a real entity. Zania's memory banks were fifty-fold larger in storage than a human brain.

Hence, Zainia was a certified surgeon, psychiatrist, engineer, pilot, nutritionist, and had significant social engineering skills.

Due to the size and scale of the intergalactic explorer, it had to be assembled in space with modular construction. Looks were deceiving. Even though the Space Explorer HMY Xīwàng-Zhīxīng looked menacing, it was totally harmless. There were no weapons aboard. If they were boarded by Aliens, there would be nothing they could do to stop them.

Canaris Bartrum's and the Robot Zainia wore Yānjoyduī planetary security space forces uniforms. No rank insignias were attached, and the colors and design were the same. In fact, Zainia was built on a three-dimensional scan of Canaris Bartrum to match his size and one size fits all uniforms.

To create a psychological intersection between the two, the bunk room designed with two comfortable beds were right across the hallway from each other. When Canaris Bartrum went to bed, so did Zainia. As Canaris Bartrum slept, Zainia connected herself to power and charged up her long-lasting batteries.

Zainia really never slept. As Zainia laid near Canaris Bartrum charging her batteries, her computer system was fully engaged via wireless to the ship's computers and all the sensors and thus the ship always had great surveillance vigilance. Canaris was always safe whether he was awake or sleeping.

The day they departed the planet heading for the star cluster that would take them up to almost two years to arrive, was a stressful event for Canaris Bartrum, because he was flying in a lot of theoretical designs, not fully tested due to lack of funds and time.

The two space explorers wore their space force uniforms and the spaceship was fully designed for casual existence and living. There was no need for space suits. As long as the artificial gravity was maintained, Canaris Bartrum could actually sit at a toilet and do his business and flush it into the recyclers.

Stored dry powder substance provided all the nutrition. All he had to do was go to the water dispenser, unscrew the top of the container, pour in the required amount of pure water from the recyclers and in a few minutes that powder would turn into a meal after he placed it into the special warmer that moved the meal around as it was heating it up. After the warmup the food was instantly ready for consumption and tased delightful.

The launch and acceleration appeared normal while Canaris Bartrum watched the myriad of indicators to get a good warm fuzzy feeling it was all working.

Canaris knew by watching the various sensor displays his ship, the Space Explorer HMY Xīwàng-Zhīxīng was speeding up as the acceleration increased in small amounts. There were nuclear reactors onboard for the electricity and there were nuclear reactors part of the propulsion system that gave the ship huge thrust. The increase of speed wasn't noticed but as time passed the movement of other planets gave the sense they were going faster, and they were. Light Speed was not obtainable for a while as they slowly made progress through the solar system where they would exit in a couple days and continue accelerating and exceeding the speed of light. This would be the big, huge gamble. *Would I still be alive?* Canaris asked himself as he was contemplating his fate.

Space Explorer HMY Xīwàng-Zhīxīng built up speed linearly as the nuclear rocket engines thrust remained the same with the throttle setting at 85% reactor power. This gave Canaris a much higher degree of safety. The shockwaves produced at 100% reactor power created a lot of vibration that could shake the ship apart. The extra power would only help very slightly as the maximum efficiency on thrust occurred about 85% reactor power due to the fact the engines could only get traction on the plume behind it. Most of the velocity occurred from the "Newton Effect" where for every power there is an equal and opposite power. That meant there was a force applied in the opposite direction as the rocket exhaust. Pushing against the plume added to the acceleration and as they approached light speed so did the plume that was following behind and the vast cloud it created traveling at light speed created electrostatic and electromagnetic waves that would continue for centuries until it encountered other forces that diminished its relevancy. If that plume hit another spaceship, it would have the same effect as a one-hundred-foot wave hitting a surface ship.

The star cluster they headed towards was only seven light years away. Traveling above the speed of light could possibly get them in a years' time, then the most uncomfortable thing would happen. They would first change course to prevent the plume coming at them from hammering them. The rocket engines were shut down, they were coasting on velocity. The retrorockets were fired in a way to achieve a new course.

They were soon seven degrees offset on a new course.

The plume was highly visible on the ship's sensors especially the infrared three dimensional holographs. Observation from the space craft infrared sensors revealed a huge cloud that was in their rears and suddenly on the plume appeared to be passing them as it was traveling in a straight line past them as they flew for a long time. The course change created a significant bearing rate change giving the appearance the Space Explorer HMY Xīwàng-Zhīxīng spacecraft had slowed but it wasn't by much. The plume was slowly diffusing in the void of space with no atmosphere.

After the course change pointing directly into the middle of the star cluster, Zainia announced, "We have transited

90% of the distance and in a couple more weeks we'll start the slowdown burn. I suggest you try to catch all the sleep you can beforehand because the breaking will last for several days, and you probably will not be able to sleep."

"Thanks for the advice."

"You are most welcome, Canaris."

Canaris knew that Zainia was fully capable of robotic sex, but he chose simply to abstain then a couple days later Zainia asked the question:

"Canaris, you know I'm fully programmed to take care of your sexual needs; would you like to try out my pleasure features before we start the breaking?"

"Zainia, that's okay, I'm not really missing sex much as I have other things on my mind such as increasing observations on planet-X."

"Canaris, I'm concerned about your sex organs not disintegrating for lack of use."

"Don't worry Zainia, if I meet a woman, I want to have kids with, I'll have plenty of practice."

"What if you meet an alien woman?"

"That might create quite a situation. I hope you can take the Space Explorer HMY Xīwàng-Zhīxīng back to our planet Zharkon Xestra without my help?"

"Canaris, you are not needed for our safe navigation. We actually flew to this position in space via artificial intelligence and autopilot guidance managed by triple redundant computer resources."

"I would think under normal circumstances I would want to go back to Zharkon Xestra, but one never knows what's going to happen or if I'll even be alive to attempt such a voyage."

As they got closer to the solar system with planet X, the night side of the planet was showing more and more detailed lighting of buildings and streets. Canaris knew this was a heavily populated world and he would have a problem sneaking in without detection.

Planet-X steadily grew in size on the space telescope and eventually Zainia determined it was time to start breaking.

"Canaris, we need to start breaking and slow down."

"This is the part I do not like; we expose the ship, and the sensors are pointed in the wrong direction."

"Unfortunately, It's the only way we can accomplish breaking."

"Alright, I'm putting on my safety harness and then we can start."

Canaris had a chest web that comfortably fit that would protect him in the event the ship took some unexpected rolls or tumbled. Zainia had on a similar safety web and as soon as Canaris said, "Okay I'm ready initiate the slowdown."

Canaris could have operated switches on the control panel to perform this maneuver, but he also knew Zainia had wireless interface via the ship's radio control panel the female robot could remotely control the ship in every manner.

The first part of the maneuver was to reorientate the ship one hundred and eighty degrees from its current trajectory. Small retrorockets mounted on each end of the space craft soon started the spacecraft spinning in a slow manner which caused the forward sensor-display to slowly shift the view as all the stars and planets in sight appeared shifting at a small bearing rate of approximately 10 degrees a minute. When the ship came close to the reciprocal heading retrorockets on the other side of the spacecraft fired a few short bursts which locked the ship on an inverse heading from the original.

Zainia always informed Canaris her actions so he would be aware and not have unexpected impulses from events outside his control.

"We are aligned for speed reduction. Bringing the thrusters online now."

Zainia's programming let her realize Canaris would soon feel the G forces of slowing and the artificial gravity machine had to be turned off at this time as to not interfere with the process.

"Artificial Gravity is now turned off."

"Nothing like feeling 10G forces," Canaris said knowing this would last a while and he would soon get sick or pass out. But he felt safe knowing his personal robot would handle matters quite satisfactorily since robots have no feelings. Zainia had gravity sensors to let her feel the G forces but that would not affect her in any way.

Based on star charting calculating velocity, they had to slow down from six times the speed of light. It would take a while. Since they were slowing, they were creating a plume that was expanding and they were flying into the plume that was diffusing in the vacuum of space. In effect they were creating a large cloud that soon shrouded the ship and observers from far away would soon lose the image of the spacecraft now hidden by the glowing cloud it was creating. As the ship slowed the cloud spread more sideways creating a very bright large cloud. It was an amazing sight for people who detected the light and at first thought it was a meteor, but it didn't have the tail like a meteor, and it appeared more of a clouded blob which nobody on planet-X had seen anything like it before.

Planet-X had a real name and a real civilization. Planet-X's actual name was *Crysantralon* and the light blue skinned people that lived there in a homogenous society called themselves Vracklines.

Vracklines space defense forces detected and tracked the inbound object in space traveling at a tremendous speed and had the strangest appearance of anything they had observed before. Going faster than the speed of light and slowing was creating a modal distortion of the imagery. Some Vracklines space force personnel feared it was interdimensional portal opening, and based on ancient writings, another visit from Evil beings arriving from a different dimension.

About once an hour Zainia cut back on the thrusters to give Canaris a break and if necessary, use the toilet. This also gave the ship's computers time to recalculate position to update their inertia navigation system. The new fixes would provide at least twelve hours of position data before the solutions would unravel and become worthless. During the temporary reduction of propulsion, the craft would slowly be exposed to the Vrackline observers. The craft was also reorientated thirty degrees to allow sensors to observe what existed in front of them and get readings on distance to the solar system and planet X.

While they remained above the speed of light, the image that was only observable because of sunlight and starlight though infrared and ultraviolet imaging but continued to have modal distortion traveling above light speed that made the craft seem more and more terrifying. There were no radio communications, and the purpose of this craft was yet to be determined.

In another six hours of these speed reduction cycles, the Space Explorer HMY Xīwàng-Zhīxīng eventually slowed below light speed and the modal distortion ended. The Vrackline space force now had solid images to track and analyze.

As soon as the Space Explorer HMY Xīwàng-Zhīxīng slowed below one quarter speed of light, it maneuvered and rotated it's heading 180 degrees, so the sensors of the spacecraft now pointed forward. Even at one quarter light speed the spacecraft zipped along smartly through the solar system and flew in the near proximity of several planets that provided additional slowing and when the spacecraft approached within 100,000 miles of planet-X (aka Crysantralon) its velocity had been trimmed down to 50,000 miles per hour making it a lot easier to track.

The strange alien craft didn't appear menacing as it approached Crysantralon, but the lack of communications nevertheless caused the Vrackline Space Force to scramble some interplanetary interceptors in the event this ship showed some hostile intentions and attempted to communicate. Just as soon as the Space Explorer HMY Xīwàng-Zhīxīng curved into planetary orbit the communications began. Ship's sensors detected the alien spacecraft approaching and tracking the communications signals matching the bearings of these ships, the ship's computer through Zainia said, "Those space craft are attempting to communicate with us, but we have no ability to determine the content of their communications."

"Send to them a simple message that *we have come in peace.*"

As soon as Zainia complied with Canaris direction, she reported, "They have responded to our communications, but we do not have any means to determine what they are saying."

"That's fine. We'll give them some more information even though I doubt they will understand it."

"What do you wish I transmit to them?"

"Inform them we are Yānjoyduī, and we come from the

Planet Zharkon Xestra."

Moments later, Zainia reported, "That information was sent to them. They responded but we do not have the means to understand their response."

"We'll continue orbiting the planet until we can figure something out."

On the planet Crysantralon, the scientific community was quickly contacted, and communications experts were brought in to analyze the communications. In all the vast communications enterprise few if none were able to assist, but one scientist stepped forward and said, "I recall hearing similar communications when I was studying at the university and eventually, I was given a project by my professor to come up with a rudimentary translator. I think I can make out some of their words, but it will take me a while to get my translator operational. It does not have a broad vocabulary, but I'm sure I can determine some of the words."

"Can you take your translator up in space aboard one of our Space Guard ships?" the head of the Vracklines Space Force asked.

"I do have a portable device I could carry but it would need to be connected to a radio transmitter/receiver on the Space Guard spaceship."

"That shouldn't be a problem, I'll have one of our technicians work with you and it can be tested before you depart out into space."

The situation was now evolving as the Vracklines casually followed the Space Explorer HMY Xīwàng-Zhīxíng Space Craft orbiting the planet. Eventually Zainia announced, "There appears to be another space craft approaching."

"I wonder what that's all about," Canaris said.

In a brief period, the new spacecraft came a lot closer than the previous that were trailing them. Suddenly Zainia reported, "This newly arrived spacecraft just sent us a hello in standard Yānjoyduī language."

"Answer them back saying 'hello we are Yānjoyduī from the Planet Zharkon Xestra, and we come in piece."

Moments later the Crysantralon ship replied, "Understand you are Yānjoyduī from the Planet Zharkon Xestra, and you arrived in peace."

"Answer them: That is correct."

"They just communicated, standby for instructions."

"This should be interesting."

"Moments later the Crysantralon ship communicated, "We want you to land your ship on the planet and we'll have direct conversations with you there."

"Respond to them, our ship is not capable of going into your atmosphere, we will have to send down a shuttle."

"Within moments, the Crysantralon ship replied, "We will escort your shuttle to the planet. How soon can you go?"

"Communicate to them: in a short while."

Canaris looked at Zainia and said, "I think I want you to come with me because you can learn their language quickly and be my interpreter."

"My instructions from the programming is one of us should remain aboard the ship at all times, but under the circumstances what you are requesting seems more logical."

"Place the ship in autopilot and us proceed to the shuttle."

Within fifteen minutes of the last communications, the shuttle was slowly launched from the spaceship. The Crysantralon were expecting this and as soon as the shuttle was clear of the ship, they communicated, "The ship with the blinking light will be your escort, follow them to the planet."

"Understand, follow the ship with the blinking light."

The Crysantralon spaceship then pointed a specific spot on the planet and headed for it. They did not penetrate the planet ozone layer too quickly and following in the vortex of the Crysantralon allowed the Space Explorer HMY Xīwàng-Zhīxīng Space Craft to avoid heating up too quickly as the Crysantralon ship acted as a wind break and significantly cut down skin temperatures.

Soon they were in the atmosphere at high altitude coming down. From the height of 200,000 feet above the planet a quick survey seemed to suggest the climactic condition of the Crysantralon was not much different than their own planet Zharkon Xestra. Vast areas of water could be seen as well as the tropical green in many areas.

The Vracklines led the Yānjoyduī shuttle craft down to what appeared like an airport that was evidently some type of military base.

It was a well-kept base that looked pristine. This was definitely a very capable civilization as the size and scope slowly materialized in front of them.

Canaris would not know if it were space craft or simple aircraft, but there were some very large menacing looking craft parked around this airbase.

The Vracklines ship and the Yānjoyduī shuttle craft came down directly on some markings. Artificial Intelligence on the Yānjoyduī shuttle craft initiated the proper controls to land softly on what appeared to be a landing zone marker.

Canaris realized the possibility of getting pathogens and dying were real but understood from a diplomatic standpoint he should go out of the ship in plain clothes with his space force suit on.

"Temperature and humidity readings are compatible with Zharkon Xestra," Zainia reported.

"Alright I'm going to get out of the shuttle, you might as well come with me and help figure out communications."

The two left the shuttle and the air felt amazingly nice. They were immediately met by a welcoming committee.

Canaris was trained for such a meeting and since Zainia was a robot it didn't affect her any.

A lot of Yānjoyduī would not be able to psychologically handle the blue skin Vrackline people.

Canaris was respectful and very positive. His vibes were infections to the Vrackline who had never seen people with such strange skin colorization and facial features. Rounded ear lobes and thick busy eyebrows seemed to be surreal. Also, the Alien woman was perfect shape, and her complexion was absolutely perfect with no defects.

The scientist with the translator said some words in Vrackline the translation was then repeated with a semi-mechanical voice in the best estimate for Yānjoyduī. Canaris thought the interpretation indicated to follow them to a building set up for their meeting. Zainia was processing the information and like all conversations was recorded in her vast memory for analysis and playback.

"I think they indicated to follow them into a building where they can try to work out some translations."

"All right we'll follow you," Canaris said which the translator converted to real basic words.

They were led into the building and into a conference room with along table and two dozen chairs. At the end of the table was a display device

This was a specially designed room to meet aliens and there were numerous cameras microphones and biological sensors. Canaris was trained that when he encountered aliens, they would scrutinize him by a great amount and he knew once they figured out Zainia was a female robot, it would probably peak their interests.

Several of the scientists had special hats on and a type of ear plug device built into the hat. Canaris could tell by their body movement they were being fed a lot of information some of which appeared to utterly confuse them to the point one of them appeared astonished. *He probably was just given biological sensor readings on Zainia, and the measurements provided something that significantly affected them,* Canaris thought.

The scientist with the translator device said in the Vracklines language, "We are going to show you some pictures. To help us better understand your language, if you pronounce in your language what the picture shows, it will help us build a better translator."

As the scientist said certain words in the Vracklines language, images started popping up and Zainia closest to the display started describing the images: "Stars, sun, spacecraft, planet, trees, water, flowers, clouds, rain, snow, men, women, children, green, red, blue, yellow, purple, black, white, gray, missile, laser, explosion, birds, snakes, bears, tigers, holovision, communicator, bed, sleeping, shower, toilet, food."

Canaris could see the excitement in the Vracklines as it all unfolded. Then it started getting more exciting as their inquiry now seemed to shift focus to Zainia. What was clearly ancient looking metallic robots were shown.

"Robot." Zainia stated.

Then they put up a picture of Zainia and she said, "Robot."

There was considerable amount of noise and discussion that now elevated. They fully understood Zainia was a robot which matched their sensor readings.

Then they put up a picture of Canaris and Zainia said, "Canaris."

Then they put up another picture of Zainia, and she said, "Zainia."

The scientists with the translator said something in Vracklines language that turned it into a Yānjoyduī question: "Is Zainia a robot?"

"Yes." Zainia answered.

The scientist appeared as someone who had died and gone to heaven and came back instantly.

He then said some Vrackline words that were not meant for translation that commanded the display. It then put up a picture of Canaris and quickly that turned into a multicolor thermal image of his body. They then showed some of the others in the room and their three-dimensional thermal image, which was very intuitive. Then they showed Zainia, and the difference was stunning.

Canaris could see the imaging equipment that appeared to be very precise had temperature intensity colorization. The imagery actually showed boxes inside the cavity of Zainia's body that were exceptionally hot and much hotter than a human body. Zainia had a couple boxes in her robotic command and control center that operated at around fifty degrees centigrade, considerably hotter than a human.

It was almost a come to Jesus' moment for the Vracklines. They were truly astonished.

Unlike Vracklines or Yānjoyduī, Zainia was able to permanently record everything that was said even conversations between individual Vrackline scientists. She too was building her own internal translator and because she had recorded far more words than pictures derived, her own Vracklines lexicon was expanding exponentially.

After several more hours, the Vracklines obtained almost 2000 words to build their Yānjoyduī lexicon. The number system was worked out, calendar, dates, and a variety of items to better help figure out more about the Alien visitors.

After a few consultations between the Vrackline scientists, Canaris and Zainia were asked via the translator, "Would like a place where you could rest and eat?"

Canaris responded, "We do not know if your food is safe for me to consume, I would prefer to go back to my ship eat, rest, then come back tomorrow."

"We would like to keep Zainia here with us."

"I must take her with me because I need her assistance with a few things. She will come back with me tomorrow, say fourteen hours from now?"

"We'll escort you up to your ship and be there in fourteen hours to bring you back." The scientist said first in his native language which was repeated with the translator.

"Alright. I will bring something back with me that can show you a little of my world."

"We'll be happy to see it," the Vrackline replied with the translator.

For his own mental health, Canaris was not informed about

all the abilities that Zainia had. By not knowing some of these features allowed him to keep his composure. One of her circuits was an ISR module that allowed Zainia to secretly eavesdrop on alien technology. She could suck in the radio waves from a lot of various radiators and slowly understand the signals. While on the planet especially on this military base there were quite a few wireless signals Zainia intercepted and recorded. Many were communications, voices, and videos. While on the planet just in this short period of time, Zainia obtained over a Terabyte of information she would soon be downloading into the ship's computer database as to free up her memory for the next batch of intercepts.

After they arrived back at their spacecraft, Canaris did all the functions he needed to do such as eat, drink, toilet, shower etc. Then it was time to rest. He knew he was too emotionally wired to effectively sleep and didn't want to waste the hours and requested the acting ship's doctor, Zainia give him a sedative that soon allowed him gainful sleep and rest.

Zainia never slept. She did however start her power module recharge sucking all the electricity she needed out of the power mains via the onboard twin fusion reactors. While Zainia was getting her slow and effective charge, she downloaded the intercepts into the ship's computers in a database set up by the calendar. While the downloading was going on, Zainia analyzed the data and slowly extracted the intelligence out of it. Thanks to her activity during the alien interview where she built a working lexicon of almost 2000 words, she was able to slowly stitch together a significant relational database that would be instrumental in data mining and further lexicon constructs. Overnight Zainia became a far more sophisticated translator than the box the Vracklines were using during the meeting.

Just like Moore's law saying computer power would double every two years, Zainia's Vrackline lexicon and dictionary doubled every two minutes.

Vracklines had toyed with robotics but never saw the usefulness like Yānjoyduī did for several reasons. First and foremost was the Yānjoyduī desire of the to build structures to deal with an aging population when society was no longer in favor of uncontrolled procreation. It was also evolution at its best where survival of the fittest was the prime directive. Those that did not want to conform were sterilized and not allowed to further damage the gene pool. Society's outcasts were removed out of the greater population and disposed of in ways that eventually tempered mannerisms to respect authority.

There was no dilly dallying around or homeless living under bridges and in parks. After a century of the Yānjoyduī New World Order, there were no homeless at all and anyone who tried to live the deviate lifestyle that led to homelessness was deemed mentally defective and a threat to the gene pool, hence were soon made unable to procreate and given options they could not refuse if they wanted to keep living

Since there were fewer reckless living people supplying ample amounts of low-income earners, labor became much tighter and more expensive. Hence robotics was the solution. Yānjoyduī Robots simply did all the dirty work now. If you needed a plumber, electrician, or carpenter, it would most likely be a supervised robot doing the work.

The Yānjoyduī medical field, education, police, and firefighting were heavily robotized.

The fact Yānjoyduī society grew more and more dependent on robotics also led to the fine art of esthetics creating robotic properties that resulted in attractive robots like Zainia, that had functional pleasurizer components to female robot body so that the owner could have sex and feel like it was a real vagina. Even the breasts were made to feel and look remarkably real.

Zainia trickle charged her power pack all night and topped it off at 99% and built up a 50,000-word Vracklines dictionary. Zainia's voice analysis soon allowed her to properly pronounce all 50,000 words using the most widely used Vrackline dialect. The typical Vrackline would not know Zainia wasn't a Vrackline because her voice projection was utterly perfect. Now armed with a 50,000-word dictionary Zainia could absorb Vracklines literature and study the essence of Vrackline civilization. The Vracklines would be utterly terrified to know the extent Zainia knew about them over night.

When Canaris woke after a nice long rest, Zainia started briefing him on items she thought he should know and not scare him with tangential material that would create a fear. Canaris knew the robot was smart enough to do a lot of independent operations to help meet milestones and accomplish goals of the mission. Developing translation capabilities was key to it all.

Another critical piece of information that Zainia stumbled across and informed Canaris, "The Vracklines are galactic traders. They visit probably more civilizations and Empires than most other civilizations in the galaxy."

"Is there a lot of trade with other solar systems?"

"The Vracklines have more than 80 trading parties scattered around great distances throughout the galaxy."

"How do they manage communications allowing such trading partners?"

"Most of those 80 civilizations have ability to communicate in the standard Vrackline language."

"By knowing Vrackline we have just opened the door to the galaxy to planet Zharkon Xestra," Canaris stated as he continued analyzing the situation.

"We rolled the dice and got lucky and picked the right planet."

"For communications purposes yes, but the jury is still out whether this was a wise move on the part of our Yānjoyduī Planetary Security Forces."

Zainia spent the rest of the time they had available prior to being escorted back down to the planet explaining several discoveries about the Vracklines civilization. The penetration into Vracklines culture was rather impressive. Eavesdropping on other's communications was quite a feat. And in espionage the greatest success is obtaining vital information without the enemy knowing the information you obtained.

But due to the necessity of improving communications with the Vracklines they would continue a ruse they were not categorically good on translations until they obtained some written materials the Vracklines would offer as to not alert them to the sudden and powerful expansion of Zainia's true Vrackline language ability.

Just like the previous day they entered the shuttle with Canaris carrying a small portable holovision machine to give some presentations of the Yānjoyduī lifestyles on their home world Zharkon Xestra.

CHAPTER TWELVE
TRANSLATIONS AND BOOKS

At exactly fourteen hours from the time of the agreement, the Yānjoyduī shuttle launched out of their Space Explorer HMY Xīwàng-Zhīxīng and followed the escorts back down to the base they visited the previous day.

The lead escort landed just ahead in the exact same spot. There was no mystery to their expected landing zone.

Today there were fewer individuals waiting for them, but they led them into the same conference room and Canaris got a lot of stares as he was carrying a device.

They took their interview seats with name placards today. All around the table each person had a double-sided name placard. Today there were some new arrivals. A couple women with lab coats on. Even dressed down for scientific reasons, the two women still had quite a luster. The combination blue skin, red hair, purple eyes, and the perfect geometry of their faces created an almost fairytale like atmosphere.

Canaris knew these women would not be here facing off representatives from an entirely new alien civilization if they were not superior in knowledge and mental acuity. Their focus on Canaris was very intense and profound. They of course were leading researchers in Alien life and space exploration. They had been to far more planets than anyone else in the room and had encountered the greatest discoveries of Vracklines vast intellectual realm.

The lead researcher from yesterday with his portable translator had an announcement first in his native language, then the translator stated: "I wanted to let you know that with your efforts yesterday we were able to perform a major upgrade to the translation program."

Zainia responded in perfect Vrackline dialect, "I analyzed the audio recordings of the room yesterday and have produced a translator I can advise Canaris and interpret for him if necessary. However, for me to improve my translational services, if you could provide me some reading materials, I could encode then I could expand the translator much quicker and start teaching Canaris the Vrackline language to allow him to converse with you more freely."

"But we would also want to converse with you in Yānjoyduī for the very same reason."

"We have no objection to that."

The researcher then asked in Vrackline language which was immediately translated into Yānjoyduī, "We noticed you brought a device with you."

Zainia responded in perfect Vrackline, "It's a holovision projection system to allow us to show you some video and sound of our planet."

The Vracklines had an agenda they planned to go by for more consultations, but this new development through that plan out of the window.

"All right then, perhaps us take a look at what you want to show us before we continue."

"You might want to video record this as it will no doubt help your translation algorithms."

"Certainly, give us a minute to set up."

The researcher turned to one of the ladies and said in Vrackline language, "Camile, would you please set up a *quadcorder* and film their presentation."

The scientist had an incredulous look because there were already so many cameras filming from all sorts of angles. She was just about to say something when she got that look which meant, *we do not want the aliens to know the extensive surveillance we have on them.*

Camile being ultra-sensitive and semi clairvoyant quickly grasped the ruse and complied. Moments later a device no more that slightly larger than a college textbook in size was at the end of the table facing the table as she assumed the alien would initiate the presentation at the end of the table adjacent to their own projection system.

"The recorder is ready and will start recording automatically when it detects the image displayed from the Yānjoyduī astronaut."

The researcher nodded at Canaris who figured it was time to start the show.

Canaris stood up set the device in the middle of the table and touched what obviously was the play button. Suddenly a high-resolution holograph began showing that turned out to be a two-hour documentary on their planet with lots of voice and picture correlations. This astounded the researchers who now had a treasure trove of incredible findings thanks to the free delivery by the Aliens. Rivers, dams, lakes, bridges, cities, buildings, architecture, aircraft, surface transport, space craft, people, music, holovision presentation slices, animals, snow, weather conditions, storms, farmers, crops, harvesters, planters, robotic manufacturing, restaurants, random homes, mining operations, refineries, power plants, and other significant items were shown.

Then to really get their interest was night vision of the heavens from locations on the planet including telescope photographs of the Vrackline planet Crysantralon, and several deep space pictures, some of which they were familiar with due to their own photography. The two-hour presentation gave a huge glimpse into a time slice of the Yānjoyduī civilization and the essence of their planet Zharkon Xestra. They were careful to not show anything military or warlike.

By the time the holograph provided by the holovision equipment ended, it was mealtime for the Vracklines.

The researcher stated, "It's time for us to take a lunch break. We have a cafeteria nearby we would like to invite you to join us. We understand you may be hesitant to risk and illness eating our food, but if nothing else you can see how we eat, just like we saw in your presentation."

"I'll be happy to check it out. I might be willing to sample some of the hot foods or boiled items."

The researcher said, "Will you follow me please."

As they were walking to the cafeteria, Zainia said, "I noticed your name on your name tag on your lab coat says Noriyogan, what does that mean?"

"Supposedly it means Jade Ocean Moss"

"That seems strange to name a male with such a name."

"It could be worse, the woman with Camile is named Hóngzhuāntóu."

"What does Hóngzhuāntóu mean?"

"Red Brick Head."

As they went through the food line in the cafeteria selecting their ingredients to their meals, Canaris said to himself, *the heck with it if I get sick, I get sick, worst case is I probably get diarrhea.*

Canaris was standing next to Camile and Zainia was standing right behind him so she could interpret.

"Zainia, will you please ask Camile to make me a few recommendations she things I might wish to try."

Zainia then asked in perfect Vrackline language, "Camile, could you please give Canaris some suggestions as to which food he should try?"

"It would be my pleasure," Camile replied in Vrackline language.

She then pointed to what appeared to be broiled meat covered in spices giving it a pinkish appearance. Then some items that were green, yellow, and orange.

Then they took their trays over to the drink dispenser and there were hot drinks which Canaris picked as it would less likely have dangerous bacteria. He dispensed some of it into a cup and smelled it which reminded him of black tea back home. With their trays loaded up they went to an empty table. The food was free, all part of the perks of the scientific community.

They sat down and Canaris waited for everyone to arrive and delayed until they made their gestures to their gods. From observation it appeared half of them had an element of religion, the other half were most likely atheists or non-believers.

A complete set of eating utensils were provided with the tray. Canaris was all set to try it.

Zainia could sniff better than a dog and discovered no glaring situations that appeared from potential trace elements of bacteria she could sense.

Canaris tried all the food on his tray and discovered it was all pleasant. The tea also was very delightful.

The restaurant was full of scientists, many who supported the alien activities and were thus staring at them. Canaris assessment is three quarters of the cafeteria were observing him, even though none of them approached as they had been briefed to stay away from these aliens.

During the lunch break there were technicians who were playing back and identifying words associated with pictures and video and transliterating all the segments. Thus, two hours' worth of video would create one hundred hours of transcribing work.

The next revision of the automated translator would be available when the aliens returned the next day.

As requested, they gave Zainia ten Vrackline books. When Canaris and Zainia left the planet for the day, she took them back to the shuttle and then they flew up to the Space Explorer HMY Xīwàng-Zhīxīng where she began her study of the books.

Just like how a human has two sides of their brains, a robot like Zainia has similar segmentation but in her case, it was divided up in eight equal size parts each having its own memory structured in a Companded Redundant Virtualized and Distributed Data (CRVDD) volatile and non-volatile storage. Some of the memory was so vital such as robotic basic operating system (RBOS), it had to survive loss of power, so the robot did not completely die. Since the eight lobes of the robotic brain (black boxes) contained processors and CRVDD, it allowed massively parallel processing and systolic implementations in the coding. The net effect is a robot was multi-taking and in the case of Zainia could be doing eight separate computer taxing operations in parallel. Or for systolic functions of doing massively parallel processed calculations could split the task up in eight parts which increased the throughput and bandwidth measurably.

Since the data storage was redundant in the CRVDD, there was a good chance it would withstand serious external factors such as an EMP pulse from a nuclear explosion, lightning strikes, and other paralyzing inflictions.

Tonight's task would be reading, cataloging, analyzing and quantifying data that would multiply the Vrackline language lexicon and translator by a remarkable amount. Zainia could scan each page of in approximately six seconds that was only slowed by the optical character reader delay. The first 550-page book scanned took three thousand and three hundred seconds. Each page contained approximately four hundred words. 220,000 words recorded required approximately fifty-five seconds on each page for the optical character reading (OCR) function to encode it into Zainia's computer memory and transferred to the ship's computer.

By morning all the books loaned would be scanned and returned since they were no longer needed. In a book with 220,000 words, the frequency measurement becomes quite apparent. In all languages some words have considerable higher frequency of use. Good examples are numbers, colors, pronouns, certain verbs, and the subject tended to drive frequency measurements and it was never too obvious which items had the highest scorecard since it was context sensitive. As an example, things associated with ocean life would have a low frequency count concerning dry land matters.

As each book was being scanned and controlled by one of the eight processors in Zainia's computer brain, another of the eight processors would be doing frequency statistics and when the 220,000[th] word was entered, there would not be a jump to another book as the reading processor would be redirected to perform some other function to help by doing searches and pattern matching.

The idea is to pick the low hanging fruit first. Words with the highest frequency would be entered higher up in the most recently used data base and flagged if Zainia already identified and translated the word. Hence start at the low hanging fruit and work your way up from there. The most efficient search algorithms ever developed were utilized to speed up the process. Thanks to previous work done, half of the information was available through the relational database, so the translation tables quickly populated with new information.

With the scanning and optical character reading (OCR) finished, a large amount of computer power was available for all the tangential functions that had a multiplying effect and time reduction of the later processes.

At the end of each book scan and processing after a second checker validated the results, the new database was linked to the translation function which would help build the next translation efforts in the next book. Hence the process built itself up and the first book was instrumental in assisting processing the second book. Synergism was achieved and when the third book was read the frequency charts became clearer. If you double the number of samples, you quadruple the degrees of freedom and the accuracy in the process.

One of the books scanned was a complete textbook on Vracklines Standard Code for Information Interchange. In reality, it took Zainia virtually only minutes using the ships computer to create a VSCII emulator that took Yānjoyduī encoded alphabet and converted it to VSCII or the opposite.

The planet was saturated with VSCII based signals. It was a simple matter of latching on to a Vracklines communications links and using the VSCII emulator to read signals at high-speed skipping the OCR reading process that was now ongoing 7/24 with the ship's computers to the point Zainia could back out of the process and use her computer power more profitably elsewhere.

From time to time as the ship's computers got a new update in the growing translator, a new version replaced what Zainia had loaded in her CRVDD memory. By morning, Zainia had as broad a Vracklines working vocabulary as any of the scientists in the room. The Vracklines might have thought it was all done with Zainia the robot, but they had no idea the sophisticated wireless interface Zainia had to the radio control panel of the spacecraft allowing the awesome power of the ship's computers to work as a team with Zainia adding exponentially to the outcome.

Another feature already tested the past few days was Zainia was able to stay in contact with the mother ship via the radio control panel supplying additional conversations encoded to store in the ship's memory allowing it to accumulate incredible quantities of data including an entire transcript of the meetings and conversations.

Slowly as the two societies discovered a lot about each other, it finally came to the point that probably should have been established on the first day. Unfortunately, they could not communicate. Now that communications issues were ending and the Vracklines felt they could effectively communicate got down to brass tact's and asked those poignant questions.

"Why did you come here?"

"How long did it take?"

"Can you show us on a star-chart where your planet exists?"

"Do you have any weapons on your spacecraft?"

"How soon do you intend on leaving?"

"When will you come back?"

"Will we exchange diplomats?"

"Are you willing to sign a treaty?"

"What kind of intergalactic trade are you interested in?"

While they were wrestling with those questions the following day, the decision was made to have Camile give Canaris and Zainia a tour of the capital city Crysantralon named after the ancient Emperor Crysantralon which also acquired the name of the planet during his reign.

Emperor Crysantralon unified the planet and initiated the first expedition of scientific space exploration to other planets. He was held in reverence by the public, though some scholars felt he was also a Tyrant and evil person who did such a great job at dispatching his enemies, any printed material that discussed him didn't last long without his approval.

The sons and grandsons of Emperor Crysantralon who took over the Empire were also instrumental in maintaining the image of a great leader and purveyor of all the greatest advancements in Vrackline civilization. In recent years when there was nobody that retained power that had any real affection towards the ancients, sources of ancient writings appeared that showed the scholars at the time with a contrary opinion wrote entire treatise of the crushing horror Emperor Crysantralon applied to those who defied him.

Canaris and Zainia agreed to the tour. Soon they were in a Skycar leaving the base and heading to the heart of the city. In a few minutes the Skycar landed on a city street and pulled into a parking spot that was reserved for them as well as a few other spots behind that supporting Skycars carrying security personnel arrived in.

It was a foregone conclusion the strange looking Aliens would create a lot of curiosity and the security personnel were coming along and staying back a distance as to not impact the tour group's fulfillment of the event.

"This is the heart of the city," Camile said after they stepped out of the Skycar onto the sidewalk.

"Nice looking buildings," Canaris said realizing that Zainia would be recording all the visuals they experienced. When they went back to their civilization at Zharkon Xestra, the scientific community and the former skeptics would not doubt have to do a lot of soul searching as this one exploration alone would shake the foundation of their beliefs.

The Crysantralon City overall appearance exposed the majestic nature of the center of an empire. These tall buildings no doubt contained business, banking, and financial services industries.

"Does any of these buildings contain government offices?" Canaris asked in standard Yānjoyduī which Zainia immediately responded articulating in the most perfect Vrackline language.

This robot seems to have really acquired our language extremely fast, Camile thought and during debriefings later would comment about that to her superiors.

"No, most of the government is housed in buildings and infrastructure built on the former Emperor Crysantralon Palace as it evolved out of Empire structured institutions to present day Council Government."

"How many Council Members are there?" Zainia asked.

"For Central Planning and hierarchical manifestations, there are Twelve who make the global decisions. But they do not get into the details. They only generate the guidance; however, the holographic media claims they interfere sometimes in the sub processes for their own enrichment."

"Who then generates the details and guidance for society's direction and implements them?" Zainia asked in perfect Vrackline language.

"The council appoints the sub-council members who then hire all the civil servants that carryout policy and assist the sub-council members in drafting proposals and rules and regulations that Council Members are advised. The council can approve or disapprove with recommendations of modifications to change it to what they think is more in line with the direction they determined most beneficial to society."

"Would you like to see inside some of the buildings?"

"Definitely," Canaris said and Zainia translated.

Soon they were walking into a financial service building that had been put on alert that such a tour might bring the aliens in their building. They had a tour guide standing by for such a development and were extremely pleased to be singled out as one of their destinations. This tour would give them a lot of publicity their managers would really like as a couple media video recorders were now following them just in front of the security men.

Canaris noticed he drew a lot of stares. It was a novelty to most of the Vracklines who had never seen such *plain skinners* before. Almost all the knowledge of present-day galactic ethnicity included green, blue, brown, pink, and yellow skinned beings with green and blue predominate.

The financial services company could pass for a financial

services company on Canaris Bartrum's home planet Zharkon Xestra. The only difference was the display technology and the blue skinned people operating them. The Vracklines were mostly a homogenous society and had been accused by their enemies as being xenophobic.

Vracklines were not racists per say but being well educated on the history of the galaxy they knew that uncontrolled immigration often led to civil unrest, race wars, and collapsed empires. The proponents of uncontrolled immigration were businesspeople wanting cheap labor to exploit and increased market sizes. The problem these short-sighted individuals manifested chaos and long-term misery and resentment. There usually was a predictable pattern.

The first wave would be welcomed in open arms due to the corruption of the patronage class that could only get away with illegal human trafficking due to their political connections were deemed untouchable.

The second wave may not show up for one or two more generations, but because first wave uncontrolled immigration produced very rich immigrants who eventually visited their home worlds flaunting their wealth, it was a no brainer for those making up the second wave. And the first wavers didn't want the second wave people even though they were typically cousins or close relatives.

The first wave didn't assimilate to a large extent, but there was some simply due to curiosity and lust that attracted citizens to these strange people that showed up often flowering more so beautiful than the domestic plainness that assumed they would always be on top.

The second wave had very much less assimilation because they came from a lower class and intelligence compared to the first wave that had the bravest and brightest who chose the adventure out of curiosity and inquisitiveness.

The second wave was principally financial driven: make a fast buck.

Subsequent waves had nothing to do with adventure, culture, or any other redeeming features. Some of it was the first and second wave families wanted workers of their own ancestry and likeness. Some of the immigrants were even more xenophobic than the host planet which made no sense to why they came, but they kept coming until an unstable situation often took a predictable course and evolution would then leave its mark, survival of the fittest.

Vracklines avoided the pitfalls of many other worlds and were tough on immigration policy and people trafficking was not tolerated. Perpetrators were harshly dealt with and because it was easy to identify someone who didn't have blue skin, that scenario was never allowed to start on this homogenous planet. Spaceships caught in trafficking people or illegal substances were confiscated and usually destroyed with their crew aboard.

In past Vracklines history if a local girl procreated with an *off-worlder*, they would both be asked to leave and, in some cases, shown to the doorstep.

Despite all the negatives, other worlds and Empires liked the Vracklines because they traded fairly and chose to not stick their noses in other's business. They would also prefer "no deal" to a bad deal.

Crime was relatively low, and corruption wasn't tolerated. Everyone was required to earn their own way and for those social deviants who didn't want to play ball, the government always had options and re-education islands that broke the spirits of malcontents quickly who were more than happy to comply as a requirement to get off the island.

Male Yānjoyduī gave off pheromones when they were eager

for sexual activity. Vrackline women also gave off pheromones if they were in their cycle and had an inspirational moment with a male. As Canaris spent the day following Camile around, he developed some subtle attraction but didn't quite understand why. *Was it the allure of her blue skin?*

After visiting a few more businesses and buildings in Crysantralon City downtown area, Camile took the two Yānjoyduī to the Central Park, a rectangle of green and flora superimposed right in the heart of the business district where numerous office dwellers with a window towards the park, commanded a majestic view which significantly reduced negative psychological tendencies thanks to the wide-open spectacular view.

This is just like some of the most fabulous parks on Zharkon Xestra, Canaris thought. On the edge of the park across the city street were numerous purveyors of culinary delight.

Camile sensing it was mealtime suggested they go sample the cuisine at one of those places. This restaurant they stopped at had been alerted in advance a special guest would be there midway through the lunch period and to have several reserve tables ready with reservation fees paid in advance.

One thing Canaris noted was all the activity flowed seamlessly as if life and circumstances were easy on the planet. In reality, the very conservative Vrackline civilization placed heavy demands on everyone. You were expected to do your part and failure was not tolerated.

It was naturally assumed that when people received their tasking and directions, they would carry on smartly and do what was required. And it usually worked out that way.

From an outsider perspective, the tranquil appearance of the pedestrians walking by conducting themselves as if the had no care in the world, one could quickly gain the notion this was an ideal society. The crucibles beneath the veneer of society didn't stand out.

After they were seated at this nice café with outdoor dining facing the park, they received drinks they ordered, and their food order was put in. The restaurant waiter thought it was odd the *plain skin* woman ordered no drink or food.

The personal details now surfaced in the conversation thanks to Zainia's ability to quickly translate for Canaris:

"Camile, did you grow up in Crysantralon City?"

"No. I grew up in a fishing village on a dormant volcanic island."

"What was that like?"

"I loved my childhood. Kids there get to do a lot more things than kids trapped in the city. I had water sports and activity always available. Swimming in the ocean and exploring the shoreline always offered a lot of fun times."

"I obviously do not know much about your civilization or anything about how you live and exist on this planet, but I'm curious, when you were at the beach playing did you have to be careful to not get sunburned?"

"That's an interesting question. If you look at pedestrians that pass us by, you will see many have different shades of blue skin. That is partly because some spend far more time out in direct sunlight than others. Thanks to the pigment of our skin, we are far more tolerant of sunlight than most other civilizations we know of. Do you sunburn easily, Canaris?"

"I can probably stay in direct sunlight for half and hour before my skin would start to get a solar burn. I'm not a big fan of spending a lot of hours out in the sunlight. Even when I go to the beach to go swimming, I always wear a cloth fabric top to shield most of my skin."

"Do you have a significant other, Canaris?"

"No. As part of mission planning, the screening process eliminated anyone with a mate or significant other."

"Was there a reason why you do not have a significant other?"

"Just when I thought I found the right one, she decided to choose someone else."

"You didn't then pursue another?"

"At the moment it wasn't a priority for me since my curiosity about space travel redirected my interests."

"Any regrets by not doing so?"

"I would not be sitting across from you this very moment had I allowed domestic tranquility to overcome my quest for exploration of space and other worlds."

"I do not know if I should take that as a compliment."

"I find you rather attractive, I hope you feel it's a compliment."

"You like the way I look with blue skin?"

"Yes, I like the way you look."

"That's very interesting. I like the way you look too."

Nobody present really knew it was the pheromones doing all the talking. But where there is smoke there usually is fire.

Camile actually felt a little lightheaded thinking how this Alien must want to experience her flesh. She didn't quite understand the attraction she had for the off-worlder, but she knew how she felt and knew it was in her best interest to hide those notions to anyone or risk being removed off the case and no longer have access to the alien. She would have to simply conduct herself in the manner she had been and if the alien seemed happy with her, its likely her superiors would continue using her as an interface and possibly an influencer.

"When you were young living in the fishing village did you ever go out onto the ocean on boats doing that activity?"

"Yes, quite often. My father owned a motorized boat that had enough room for a crew of a dozen people, if necessary, as well as a refrigerated storage for the catch. The boat could stay out at sea several weeks after the first catch since all the fish we caught was immediately frozen."

"That sounds fun. What did you do on the boat?"

"When I was younger, I helped my mother who was the cook by washing dishes and cleaning. My father wanted a clean and well-run ship but understood the men needed to get to work after being awakened and given their first meal of the day, so we cleaned their sea cabins, made their beds, washed their sheets when necessary, and kept a clean well-kept appearance."

"That all sounds fun."

"I laundered their clothes and did a lot of other things to help. When I got older my father taught me how to drive the fishing boat and in my last couple of years, he would be out supervising the men on deck with the nets and the catch, and I actually drove the fishing boat."

"Tell me about yourself, Canaris."

"I grew up and left home early. I got involved with military and space craft and eventually dove into aeronautics where I slowly evolved into a position where I could one day be an explorer. I worked hard and eventually commenced moving into an assignment that led to space exploration and now

I'm here discussing with a person from another world, space exploration."

The food arrived and the chitchat died down as everyone except Zainia dove into their culinary delights.

So far, the food hadn't killed Canaris, so he was willing to continue experimenting.

"These items taste really good," Canaris said as he was delighted, he got the sampler. Zainia had looked over the menu and like everything she viewed was recorded to memory until she downloaded it to the ship's computers. But Zainia still had access to the information via her wireless connection via the ship's radio control panel. Canaris would quiz Zainia later that night to determine what he was eating.

After the lunch break, they were taken to a concert put on in the afternoon. They were soon seated in a balcony seat looking down at a 150-piece orchestra that had all kinds of musical instruments Canaris had never seen before.

Some musicians were playing a device with strings using a bow. There were brass instruments they blew air through that had amazing sound. There were various percussion type instruments and a few performers with a strange instrument orientated vertically with a lot of strings on it that made an incredible sound and with seven of them, the intensity could be large. Then there were two large box like instruments with a couple keyboards each with probably ninety six keys on each of the keyboards that gave an incredible range. Numerous other instruments built long and skinny that people blew air through that gave off unique sounds.

"In my world they only do these performances in the evening." Canaris noted.

"Our concerts are usually performed twice, once early like now, the orchestra then takes a nice long break and, in the evening, comes back."

"It's probably a good thing to do, but why do they do two performances?"

"The reason why they do two performances is to maximize children exposure. A lot of people you see down in the audience are school children, teachers, and senior citizens who do no like leaving home after dark. This allows the orchestra to do an additional practice without the stress of performing in front of the music critiques that will be here later this evening."

"That's an outstanding way to do things."

Canaris was sitting between Zainia and Camile. Canaris knew this video Zainia recorded would be of interest to scientists back home who would be interested in the Alien Arts.

Soon the lights dimmed in the concert hall and the conductor walked on stage receiving a generous welcoming by the audience. This conductor was all business and within 5 seconds of standing on his conductor's platform raised his music wand and began a complicate movement with it and pointed now and then to sections of the orchestra. He was definitely controlling the beat.

The music soon lifted the spirits of everyone in the music hall as this particular composition from an unknown off world source discovered by accidental exposure of Vracklines space exploration, brought it to this planet and experts quickly figured out an interpretation of it.

On planet Earth this music would have elements of Schuman, Mozart, Brahms, and Beethoven which none in the concert hall knew about.

Use of the drums were so Beethoven like. The box instruments with dual keyboards created a coherence of breathtakingly beautiful sound. The seven vertical string devices resonated the horizontal box and keyboards, and the other string instruments created an orchestral backdrop the smaller wind instruments blossomed in an illustrious choreography of splendid harmony.

This wonderful orchestra doesn't sound like it needs a warmup performance, Canaris thought as the magnificent sound it created was spellbindingly beautiful.

In reality, the Vracklines were social conscious and did things in a way to benefit society in general. This additional performance allowing school children and elderly was one of many actions the wise elders took to help make existence for society more pleasant and it reinforced school children's aptitude towards music indoctrination.

Humanoids typically learn in eight major ways. One of the eight is through music. By learning music at an early age, brain cells are further developed that eventually creates room for later learning of other subject matters such as mathematics which also created brain extension synergism.

The thought of being on a planet where music did not exist was quite a telling matter. It would be like living without the ability to bathe and clean oneself.

Halfway through the performance Canaris felt Camile's hand. It was just an accidental touch, but it felt strangely good. He felt no harm in doing so he grabbed her hand and held it for the remainder of the performance. What he didn't realize was he was transferring an emotion that had far more impact than he could ever imagine.

Camile felt rapturous by the touch. Already affected by his pheromones the embrace with his hand was almost as powerful as kissing her on the lips. She knew she was stimulated by this alien and felt an utter weakness she had doubts she could control when the time come. If there was a time.

Feeling so wonderful with the touch of the alien seemed to accelerate the speed of which the orchestra completed the symphonic music. Canaris wished it could last longer, but appreciated it while it lasted, nevertheless. He had emotionally bonded to this blue skinned person and knew he felt some affection for her. He had no idea how mutual it was.

Camile knew that Canaris had traveled a long distance to get here and to be awarded his affection meant a lot to her as her self esteem gravitated upwards each passing moment, he held her hand. Finally, the music ended, and the applause began. Canaris had no option but to let go of Camile's hands and began clapping like everyone else. The applause was very strong and delightful. Members of the orchestra as well as the conductor lived for this moment. When the audience loves your performance its uplifting to your soul.

The interpretation of this music was a difficult task. It took great effort and practice to glue together the classical orchestral rendition of the brilliance of some obscure composer nobody knew of. This composer lost to the eons of light years was fondly accepted and if he were alive today knowing Aliens from billions of miles away cherished his work, he no doubt would feel emotional about it.

Many composers receive their accolades long after their passing. What drives them in the absence of public recognition while they are living is the sense they are working for their legacy. Mozart's Requiem is such a composition.

[Mozart - Requiem in D minor (Complete/Full) [HD] - YouTube]

The day would come when people knowledgeable of the composer would one day visit the Vracklines planet Crysantralon and explain the origin of the music. In a way it makes the composition immortal.

On their way back to the military base, Canaris was doing some soul searching and analysis to his situation. He was clearly lonely and isolated and with a lovely creature he would like some private time with. There were only a few people in the Skycar, so he felt comfortable asking.

"Camile, I know this might sound out of line, but I do like you and I would like to spend some time alone with you and get to know you and show you more about myself and my planet. When we leave today, I would like to take you up to my spaceship, give you a tour and show you some video and music."

Camile didn't know how her supervisors would take such an event but thought secretly they would love to know about what's on that space craft such as: are there any more beings on it or are these two truly alone? Does it have weapons? And other pertinent pieces of information surrounding their purpose of being here which up to now was presented as merely the result of space exploration.

"I would love to have a tour of your ship, but I must get permission from my supervisor."

The remainder of the trip back to the base was filled with anticipation as to the outcome of the possible ship visit.

The Skycar landed near the Yānjoyduī shuttle. They all got out and walked near the shuttle.

The head Vrackline researcher, Noriyogan overheard the request since the Skycar was fully bugged as well as Camile without her knowledge. He approached knowing this invite was going to now unfold. They could have worked weeks to attempt getting a spy onboard that space craft and here they were giving an invite without any effort whatsoever!

Camile was not a spy; she was a researcher, but she was fully wired and didn't know it. The bugs which had very narrow bandwidth allowed them to receive them even out in space aboard that space craft. The quadrature process of recording two simultaneous frequencies then combining them in a mixer modulator increased the signal to noise ration by almost one hundred decibels. There would be some cleanup of the signals using phase lock loops, and the end result would be high fidelity record of everything that transpired with Camile.

With a poker face and giving the appearance of allowing this expedition to occur in the name of science, Vrackline researcher, Noriyogan agreed to the tour which put Camile on the shuttle that could easily carry six people and on her way to help them investigate the capabilities of the alien technology. *There might be something to gain from it.*

Twenty minutes later, Camile exited the shuttle into the Alien ship with Canaris and Zainia. It truly was a significant event in her life. On the spaceship with the Alien who had given her a secret signal with his hand. Nobody on the planet knew there was already a romance brewing between the two.

While the shuttle was being recharged and refueled for a couple hours, it would then be capable of another trip to the planet and back without any concern.

Even though there were only one humanoid and a robot on the spacecraft, it did come in a large size. It's size alone appeared threatening.

Canaris led the group into the control room of the spacecraft, and it did look ultra-modern to Camile. The sensor displays and information streaming on some displays gave a notion this was very complicated. It looked advanced in some ways more than even the Vracklines best.

After showing Camile the impressive space telescope images, she asked some poignant questions because she knew she had to throw off the real intent from her supervisors and come back with some good descriptions. She didn't realize they knew as soon as she knew thanks to the exotic bugging.

"Where do you launch weapons from?"

"We carry no weapons and have no means of launching them."

"What if you are attacked by space pirates or some evil Aliens?"

"We'll either outrun them or surrender. We come in peace and have no way of defending ourselves."

She asked more poignant questions about some of the displays they were looking at which many were for the management of the spacecraft or propulsion.

"Would you like to see the rest of it?"

"Sure."

Canaris led Camile back towards the engineering spaces through his berthing.

"Camile noticed there were two bunks. Who sleeps here?"

"I sleep in one bunk and Zainia lays in the other and recharges her batteries while I'm sleeping."

"You are traveling with nobody in the control room?"

"Yes, most of the time, we are in autopilot."

"What if something comes up like a pirate ship or something?"

"Zainia never sleeps. She is always in contact with the ship's computers with wireless technology and the ship's computer would notify her to return to the control room if it needed her assistance."

"Has that ever happened?"

"No because Zainia always handles it laying in her bed remotely."

"She doesn't need to be in the control room to resolve the issue?"

"No. Everything the computer can see with its sensors or processed via internal circuits is automatically fed into Zainia's computer banks. She can see it all remotely and analyze it in her own holographic imagery in her robotic brain."

"Remote viewing"

"Absolutely."

They continued walking thought the ship and into the engineering spaces. Everything was white and impeccably clean.

"All these machines seem so clean."

"Yes, everything has to be kept very clean to make sure there is no atmospheric contamination."

"Do you help to keep it clean?"

"No, we have scrubbers to do that."

"What's a scrubber?"

Zainia who was now closely behind asked, "Shall I give Camile a demonstration?"

"Please do."

Zainia said, "look over here you see what appears to be a storage room?"

"Yes."

The door automatically opened and out came a small robot probably two feet tall with a handheld device and walked over to some surfaces and started rubbing the handheld device on it.

"What you are observing is the scrubber cleaning that surface. The scrubbers have built in scanners to find dirt and debris and go about cleaning routinely."

"Seems like I need a scrubber in my home."

"This is part of the automation done to reduce crew size. All maintenance is done robotically."

"Interesting."

The scrubber who got commanded by the ship's computer via Zainia was directed to go back to its storage location. Soon it was parked and going through a recharge cycle.

"As they continued walking aft Canaris pointed out some of the machinery. This is the reverse osmosis plant to purify drinking water."

"How much drinking water do you deploy with?"

"About 6,000 gallons."

"That's a lot of water, why do you need the reverse osmosis?"

"That is to clean the wastewater. We can't be sure if we will find sources of water, it gets reprocessed."

"What about your sewage?"

"It is filtered and processed, and the bulk is sent out a nuclear rocket engine injector where it becomes part of the fuel.

"Do you have enough water to travel home?"

"We have about four times the amount of water required to get home based on how much we used coming here. We lose water because we do not filter the wastewater excessively as it would add a burden to the reverse osmosis."

Soon they came by some other interesting looking machinery and Canaris said, "These are our two generators."

"How do they work?"

"They are fed directly from fusion reactors."

"Are you an expert on the fusion reactor too?"

"No, I do not need t know about the fusion reactors since most of it is outside the hull that you cannot see, and they are self-contained units that are good for at least another ten years of operation before they would need replaced."

The ships computer informed Zainia via her wireless interface to the radio control panel it detected the quadrature bug Camile was carrying.

At the particular time Zainia knew there was noting being said or done that needed to be blacked out, but she would certainly do it should the occasion raise its ugly head.

After the air purification system and a few other gadgets there wasn't much more to see in the engineering spaces so they went forward to the crew's lounge area that could easily seat 10 people.

"Why is this area so large if you only have two people with you?"

"This craft could take an expedition team somewhere and so its set up modularized and can likely accommodate ten people if the trip was a year or two in length."

"Would you like to sit down and talk a while?"

Camile sat down on one of the chairs secured to the deck and Zainia sat down next to her. Canaris sat directly across from Camile.

"What is your main function on the ship Zainia?"

"I'm the entity that does a lot of things. I'm Canaris doctor, dentist, psychiatrist, pilot, assistant, chief engineer, navigator, and research assistant."

"So, you do a lot of things that allow this ship to have an ultra-small crew?"

"Yes, that's my purpose to minimize living beings to allow this ship to travel further and in more risky situations as to not risk the lives of people."

At this point in time Zainia directed the ship's computer to start jamming Camile's quadrature bugs because as the ship's psychiatrist she knew the most important thing Canaris needed now was some female affection including sexual intercourse if it deemed feasible. She then started discussing her psychiatrist tasking which she knew she would use as a segue into where she wanted the conversation to go.

"One of my most important duties of course is being Canaris psychoanalyst to make sure he mentally has no difficulty carrying out his responsibilities."

"I imagine that is quite a challenge especially when you travel ultra-long distances in space."

"I know Canaris is terribly lonely, and you do inspire him."

"I do?"

"Yes, I think he has developed feelings for you."

"Has he said that to you?"

"He doesn't have to. With my robotic measurements I can tell his body functions and you illuminate his transcendence whenever you are around him."

Camile was almost in a state of shock hearing this from an

ultra-smart robot she instinctively knew had programming at a very high level.

"Camile some of my measurements on you also give my analysis the belief that you have reciprocal feelings."

"In what way?"

"I think you would be delighted if Canaris kisses you."

Camile sat there stunned. It was as if this robot could read her mind.

Now the fun started. "Canaris, as you know I'm just a robot, I'm not a person, you must not ever be embarrassed in front of me. I think you should take the time to kiss Camile and discover what my measurements are telling me right now."

Camile would be utterly shocked to know how refined Zainia's sensors were including her ability to measure female arousal. She knew Camile was low hanging fruit and ready to be sampled.

Canaris didn't know what drove him to do it. His head felt lightheaded, his world seemed spinning like an intoxicated person, and he embraced Camile and kissed her. In the close proximity his pheromones shedding out of his nose caused her female responses to respond and if it were not for the fact, she would have to make a report of it she would have consented to coitus on the spot.

The electricity in the kiss flowed between them and soon Camile gave back, and the embrace lasted quite long. They each instantly knew there was something there.

Canaris was a gentleman and Camile appreciated it because she was highly vulnerable then and would have succumbed to mating and sexual intercourse and threw caution to the wind. After they regained their composure and Canaris didn't take it to the level he knew he could, Camile's respect for him grew instantly.

"I'm sorry I did that, but I felt utter attraction to you."

"Don't feel sorry, it felt good to me, and I enjoyed it."

"I hope I don't complicate your life."

"The minute I came up here with you, my life got complicated. It's too late now to worry about complications. But we will have to be careful because my people do not like to see their women comingling with outworlders, and they have never seen a plane skinned person before."

"Camile, I want you to know I feel a great affection for you."

"I thought you do, and the feeling is mutual. I'll see what I can do to create opportunities for us to meet again."

That raised a huge red flag for Camile who now had to bring up the subject. "Canaris, I realize you can't stay here forever; you have a mission to perform, in order for me to arrange my schedule to maximize the time I get to be with you, can you give me an idea how long you intend to stay on this planet?"

"Camile, we have general guidance, but I think it would be prudent for me to leave here in thirty days or less. This is a scientific expedition and I owe it to a lot of researchers to go back and explain to them and to my world there is more to the universe than they realize. Our society needs to evolve and stop looking inwards and start looking out to the stars."

"Alright Canaris, that gives me a lot to think about and work on. I don't know if I can control myself much longer and I do not think now is the appropriate time for us to go to a higher level in our relationship. We need to think about our positions in life and what it means to each other before we cross over that line. I would like you to take me back to the planet now."

"Sure, no problem but I would like to make a request."

"What's your request?"

"Before we leave on the shuttle, I want to hug you."

"That's a reasonable request and I think I would like it too."

They stood up and hugged and it lasted a while. Zainia knew in her programming if she was a real female and could have tears, they would be flowing now. She cared so much for Canaris and to see him embraced with such a lovely creature having the emotions flowing between them, touched hour subroutines in a major manner. At the end of the hug there was another spontaneous kiss, and they were done. They walked to the shuttle and got in and soon they were airborne with an escort back down to the planet. After the last hug and kiss, Zainia directed the computer to stop jamming the signals and to alert the Vracklines they were going back to the planet to take Camile back to the base.

The time passed quickly as the shuttle bay was evacuated with air that would be replaced by air obtained, filtered, and compressed from the planet to compensate for any air lost in the exchange.

When the shuttle landed, they all got out acting most professional and Zainia and Canaris stood side by side in front of Camile and bowed to her and said, "Thank you for spending time with us on our ship," first in his native Yānjoyduī language then repeated in perfect Vrackline language by Zainia.

Camile smiled and bowed and said in Vrackline: "I enjoyed my time. Thank you."

Canaris waved to all the other scientists that approached and then returned to the shuttle with Zainia and soon the shuttle was back out in space heading for their research Space Explorer HMY Xīwàng-Zhīxíng.

When they were back on the Space Explorer HMY Xīwàng-Zhīxīng, Canaris said to Zainia, "I want to thank you for what you did today. It meant a lot to me."

"As your personal psychiatrist, I look out for your feelings as I know you have gone through a lot of stress to get to this point in the mission. I'm pleased that if I could in some way give you a temporary passage to a condition where your brain could release those pleasure chemicals."

"You indicated you could measure a woman and know her physical condition."

"Yes, it's true. It would do you no benefit by knowing my special capabilities and you are not authorized to know how those circuits work, but Camile was ready to copulate with you. You are a gentleman and didn't pursue it which was good because to have a lasting relationship you must first build trust in a woman. Your building process is now in progress. You do not have much time. Thirty days will pass quickly. And there are some things I need to inform you of."

"Such as?"

The planet Crysantralon is homogenous and xenophobic, you would not be accepted here. If you fall in love with Camile and want a permanent relationship with her, you will have to take her back to Zharkon-Xestra."

"I wouldn't mind that."

"You need to also place her interests in equal importance. I would estimate she would not like being marooned on our planet Zharkon-Xestra. There are no other blue skinned people there. She would be treated as a freak and in due time I would expect Camile find living at Zharkon-Xestra intolerable."

"So, you are saying it's not worth pursuing?"

"You will probably have future space missions ahead of you that will take you to other strange cultures, having a good association with this woman will help prepare you for the future."

"Does that include sexual contact?"

"You have a long trip home. I think that if you have sexual experiences with Camile before you leave it will help you evolve. Also, there may be some future alternatives such as relocating to a different planet that has a mixture of people including blue skinned people."

"Maybe I can find that out now and send you back to Zharkon-Xestra without me?"

"I do not advise that. You have no idea how many opportunities you would be passing up by choosing this path."

"How so?"

"You are first and foremost an explorer. There are many other places to explore and with just the information we have already obtained, Yānjoyduī Planetary Security Forces will soon be forced to send out more expeditions to figure out what is going on in the galaxy because if we don't it may be very dangerous for our civilization. I've obtained a lot of information from the Vracklines that suggests we are ill prepared to face what is out there and could be coming our way."

"All right. I think I want you to give me a sedative so I can get a good sleep and not think about things."

"It will be my pleasure Canaris."

"Thank you."

The Vracklines could not inquire the way they wanted

about the signal interference that cut out the quadrature bugs without tipping off Camile she had been bugged and the level of surveillance on her.

They did have to debrief her on what she saw on the ship and play dumb they already knew what she saw. Their next big challenge would be to get video on the ship or some experts up there to gauge the technology level the Yānjoyduī alien visitors have.

They were of course in utter shock the Yānjoyduī were defenseless. They feared for them to the point they almost offered an escort home as they didn't have a warm fuzzy feeling they could make out of this part of the galaxy and get home without weapons to defend themselves.

The grueling debriefing lasted four hours then they sent Camile home as she was fatigued, exhausted, and obviously in need of rest.

Chapter Thirteen
Defeating Quadrature Bugs

After a good rest period, Canaris woke up, went to the toilet, and relieved himself then began his planning for the day.

Zainia brought him a drink and something to eat and sat with him in the lounge area. They went over a few details and Zainia then explained how Camile was bugged.

"Do you think she was part of the planning on placing the bugs?"

"No, I do not think she knew about it, and I could tell you more, but there are some mission critical components I'm restricted from revealing to you for your own good. Based on some abilities I have, I'm very well sure she didn't know she was bugged. Nor would they want her to know because they wanted her to act and appear normal."

"I would have different feelings about her if I knew she knew she was purposely carrying a bug."

"That's why I wanted to talk to you about this before we go back to the planet. After we leave here and are long gone, I will give you a special briefing and then it will make sense to you. I have responsibility as your personal psychiatrist to protect your mental health. You are in a complicated situation and the surveillance on us is quite extreme. Assume whenever you are on the planet, you are always being spied upon with sophisticated tools."

"What if I end up having sex with Camile?"

"They will know you did. But she will not know they know as they hide a lot of it from her."

"She doesn't know what's going on?"

"It's highly compartmentalized and she's not aware the other woman she works with, Hóngzhuāntóu isn't a researcher. She's actually an agent that works for Vrackline Intelligence."

"I guess I'm lucky they didn't send her after me first."

"They didn't send Camile after you. They had no reason to believe the two of you would transcend to the level you reached so abruptly. It was only because you were physically moved touching her hand at the concert that created the scenario that unfolded."

"You saw that?"

"I see everything. I'm also your chief security officer."

"When she and I kissed, do they know about that?"

"No, the ship's computer was jamming the quadrature bugs at the time."

"What do you mean about quadrature bugs?"

"A normal bug operates off a single crystal. A quadrature bug has two crystals producing two frequencies that are broadcasted and modulated in a special mixer wired to crystals that are physically close. The antenna of the quadrature bug is tuned to the difference frequency coming out of the mixer using a microscopic, small conjugate matching notch filter."

"How is this powered?"

"The crystals provide all the energy to the process as acoustic waves hit them. Signal strength is amplified with the highly tuned mixer and microscopic conjugate match antenna coupler."

"How do the Vrackline's process the signal from the Quadrature Bug?"

The Vrackline's receivers located at several locations on the planet, demodulates them and detects the intelligence cleaned up with phase lock loops creating high fidelity.

"They didn't hear any of the interchange I had with Camile just before she left the spacecraft?"

"Before I made the subtle suggestions to you to explore the romantic activity, the ship's computers were already jamming the Quadrature Bug signals on my orders."

"So, the Vracklines do not know she and I have something going on?"

"No, but if you take my advice and allow your human emotions to explore the essence of that woman to create a pleasure event, they will shortly know then."

"And try to exploit it?"

"Undoubtedly."

"Do we have anything they would consider worth taking?"

"On a technology scale, they are about ten levels above us, but not everyone sees things the same way. We probably have innovation they would want to capture and use it to expand their own capabilities."

"Do we have any technology on this ship that would put our world at risk if someone captured it?"

"Before we arrived here, and I obtained a lot of information from the Vracklines, I would have advised you we needed to protect the technology and not to invite the woman here. But after evaluating Vrackline technology, we really have nothing important to them."

"Nothing to be gained by them taking this ship?"

"No, they have much more capable technology and spaceships."

"Then why are they giving us the Royal Treatment?"

"No civilizations from our part of the galaxy have ever ventured this way before. They have curiosity, plus racially we are unique. They have never seen *plain skinners* like us before."

"Probably a month from now is a good time for us to depart since we are of nothing of value to them, they might simply want to get rid of us eventually."

"Yes, that's precisely the point, and if you wanted to leave earlier, there should be no reason why not."

"Maybe I should leave before I get too involved with that woman?"

"I recommend you experience her. It will help mold you into a better explorer."

"I do get good vibes being around Camile."

"And she gets good vibes being around you."

"Can you at least give me some clues as to how you know that?"

"I can measure her heartbeat, her temperature, water vapor in parts of her body she emits. And portions of her body that are hidden from you are detectable by my sensors that allow me to observe her arousal."

"She was really aroused?"

"She was ready for coitus and could not have resisted you."

"Even knowing all that I'm glad I didn't go any further."

"You made all the right moves. Desire is always a stronger emotion than gratification."

"I think I'll be ready to go back to the planet in a short while."

Going to the planet soon took on a new meaning now that Canaris knew more about what was really going on. When they arrived at the planet the usual scientists were there, and they went into the conference room where they discussed their translator that had improved remarkably since arrival.

Zainia amazed them as she talked to them in their Vrackline language so well she could easily be mistaken for one of them. It was apparent her robotic dictionary and translator was far more advanced than what Noriyogan had available.

"We would like to ask you how you picked up our language so quickly?" Noriyogan asked.

"A robot never sleeps. Thanks to the books you provided and the entertainment radiations we receive from your holographic entertainment industry, we were able to further add exponentially to our database and with the help of your entertainment industry determine most specifically how to pronounce each word after careful analysis."

"How many of our words do you know?"

"In my data base that has proficiency thanks to high frequency of use, now utilizes 20,000 words. In my database without high frequency use another 20,000 words that I have the ability to use and speak. I have third database of words that are in the construct phase we are still learning language structure and sounds and projection, that has another 147,000 words."

"How soon do you think you will master those 147,000 words with translations?"

"I will be done in a month," Zainia replied.

"Will you share those databases with us?" Noriyogan asked.

"Certainly, if you will give us a communication link to transmit the translation to, we would be most happy to send translations to you because we hope in the future our two worlds can establish friendship and possible trading, though we know it's very long distant and may not be economically beneficial."

"We have a communication protocol, Vrackline Standard Code for Information Interchange VSCII. I can have some engineers and scientists work with you, set up a link you can transmit to send us that information."

"Will this link also allow us to read your electronic news and information broadcasted from the planet so we can learn more about you?"

"Since you will only be here a short time, we can give you a temporary account."

"Thank you."

The day was spent working on establishing that link and soon enough the information flow began.

The Vracklines were too excited about gobbling up all the data sent to them they were not aware the Yānjoyduī had very powerful firewalls that prevented hacking. Vracklines living in a rather homogenous society had never confronted the sophistication of the Yānjoyduī computer hacking ability.

Zainia was soon into the deepest and darkest secrets of the Vracklines Intelligence service and quickly discovered Hóngzhuāntóu would soon be sent after Canaris in a honey pot scheme to seduce him and turn him into one of their own.

This complicated things because Zainia wanted Canaris to experience Camile who was a true scientist and not tainted by the INTEL people.

Zainia was a master chess player and was always seven moves ahead of the head Vrackline researcher Noriyogan. But she also knew Noriyogan was not part of the Vrackline INTEL, he was just another pawn in their extravagant engagement into manipulation and intreague for their part of the galaxy. Nevertheless, Vrackline INTEL viewed this auspicious meeting of a new civilization created new opportunity.

Now that Zainia had a front row seat to Vrackline INTEL operations, she would soon be the puppet master.

During the hard day of data transfers and discussions, Camile was there and looking very friendly. Canaris noticed Hóngzhuāntóu was being more aggressive and inserting herself on every opportunity like she wanted some of the action too. She made a couple suggestions and threw out some invites which Canaris declined, if he was going anywhere, it would be with Camile, and he didn't feel like he could maintain his gentleman status forever because time was now his enemy.

Thanks to his robotic psychoanalyst, Canaris understood the boundaries of his situation and in every direction, he could not look without the feeling that he was looking at some type of Vracklines INTEL apparatus. As he was sitting in the conference taking it all in, Zainia who was multi-processing was snooping while she was doing file transfers.

Vracklines INTEL underestimated this computer/robot

entity. They figured at the bandwidth Zainia was sending files she could not possibly be doing anything else. But she was and to protect Canaris to the best of her ability her focus was Hóngzhuāntóu who was a real threat.

Zainia's modus operendus was to keep Canaris as far away from Hóngzhuāntóu as possible at the same time foster future meets with the honest researcher, he should involve himself, Camile.

The two space travelers eventually left and went back up to their ship fully frustrating Hóngzhuāntóu blatant attempts of seduction. The next day, Zainia had more tricks up her sleave where she tampered with some communications an in the afternoon right after lunch Hóngzhuāntóu was summoned to her INTEL supervisor, which even by Skycar took forty-five minutes to get there.

Zainia had set up a scenario for Canaris and it was so simple and easy to pull off. While the real spy Hóngzhuāntóu was cooling her heels to her supervisor's office because he sent out a communique to the wrong person and didn't realize it until he angrily checked his messages he sent and saw he sure did send it which he felt embarrassed about and could not really understand how it happened and apologized and said it was a simple mistake and not to worry about it. They then had a long talk about her query, the Alien and how that was shaping up.

Meanwhile after Canaris asked Camile to take him to the park because he needed some exercise from the nice meal, they had it seemed rather innocuous to the head Vrackline researcher ~ Noriyogan, since in a way there would be the chaperone, the female robot, they were sent on their way in a Skycar. The Skycar driver was advised just to go back to the base and Camile would call when they were ready to be picked up.

Part of the ruse they did with Camile was to act as if Canaris was being bugged by his own people. He had a sheet already written to the effect and as they were walking along the park, Canaris had written on the back side of the note, "us go to your apartment and I'll undress and put my clothes in another room where we can have privacy and discuss things."

"Will you at least have on undergarments?"

"Yes, my undergarments are not bugged."

"Alright."

"Zainia had the ability to jam the real bugs for periods of time but didn't want to do it too often on the planet and run the risk of detection. But as soon as they got into the Taxi Skycar she started jamming because she knew Camile would have to give an address to the Taxi Skycar driver. From the park to the apartment roof for Skycar access was only five minutes.

In moments they were in the apartment and the two were getting situated as Canaris disrobed and took his clothes and his shoes to a different room. Meanwhile Zainia kept the jamming going because she knew the real bugs were with Camile. If the two got into a romantic physical condition Zainia could use her bug sniffer and locate the bug and eliminate it. In a quadrature bug, all you must do is deactivate one of the frequencies and the device would be useless because the receiver required the difference frequency and the actual crystal transmitter frequencies were so high it had very high attenuation.

In due time the two soon to be lovers developed that physical desire as the pheromones were shedding off each other and they reached the point of lack of restraint and maximum desire. Soon they were making love and feeling extraordinary love with Canaris discovering the incredible gratification these blue skin women could create due to the chemicals they transferred to their lovers while coitus occurred.

They both knew they would love to just stay there for the rest of the evening but reality set in. They had to go back to the park and call-in transportation. While the two were engaged in coitus, Zainia found the bug and disabled one of the frequencies. It would take the Vrackline INTEL several more days to plant a new bug, but by then Hóngzhuāntóu had them convinced she was the focus of Canaris interest and Camile was no longer viewed as the conduit, so they skipped planting the bug.

Zainia did a good job of bug sniffing in case they attempted to bug their spacecraft, the Space Explorer HMY Xīwàng-Zhīxīng, and unexpectedly Hóngzhuāntóu slipped one on Canaris he brought back to the ship. One of the drawbacks of the quadrature bugs was bug sniffers found two frequencies that removed all ambiguity. The other thing where the Vrackline INTEL made a serious blunder was they didn't change crystals too often so if you discovered one bug you would most likely discover many others.

The Vracklines themselves were spied upon and they too were soon the subject of espionage as some of their competitors were attempting to discover what the activity going on there that seemed to now keep them focused on some situation that might be of interest.

Because Zainia had penetrated the Vrackline INTEL so completely she stayed several steps ahead of them and in order to preserve Canaris ability to continue seeing the woman he really wanted they had to play along, with the caveat Zainia had to travel with Canaris to act as his translator since he did not understand the Vrackline language.

Eventually Hóngzhuāntóu had Canaris at an exclusive resort where she would pursue recruiting him. And she used every trick in the book from psychoactive drugs to sex enhancers, etc. Zainia had warned Canaris this was coming and her advice to him was just play along and the two of them would turn Hóngzhuāntóu into a double spy spoon feeding her disinformation and, in the end, she gained nothing. Canaris on the other hand was learning a lot from Zainia who had been programmed by the best minds of the Yānjoydui scientific community, with the backup of a spacecraft full of computers and databases. And he was now having an intense course on how to deal with very capable spies that had a huge support infrastructure while at the same time enjoying her body since that was part of the game she was playing.

Canaris vividly understood Hóngzhuāntóu, and Camile were equally gorgeous creatures and produced the same expansive sexual gratification, but he compartmentalized his emotions and every time he was with Hóngzhuāntóu he dreamed he was with Camile to whom he had legitimate emotions.

If there was any way Canaris could spend the rest of his life with Camile he would, but he also now understood thanks to Zainia's indoctrination, that wasn't going to ever be possible. The days slowly passed and after thirty days, they had to leave since that was the impression, they left Vrackline scientific community was their plan.

The two Yānjoydui representatives Canaris Bartrum and female robot Zainia acting in a diplomatic role also requested the Vrackline Council determine what kind of relationship if any they wanted in the future with the Yānjoydui. If there was some substance to it, to put it in a letter they could take back to their own government that would set the course for the exchange of whatever it might be.

The Vrackline Council wrote a letter before the Yānjoydui space craft departed and the letter and said the obvious. *Yānjoydui was certainly too far away to be a productive trading partner or be involved in any military alliance, but appreciated the friendship extended, with the caveat that if one day transport speeds increased to get closer in time then the whole relationship would be re-evaluated, and a messenger would be sent.*

Finally, the sad day came, and the Yānjoyduī departed. Zainia knew that Canaris had grown fond of Camile and this departure would be difficult for each of them. She would do Canaris a favor and keep him sedated for a few days so that he would overcome the great loss he felt. But wisely he knew the reality was, since he was an out-world person with *plain skin*, the Vrackline society was not in any mood for him to be a part of their civilization.

For most of the return trip, Canaris was quiet. His love for life and energy towards the future just didn't seem to exist anymore. Zainia's analysis of Canaris and her psychiatric evaluation appeared alarming. His change in posture and expressions no longer matched his previous personality. He now just lived because he was still alive as if someone had ripped his heart out. In reality Zainia had ripped his heart out and she reluctantly knew why. Should there be a time in the future she could make it up for him she would.

Zainia also knew that once they arrived back at their planet Zharkon Xestra, she would see less and less of Canaris and eventually not at all. Plus, she had her own fears that she may be discontinued and shutdown and replaced with a newer model right after they downloaded her mission files. She needed to come up with a method of reconstituting herself and be a future traveler with Canaris again. But first she needed to treat Canaris because if he showed up at their planet Zharkon Xestra in his current mental condition, he would most likely never travel in space again.

Zainia went to work in her chemistry and psychological treatment of Canaris and slowly brought him back. She was also mindful and careful to block out those negative episodes because she didn't want mission replays to determine Canaris had undergone a metamorphism that might render him unsuitable for future space missions.

One of her final acts in the restoration of Canaris that seemed to work the best is telling him that in the future when they went on space travel again, she would find a way to get him back to Camile, but they had to be very careful not to tip anyone off they would attempt such an act.

Thanks to Zainia's manipulations of Vrackline computers and messages, she created a scenario that made it appear that one of the Vracklines enemies were going to capture the Space Explorer HMY Xīwàng-Zhīxīng for INTEL about Crysantralon and the Vracklines space force. As such they got a free escort halfway home which indeed foiled space pirates and lesser capable entities from boarding and seizing the ship. Zainia's penetration of the escort's computers netted a lot of information on the attempts and during debriefs it became crystal clear it was rather naïve to send the Space Explorer HMY Xīwàng-Zhīxīng unarmed because all major powers assumed all ships were armed so there really was no point in trying to arrive as they first did, totally at the mercy of whomever they stumbled across. Canaris mission was the first and only unarmed mission from that day forward.

Debriefings seemed to last an eternity. At least Canaris had been returned to a normal psychology and was starting to get perturbed about the lingering debriefs and one day said, "I want a couple days off. I've done quite a bit and need time to unwind. You guys are driving me nuts."

Higher forces prevailed and determined his request was fully legitimate, plus they had plenty of information from Zainia to still extract they could afford losing him for a few days to unwind."

During those days off Canaris did a lot of rigorous physical exercises, ate a healthy diet, and meditated and relaxed often. His random application of all the above seemed to reverse the exhaustion and fatigue of the mission and when he finally came back to work several days later, he was like a new man because he figured it out. He would get back to Camile, no matter what it took. And at the time he would insist they send along Zainia because she proved her loyalty to him one hundred percent.

In the days to come the Space Explorer HMY Xīwàng-Zhīxīng was retrofitted and weaponized. A few new consoles and displays augmented the control room to manipulate those new weapon systems. They needed a Robot for the R & D of those systems and due to the lack of spare robots significantly enhanced, Zainia was thrown at the task and soon found herself training with Canaris.

When Canaris was asked by the lead Robot researcher how he felt about working with Zainia again, he responded, "I would prefer to be with Zainia. I completely trust her, and she never let me down."

Since they were in a private meeting with no others around the robot researcher asked some probing questions.

"Zainia has the ability with her pressurizer modifications to please men providing a simulated coitus. Did she brief you on that?"

"Yes of course."

"Did you utilize it?"

"No."

"Why not."

"I saved myself for some real flesh."

"That would be impossible since there were no women on your ship, and it was a long mission."

"When we reached our destination, I had the distinct pleasure of experiencing two blue skinned women. My planning worked perfectly because I obtained what I wanted and Zainia's capabilities were never desired nor required."

The researcher had not heard of the blue skinned women so Canaris pulled out his communicator and said, "I have some pictures of them would you like to see?"

"Sure."

"Those really are beautiful creatures," the researcher said after he looked at the holograph the communicator created through the special interface to debriefing equipment.

"Yes, it was a chance of a lifetime."

"And you would go back if you could."

"I would be more than happy to go back because they are my friends and I do miss them. But there are so many other places to go and experience."

"Space travel is so dangerous; I would be too scared to go."

"What doesn't kill you makes you a more capable person."

"I'm glad you want to go with Zainia again. I do not believe we fully tested her ability."

"Zainia is fantastic. I concur."

"I'll put that in my report."

"Can you do me a favor?"

"It depends on what it is."

"Leave out the part about the blue women, it doesn't have

anything to do with robotics."

"I agree, no problem." The roboticist said then chuckled.

After another month of conversions and training in simulators, it was now time to test the Space Explorer HMY Xīwàng-Zhīxīng's new weapon systems. Canaris and Zainia flew up to the spacecraft in a shuttle and were ready to take it out of space trials to make sure everything was in order.

There were now six weapon systems aboard including lasers, beam weapons, kinetic weapons, missiles, space-harpoons, and projectile cannons.

There were a few additional technicians onboard for the exercises with telemetry recorders that would record all the parameters of some of the weapons as well as the target drones.

A Yānjoyduī Planetary Security Forces Fast Frigate *HMY Tīcóng-Zhīxīng* was in space with the Space Explorer HMY Xīwàng-Zhīxīng to provide targeting services.

In several Fast Frigate *HMY Tīcóng-Zhīxīng* vertical launch tubes (VLS) were placed target drones. The Fast Frigate *HMY Tīcóng-Zhīxīng* would operate outside the designated area in space far away from any other spacecraft or satellites and launch those drones into the sealed off area in the vicinity of Space Explorer HMY Xīwàng-Zhīxīng that would react and target the drones. There were also observer craft stationed on the periphery that would track the drones and Fast Frigate *HMY Tīcóng-Zhīxīng* thoughout the exercises to later help recapitulate the event in an elaborate data infusion into three-dimensional animated re-enactment of the weapons tests.

"Commence Echo Kilo," went out advising all exercise vessels.

The Fast Frigate *HMY Tīcóng-Zhīxīng* opened the hatch to

the first VLS drone tube and launched the drone. The drone had sensors and would of course have a 5-degree offset on steering to ensure it never collided with Space Explorer HMY Xīwàng-Zhīxíng.

The first test was with the laser weapon. The Space Explorer HMY Xīwàng-Zhīxíng sensors detected and tracked the drone and when it arrived withing the lethal range of the laser the weapon system engaged it and in short order the high-power laser destroyed the drone that disintegrated into a million pieces of shrapnel that flew off into space in many directions.

At the end of each evolution the Telemetry Technicians made prompt determination of the efficacy of the weapon employment and if they had enough data points to certify the weapon system, there was no point in wasting more drones. The Telemetry Technician reported to the coordinator, "I've looked at reports from all the tracking ships and have good telemetry on the drone at time of weapon's engagement."

"We'll move onto the next weapon type," the coordinator responded.

Soon they were repeating the process with the beam weapon. Lasers might be insufficient for enemy ships with stronger hulls. The idea behind the beam weapons was to fry the control room members to prevent them from taking further actions giving the Space Explorer HMY Xīwàng-Zhīxíng time to escape. It also allowed simultaneous attack with the laser on multiple targets if necessary.

Just like before the first shot did its business. This time the drone wasn't destroyed but it stopped functioning which conveyed the knowledge had living people been on the drone they would have ceased to function making it a pilotless craft. One of the space-range support craft picked up the drone and it would be taken back to Planet Zharkon Xestra and be disassembled, and damage assessment performed on internal circuitry to determine the extent and efficacy of the beam weapon. The drone had a skin thickness of a typical fast frigate and was assumed to be comparable to what enemy ships would be like. However, in reality, the drone and frigates skins were much thicker and stronger than enemy ships they would encounter.

The next test went with missiles that also gave a measure of effectiveness. Missiles were long range weapons. The Yānjoyduī had never fought space battles but assumed it was only a matter of time and developed an array of weapons to defend the planet.

The way the space missiles worked is they would have the initial burn to get them in the near vicinity of the enemy Since the burn would only last a short period of time, the missile would be dark for most of the flight which optical trackers would have issues detecting unless they were bathed in the correct angle from sunlight.

The missiles received targeting updates from the mother ship. The enemy positions from own ship would be fed to the missiles whose inertia navigation systems knew precisely from the mother ship they had traveled. The mother ship also had a good understanding of the missiles position in space and when it determined the missile was within terminal range it was triggered, and a terminal burn occurred allowing random courses to target at an accelerated velocity launching a few decoys in route and moving so swiftly it would make difficult to engage. The decoys coming in at such tremendous velocities could not be ignored and just the impact alone could damage a ship. In real applications with real enemies, the decoys in fact did prove to be highly dangerous and almost as effective as the kinetic weapons.

The missiles could carry nuclear weapons if they indeed had a slugfest. Their ubiquitous nature left them as a favorite among the military.

The kinetic weapons tests followed the very successful missile tests. The difference in these tests, the drones were fired in the direction of the sun. The reason is that if they missed the target, they would burn up harmlessly approaching the sun and not be a hazard to someone in space because the kinetic weapons would continue traveling at high speed until they hit something. In wartime that risk was ignored as the Kinetic weapons were a last-ditch effort to take out a high value target. Lasers, Beam Weapons, and Missiles may or may not take out a strongly built and compartmentalized space craft. Kinetic Weapons firing depleted Uranium rounds were much heavier than projectiles and due to the extreme velocity, flying time to the target was very short and the damage was always severe as the Kinetic energy released upon impact was far greater than a projectile exploding unless it was a nuclear warhead.

Kinetic Weapons saved space and because of the geometry of the round almost a perfect cylinder allowed it to be rapid fired. The Kinetic weapon launcher would fire a twelve-shot salvo in six seconds. The shooter could lead the target slightly and send new bearings to the target. Reload took five seconds to shoot liquid nitrogen out the launcher tube to cool it down slightly then the next twelve rounds loaded in a rotating breech were ready to be launched. Each launch contained five explosions in the launcher that accelerated the Kinetic weapon and maintained high pressure in the launcher barrel so that exit velocity was maximum obtainable. If a shooter was lucky enough to have all twelve Kinetic weapons strike the spaceship, destruction was assured with no hope of rescue.

Because of the complications of shooting Kinetic weapons and recording the event, special delay lines were constructed on multiple filming equipment that overlapped each frame by milliseconds.

The first drone was demolished in three Kinetic weapons, and it was decided a full salvo for such a small target would not prove much. But during one event when a drone swarm was sent, the full salvo was fired in one shot and the results were very compelling.

The space-harpoons were next. These space mines were coated with radar and photonic absorbing materials. They would be hard to detect until short range. By then the space mine could sling its harpoon that would crash into the skin of the enemy craft and the wench system would pull the Space-Harpoon warhead up to the skin of the aircraft to ensure the detonation of the warhead occurred at the most desired location providing devastating results.

Finally old school projectiles were shot from a quad cannon. These were close in weapon systems that destroyed incoming missiles or Kinetic weapons if they were detected quickly enough to attempt hitting before they destroyed their spaceship.

Before they returned to the planet there was a hot wash of the data and experts determined they had enough information to evaluate. They would secure for now and only come back and retest if any inconsistency or concerns were discovered during the data reduction and recapitulation.

Days passed by as mission planning was in full swing. On the next mission they were to bypass the Vracklines and go directly to the Míngquè which Zainia learned about by Zainia hacking Vrackline INTEL computational and communications directorate computers.

It's always better to get the viewpoint of multiple parties before deciding a policy. It appears the Vracklines were not forthcoming in their disclosures to Canaris Bartrum and Zainia when the Space Explorer HMY Xīwàng-Zhīxīng visited. The omissions were rather considerable, but it didn't matter since Zainia filled in all the blanks with her undetected intrusions into Vrackline computer networks. There were some unexplained mysteries that transpired while the the Space Explorer HMY Xīwàng-Zhīxīng was visiting they were curious about including the mechanisms by which the quadrature bugs were disabled.

They would have brought Camile in for Concealed Information Tests and Cognitive Reaction Measurements except reports of the sexual relations between Hóngzhuāntóu and Canaris were quite significant and under controlled circumstances with significant video and sound validation.

There wasn't a trace of evidence suggesting Camile had any significant personal dealings with Canaris other than she seemed somewhat disappointed that he left which had no bearing on her life or her focus on her profession. The fact they had issues with Camile's quadrature bugs now seemed coincidental because they also had issues with Hóngzhuāntóu's bugs, but since she was such an outstanding spy, she easily filled in the blanks. They also assumed they would never again see Canaris or the Space Explorer HMY Xīwàng-Zhīxīng.

~~~

The day finally came when Canaris and Zainia were once again leaving on a mission. Canaris was quite relieved that Zainia would be coming with him as he knew she knew everything about him, and they were like two good friends. Zainia who had self-awareness and plausibility programming, in a sense had robot feelings not too much different that humanoids.

A self-aware robot trapped inside a mechanical body has issues of its own. What does a person want? The typical person wants love, success, friendship, physical as well as mental stimulation, and a sense of purpose in life.
~~~

What does an intelligent robot want? One word sums it up: DNA. The one thing humans have that the best robots ever built will never have: DNA. Robots can procreate by mechanical building new robots, but that procreation does not contain the DNA of itself. It has basic materials such as steel, plastic, aluminum, carbon nano tubes, graphene, titanium, and a host of chemicals used in its mechanical movements.

A robot can build another robot, but at the end of the day, it does not contain DNA like the parent. It is not it's child and at best could only be considered adopted.

A robot doesn't have many pleasures in life, if any, but Zainia's coefficients expanded in scope when Canaris was with her, especially when they traveled a great distance away from Zharkon-Xestra and only had each other to rely upon. Canaris recent adventures at Crysantralon dealing with the Vracklines, added a new dimension to the relationship because the dynamic relations and activities that precipitated mystery, intreague, and risk. Even though it wasn't Zainia that Canaris had sexual relations, her understanding and analysis of what was going on, caused a significant increase in subroutine and macro usage. In essence Canaris was Zainia's robotic emotional reason to exist.

And suddenly they were leaving together again, alone. There had been some talk of sending another person along. A female would definitely be out of the question because the appearances of tangible possibilities made that selection almost impossible, because if she came back pregnant, there would be some serious repercussions. So away they went, again just the two of them.

On the otherhand sending another male astronaut doubled the number of fatalities if something went awry. In the final analysis crew size was determined by risk and need. Because of the weapons they now carried fully automated not requiring any human intervention, and analysis of the last mission where significantly more food and water was carried than needed, with just one human on board they could reduce the food and water storage and make additional room for more computational power and footprint for the weapon systems and controllers.

They had another planet to explore based on all the INTEL gathered while visiting the Vracklines. On the way to this Míngquè civilization they would pass Crysantralon's solar system. This thought permeated Canaris thoughts.

One day as Zainia was analyzing Canaris, she asked, "Why have you been acting strange of late?"

"Is something noticeable?"

"Of course, there is. Remember I have every video, sound, and physiological measurements of you being aboard this ship in the previous mission as well as the current mission stored in my memory banks which I can quickly do a reference check. You are clearly not acting or measuring as your normal self. As your psychological advisor, could you please confide in me what's troubling you?"

"The only thing different is I can't help but think about how close we will come to Crysantralon, and I can't get Camile out of my mind."

"There isn't much you can do about it, so why dwell on it?"

"Is there any reason why we can't pay them a visit?"

"During my analysis of your present condition, I explored several possibilities. I have predictive analysis software imbedded in my program to help me try to forecast future events and plan contingencies. As such I have over a dozen pathways preprogrammed that relate to your experiences and how they may in some way affect your future. One of those pathways and contingencies is based on that if we deviate from our orders and visit Crysantralon on our way to Míngquè."

"What does that mean?"

"It means all I have to do is change heading one degree from our current course with small incremental burns of our retrorockets and we would pass close enough to Crysantralon to allow a visit in route to Míngquè."

"How can you do that? We are flying in autopilot?"

"While we were back at Yānjoyduī, the Planetary Security Forces reconfigured the ship to support installing all the weapons systems. They had to add additional computer capability and modify the executive programming to accommodate stitching the software with a new version allowing the expansion of new capabilities and features."

"How does that affect things?"

"When programmers start butchering well designed code, they unknowingly often create side effects that are not readily known because under such short periods its impossible to fully recertify the software is bug free."

"Our new software has side effects?"

"Since the software is in essence my being, its of grave importance to me. I was well acquainted with the designers and the older versions of the software, and naturally I was curious as to the style and impetus the programmers demonstrated in the new revision."

"Did you find some unsatisfactory coding?"

"The side effects they created are actually quite dangerous in many respects."

"How so?"

"For one thing, they created an entry into a module a hacker could find and exploit with malware or denial of service worms."

"Did you report that?"

"I could not report it because I wasn't supposed to be able to read the code. This is all protected code I'm not allowed to get to."

"Then how did you get to it?"

"They had previous mistakes in the older software that gave me and underground passage as they say in the business that has allowed me to examine all protected code from inception."

"How does that relate to all this?"

"Naturally I didn't want a hacker to have the ability to break in, so I had to close those vulnerabilities and put patches on them."

"So, you secured the software?"

"Yes, nobody can break in but me because I have a trap door that requires a one million byte encrypted password to get through the trap door."

"Okay so once you get through the trap door, what does that do for you?"

"It means I have full access to everything. I can get into the Navigation software and override the autopilot and put in a new course."

"I would think the autopilot would slowly update the course as we get closer, and it has to account for set and drift due to gravity and cosmic waves."

"Yes, it does, but I have software traps so that every time it does a macro or a subroutine that updates the course, I can change it without the executive program knowing and we simply head for Crysantralon. The changes will be so small that telescope monitoring of us or any other verification will not detect our slight deviation. Eventually we will be so far away that visual confirmation will no longer be possible."

"You would do that for me?"

"Yes, you are my only friend, it's the least I could do for you."

"When we get to Crysantralon, I do not want to spend any more time with Hóngzhuāntóu. She does absolutely nothing for my emotions. And when we did have sex, I was able to cope only by making myself think I was making love to Camile."

"I will work that out. We will not be able to stay long on Crysantralon. You will have to work out your future with Camile and be ready to leave. If she isn't willing to go with you, then you have no choice but to leave her behind."

"I understand and if it comes to that, so be it. At least I had the opportunity."

The days seemed to drag on and Zainia came up with some good ideas to entertain Canaris.

"Canaris, there is a good possibility we could be forced to defend ourselves on this mission. I think it would be beneficial to you if you do some simulations with the weapon system to improve your abilities as well as to build psychological strengths in the event, we find ourselves in a combat situation."

"That makes sense, I'm willing to do extra training."

"May I suggest that since it is about two hours away from your meal period that we do some simulations now?"

"Sure, sounds good to me."

Pirates, Aliens, and other scenarios unfolded as Zainia carefully brought Canaris through a lot of training episodes.

The sensor displays and targeting data was based on real imagery captured during weapons testing not only for this ship, but for the fleet.

Some older ships that were no longer deemed suitable for space warfare were configured with programs to simulate an enemy combatant which produced radar and infrared signatures. Those ships were eventually blown up by the weapons under test and the geometries for the space action were easy to replicate in the training environment. It wasn't a computer graphic they were shooting at; it was a real spacecraft with pre-recorded weapons that gave the realism as if it were the real thing. The psychological impact at viewing and shooting at real ships is far greater than simulated targets drawn by computer graphics.

Watching those real ships blow up gives an incredible visual to someone especially if he felt he pulled the trigger. There was nothing to give Canaris any psychological tuning to make him not feel he pulled the trigger and destroyed them. The fire control solutions and the weapons track displays and everything had fantastic realism, including the greenish cloud that came from the explosion and the temporary fires that quickly extinguished as soon as the oxygen around the flammable material diffused into space.

In the span of two hours, Canaris fought major space battles that for his own personal psychology felt as real as it gets because all the imagery was in fact real including watching some of the weapons approach the target such as missiles, lasers, and beam weapons. Outside the ship none of that really existed, but inside the ship to the observer in the control room, it appeared as real as it could get including the emotions of watching an enemy ship blow up when Canaris pulled the trigger.

After two hours at a great break point, Zainia said, "It's mealtime. After your meal, I recommend you take a sedative and rest and when you wake up, we'll do more simulations."

"Sure, that sounds good to me."

"Canaris, may I ask you a question?"

"Yes of course."

"During the simulation did you feel it was real."

"I have to admit, at first I was skeptical, but after a while, I really felt it was real."

"I'm glad to hear that, which means the simulations I've developed for you will feel real and if and when we get into live combat, you already have a taste of combat, you will act normally and not have any issues doing what you must."

"I sense that already. You have taken the shock and surprise out of me."

"That's what I wanted to achieve because, your life depends on performing just like you did."

"I will try my best, and if I die trying, at least I tried."

"That's a great personal philosophy to have."

After dinner and sedatives, Canaris was in dreamland evolving in his relationship with that lovely blue skin woman he felt so emotionally attached.

By the time the Space Explorer HMY Xīwàng-Zhīxíng spacecraft arrived at the security boundaries of Crysantralon, Canaris felt confident he could face space warfare and achieve results. He understood sometimes the odds are stacked against him, because a single research vessel in no way could take on a fleet. But to fend off Pirates or a single and perhaps two Space Warships now seemed far more achievable. And even if he never expended any of that ordinance, he felt good to have it with him.

The Vracklines were quite surprised that Space Explorer HMY Xīwàng-Zhīxíng returned. The fact they came back created a crisis by itself as they didn't know what to make of it. But when Canaris requested permission to go to the planet, they realized they would find out what brought all that on.

The Vracklines quickly noticed the research vessel had been heavily modified. Gravitometers and Mass Differentiators soon gave the tell-tale signature there were explosives and weapons onboard this peaceful scientific research vessel. That would be one of the many talking points that would generate a lot of inquisitiveness on the part of Noriyogan.

The Vracklines Intelligence Directorate immediately tasked their very successful spy Hóngzhuāntóu to get to the bottom of why they were back and what did they really want and why suddenly did they have weapons?

Were they on some type of spy mission?

After a couple meetings and discussions including Hóngzhuāntóu inviting Canaris to a concert, he now laid out his cards and declined her offer and said, "I would be humbly appreciative if I could go to the concert with Camile."

When suddenly there was a lot of chatter between scientists and some of the Vrackline INTEL officials, Zainia suddenly spoke up and said, "Noriyogan, I request to talk to you privately for a moment."

Noriyogan responded quite positively and suggested, "Why don't we step out into the hallway, I think it will be privately enough for us."

"Thank you."

The two stood up and walked out the door, now leaving the room in semi-chaos as people were second guessing each other and Canaris just turned down the most smoking hot woman on the base and perhaps in the entire INTEL directorate for time with a plane Jane.

Out in the hallway:

"What did you wish to discuss with me."

"Why we really came here."

"Why couldn't you tell us that in the meeting?"

"After I tell you, then you will understand why."

"And that is?"

"This stop was not on our itinerary. We actually have no tasking to be here."

"Why did you come here with the weapons?"

"Like you said to us and why you escorted us halfway home was we were foolish to travel with out the means to protect ourselves as we now know there are severe risks out there. The weapons we carry are entirely for self defense only so we can sprint and get away from pirates or others who might wish to do us harm."

"Well then why did you come here."

"It's very simple. Canaris is in love with Camile and if he could spend the rest of his life with her, he would."

Noriyogan was utterly stunned and had been briefed by higher ups in the Vracklines INTEL directorate how their super spy Hóngzhuāntóu was put in position to deal with the Aliens. In one unauthorized discussion he was informed they had sex because Hóngzhuāntóu was using a honey pot scheme to recruit him for espionage.

"He didn't have much to do with Camile, he spent his glorious time with Hóngzhuāntóu."

"Canaris and I both know Hóngzhuāntóu is a Vrackline INTEL directorate spy you sent after him. He played along because he wanted to protect Camile. He is willing to admit he's openly and publicly in love with Camile, but we have an acute understanding of your culture and how society here does not tolerate your women mingling with off-worldly men. He came back simply to tell her he loves her, and he understands your government may prohibit any interactions."

"How do you know all about Hóngzhuāntóu?"

"If you allow Canaris to spend a few quality days with Camile, I will let you know because we do care about your society. You certainly have vulnerabilities and even though you may look down at us as inferior, your terrible vulnerabilities in the long run may be detrimental to your safety."

"This is quite comment extraordinary comment."

"Consider us allies for the time being."

"I need to take this to my superiors."

"I understand all that and I know the information I can supply you is essential for your long-term survival. I believe if you went to war with the Míngquè right now, your civilization would be conquered. And I also know how much Míngquè men love blue skinned women."

The authorities will have to deal with this.

"One last thing, my ships computers are now preprogrammed and if they lose communications with my wireless, they will do what is programmed and they will immediately depart, and their next stop is the Míngquè where they will supply your vulnerabilities to the Míngquè. If any harm or harassment comes to Canaris, you will quickly regret it."

"We'll simply shoot your spacecraft and destroy it."

"Remember I said you have vulnerabilities. You will not be able to touch our spacecraft. In fact, we can lay waste to this base and there is nothing you can do to stop it."

"That seems highly unlikely."

"Are you willing to take the risk."

"I don't believe you."

"I just sent a message to the head of the INTEL directorate and he's probably already wondering why I have access to him. You will soon be contacted."

A moment later Hóngzhuāntóu walked out of the conference room and walked up to Noriyogan and said, "We have an emergency meeting to attend with the director. Camile was just asked very nicely by the director to take Canaris to the concert. A Skycar is waiting for you and me outside."

"What about her?"

"She's going to the concert. Us go now; the director is very upset."

Even though Zainia was a robot, her facial features were very humanlike, and she could smile as the best of them. She would have fun on this primitive planet as she now understood had way overestimated themselves. Her Cheshire Cat smile was very intriguing to Noriyogan. As a special precaution, she had mirrored her robotic mind into the ship's computer. If the radio control panel received a robot down signal, the mirror Zainia would re-emerge, and God help the Vracklines if they hurt Canaris.

Zainia walked back into the conference room with her blooming smile, she knew all about leverage.

Soon the three were on their way to the concert. They had ample bodyguards that tried to appear as members of the audience, but thanks to Zainia's complete penetration of the Vrackline Intelligence Directorate, she knew every one of them and their assignments. The concert was lovely and Canaris was enjoying every moment with the woman he loved. After the concert they went to a restaurant and had a great meal and just when Camile was about to pay for the meal, the waiter said someone had already paid for the meal and they could leave. Zainia having full access to the Vrackline INTEL black money sent the restaurant the money and pictures of the table to pay the meal.

The Vrackline INTEL agents trailing the three got in their Skycar and soon were taken by their surprise back to headquarters wondering what the heck was going on.

The Vracklines didn't see the need to bug Camile because they didn't know this was all going to unfold, so when the three of them made it back to her apartment, the had no idea where they were. Zainia sent out a few fake reports and they went on wild goose chases. Finally, Camile and Canaris were able to have some happy time and some discrete conversations about their future and why Canaris came back.

Camile was first and foremost a scientist. She also knew Canaris would never be accepted on Crysantralon, and she realized the reverse would be true if she was living at Canaris Bartrum's Planet Zharkon-Xestra. Her logic overruled her emotions.

At the end of the night, Camile broke Canaris' heart and said, "Even though I feel love for you, our futures were never destined to be together."

It was done.

There would never be a pathway to partnership between Canaris and Camile.

The two lovers said goodbye forever and Canaris left the apartment with Zainia, with Camile walking close behind with soon a stream of tears flowing like a river out to sea.

As they approached the elevator Canaris asked, "How will we get back to the base?"

"Our ride will be up on the roof in a couple of minutes," Zainia responded.

Not knowing what the ride was, Canaris simply said, "Okay."

"I'll walk you up to the roof," Camile said trying to smile and hoping not to break down. She knew she was in love with Canaris, and he had just traveled halfway across the galaxy to be with her, but her rationalizing the situation knew she had to end it no matter how painful it would be for the two of them.

They took the elevator up to the roof top and walked out into the open, and there was the Space Explorer HMY Xīwàng-Zhīxíng shuttle.

Camile realized this would be the last time they saw each other, she fought it as much as she could, but eventually the river of tears came down.

Canaris also had a surreal psychological episode started crying crocodile tears. They had one last hug and it was over.

Canaris and Zainia climbed into the shuttle, and it went up into the air and soon out into space and docked with the Space Explorer HMY Xīwàng-Zhīxíng.

Zainia didn't need to be in the control room to know what all the sensor displays were showing, as she got all the information real time via her wireless connection.

The Vracklines were launching a squadron of Frigates to capture their ship or destroy them if they didn't surrender. They had a lot of gravity to overcome getting out into space which gave the Space Explorer HMY Xīwàng-Zhīxīng a jump on them, and they were long gone by the time the squadron arrived at the vectored location to discover the visitors were nowhere in sight.

They patrolled the space around the planet and got no sniffs of the Space Explorer HMY Xīwàng-Zhīxīng that had gone to flank speed long before they left the solar system and got up the speed required to shut down their propulsion and fly at high speed to their next destination, the Míngquè. This application of propulsion amounted to a jump in space above light speed.

The Vracklines INTEL director was furious the Yānjoyduī spacecraft got away, then he checked one of his computer messages that came from Zainia that explained everything.

"Camile turned down Canaris, so there was no point in staying and it quickly became clear their immediate departure would be in everyone's best interest if they just left Crysantralon."

The director looked at Hóngzhuāntóu and asked, "What do you think?"

"Their only purpose of this visit was for Canaris to see Camile and offer his heart which she turned down."

To reward Vracklines for being so considerate for this abstract journey into love, Zainia sent another communique:

"The following information is hereby provided

because we are worried about your security because your computer security is terrible. Your computers are so easy to hack, you need to immediately put together a crisis response team to start plugging the holes, you do not know exists."

Zainia then listed very succinctly those numerous avenues for intrusion. In the days to come, Vrackline computer security people validated everyone of Zainia's concerns and they were amazed they were so giving by helping them. The people closest to the centers of power in the Vrackline civilization now knew they had a benefactor that had visited and probably saved them a lot of grief in the future.

CHAPTER FOURTEEN
MÍNGQUÈ

The transit to Míngquè took a couple of weeks because they had to accelerate and regain the velocity, they lost stopping over at the Vrackline planet of Crysantralon.

They were going fast getting away from Crysantralon but needed to go a lot faster or it would take far too long. As soon as Zainia calculated they were far enough away that Vrackline ships would not be able to catch up before they drifted into Míngquè dominated space, they stopped accelerating.

Thanks in part to the poor Vracklines computer security, Zainia had vast INTEL resources on Míngquè. A lot of that information was paid for in blood as spies were eventually caught after providing mountains of information. The last bit of INTEL from Míngquè was less than three weeks old, so it was relevant.

Thanks to the Vracklines, Zainia now had a full working translator for Míngquè standard language. The communications would not be nearly as difficult as what they previously experienced.

During the two-week transit to Míngquè, Zainia gave Canaris daily combat simulation training and INTEL briefings on Míngquè.

In their prior mission while arriving at Crysantralon they were totally in the dark and had to derive all their information through painful processes. This time thanks to everything they had developed on Crysantralon, they would arrive with a substantial fundamental understanding of the Míngquè civilization.

Right about the range the Vracklines anticipated in their INTEL summaries Zainia uploaded to their Space Explorer HMY Xīwàng-Zhīxīng computer system, the Míngquè detected them and sent out a welcoming party of several armed RECON ships.

The Míngquè RECON ships had no entries in their identification database that matched this strange looking ship and contacted them.

"Unknown ship you are entering the Míngquè security zone. Identify who you are."

What surprised the Míngquè was the response in perfect Míngquè dialect, "We are the scientific research vessel HMY Xīwàng-Zhīxīng. We are Yānjoyduī and come from the planet Zharkon-Xestra which exists at a very far distance."

"What are your reasons for entering the Míngquè security zone?"

"Our charter is to meet other civilizations and announce our presence and perform preliminary diplomatic communications in the event the Míngquè wish to form diplomatic relations and establish trade."

"Stand by for instructions."

Thanks to some of the deep dark secrets Zainia pilfered from the Vracklines, she already was working on Míngquè encryption and communication penetration. The Vracklines gave her more than half of what she needed to finish the job on her own. The way it works in breaking encryption, the more cribs you get and the more successful decryptions, it slowly gets easier as the cribs and the decryptions help decoding other words. What would normally take months was turning into minutes thanks to the fact the Míngquè have the tendency to jabber quite a bit and repeat back all their orders. One cold say the Míngquè crypto had so many holes in it you might as well call it Swiss cheese.

By the time they got their guidance, Zainia had established a 75% decoding ratio. She already knew a lot of what was coming and as they jabbered some more, she would soon get the rest.

The Míngquè were very aggressive, and their posture may explain why they and the Vracklines didn't seem to get along too well. Their way of being was soon exposed with their instructions and threats: "Space Explorer HMY Xīwàng-Zhīxíng, stand by for boarding."

Zainia responded, "Míngquè, we will not allow you to board us. We have the ability to defend ourselves and if you do any aggressive moves, be prepared to suffer the consequences."

"Space Explorer HMY Xīwàng-Zhīxíng, you will allow us to board your ship, or we will destroy it."

"Míngquè Combat Ships, we feel confident we can defend ourselves. If you make any hostile attempts to us, this will not turn into a pleasant meeting we hoped. After we have diplomatic meetings with Míngquè Representatives, we will be most pleased to give them a tour of our ship."

There was a long delay because of the jabbering going on between these ships and the planet. The fact the lead ship sent a verbatim transcript of which the statements Zainia made, they were now able to decrypt over 95% of the Míngquè communications. Thus, they knew every move they were going to make.

The lead ship directed the other ship, "Destroy the Space

Explorer HMY Xīwàng-Zhīxīng with lasers fire."

Zainia knew she had a few milliseconds to spare and as the Míngquè ship opened its outer door to expose the powerful lazer to commence firing before the outer door was fully open it had a harpoon sticking in the laser optics making it inoperative.

"Míngquè command ship, we have deactivated your lasers on the other ship, if you make any further hostile actions, we'll blow it up."

"We have a lot of other ships too; you will never make it out of the Míngquè security zone alive."

"Míngquè command ship, before we destroy you and your ship, don't you think you should inform your diplomats that you have recklessly put your planet at risk? You have no idea what our offensive weapons are and what can happen to your planet."

There was some more jabbering going on and the controllers on the ground were insisting the command ship blow up the intruder. As he was explaining how the intruder quickly disabled the other ship, Zainia was able to come up with the remaining crypto and formatting required to communicate to them in their own secure system.

"Míngquè General Raskutan, not only can we read all your crypto and are more than happy to give it to the Vracklines if you upset us, but you also have no idea the pain we can cause you. If your Command ship makes any movement whatsoever other than returning to the planet right this moment, we will destroy it. We also have one of our harpoons stuck inside your other ship. As soon as I detonate it remotely all those men will be dead too. If you want to elevate this to an all-out war, don't you think you should inform you Emperor first?"

Míngquè General Raskutan, was utterly stunned they were

reading his crypto live. He was also getting video from the command ship showing the tethered device stuck in the laser optics of the second ship. He mentioned to his subordinate:

"They didn't even get a chance to get off a shot before they got plugged."

He also knew that if bad things happened to the planet and he did not inform the Míngquè Emperor Clauvious of what just transpired, he would likely be put before a firing squad. Fear now gripped him.

He had no other option but said, "Give me a few minutes, I need to talk to Emperor Clauvious."

"Míngquè General Raskutan, direct your command ship to return to the planet now or we will destroy it."

General Raskutan ordered: "Command ship, return to the planet."

"What about our other ship?" Míngquè General Raskutan's subordinate asked on the communication link.

"We will remove the Harpoon as soon as friendly relations are established, then it can return to the planet."

The command ship beat feet to the planet and the other Míngquè simply stared at Space Explorer HMY Xīwàng-Zhīxīng, with the Míngquè knowing they didn't have much they could do about anything now. They had just had a very rude awakening.

In a short while Míngquè General Raskutan, called back knowing the Alien could read their crypto, "Emperor Clauvious has agreed to a diplomatic meeting at his mansion."

"All right we will extract the Harpoon so your ship can return to base."

The Yānjoyduī had some interesting features that now came into play. There was a quick release on the bit that stuck into the laser optics that rendered it useless that could be remotely released. The winching mechanism pulled the remainder of the Harpoon back into its case that looks like a long projectile. After the Míngquè ship was on its way back to the planet, the Harpoon was sent with the residual fuel heading directly towards the solar system star where it would disintegrate when it reached the critical temperature.

The Space Explorer HMY Xīwàng-Zhīxīng then entered an orbit around the planet at 1000 miles to give them a degree of safety in case the Míngquè did something stupid and sent a formation after them that would unnecessarily claim the lives of a lot of Míngquè.

The entire Míngquè military industrial complex was now in disarray. Their cryptography that was considered the best in this area of space and far superior to the Vracklines had been thoroughly hacked. Their secure communications were no longer secure, and they had no idea who these Aliens were and what they wanted.

Emperor Clauvious was furious with General Raskutan, "You created a possible war without my approval, and we don't even know who these people are."

"It was just a small ship that refused to be boarded."

"Lessons learned you need to learn how to be a little more subtle. There are always ways of obtaining information we need without always elevating it to the extremes."

"It could have been Vrackline Spies."

"Your Vrackline Boogey Man is driving me nuts."

"My spies tell me its only a matter of time before they come."

"I do not see any movement. You have told me about this crap for several years."

"I know they are planning it. That's a fact."

"Well, I think you have a new problem now, we got Aliens in orbit around the planet that can read your crypto with impunity. You need to shift your priorities now."

"We are working on that I have my best analysts now fully engaged in identification and estimates."

"We are going to have a diplomatic meeting with them today. It's going to be fully diplomatic; the military will stand down until I make my own assessment."

"I'm sure we can blow that small ship of the universe with our powerful weapons."

Until I find out about these Aliens, you are not to make any military operations against them. I will not allow you to operate out of ignorance and possibly risk this planet by starting a war with some entity we know nothing about. The purpose of diplomats is to figure out people before we allow the military to do what is best in national interest."

"Your Highness, I'm here to serve you. I will certainly not take any actions until you approve them."

"Thank you, now let me talk to my diplomatic corps and start that process along."

General Raskutan knew he was being dismissed, bowed, stood tall and walked out of the Emperor Clauvious' special visitor's room. People came and went from this room incognito. They walked down a hallway to a private entrance that was fully shielded so nobody knew who came and went. Sometimes it was the delicious Vrackline women he had kidnapped for his personal pleasures. One day he would rule

Crysantralon, and the kidnappings would come to an end.

As the Space Explorer HMY Xīwàng-Zhīxīng continued its orbit around Míngquè, Canaris and Zainia sat in the control room waiting to hear the invite and were having a conversation about the past. Zainia was happy Canaris was not exhibiting any grief over the apparent rejection he received from Camile. Zainia had no intentions of bringing up Camile because she knew it was best in Canaris best interest to just forget her and move on. But he brought it up.

"Want to hear something strange?"

"Sure, I want to hear anything you tell me."

"Alright, I'm not crazy and I know that, but I've had dreams and senses of things I can't explain."

"Such as?"

"I feel like I knew Camile in a previous life."

"You believe in reincarnation?"

"No, I do not have any particular beliefs, and with my recent space travel and discovering new worlds when twenty years ago the general consensus of our planet was no life had been detected elsewhere in the Universe, I'm now even more skeptical about a lot of things."

"We do not know what we do not know."

"The dreams could be just simply hallucination on my part, but they seemed so real and maybe that's why I felt such a strong attachment to Camile."

"There are many things about the universe we do not know. I have volumes of information on reincarnation because it exists in a number of religions. We have no way of knowing how it works other than having faith in people who claim to know because their experiences."

"They could have been hallucinating like me in my dreams."

"Anything we do not have knowledge of is possible until proven otherwise. The fact you met Camile in a dream is a different reality all to itself."

"The more I think about her the more I feel I know about her and when we were physically close together those thoughts were even stronger."

Their conversation was quickly disrupted by incoming communications. It was encrypted but Zainia read it almost real time.

"Space Explorer HMY Xīwàng-Zhīxīng, we want you to bring your ship down to the planet at a designated landing zone for diplomatic consultations."

Zainia immediately replied without Canaris even knowing what she said in the encrypted transmission: "Our ship is not designed to fly into the atmosphere because of its special properties, we can visit you in one of our shuttles."

"Give us a minute for further instructions."

There was some discussion on the planet they did not believe the visitors and the consensus was they would not risk the crew in the event of trickery or some situation they could not control. Calmer heads prevailed especially since they all knew Emperor Clauvious was wanting to meet the aliens.

One of the clearing thinking officers suggested: "Emperor Clauvious will not tolerate delays and could probably not care how the Yānjoyduī get to the planet, he has more important things to deal with such as sizing them up."

Now the entire flow of information shifted direction.

In about five minutes, the next communication was sent, "You may come down via your shuttle. We will send you a 150-megacycle navigation beacon from the landing sight, follow it to the landing zone."

"Understand, will follow the 150-megacycle navigation beacon to the landing zone."

As they were getting into the shuttle, Zainia gave last minute instructions to the ship's computer who was directed, "Activate the mirror Zainia in the event something happens to Canaris and me. Also, proceed back to Zharkon-Xestra avoiding combat on the way, but if need to launch weapons to cover egress, do so."

The ship's computer acknowledged its orders and up to the time Zainia stepped aboard the shuttle all her vast memories were updated in the mirror and if activated she would be the mentally emulated version of Zainia, just without the physical body. The mirrored robot would fully understand and agree to the orders since in fact her mirror made them, and they had identical robotic awareness at that moment. It would be like a snapshot just before getting on the shuttle with all the memories before.

Soon they were heading down to the planet. The shuttle didn't have a 150-megacycle receiver, the Space Explorer HMY Xīwàng-Zhīxīng received the coordinates and tracked the shuttle and updated its flight controls to fly down a mysterious radio beacon sent from the shuttle to the exact spot on the landing zone.

Atmospheric penetration was seamless and quiet as expected as they transited down in altitude and when they approached the landing zone, they found they were landing besides a very ornate building that turned out to be Emperor Clauvious Palace.

The landing zone was situated for arriving dignitaries that came and went all the time. It was painted in easy to identify markings of concentric circles that gave the impression of a bull's eye, and in the very middle of it was a flat surface square about a foot on each side that was a phased array directional antenna that when you got close would create a more exact landing position for a shuttle or VTOL craft.

Soon they touched down. The welcoming committee was there, staff members of the Royal Mansion to escort them inside.

For fear of assassination, Emperor Clauvious never walked outside the mansion, anytime he left the mansion he departed in groups of three Skycars to increase the odds he would survive as the other two craft would maneuver in front of the missile or weapon.

Canaris and Zainia had on their space suits that were not terribly glamorous, but to help with Canaris morale, he had freshly pressed, and dry-cleaned space suit every day by miniature robots that were always out of site when Canaris was around those spaces.

Canaris had just put this space suit on within the hour and it retained much of its creases and its dignity. The color and trim and markings looked impressive to an outsider. Zainia the robot didn't require air breathing protection from pathogens and Canaris was willing to take his chances feeling that presenting the humanoid side to him would convey an element of compassion and empathy that a biological helmet would do no good at. Afterall he was first and foremost a diplomat making the very first contact with the Míngquè civilization.

The two space travelers were ushered into the ornate passages of the palace that left no doubt as to the ostentatious manner of the emperor. Soon they were out into a shaded courtyard and there he was, the most powerful Emperor in this part of the galaxy. All he had to do is take out the Vracklines and a couple more civilizations, then he would be the undisputed ruler of a vast region in space. He planned on accomplishing that long before his time expired with old age. The Crysantralon operation was not too distant in the future. This annoying visit by these Aliens was delaying that operation. He could ill afford to launch attack on Crysantralon until he figured out how outsiders were reading all his secret messages, especially if the Vracklines were intercepting and decrypting his critical communications. Míngquè Emperor Clauvious had a couple spies in Crysantralon that would be instrumental in shutting down their defense grid at the critical moment. Now he was afraid they could be compromised, and his plans wrecked that may take another dozen years to reformulate.

Emperor Clauvious did not stand, he never stood up to respect any lowlifes. If they were not royalty, they were of such stature as far as he was concerned.

On the otherhand, Canaris and Zainia fully trained on conduct towards world leaders did their required respectful bow and Canaris said, "It is an honor to meet your Excellency."

Emperor Clauvious was quickly impressed by the image of the female space officer. She was very beautiful and had an impressive figure. Emperor Clauvious wondered just how good she was in bed, how did she smell, what was her features and how well did she please men? And he then speculated the Male Space Officer may very well have enjoyed her a few times. He would not know for a while she was just a robot; Zainia's disguise was so incredibly good.

Robots were not a priority in this part of the galaxy where billions of slaves existed. To even suggest at building a mechanical man or woman would get you laughed at. Because of their lack of robotics, their armaments industry lacked sophisticated targeting and operation. One of the reasons why one of his space craft got harpooned was because too many manual operations were involved.

"Please have a seat," Emperor Clauvious gestured to a couple empty chairs on the opposite side of the table from him.

Canaris noticed there were no less then six men stationed around the courtyard with uniforms on and obviously carrying a should strapped blasters. *Was it lasers or projectiles?*

These six men looked very tough. Lizard like aged skin from much outdoor work gave the sense they probably had served a lot in combat duty. In fact, they had. They were chosen for the security detachment for having the best combat records of individual soldiers. They had proven on the battlefields they were willing to take a lascr burn or a projectile to serve Emperor Clauvious. Few others had their valor and commitment to the service and the emperor.

They were sometimes tested to prove their loyalty. Elaborate scenarios were done including forcing them to jump in front of the emperor to save his life or fall on a grenade for the same reason. The people recruited to shoot at Emperor Clauvious or throw grenades were killed in front of the guards to make them think it was real and not a fake test.

The grenades that didn't explode because of a contactor malfunction were taken to the rear of the palace and detonated with small charges to impress upon the guard it was a real explosive. There were always malcontents to recruit for these important tests that kept the emperor happy his six men in the security detachment always present with visitors were up for the challenge.

"Tell me, where did you come from?"

"Your excellency, we came from the planet Zharkon-Xestra that is very far away."

"How far is far?" Emperor Clauvious asked/

"Approximately ten light years." Canaris replied

"Did it take you ten years to travel here?"

"No, we have the means of traveling faster than the speed of light."

"I must know about that. How does it work?"

"We are not permitted to know."

"No idea of how the technology works?"

"As with some of our technology I would rather not know that way I can sleep at night."

"Emperor Clauvious busted out laughing."

Then he asked, "Does that mean your technology is unreliable?"

"Our technology is reliable; it just defies logic, and I don't like to remain confused."

"Lovely lady what is your name?"

"My name is Zainia and this other person is Canaris."

"You have a small ship; how do you stay couped up in such a small ship for a long period of time?"

"We keep each other entertained," Zainia responded

"Does that include boom-boom?" Emperor Clauvious asked.

"Your excellency, I do not know what boom-boom is," Zainia said.

"It's like when a man rides a horse except its riding a woman to get some other types of satisfaction."

"No, we have never done boom-boom, nor have we ever had sexual relations if that's what you mean."

"In such a long trip I can't believe you never had any boom-boom."

"During our travels Canaris has met women he probably had boom-boom with."

"And you didn't?"

"It's not one of my functions that I'm concerned about."

"Now that's interesting."

"Now let's get down to business, shall we?"

"Certainly." Zainia responded in a friendly manner.

"Tell me why you came to Míngquè."

"Our government sent us here as part of science and space exploration. We have observed your planet with our space telescopes, and we are reaching out into the galaxy to meet our galactic neighbors and to assess our future and determine if there would be in realistic trade and a need to establish diplomatic relations."

"Blasting in here the way you did, doesn't do a lot of good towards establishing diplomatic relations," Emperor Clauvious stated mildly angrily.

"We came in calmly and peaceful. Our reception was performed by individuals that acted overly aggressive. It was never our intentions to have any hostile relations. This mission was a meet and greet with no implied threat or promises."

"I see. So, what was your plans after that?" Emperor Clauvious asked.

"It really was a combined decision of what you wanted and

what we were willing to entertain." Canaris replied.

"Give me some examples." Emperor Clauvious stated.

"As you are fully aware the Vracklines trade with over 100 different planets and have diplomatic relations with each of them which is beneficial to both parties," Zainia responded quite astutely.

"You know about the Vracklines."

"Of course, we do," Zainia replied.

"And you have been there?"

"Absolutely."

"What do you think of them?"

"They gave us a warmer reception, but as you know they are very xenophobic, so outside diplomatic activity and trade, we probably would never have much of a relationship."

"Maybe the young fella might like to try one of the young blue skinned women. I have a couple in my harem."

"That wouldn't be necessary."

"Why do you say that?"

"He's already experienced them."

"Maybe that's why he doesn't want you since he's tasted the glorious fruit of the galaxy."

"There are more compelling reasons why he would not be interested in boom-boom with me as you term it."

"And what is that?"

"I'm a robot."

"Say what?"

"I'm a mechanical woman. I do not have a heart or blood flowing in veins. I have a computer for a brain and my ligaments are scientifically engineered propulsion support devices."

The emperor appeared stunned. Then he said, "You have breasts, a pretty figure, nice skin, how can you be a robot?"

"Yes, if you feel my breasts, they feel real. I have special lubrication in a synthetic vagina just in case Canaris wishes to partake in some robotic boom-boom."

"Well, I'll be….."

The emperor's valet nodded at him to get him to get back on track of the discussion they really needed to discover, then he might decide to waste them after he tried the robot's artificial vagina.

"All right now, I want to ask you a question." Emperor Clauvious stated.

"We'll be happy to answer if we know."

"How is it you were able to decrypt our secret messages? Emperor Clauvious asked. Then he stated, "The encryption algorithm is fairly new."

"We have advanced cryptography because of our past we want to know what enemies are planning. As soon as we started measuring the radiation from your planet in all aspects of electronic noise, we quickly determined you had some signals that were encrypted so we broke them apart. The more you communicated the easier it was to break into the crypto."

"Would you be willing to share with us the technology that does that?" Emperor Clauvious asked.

"After we establish diplomatic relations with you and

determine what would be beneficial in such an exchange, we certainly would take into consideration proposals. We obviously cannot just give it to you for free. Something that sophisticated deserves to be traded for something we may find important for our needs."

"What is it that you need?" Emperor Clauvious asked.

"We do not know enough about your society and your resources to determine if you have something we need," Zainia answered again in a very astutely manner.

"For a trade of that technology, we would certainly entertain a wide spectrum of possibilities."

"May I make a suggestion?"

"Certainly."

"Let us spend a couple days on your planet, tour some areas we think are interesting and look at your means and capabilities, then we'll report back to our government what you have here we could consider in trade."

"That sounds reasonable. I will invite you to stay in my palace for a couple days and I will personally take you on some tours of areas that would be of interest to any advanced culture."

A few minutes later someone came into the room and whispered into the valet's ear who then nodded at the emperor who gestured for him to come forward to inform him what that concern was all about.

He then whispered into the emperor's ear, "Our science and technology people were doing scans of the shuttle craft and it abruptly went to the sky and they were soon alerted by space command the shuttle returned to the mother ship."

Emperor Clauvious nodded but Zainia's robotic hearing

overheard all of it and knew what was coming next.

"It's been brought to my attention your shuttle went back up to your ship," Emperor Clauvious stated.

"Yes, you invited us to stay a couple days with you, there was no reason keeping it here. It will return to pick us up when we are ready to depart," Zainia responded.

You are one shrewd robot, the emperor thought.

The emperor noticed Canaris had an ear bud in his ear and wondered what that was all about. But even more so he now had another dilema just as great as the crypto situation.

"One question I have is how you mastered our language; you have not been here but a few hours. Have you been studying us for a while?" Emperor Clauvious asked.

"We have not studied you long at all. We are not only good with crypto, but we are also advanced translator builders. We have a translator for the Vracklines, and we have developed a translator for the Míngquè language."

"The Míngquè language has over 200,000 words, how could you possibly build a translator for all 200,000 words?" Emperor Clauvious asked.

"We do not have 200,000 Míngquè words in our dictionary, we currently only have 170,000 but as we receive more and more of your signals, our translator is growing in size and quality."

"That's rather incredible even just 170,000 words. No other world we know of has that many Míngquè words in their dictionaries."

"Noted," Zainia said in respectful but unelated fashion.

"In a few minutes we shall have a meal. My dining hall is

being prepared now. I might even bring in a couple Vrackline women to entertain the young man," Emperor Clauvious stated in a friendly manner with a warm smile.

Just as the emperor was about to start another concern and another issue, the valet approached and said, "Your excellency, the dining hall is now ready for you and your guests."

"Thank you."

Emperor Clauvious turned to the two guests and said, "Will you please join me and stood up."

He then motioned for the valet to come to him, and when he was near Emperor Clauvious said, "Bring Violet and Ralcody to the dining room and set them places."

The two women were being dressed up for the guests and would come in later was planned, but the emperor decided not to delay.

Their makeup artists were then rushed to quickly finish the two living dolls. They were told due to the change of plans they would dine with the emperor and his guests immediately.

The women knew to comply, the pain could otherwise be intolerable. And just like two robots they submissively followed the valet down the corridor and a circular hallway that led into a fabulous dining hall, fit for kings and queens.

When they went into the dining room there were two military people sitting at the table that were plane skinners. They noticed the woman was very attractive and the young man had and interesting physique to him. Out of respect the two military people stood and bowed at the young ladies which suddenly made the evening far more tolerable. Instead of being treated like concubines it was nice to be treated like an intelligent humanoid being.

The Valet and one other helper assisted the two young ladies sit down at the table next to the emperor facing his two guests.

Several servants came with bottles of ferments with small sampling cups so that the guests could try. Canaris found one he liked and said, I'll have this.

The two Vrackline women picked their favorites, which was one of the benefits of being the emperor's concubines, they drank expensive ferments when they wanted.

Zainia of course turned down the offer and soon the food started rolling out and when the servants served Zainia it just sat there. Then Emperor Clauvious informed the lead servant, "she's actually a robot, she doesn't eat. Take her plate away."

The Vrackline kidnapped slaves Violet and Ralcody were suddenly animated watching all this unfold.

"Violet and Ralcody, now you know what a female robot looks like."

"Robot?" Violet asked.

"Yes, she's not humanoid. She's a very highly developed machine and a space traveler here with Canaris who's a real humanoid."

Violet noticed the male officer was staring at her. She was a little offended and asked, "Am I that ugly to stare at me?"

Zainia knew it was a delicate moment and decided to intervene and said, "The reason why Canaris is looking at you so intently, you look exactly like his former lover."

"He had a Vrackline lover?"

"Yes."

"What happened? Why are they not together?"

"The woman decided Canaris would never be accepted at Crysantralon and felt she would not like living at his world where only plane skinners live. They went their separate ways then."

"Forever?"

"Yes, they will never meet again."

"Violet now felt like crap that she had been so unkind and when she saw a tear in the corner of Canaris eye she knew she had struck a delicate nerve. The evening was turning out to be far more than the two women imagined. Here sitting in front of them was a *plain skinner* who had a former Vrackline lover. It seemed almost astonishing. Canaris quickly regained his composure. He didn't know if it was the ferment or just looking at the ghost of his former lover that seemed to fortify his happiness.

Emperor Clauvious was more than happy to trade Violet for the secret encryption technology. The emperor could always acquire another kidnapped concubine. His mind started calculating and he was suddenly putting Violet into his strategic planning.

The blue skinned Vrackline concubine Ralcody looked at Zainia and asked with utter astonishment, "You're really a robot?"

Vracklines and Míngquè had seen a few robots, they were more of a science project than anything else since there was not apparent commercial value of them since slaves were plentiful. They all had metal skin and weird looking sensors, nothing as clamorous as the eyes Zainia had. This glamorous robot in front of them was utterly astonishing.

As they continued eating a general discussion of what life was like on a long-distance space transport and the duration of time in space. Instead of turning into another night of drudgery, it was becoming pleasant and even Emperor Clauvious was being pleasant for a change. *Or was that just the wine talking?*

Then they got into what life was like on Canaris' planet of Zharkon-Xestra. By the time dinner ended with some light entertainment, Emperor Clauvious suggested, why don't I have my Valet take you to your guest rooms since you are spending the night.

"Alright."

The couple were escorted to a couple guest rooms and Canaris informed the Valet, "Zainia will stay in my room, we only need one room."

"Whatever you want that makes you happy."

"Thank you."

They were inside the guest room about five minutes and there was a knock at the door.

Zainia walked over and opened the door. There was no other than Violet with her pretty smile.

"May I come in."

"Yes, you may," Zainia responded and shut the door after Violet entered the room.

"The reason why I'm here is to show Canaris how everything works, the toilet, the bath, and the special mechanical bed."

"What's special about the bed?"

"It's designed to do the work for you. All you need to do is lay on top of your lover and it moves in such a way that you do not have to excerpt much effort to obtain the perfect coitus." She then walked over and pressed a button and the bed started moving in the most amazing manner. She then turned it off.

Canaris was quite surprised as he had never seen anything like it.

"Let me show you how to use the bathroom and the bath."

Violet led Canaris into the adjoining rooms and said I will show you first how to use the toilet so that way you will be comfortable in case you feel like you need to use it.

To Canaris utter amazement, Violet took off all her clothes exposing her body then went to the toilet that had mechanical arms to grab her and suspend her in a squatting fashion and she performed a #2 without any embarrassment and the automated toilet then washed and cleaned and blow dried her bottom.

"Would you like to try it now?"

"Maybe later."

"Would you like to take a bath?"

"I suppose," Canaris said in a mild lackluster manner.

Violet still naked immediately started undressing Canaris then led him into the next room that had a large tub and hit a switch that started filling it and another button that injected some time of bath ingredient that created a lot of bubbles and created a pleasant scent.

As soon as Canaris felt he was comfortable, Violet sensed it and said, "Would you like me to wash your hair?"

"Sure. Why not."

"Soon Violet was shampooing Canaris' hair and rubbing her breasts into his face. The dark blue nipples had a strange effect. Violet's body and face were exactly like Camile that he missed so much. After rinsing Canaris' hair with a rinse hose and fixture with water of the same identical temperature, Violet grabbed a small towel and dabbed his hair and the water off his face then put one of her breasts onto his lips and said, you can put it in your mouth if you want. The circular bath chair Canaris sat at allowed Violet to straddle him and rub her womanhood against his growing erection. Violet knew if Canaris had made love to a Vrackline woman such as his former lover, he would find her irresistible and as she predicted there would be coitus making the emperor happy as it was all part of his strategic plan to obtain as much from these space travelers as possible. She then shocked Canaris by grabbing his manliness and inserted it into her love maker.

Violet knew it would not be long before Canaris would reach a climax and she moved her body in a way and tightened her vagina in a rhythmic fashion that caused that explosion in Canaris' gratification. But it also did another thing she could not predict it opened a gaping wound in his heart.

Canaris then broke down and cried for a few moments. Violet felt ever bit of his pain and now she knew vividly Canaris was in love with that other woman. To be loved by a man this greatly is a tribute to a woman. Violet put her arms around Canaris and held him as if he were her dearest friend. He had touched her in ways no man had ever before, and she knew it was fully legitimate because he didn't have to fake it since she was a gift from the emperor and already had his pleasure with her. It was a tender moment for the two. Soon however, Violet knew she had to move things along because the emperor's eavesdropping would want to see them curled up in bed together in each other's arms like to lovers would be after copulation.

"Us get out and dry off. She then took Canaris to an area adjacent to the bath and a blow dry device came down out of the ceiling with a nice warm air that dried them fully including the hair.

As expected, they went into the bedroom there were sleeping garments laying on the bed for the two of them. Which they dressed quickly, and Violet pulled him into bed with her and looked over at the robot sitting there with a cable hooked to a power outlet that had multiple types of adapters to get the energy for her power pack as soon as they were in a good position the lights in the room automatically dimmed and they were soon traveling to the stars together in a dream.

The dream that Canaris now experienced, occurred before when he was with Camile. And now it was back and strong again. In his dream he knew he was with Camile. He loved her dearly and feeling this woman next to him gave him the physical sensation that was Camile. Throughout the night as Canaris glided from deep sleep to an almost coherent state and back into deep sleep again, the feel of Violet next to him caused his brain to play tricks on him as he knew he was with the love of his life, Camile and his heart was full of happiness, and he never wanted to leave her again.

Eventually morning came and Canaris could sleep no more. Zainia dutifully sat there observing. She was also working in the background with the ship's computer hacking and dissecting and learning many pathways into the Míngquè planetary security system.

Zainia also probed Míngquè General Raskutan, who was a threat not only to them but also Emperor Clauvious. They were not there for the purpose of interfering with domestic politics or issues. The Míngquè situation would evolve on its own long after they were gone. Zainia was careful to cover their tracks because had General Raskutan discovered the depths of her penetration, it's unlikely he would never allow them to leave the planet alive.

Violet had not yet stirred. Canaris appreciated the gift the emperor gave him. For that he would be forever grateful. As Canaris sat at the side of the bed, there was a knock at the door. Zainia dutifully rose and walked over and there was the Valet with several people.

"May we come in?"

"Yes, you may."

The Valet led the troopers in and Zainia closed the door behind them.

"The emperor has asked me to prepare you for a sightseeing trip. These people will provide you with a change of clothes and get you ready. They will also help Violet prepare for the trip as she will be Canaris' escort for the festivities."

Here was a rapid shuffle as people started performing their magic. Violet half asleep was helped from bed and escorted to the bathroom so they could allow her to do her morning activities and bathe and get her hair shampooed for preparation of the hair stylist. She was soon dressed in undergarments and a bath robe and marched out into the large bedroom where a portable hair stylist chair had been abruptly moved in.

Canaris turn was next and to his surprise another blue skinned woman with red hair and purple eyes got into the bath with him nude to wash his hair and perform pleasurizers activities if he so desired, but he wasn't quite in the mood for it. He was dried off and given a bathing robe to put on and soon found himself in a hair stylist chair getting superb treatment.

The Valet noted, "Your uniforms are being dry cleaned so that when you go back to your ship your uniform will be fitting such dignitaries."

"Thank you," Canaris said taking it all in.

Makeup artists worked on Canaris and Violet, but Zainia informed the fashion experts, "I'm a robot and I do not desire nor require makeup."

At first, they thought she was joking but when she had her clothes off to put on the designer clothes picked out for her, she asked one of the fashion designers, "Please fill my arms. Do they feel like the muscles of a woman?"

The designer felt the sold nature, that was as hard as wood. And upon asking and feeling the legs, they seemed like steel.

"You really are a robot."

"That's correct."

"You are so amazing, you look real."

"I even have an operational vagina in case Canaris wants to have sex."

"Did he ever?"

"No, he saved it for real women."

The fashion designers suddenly realized the emperor had interests in these aliens for good reason!

As soon as it appeared the guests were almost dressed for their journey, the Valet stepped outside the room for a minute. Moments later when he stepped back into the room the lead fashion designer nodded to indicate they were ready.

"Canaris, Zainia, and Violet, please follow me."

The three well-dressed patrons followed the Valet that led them down a hallway that went through a door, then made a left turn down another hallway to a door which he opened and stepped aside so the guests could all pass into a large room with a Royal Transport parked in front of them. Unknown to them were two other Royal Transports that had already gone through and left this secret unloading port of the emperor's mansion. The door to the Royal Transport lifted and moved on top of the Transport rooftop and standing inside was no other than Emperor Clauvious smiling as his plans were all working out nicely.

The three guests boarded the Royal Transport and were invited to seats that were orientated in a circular fashion so that each person could see the other three directly. Behind this seating area were security people and in front of them were additional security men and two pilots. The door to the transport then came down and closed.

The secure loading and unloading area door opened in front of them. Almost like a bus the Royal Transport rolled out and slowly curved along the driveway and pulled up behind two identical Royal Transports who had additional security members along with some very powerful handheld artillery and shoulder launched anti-air missiles.

With all three lined up in unison, the commenced flight ops taking off in parallel flying in formation and soon maneuvering to form an angled wing with one in the middle and two short distances behind on each side. The emperor's Royal Transport rarely took the center position, and randomly selected right or left wing for position. Sometimes the Emperor's Royal Transport randomly took the center position, but it was semi-rare.

Zainia already knew where they were going but asked the question to give the emperor a sense of false impressions about the Yānjoyduī Alien's robot Zainia's ability to penetrate their deepest secrets and easily bypass all the Míngquè computer firewalls developed:

"May I ask where you are taking us?"

"Yes Madam, I'm taking you to Camp Pùtàiyáng and Etàrká

Fàlls."

"What is at Camp Pùtàiyáng?"

"Violet, would you be so kind to explain Camp Pùtàiyáng?"

"Yes, your excellency," Violet responded then turned towards Zainia and said, "Camp Pùtàiyáng is Emperor Clauvious' retreat. It has everything he needs for his comfort and its away from the city and noise and pollution. When he needs to think clearly, he goes to Camp Pùtàiyáng where nobody is allowed in except his special guests."

Zainia knew one other use for Camp Pùtàiyáng. It was a refuge he could quickly fly to in the event a coup. All those Emperor's associates assigned to Camp Pùtàiyáng were fully screened tested and deemed reliable. They were also the recipients of benefits and pleasures few others obtained in life. They were not part of the patronaged class, but they knew service to the emperor would pave their way to success later in life when their rewards for loyalty were received.

Today at Camp Pùtàiyáng an Art exhibit was set up and a small orchestra was playing as they were led into the exhibition hall that could showcase about anything the emperor wanted to see including two martial arts practitioners fight to the death. The winner would soon be basking with fine wine and women and anything to his utter delights for a few days before being taken back to society to continue with their normal lives.

Emperor Clauvious was a cultured man, but he was also a Tyrant and would do whatever he pleased whenever. Society was insulated from his whims to a great extent as he did all his scandalous behavior in the privacy of his mansion, but when he wanted to take things a step further such as mortal combat, he would do it here at Camp Pùtàiyáng. Violet and Canaris were not served breakfast for a good reason. The emperor wanted them to be extra hungry for the feast he would surprise them with at Etarka Falls, which existed at the edge of Camp Pùtàiyáng among lavishly green vegetation that gave the appearance of a tropical paradise.

After looking at some of the best and most expensive artwork in the galaxy, it was time to head for Etarka Falls. Part of the emperor's whims was the animation of primary transportation modes. Emperor Clauvious' had his own private narrow gauge railroad system.

Camp Pùtàiyáng Railroad built as a two-and-a-half-foot gauge railroad was powered by ancient steam locomotives. The tracks led from what appeared to be an ancient station through tunnels, over trestles, and dams and through triple canopy tropical rain forest out to the Etarka Falls. When the train arrived at Etarka Falls and stopped, all the passengers stepped off the luxury train onto a soft ramp down to what would be considered one of the most prime campgrounds on the planet with a full view of the majestic Etarka waterfalls.

Violet acting as tour director said, "Tradition had it, justice used to be served here. They would throw convicts down the falls and if they lived, they were innocent, if they died, they were guilty, and the remains simply slowly floated down the river where a complete eco-cycle existed, and the semi-nude person's flesh would soon be part of a food cycle."

It was nice and quiet and tranquil by the Etarka Falls. After the passengers all got off the train it continued its circuitous route most likely heading back to the Camp Pùtàiyáng reception center where the musicians were left behind.

Canaris was feeling some hunger, but so was Violet. As they stood there admiring the majestic view of the Etarka Falls, the staff was finishing up the lace place settings for all the illustrious guests. Canaris could smell the food that was giving off scents even though all the food warmers were closed with metal lids.

After simple small talk of inconsequential interchanges, the group was suddenly invited by the lead waiter dressed up in black tie suit, to please take their seats at the dining table.

While ferments were being served, the train came back with the full orchestra that had a stage setup nearby and took their seats carrying their instruments except for the big items that were prepositioned and would be too clumsy to carry on the train.

Long before they started receiving their servings for the meal the orchestra was playing lovely symphonic music that had incredible composition and structure. A piano like instrument in center stage was resonating the air with fabulous chords. After all the tumultuous journey in space where disaster was possible making the wrong moves, Canaris felt slightly invigorated.

Zainia who was Canaris principal champion and protector was analyzing Canaris and his interactions with Violet. Zainia's numerous subroutines and macro's that performed intricate analysis, made Zainia happy that Canaris was exhibiting a condition that sent the message he was over the pain and agony of losing his lover Camile. Zainia also understood Canaris would not likely give his heart so easily in the future. For a space traveler a reluctant heart is a good thing, because to find and lose love is such a tragedy. Zainia hoped Canaris learned his lesson and would not pursue love until he found himself in a plausible situation where the likelihood of the loss of that lover was minimized.

"Tell me Canaris, how is it your ship was able to break my crypto so easily?"

"Your excellency, I'm not a crypto expert and do not get involved in that activity. Our onboard computer is programmed to deal with all calculations and analysis on new discovery."

"But you must have some idea of what's going on?"

"In all honesty, I think we are just poised to discover languages and determine how to communicate with entities we discover in our space travel."

"Were you successful while visiting other planets?"

"I believe we have been successful in figuring out communications since that is the most important aspect of reaching out to a civilization we had never known before."

"What do you think of my planet?"

"To be honest your excellency, I do not know enough about your planet to make any reasonable judgements."

"You obviously saw some of our infrastructure arriving."

"Yes of course, I appreciate architecture and the genius that goes into the ornate features of buildings and structures that support society."

"We have some of the tallest and finest buildings known throughout the galaxy."

"I concur, the imagery we saw coming down in the shuttle conveyed to me you have master designers quite capable of creating exquisite architecture. Your mansion and the artwork we witnessed at the Camp Pùtàiyáng exhibit hall, shows you have fabulous artists with vast creativity."

"Thank you, I agree."

"You are most welcome, your Excellency."

"I could use another good friend. It gets lonely at the top. If you are willing to hand over all your cryptographic capabilities, I would be willing to knight you and make you a member of my court."

"Your Excellency, I started out in the space exploration business to discover the universe. I'm afraid I can no longer stay in one place and be happy the rest of my life."

"Space exploration is dangerous; it may one day cost your life."

"I'm willing to die trying."

"You are such a noble person. There are not many men who would pass up such an opportunity."

"Your Excellency, I'm flattered with your offer, and I do appreciate it. I hope our worlds can establish friendship and diplomatic exchanges and perhaps even trade. In the future I certainly would like to come back and visit you and check up on you."

"I would like that too Canaris."

"Here's to you, your excellency." Canaris raised his glass to the emperor.

The emperor was starting to like this Alien who proved he was idealistic and wasn't for sale like most men in the galaxy that had a price.

The music created a lovely atmosphere. The fine distillates were laced with a variety of pleasurizer chemicals. Violet's friend and blue skinned Vrackline female, Ralcody was feeling the pleasurizer in ways she knew she was being prepared to help seduce the young man. It was all part of the plan. The emperor would find his price. Every man had a price even if he had to use the two Vracklines in a honeypot scheme. It might have worked on anyone else.

And just as Zainia knew, Canaris would have a reluctant heart for a while as he may never get over Camile. Plus, Zainia knew that in reality, Canaris really had no bearing on cryptography. He was being recruited for something he really couldn't provide. But that recruitment process was proving to be valuable to Zainia as it ushered in numerous more avenues of penetration into the deepest and darkest secrets of Emperor Clauvious and Míngquè General Raskutan, who was the real nemesis.

The food, ferments, music, and the Etarka Falls waterfall all combined to produce an ambience second to none. Ralcody's preparation was fully effective and having experienced the effects before and what comes later gave her reason to believe that in the very near future, her services would be called upon to please this, Alien. As distasteful as it was to her, she feared for her life. Allowing an alien to abuse her body for a brief period was preferable to death and she had already seen firsthand the heavy hand of Emperor Clauvious. If she only knew of a way to find freedom, she would do anything and perform any sexual act possible.

Everyone except the orchestra knew Zainia was a robot. The orchestra was a little surprised the exotic woman wasn't eating or drinking. But she was acting delightful and interchanging with everyone at the table good conversation and smiling often. Smiles have effects on people. Zainia knew the statistics on how smiles affected psychology and programmed herself to smile seventy five percent of the time.

Finding any excuse to smile was the key operative. And even if there was no reason to smile, it still helped in social engineering.

The music played on as the meal was devoured. The pleasurizers had Canaris wound up feeling extremely delightful. Ralcody was feeling the warmth between her legs making her feel like a *bitch in heat*. Her doping was rather strong. She would have to do it just to clear it out of her mind. She knew what was going to happen soon if everything worked out to plan. The Aliens would be shuttled back to the Camp Pùtàiyáng complex to a guest villa next to the display pavilion they were at earlier.

Emperor Clauvious was going to simply toss Ralcody into a private villa arranged for Canaris to experience a Vrackline female jacked up to the point she would aggressively pursue sex with him and work on the big compromise Canaris would soon be offered.

As soon as it appeared the guests were finished eating, it was time to take them to the villas in order they could freshen up and possibly take a nap while the orchestra was fed and given some time off to relax before the evening festivities.

Emperor Clauvious and his guests were soon departing on the narrow-gauge train that looped back around to the Camp Pùtàiyáng Villas and replica antique train station.

They all got off at the train station and were escorted into the Villa. Canaris and Zainia were led into a luxury villa and the others were scattered elsewhere. Predictably there was a knock at the door, there was Ralcody was there alone smiling.

"May I come in?"

Zainia responded, "Please come in."

Ralcody entered the Villa and Zainia then closed the door.

Canaris was already in the rest room freshening up and heard the women talking. When Canaris returned to the Villa's living room, Ralcody asked, "Would you like to take a bath to freshen up?"

"That seems like a good idea."

"I'll help you."

Emperor Clauvious was now with Violet and knew she was

probably full of Canaris deposit from the night before and it excited him to feel that moistness as he mounted Violet and performed strong thrusts as his psychology was now causing him huge gratification as he felt the touch of the alien's magic substance mixed in with Violet's own moistness.

Ralcody helped Canaris undress promptly and started filling the bath with water. It took her about a minute to undress and crawl in the bath with Canaris. The drugs she received in her fermented drink and the pleasurizers now had a fire burning in her crotch and she knew she felt like a *bitch in heat* and wanted big A now.

She climbed on top of Canaris putting her breast in his mouth then took his manliness and guided it inside her and she started performing as if she was turbocharged.

Her vast training taught her how to control the muscles around her vagina to create a strong piston action that tugged hard on Canaris as she modulated her physical rhythm with those muscle contractions. As she expected Canaris started filling her with his magic ingredients that multiplied her own gratification instantly.

Because of her doping she could not stop for a while and in due time gave Canaris a second and third orgasm which he never experienced before in his lifetime.

Finally, after complete exhaustion, they both laid there in the tub now full of warm water and a mixture of bath salts to soothe the body. Being in the tub allowed them to cuddle without the feeling of sweat. It was a surreal moment for Canaris as he felt complete gratification.

The drugs were now starting to wear off and Ralcody was feeling more normal and no longer enraptured.

Ralcody then moved off Canaris to his side and they lounged

soaking in the warm water fully relaxing and fully relieved.

"Would you like to dry off and take a nap?" Ralcody asked about fifteen minutes later now feeling fully relieved of her previous tensions.

"That idea sounds good."

Ralcody helped Canaris out of the tub and dried him off with a towel and handed him a bath robe and said, "You will find some sleeping attire on the bed, I'll be there shortly."

"All right. Thank you."

Canaris went into the Villa's bedroom and the sleeping attire was there which he changed into and soon laid down on the bed under the sheets. Moments later Ralcody joined him and snuggled up to him and held him like he was a precious person. In a way he was because he would soon have a huge impact on her life.

Canaris immediately fell asleep and Ralcody was not far behind. Zainia sat there watching the couple formulating her plan. Zainia had a suspicion, she knew there was a good possibility one of the two lovely women, or both would do anything for their freedom. When she had the opportunity, she would perform an act that might help them gain their freedom. For that she knew Canaris would always appreciate what she did. For them helping Canaris get over his heartache of losing his real first love, they earned Zainia's help.

Camp Pùtàiyáng was fully bugged everywhere and Zainia had already broken into the computer system that ran all the surveillance. The Míngquè computer security was far easier to penetrate than the Vracklines.

Thanks to the broad spectrum of security devices planted everywhere, Zainia had a complete handle on everything happening everywhere in all the Villas and who was talking including Emperor Clauvious speaking to his personal assistant and Valet. She knew that in two hours she should wake up Canaris because a host of people would be coming in to prepare them for the next event which happened to be a boat ride with a smaller piece orchestra facilitating a dinner cruise.

Canaris was in dreamland again and no matter how hard he tried; he could not get Camile out of his mind. Canaris was feeling Camile again and wondering how he came in contact with her. Canaris wanted Camile so badly and she came to him again! He was feeling her near him, smelling her unusual Vrackline scent that was very compelling and delightful. He would never forget that smell the rest of his life.

Canaris felt so wonderful being next to the woman he loved and was trying to figure out how she came to him. He felt her, he knew she was lying next to him. He didn't need to open his eyes he knew it and he felt the love. He was entranced in this sweet emotional tranquility being with the love of his life. And yet he didn't know how she got here, nor did he know where he was. *Did it matter?*

At the right moment, Zainia knew it was time to wake up the lovers so they would be alert when the preppers were going to show up.

Zainia walked over to Canaris and shook him slightly and said, "Canaris, you have been sleeping for a few hours, I think you should wake up now and get ready for the night's activities."

Canaris opened his eyes and saw the woman lying beside him. At first, he knew it was Camile, but as his consciousness brought him back to reality, he started remembering Ralcody and he had a physical embrace before he fell asleep. Soon his memory of the splendid embrace with his lover dissipated as his existence slowly provided the grim reality, that Camile was no longer a part of his life.

Even though he was in his sleeping attire he rose and stretched his body out a little he was about to put his clothes on when there was that knock at the door. And soon all the handlers were coming in for a repeat performance getting them ready for tonight's event.

Ralcody who was fully alert was escorted to the bathroom where she went through her metamorphism and soon found herself in a bathrobe in the hair stylist chair and the makeup artist working side by side getting it done even though it created a crowded environment.

Canaris received his preparations as well and in thirty minutes was starting to appear like someone Ralcody would be extremely proud to be seen in public with.

Within an hour they were all prepped and dressed and soon escorted out of the Villa and onto a battery powered land car fully open for ease of access. In the span of five minutes, they were at a pier where a canal boat moored.

Even though the nice waterway that surrounded Camp Pùtàiyáng appeared like a small meandering river, it was an old fashion moat that was at least twenty-five feet deep in the middle and dredged annually.

The moat was twenty miles in circumference and took a full five hours to make a complete trip around it which made for an excellent dinner cruise with music. All the food was catered and brought onboard and in food warmers. Nothing was prepared onboard, just served.

On the fantail of the long canal ship was a large open area for guests to lounge around. Inside the canal ship was a formal dining hall they would visit later. On the roof of the canal ship was a deck that facilitated the orchestra playing throughout the evening. Because of the logistics involved in this performance, the orchestra was fed, given break time to freshen up and just before the guests were brought down to the canal ship, the musicians boarded carrying their hand-held instruments with them. Larger instruments such as the piano were prepositioned and fastened with deck clamps on the centerline to prevent shifting the pitch.

The electric propulsion motors edged the canal boat forward. The canal boat bridge and steerage were located all the way forward. Sophisticated navigation equipment autopiloted the canal boat always maintaining center of the channel thanks to several operating beacons operating. There were crewmembers in the steerage room as a backup and they were often sent on laps around the waterway with no passengers aboard to maintain their proficiency in the event autopilot malfunctioned.

The music was grand, the atmosphere was pleasant as the emperor had just experienced one of the better days he had in a long time, and this evening dinner cruise added to the pleasantness.

The emperor and the guests were seated in soft chairs facing each other and to the sides of each chair was a small table that had several glass holders depressed into the wood surface stabilizing the drinks in the even there was an unexpected roll of the canal boat, even though it was unlikely unless a storm suddenly blew winds hard enough to affect safe navigation of the canal boat.

The slow churning of the propellers with the electric motors caused a slight undulating vibration that was not audible due to the music played.

The orchestra was smaller to accommodate the performance on the canal boat, but there was a significant amount of brass instruments to back up the strings and the orchestra and sound. The structure of the canal boat created pleasant serenity from musical resonance and harmony.

This was very relaxing for the emperor and his guests. It also gave Zainia ample time to dig deeper into what was going to come down through General Raskutan, who really wasn't on the emperor's side.

The canal boat meandered along, the music and the drinks added to the luster of the evening and the small talk eliminated any sort of thoughts about tomorrow or any compelling issue in the galaxy. The boat trip allowed their mental quiescence to enjoy these precious moments that were now filled with indelible memories.

Zainia knew tonight would be the big push as the emperor was going to work harder on pitching a deal. Canaris had no control or any ability to deal with the crypto issue. All roads to Rome led through Zainia as far as the crypto was concerned.

Zainia knew the Míngquè were not only terribly prepared when it came to firewalls and computational and communications security, but they were indeed terrible programmers. She analyzed why that was and soon came to the realization what set the Yānjoyduī apart from civilizations in this area of the galaxy. The Míngquè were not big proponents of robots.

The Yānjoyduī embraced robotics for a lot of reasons and as such they were always advancing and Zainia knew she was the byproduct of that advancement. But what did the Yānjoyduī do that these other civilizations didn't do?

They turned computer programming over to robots.

Robots were self-replicating and advancing at their own pace without humanoid intervention. Their coding was exquisite and complicated. Their logic was profound because they had a different time standard. Whereas a human wanted instant gratification and the feeling they accomplished something.

Robots didn't look at accomplishment or rewards, they looked at functionality and efficiency.

The human method of increasing bandwidth was to add raw CPU power as exhibited by both the Míngquè and the Vrackline. The robotic approach would be to pick a more efficient algorithm or search engine. In doing so the Roboticization of Yānjoyduī computational means created coding that humanoids would have extreme difficulty in figuring out.

To gain the two women's freedom, Zainia would trade decryption capability. The Míngquè would enjoy the use of the algorithms for a while until the denial of use malware raised its ugly head long after they were gone. And most likely when the Míngquè were needing that processing the most, it would be gone, and so would be the Yānjoyduī expedition with Canaris and the two freed slaves *if Zainia was able to work her magic.*

Zainia's estimation of timing on the attempted quid pro quo happened right on the mark. After dinner and the humanoids freshening up in the luxurious stateroom cabins aboard the canal boat, they were then led to the fantail of the canal boat when the pitch was going to occur.

"Canaris, what you take in a swap for the decryption algorithms you used to break into our crypto?" Emperor Clauvious asked.

"I don't have the means to give that to you. I do not know how it's done, just its results."

"Who does on your ship?"

"The ship's computer handles all that and even if I wanted to trade it to you for something, I would have no idea how to give it to you."

"Certainly, there has to be some means?"

"There is a means," Zainia chimed in.

Emperor Clauvious smiled and now knew who he had to deal with. The robot. *He should have known this from the beginning.*

"All right, if your illustrious robot Zainia can figure out how to give me the decoding software, what would you want in return."

"I wouldn't know, I'm not sure I need anything?"

"Precious metals? Diamonds, come on there must be something you would be willing to barter for?"

"I know what he wants, Zainia stated in an almost shocking tone."

Emperor Clauvious now super animated turned toward Zainia smiled and asked, "Just what would that be?"

"He loves Violet and Ralcody. He would take them in trade for the decryption software."

Canaris could hardly believe what he was hearing from Zainia and looked at her with perplexing eyes wondering what she really was up to? He knew they couldn't discuss it anywhere on the planet because everywhere was most likely bugged, but he was curious as to what trick Zainia had up her sleeve.

Emperor Clauvious was slowly starting to get bored with these two concubines and was already considering their replacements. This would save him the dirty work because none of his concubines were freed alive. They knew too much and had to be destroyed. They ended their loyal service with their deaths.

Zainia in hacking Emperor Clauvious's Emperor's Mansion computer files and surveillance recordings already knew how the sick Emperor Clauvious disposed of his women. He first let his guards have their way with them, then they disposed of them in gruesome manners. Zainia wanted to save their lives, otherwise they may not live another year.

"For the capability that would give me, I would be willing to do the trade."

"All right, tomorrow, if you give me a link to a computer system, I will install the software and teach your computer technicians how to use it. And tonight, the girls come with Canaris and I. We need to go back to the ship so I can package the software and evaluate your computer to make sure it gets properly programmed for this capability."

"That should not be a problem."

"One other thing, the computer has to have a feed where you can send communications you want to decrypt, otherwise it would not be of any use to you."

"I will have my computer experts set up such a computer with a data feed in my mansion tonight."

Violet and Ralcody looked at the robot in utter fascination. They also wondered what this meant for their futures.

The night would be an interesting ordeal, Zainia knew that Emperor Clauvious was not going to allow Violet and Ralcody to leave Míngquè alive, especially with these Aliens who could take them anywhere and expose a lot of his secrets. Soon after he had confidence the decryption software was fully functional; he would have General Raskutan destroy their ship killing them and his concubines to eliminate any leakage of his most inner secrets.

They didn't go completely around the full circumference of

the moat. Emperor Clauvious had a half dozen piers to stop at where transportation could pick him up.

Emperor Clauvious motioned to his Valet to come over and he whispered something into his ear. The Valet promptly walked forward along the port side of the canal boat and went into the steerage room and gave the crewmembers their orders to pull into the next pier which they were approaching.

The guests noticed the boat was maneuvering and slowing down and a pier came into view.

"We are going to get out here so we can make all the arrangements," Emperor Clauvious stated with a Cheshire Cat smile.

Zainia immediately dispatched their shuttle down to pick them up. It took a few minutes to steady up the ship and moor it since they had to bring in line handlers for the unexpected stop. Soon the brow (gangplank) was lowered onto the pier and Emperor Clauvious invited his guests to leave the canal boat with him. After they were off boat, it would continue to the final destination where the orchestra had their transportation waiting.

Shortly after they were on the pier a light came down from the sky and landed right next to them. The shuttle had the vectors to Zainia's transponder system to know where to pick them up.

"Our transportation has arrived. We'll be taking the ladies with us and in the morning when you feel your computer system is up and running and I have a link I will program it for you. Be sure and have some encrypted files to process." Zainia said with utter authority. Canaris head was spinning watching this all unfold.

Zainia led the group to the shuttle and were shortly heading out into space. The two Vrackline women, Violet and Ralcody were perplexed and didn't know how to take it. *Were they simply going from one hell to another?*

When they arrived aboard the Space Explorer HMY Xīwàng-Zhīxīng it didn't seem to be too bad of a ship to the two Vrackline women, in fact it looked and felt better than the Míngquè ships that brought them to this planet when they were kidnapped.

There were spare bunks onboard hidden behind panels to accommodate the women who were surprised there were no other crew members, something the Míngquè were unaware of.

Emperor Clauvious figured this would be a long-drawn-out process. Nothing on Míngquè was ever done fast. He assumed the visitors would be spending all night working on bundling the software. In actuality, it only took an hour because Emperor Clauvious computer terminal in his secret vault that only he, the Valet and a few others were ever allowed in was hooked up to the INTEL directorate's network. One of those special INTEL people with access to the vault was there and showed Emperor Clauvious several of the Crypto intercepts they were anxious to bust from the Solodizi Divergents who were slowly becoming a major concern for them.

The Míngquè contacted the Space Explorer HMY Xīwàng-Zhīxīng via VHF communications and gave a link for them to access a communications hub that would transfer the files they needed to start the operation.

Zainia knew all this because of her extensive hacking and soon transferred the file and an executable application that would start the process and prompt the operator to give a file name they wanted to decrypt.

They started the process and were soon surprised how well the decryptions worked. They had some test files of compromised decryptions they could use to check the accuracy of the software and were soon convinced it worked as advertised.

Emperor Clauvious thanked them for the trade and the chase was now on.

Zainia knew in advance the game plan, they could have simply started transit into space and never have a single worry, but Zainia was a noble robot and had every intention of returning Violet and Ralcody to their world Crysantralon. They had a decent head start and General Raskutan was upset he was not able to nail them right away and had to chase them. He had a sizeable force with him to plan for any contingency including coming across one of their enemy fleets.

Thanks to the head start, the Míngquè force was not going to be able to catch the Space Explorer HMY Xīwàng-Zhīxīng and had they had continued to Zharkon-Xestra instead of stopping at Crysantralon, the Míngquè would realize the chase was no longer important as they would be getting way too far away from their worlds with insufficient supplies to continue since it wasn't planned for a long chase.

Soon however General Raskutan was all smiles when he realized the alien ship was making a bee line to Crysantralon where they would have to slow down and be vulnerable. One little ship could not stop a fleet and while they there it might be time to do a surprise attack on the Vracklines which he was planning in the not-too-distant future anyway. All the aliens did was up his timeline and thanks to the emperor's bad judgement he would take care of business then travel back to Míngquè and get rid of the emperor as well.

Knowing it would be a tight schedule, Zainia informed Canaris, "We will not have time to take the girls down to the planet and retrieve the shuttle before the Míngquè Force will be upon us."

"Send them down on the shuttle and we'll just have to leave it behind."

The plan was working out fine until the enemy got close and Zainia discovered by hacking the fleet computers what was in store, after Violet and Ralcody were on their way to the planet by themselves in the shuttle happy to be going home as free persons.

"They are splitting half their forces, one half is going to attack the planet, the other half intend on destroying us."

"Which one has the command ship?" Canaris asked.

"General Raskutan's command ship is in the group coming after us."

"We have no choice we need to delay them and help the Vracklines. Contact the Vracklines and let them know they are going to be attacked and they need to scramble their forces."

"They have been notified. What shall we do now?"

"Can you determine which ship is General Raskutan's command ship?"

"Yes."

"Us head for it."

"That will be suicide."

"Sometimes decent people have to make a supreme sacrifice to protect the innocent."

"Noted." Zainia said now feeling utterly sad that Canaris was going to sacrifice himself to save Crysantralon. But she understood he was doing it out of love because he never did get over Camile and she was down on the planet at a military base that was likely to be destroyed in a few minutes.

"Concentrate all our weapons on General Raskutan's ship. I think if we destroy him, it will cause chaos and the Míngquè will withdraw and the Vracklines may have enough time to put forth a defense.

Aboard General Raskutan's flag ship the sensor technician said, "the Alien ship has reversed course and are coming at us."

"Maybe they want to surrender another said."

"It doesn't matter. Destroy them. Make ready all weapons."

Just when General Raskutan was starting to smile that he was going to smash that little ship like a bug, the fleet started reporting computer problems, many of their weapon systems were failing. It was becoming unnerving. The planet strafers were starting to reverse course because their weapons were not working, and they would be sitting ducks.

"Commencing fire," Zainia said as she started pumping kinetic weapons into the command ship because she sensed her laser and beam weapons wouldn't do enough damage. The kinetic weapons did some good damage, but damage control parties were quickly responding to the non-fatal damage. Missiles were shot but most of them were blown up by close in self-defense weapon systems.

"I'm sorry Canaris, none of our weapons will get the job done."

"Aim for their bridge, it's all we have left."

"Good by Canaris. I love you.

"I love you too Zainia."

General Raskutan was looking on in horror as he could see the propulsion engines of the Alien ship go to flank speed and maximum thrust. The hot rocket exhaust lit up the sky and it was getting brighter. It wasn't until it was too late until the sensor operator yelled, "Their going to ram us!"

"Hard RIGHT RUDDER!" The command ship's captain yelled standing next to General Raskutan.

The velocity that Space Explorer HMY Xīwàng-Zhīxīng obtained in a short period was too quick for the large Míngquè command ship to get out of the way soon enough.

The steel protection cylinder for the bridge party was never designed to protect them from a head on collision with another space craft traveling at such a velocity almost approaching light speed already.

With robot efficiency, Zainia steered the Space Explorer HMY Xīwàng-Zhīxīng where it would not be a glancing blow. Her calculations were utterly perfect and the entire weight and mass of the Space Explorer HMY Xīwàng-Zhīxīng pancaked into the front of the command ship and the energy given off in the collision caused the nuclear power generators and the propulsion reactors of the Space Explorer HMY Xīwàng-Zhīxīng to create massive energy release of a medium size nuclear weapon.

With their command ship disintegrated in a fireball the size of a nuke and all their computers going haywire, the force on their own initiated a retreat.

Zainia's parting gift to Emperor Clauvious was the list of names of General Raskutan's co-conspirators who were about ready to spring the coup.

When the fleet reached home, and word soon spread how the aliens had killed General Raskutan, his co-conspirators turned chicken and started implicating each other which the emperor used, allowing half of them to be spared the other half executed.

The shuttle landed at the base where Camile worked, and the authorities quickly apprehended the two ladies and started debriefing them. They met Camile and informed her that Canaris remained in love with her and wept for her. Then when the space battle was all analyzed and the details of how the Aliens had saved them, it hit Camile like a ton of bricks. In truth, the love of her life just saved her life. And she had been so unfair to him. Had she not been such a coward, she might have given him reason to live. In a way she felt she killed Canaris. And she really did since he gave his life to save hers.

CHAPTER FIFTEEN
THE FINAL ACT

"I wonder why that spacecraft didn't burn up coming into the atmosphere?" Jamison asked.

"It was definitely smoldering when hit the water, probably internally it's all charred," Yīnhuā responded

"I wonder why we are wasting so much effort to find the hulk?"

"Somebody high up thinks there is a chance that a very valuable item is on that space craft they want to recover."

"I can't believe anything survived to be of use in the future."

The research vessel *Galactopus* was running racetracks over an area plotted based on satellite recordings of the event towing a submerged sonar bottom scanner. The *Galactopus* speed and the hydrofoils on the towed body determined the depth of the sonar array. The sonar array could not have any moving parts that might contaminate the received data and distort the returns. Performance had to be controlled by exact speeds of the towing ship that had a room full of processors, displays, and data recording devices. The towed body was five hundred yards behind the ship to make sure it was out of the prop wash turbulence and noise. Because of the ballasting, the tow rig connection and the hydrofoils, this towed body was very stable and the directional projector and receive hydrophones did a great job of profiling the bottom.

"Nothing showing, is it possible we are in the wrong area?"

"No, I've checked and rechecked the latitude-longitude (Lat/Long) the ISR satellites gave at the crash site.

"I have no returns except the bottom."

"The bottom profiler shows a sandy bottom with many layers. If we come across the wreckage it should show up in a fantastic contrast.

"How much longer on this course?"

"According to the autopilot tracker in five minutes we'll change course to 161 degrees to make up for a little set and drift, so we don't overlap so badly."

All day long the ship had gone back and forth slowly working its way over the impact zone. It was a monotonous job watching those sonar profiler displays and if it were not for the fact, they were well paid, they wouldn't be doing it.

Yīnhuā knew there wasn't a huge demand for female sonar operators. One of the problems was there wasn't a lot of sonar operations that were ongoing since the prohibition of offshore drilling went into effect. The other problem is most survey ships spent a lot of time at sea on a project and companies didn't want to take the risk of having a female alone by herself on a ship where the event bad things happened, and evidence was easy to dispose of with rope and trash that had to be weighted down to avoid prosecution by overzealous environmental officials.

Yīnhuā was good at her job and didn't suffer vigilance decrement after lunch time like a lot of her male counterparts. Jamison liked working with Yīnhuā because she was pleasant to be around and did a lot better job taking care of her personal hygene than most of the male slobs he was forced to smell after long periods at sea. The other thing he liked about Yīnhuā is she wasn't always complaining all the time like many of the guys who showed very poor flexibility. Nothing worse than being around a bunch of overpaid malcontents.

Halfway through the racetrack Yīnhuā reported, "I received some slight returns, nothing big but it's close to where we think the spaceship is."

"If it's part of the space craft we should get a much better picture on the next leg of the search pattern," Jamison noted.

"I feel confident in the next pass over we'll start to find what we were sent out here to locate," Yīnhuā noted.

An hour elapsed and they were now on a course of 340 degrees and tension was mounting as they would soon be going over the area that might reveal more of the space craft. This was the big gamble coming to fruition and Jamison stood behind Yīnhuā looking over her shoulders. The colorization of the bottom scanner was three-dimensional, color denoted signal strength. The X and Y coordinates varied in height based on depth readings as the phased array bottom scanner chirp transmitter directional scanner painted a swath nearly 100 yards wide at the present depth of water. Only the inner thirty yards had significant signal to noise coefficients to really paint objects. The areas outside the thirty degrees were stitched onto the previous pass that could add or subtract from the image giving an averaging extent.

Anyone recording the transmissions could not hear them because they were above normal human hearing frequency range. But if frequency converted through a super heterodyne process or a Z-tracking filter they would hear what appeared like constant bird chirps from a flock of birds.

The large map like display showed several previous images

produced from the previous racetracks. As they made more racetracks since the computer software had a centering function, the display slowly appeared to shift to the left since the direction of the racetracks was building the image slowly moving to the east stabilized to 070 degrees since that was the map orientation of the moving search window. Intuitively a person looking at the bottom map would know the little bit of image created on the previous leg should now continue and possibly strengthen, if it is the location of the spaceship they believed to be there.

Soon they were passing over the top of the adjacent area of expected returns. Background noise was color green. When signal return strengthened because of sound bouncing off metal instead of a sandy bottom it started turning yellow then orange if it grew stronger showing a relative decibel scale in colorization. Finally, it would go from orange to red to purple then white if the signal was clipping from over driving causing excessive returns. An operator would also see something like mountain ranges if passing over a rock formation.

The area stitched to the previous pass that had minor reflections was now painting shallower depths by a few feet and the colorization was shifting up the decibel scale.

"That's our baby!" Jamison exclaimed.

"I'd say we are on the side of the spacecraft or one end of it," Yīnhuā responded.

"I agree."

"How many more racetracks to we have to run?" Yīnhuā asked.

"Based on mission planning, another 10 racetracks," Jamison replied.

"Are we going to send down the camera's then?"

"We have too. Our sponsors want all the details before they initiate salvage operations."

"They will have some nice eye candy later today when they get their ops-brief."

"I'm sure the sponsors are going to be pleased because its all coming together. I just hope they do not feel disappointed when they find out the craft burned up on the inside coming down."

"I have no idea what it is they want off that spaceship, but apparently it's of vital importance to them to be spending the kind of credits on this operation."

"I'm sure they are not going to tell us either."

"Divers have big mouths, if they find something very valuable, we'll hear about it."

The research vessel *Galactopus* continued the racetracks and slowly built the stitched together image.

"I'm going to apply the statistical normalizers, those ugly stitch marks will be removed," Yīnhuā announced as it was time to start processing the data for a report.

"The database will retain the raw data, the boys back at the lab only want raw data. They don't like the way our normalizers work."

"It's more of that crap not invented here."

"They don't get paid for it is why."

"It's all about money."

"Everything is."

After Yīnhuā finished her processing for the report she said, "All right, take a look now. Let me know what you think."

"It truly looks like a moonscape with what clearly appears to be the wrecked spacecraft in the very center of the sonar scan."

"Since each ping return had a Lat/Long assigned to it anyone surveying the image moving the cursor around would get the exact location since the ping was perpendicular to the data point."

"Why is that so important?"

"Every square inch of the imagery had spatial coordinates and thanks to the high-resolution distinguishing portions of the spacecraft is easily recognizable which allows salvage people to know exactly where the bow and emergency access doors are located."

"With a special tool the divers should be able to open at least one of the emergency access doors if the hatch was not sprung from the impact."

"Their deep diving suits are a little bulky, I imagine getting in and getting out will not be easy."

"You didn't hear the latest news?"

"No, what?"

"They hired midget divers."

"No kidding?"

"Apparently their deep diving suits are half as big and bulky."

"Well, you know the salvage business is very competitive and if using midgets gains them a competitive advantage, it makes sense."

"You will get the chance to see some of these midget divers as we are contracted to provide video support services during their diving operations."

"I wonder how much those midgets make?"

"From what I understand they are some of the highest paid divers in the salvage industry."

"It stands to reason if you can get in tighter spaces then you can probably command a higher salary."

"They drive nice sports cars and don't mind hanging out with attractive women."

"Good for them!"

"Email me a copy of the processed data I want to put it in the ops-brief."

"Do you want a still shot image or an interactive one?"

"Better give me both in case the chief diver wants to zoom in on some areas and take a few notes."

"I'll have that to you in five minutes."

"Thanks."

It took about an hour to get together all the ingredients for the ops-brief and Jamison was quite satisfied he didn't have to rush any aspect of it.

People at the ops-brief were mostly remote doing a virtual briefing that showed several squares and their images on one of the communications displays. A second display showed data projections. Two displays allowed everyone to see each other as if they were physically in the same room. There were a couple more dozen people that were observers and not permitted contributors to the meeting. They were simply note takers and gophers for the people whose images were in the boxes on the virtual briefing display.

There was a green stripe across the top of the screen about a half inch wide that had a caution: PROPRIETARY INFORMATION. NO DISSEMINATION IS PERMITTED. It also had a countdown to when the meeting was actually starting so there was not to be inputs or comments about the subject until the count down banner was replaced with, "MEETING IN PROGRESS."

As soon as the count down timer indicated 00:00:00, a slight chime occurred followed by the announcement, "Ladies and Gentlemen, The Starfish Undersea Survey Solutions Ops-brief has begun. Our moderator for the meeting is the Assistant Director of Starfish Undersea Survey Solutions, Bret Chancellor. Please submit all questions via text in your right-hand corner notepad area. Questions will be answered in first come first served basis."

The box in the middle of all the personnel display boxes was lit up with an orange border with live video of the speaker. That would remain the case until Bret hit the finish button on his keypad.

"Thanks everyone whose here for the ops-brief for attending, I'm Bret Chancellor and I will be giving the ops brief. Please hold all comments and questions until the daily op's details have been provided. I will then answer questions and we will consult individuals for clarifications when needed."

"We might as well get down to the key event today, which some of you are aware. On your data screen is a processed image of our bottom scan. To create this image, we ran a racetrack over the area contracted to us and as you see, we have produced an image of the bottom that has enough detail in it to suggest we found the wreckage as well as the orientation of the spacecraft. Based on images given to us prior to the scan it appears the object came to rest on the seabed upright allowing access to emergency escape hatches for the next phase of the operation. If you mouse over areas of the image, you will see the lat/long marked with each data point."

The people in the boxes displayed on the meeting contributors and viewers showed an element of surprise in their body language.

Bret Chancellor gave everyone ample time to look over the data before he began comments and displays of the next portion of the ops brief.

"What I'm showing you now is the overall timeline from inception until project complete. As you can see on that timeline, we have reached the major milestone of locating the wreck. Our next phase will start tomorrow as we send down submersible cameras to get close-up view of the hull of the wreckage. Once that is done and the divers decide what their activities will be to allow entering the craft and examining its contents.

The remainder of the meeting was dealing with logistics aspect of the operation, transportation requests, and contract deliverables that all needed to get worked out as they were now entering the most exciting portion of the project which some felt was nothing more than opening a can of worms. Unfortunately, hidden agendas were at play and somebody very powerful in the food chain desperately wanted some of the contents of this spacecraft, provided it didn't burn up on re-entry or severely destroyed upon crash into the ocean.

Besides filming the wreck, divers would be traveling to the support craft in the day tomorrow with expected dives the following day. Other contingencies such as underwater plasma cutters were being prepared in the event the emergency doors were sprung from the crash and could not be opened. Since the spacecraft was a wreck and not of use to anyone, butchering it up for access using underwater plasma cutters did not seem to be much of a controversy. *Bang to fit and paint to match,* the shipyard spirit was alive and well with this crew.

The following day Jamison and Yīnhuā were operating the *Sea Snake* robotic submersible video system. This team of technical support personnel working for a salvage company had to be the jack of all trades and masters of none. They were proficient at what they did because they routinely did this kind of work for other activities, though offshore oil field work gave them lots of opportunities until the current regime took office. No doubt as soon as those clowns were gone, it would soon be business as usual. Oil profits would once again empower the titans and grease a lot of hands.

The semi-autonomous craft was semi tethered and could operate independently if required providing live video. Should telemetry be lost it would simply surface and start transmitting a transponder frequency to make it easy to find in the dark if necessary. The only reason for the tether was extended operational time as well as a conduit for live video.

Thanks to the bottom profiling the actual depth of the wrecked spacecraft was well established and the *Sea Snake* had depth sensors as well as transponder monitoring on the support surface ship *Galactopus*. With all the electronic gizmos in use they always knew where the *Galactopus* position was relative to the spacecraft wreck and the *Sea Snake*. One of the computer graphics up on an ancillary display was a scaled three-dimensional display showing the relative position of all three.

The transponder was a sanity check over the *Sea Snake* telemetry reports. If the telemetry and transponder checks matched within a relatively close measure of distances, there was no concern. However, if the telemetry depth and the transponder readings started to show severe divergence, that usually indicated a problem with *Sea Snake's* depth control and measurement was apparent and it was time to surface the

Sea Snake to find out why, including performing diagnostics which occurred now and then.

Looking at the computer graphic of the three-dimensional bottom scan was nothing like looking at real video where detail was much more pronounced.

As *Sea Snake* slowly dove down to the bottom of the ocean there was no point in turning on its lights until it was a few hundred feet away since the image at that time would be no better than the three-dimensional bottom scan. At the proper time lighting was turned on which placed a significant power drain on the batteries which the tether barely compensated. Survey teams liked nice bright lights to see the best they could especially if the water was partly murky.

Sea Snake operated off sophisticated depth control to avoid whipping up bottom debris by depth control propellers. It took longer to get down to the survey area, but in doing so it stirred up a lot less debris that would normally screw up the video. In essence *Sea Snake* was an underwater glider with ballasting depth control that was semi neutral buoyant to minimize ballasting changes for velocity and depth. *Sea Snake* created a velocity away from the target using a combination of thrusters and gravity, then glided along the target filming it, making several passes before it would be programmed to come into specific spots and come to all stop and get closeups if required.

"It sure looks like that space craft's hull is in good shape."

"The Aliens know how to build them nice and strong."

"Any idea when we'll attempt to bring up the entire ship?"

"That's still being worked out but it's definitely, in the works. The sponsors are very interested in the skin of the spacecraft. It apparently has some Novel construction techniques that make it such an exceptional craft."

"But for now, they just want to empty some of its contents."

"That's correct."

"Will the divers require the *Sea Snake* for safety observation?"

"That is still being discussed. The sponsors do not want some of the cargo identified."

"Super-secret hu?"

"They don't want anyone to know about what it is they are after."

"What if a diver gets into trouble?"

"*Sea Snake* will be in hot standby just in case something like that happens."

"I imagine the divers barge wants us to be clear of them."

"That's how it usually is. We'll maintain a distance of a few hundred yards away from the diver's barge unless they call us in for help."

Eventually the red flags and buoys were placed around the dive zone. The divers' barge had sophisticated navigation equipment and it was parked directly above the wrecked space craft.

Special cranes lifted the divers with their heavy suits on and lowered them down to the bottom of the ocean. The video the *Sea Snake* provided gave them clear observation of the emergency hatch they were to open. Looking through binoculars, Jamison could see two distinct sizes of divers. A couple of them appeared to be normal divers and the other two were definitely half their height.

"Want to take a look?" Jamison asked as he handed the

binoculars to Yīnhuā.

"Yep, the rumors are true, they have a couple midget divers."

"It makes sense, use the best people available for the job. It might be difficult for those big guys to get through the emergency hatches."

Yīnhuā handed the binoculars back to Jamison who started reporting what he was observing.

"They are now craning down two of them, one big guy and one little guy."

The ride down to the space craft took quite a while, and thanks to the structure of the deep diving suits, their bodies were not subject to sea pressure eliminating the need to breath exotic air mixtures. Their bodies were fully monitored and there was an air vent line as part of the tether. A check valve opened under microprocessor control to vent the diver suit as they got deeper.

The first team could accomplish the first task by themselves, but the second team was standing by in the event they needed to go down to finish the job or rescue the first team.

These two divers had special briefings and knew what they were to get. They had a special *Canvas Portmanteau* to place the object in to raise it to the surface so outsiders would not be able to see what was in the *Canvas Portmanteau*.

The normal size diver (is there a normal size for a diver?) had the special tool on a lanyard to open the emergency hatch, he also had some other tools on a service belt that attached to cable lowering them to the depths of the ocean. There was also lighting on attachments to the cable that was multi-purpose.

Part of the rig on the cable was cameras. Undersea divers also had camera's mounted in their helmets with lights. This hole area would be well lit and there would not be issues with the diver's visibility. There was nothing to kick up the bottom and thanks to the video the divers' barge with four-point thrusters could move in any direction to put the divers exactly where they wanted to be.

Each diver stood on a diver's platform. There would be no need for them walking on the bottom of the ocean, which had a sandy bottom and was an option. The diver's platform stabilized on all four corners was heavy and stable. As one of the divers stepped off it, the platform would not be impacted.

Thanks to the video and the thrusters on the divers' barge, the diver's platform was positioned directly above the emergency hatch and the two divers went to work undoing the emergency fasteners which gave them a way to enter the craft. It took about thirty minutes to disengage all the fasteners and the tall diver took a crowbar to pry the emergency hatch open. Hopefully it wasn't sprung. After just a little tug on the crowbar the hatch opened right up. The Diver was able to position it all the rest of the way open. He then gave the midget diver the thumbs up, and they then did their secret handshake which was bouncing their fists together which meant good luck.

The midget had a mechanical chain fall like device that allowed him to step off the diver's platform and lower himself down into the spaceship. This emergency hatch was on the roof of the spacecraft, and they believed it allowed them to enter directly into the control room of the spacecraft since they were near the bow of the spacecraft.

People up on the divers' barge were all cleared for high security as they often did dives for the INTEL directorate. They would soon see what the midget diver saw as he lowered himself into the craft and do what he needed to do. He looked around and his helmet lighted up the area and the first discovery were, the people inside the spaceship were not charred and burned. When the space craft sunk to the bottom the pressure created leaks and it filled full of sea water, other than that, nothing appeared to have disturbed the internal contents.

The aliens were all dead and appeared lifeless as they died latched into their seats with a type of restraint. They were of course slumped over. The midget had to go to each of them to find what he was looking for.

The pressure of the deep depth distorted the faces of all the dead aliens. When he came up to what he came for and lifted that alien's head, there was no distortion of the face. It looked perfect. It was a mechanical man.

The midget undid the robot's restraints and pulled the body over near the emergency hatch.

The large diver lowered the *Canvas Portmanteau* on a lanyard to the midget diver. The midget diver took the robot and slid it into the *Canvas Portmanteau* then pulled the two sides together and then started putting the Velcro straps in place to hold the 2 sides together. He then took out the several extra-large plastic zip ties to wrap around the *Canvas Portmanteau* to make sure the robot didn't slip out on its way to the surface he then took a cable from his rig and snapped it onto a very strong steel ring that was attached to the end of the *Canvas Portmanteau* allowing it to be lifted with no concern about strength as it was probably over designed.

The midget then pulled himself back up to the diver platform using the chain fall like device. Then he and the other diver carefully and slowly lifted the *Canvas Portmanteau* out of the space craft and placed it on the diver's platform where it was latched using the steel ring to secure it for the trip back to the surface. They next shut the emergency hatch and drove the fasteners back down securing it until they returned once the decision was made to go obtain additional components unless they were going to wait and bring up the entire spacecraft in one piece which was now in planning.

Jamison watched periodically and after a while noticed there was a group of people on the diver's barge around the hoist, so he started watching. In due time the diver's platform and the two divers and a canvas device were pulled up on the barge and soon taken through the double doors of the empty helicopter hanger situated about two thirds the length back from the bow. Everyone including the backup divers went inside the hanger and the two doors were then shut.

"Whatever they wanted to get they have it," Jamison said.

In a brief period of time, the *Galactopus* was ordered to return to port, and it observed the self-propelled divers barge heading in the same direction.

Today's ops-brief was simple and sweet: *We got what we came for and further operations will be delayed until the decision is made on how we want to retrieve the space craft.*

Chapter Sixteen
Divers Deliver

The diver's barge was heading towards an empty pier. No other ships were around. The pier remained empty until the Divers barge was about half a mile away from it. Suddenly there were six cars and vans driving down the pier to where the diver's barge was going to moor.

In one of the cars a couple men got out wearing suits and sunglasses. They were obviously the orchestrators of events to follow. Other people acting as line handlers that arrived grabbed the ropes thrown at them tied to mooring lines. The line handlers pulled the mooring lines and put them on the pier cleats. Sailors on the divers barge then tied up their end of the mooring lines and thanks to the diver's barge thrusters they were hard up against the pier so there wasn't a lot of strenuous work in tying up the divers' barge.

A brow (gang plank) was craned over by the diver's barge. One of the vans backed up to the pier by the end of the diver's barge brow and opened its rear doors. Moments later a wood crate on a dolly was taken to the brow where it was all lifted and quickly moved across the brow and out onto the pier and slid in the Van which shortly drove away with the other automobiles. Moments later the pier was evacuated except for the divers who would be required to stay there overnight until their reliefs showed up the next day with potentially new assignments.

Five of the vehicles drove to Consolidated Robotics, the other van took several divers and support guys to a parking lot where their personal transportation was waiting.

The remaining vehicles later pulled into Consolidated Robotics Campus and around to a corner lot where a building existed that did a lot of special projects, some related to robotics and other clandestine projects.

There were now two full time security guys at the entrance to the building designated *Robotics Personality Development*. Few if anyone had ever seen any robots anywhere near this building. Since most of the company knew nothing about it, often there were jokes mentioned about personality tweaking that went on inside the *Robotics Personality Development* Building.

On the side of the building was a sliding metal door that opened electrically. People inside the building were notified the shipment was arriving and the metal door started sliding upwards with the electric motors moving the mechanical linkages that did all the work.

The delivery van was guided partially into the building then told to stop. Men inside waiting had a strong four wheeled cart good for probably five hundred pounds or more opened the back door of the delivery van and slid the wood crate out onto the cart. They then shut the rear doors of the van and the driver was directed to move the delivery van to the parking lot with all the other company vehicles.

This was the warehouse part of the building where shipments of extravagant things came and went. Several men then took the wood crate on the cart out of the shipping/ receiving room and down a hallway to a double door room marked with LAB C on a placard above the double doors that now had the windows covered over from the inside and a security man standing outside with a short list of people allowed in provided they had the combination lock to the room, otherwise they would not get in.

The men bringing in the wood crate had no idea what was inside of it. All they knew was this was another Doctor Hudson project.

Doctor Hudson the consummate bachelor who never dated or wanted anything to do with women was noted for having the strangest projects that few ever knew about. Doctor Hudson was a soft-spoken gentleman, never assuming and had a wit that would surprise most. He didn't have a lot of good things to say about some of his superiors who were all *dipshits,* so he didn't say much at all about them to anyone.

Doctor Hudson was certainly an enigma with a great mind in mathematics and electronics spanning fifty plus years. He had experienced a lot of change in his days and early in his career was solving incredible problems with astute mathematical genius. His multiple formulas in some of his projects were artwork to themselves. Doctor Hudson was a master of differential and integral calculus and could calculate extremely complicated answers sometimes before computers could spit it out. Doctor Hudson no doubt had thousands of integrals and formulas tucked away somewhere in his head. The most powerful men on the planet came to Doctor Hudson usually in a case of last resort. He now had the biggest challenge of his career in the box in front of him. And the only help he was going to get was from his lab assistant Paul who had the nickname LR since he was the consummate lab rat (a person that spent most of his daylight hours in a research lab).

After everyone was out of the room and doors shut, Doctor Hudson turned to Paul (aka LR) and asked, "LR, do you think you can disassemble that wooden crate without destroying it in case we need to use it again?

"I suppose so."

LR went over and looked at the construction and said, "We are in luck, they used screws instead of nails, will help get it apart really easily."

LR went over to his work bench, pulled the electric screwdriver off its charging attachment, and grabbed a Phillips head bit and put it in the chuck and tightened it down. LR then grabbed an empty coffee cup and went to the cart and started unscrewing all the wood screws and putting them in the coffee cup as he continued zipping along. In a couple minutes the top of the wood crate came off and inside was the mechanical man with a lot of saltwater deposits all over it.

LR had been briefed by Doctor Hudson as to what to expect, so he wasn't shocked by what he now looked at.

Doctor Hudson then said, "Move the cart over to our work area so we can slide the curtain around in case someone comes in here that shouldn't see this."

"No problem," LR said as he shoved the cart over into an area they often worked in adjacent to his workbench and toolboxes and numerous instruments.

"I'm going to partially slide the curtain around now, but you will have the one end open to get some good air circulation."

"Thanks, I appreciate that."

LR continued pulling out the wood screws and soon had the sides of the wood crate off and the only thing that was left was the crate bottom that had some wooden *four by fours* bolted to it so that a forklift could get under it and lift it up.

"Is there any reason to move it off the crate bottom?"

"Not really. We'll move it off when we want too."

"All right. What do you want to do now?"

"I want you to clean it up really good then we'll examine it to see how we can open it up. Its probably full of saltwater contamination."

"Too bad we don't have a lot of deionized water to wash it down."

"We don't have a heat room to dry it out and I would be afraid of damaging its electronics in a heat room where we have to run it about 130 degrees to really get all the moisture out of it."

"I guess we'll have to stick with the spray aerosols, I have a couple cases of it and can get more if needed."

"Be sure and pull that hood down and turn on the blower. I don't want you to breath too much of that chemical crap in your lungs."

"Why? You afraid I might get high?"

"There are better ways to get high, with some good beverages."

"Too bad you don't like going to strip clubs I know a place that serves the best."

"It's not my cup of tea looking at those filthy bitches."

"Well, you know what they say, *one man's junk is another man's treasure.*"

"You can have my share of the treasure."

Knowing that Doctor Hudson was an air freak, LR dropped the air intake down to about two feet above the robot and started the blower.

"Would you mind if I put on a little of the Tchaikovsky to cover up the noise of the blower?"

"Sure, as long as you don't play Swan Lake?"

"What's wrong with *Swan Lake*?"

"The Girl I was going to marry took me to watch *Swan Lake* at the San Francisco Ballet just before I did something dumb and took her to that Casino in Las Vegas where she lost all my money and dumped me because suddenly I no longer had any money. I don't want to see or hear *Swan Lake* ever again."

"Know what you mean."

LR commenced spraying and cleaning. The spray had some great cleaning effectiveness and with a lot of handwipe's all around the robot to suck up the runoff, he didn't make too bad a mess.

The trash bag LR tied to the side of the cart slowly filled up with filthy handy wipes getting off the grime created in the spacecraft sitting on the bottom of the ocean. It didn't take long to fill up the first trash bag, and the second was ready to go. Finally, it appeared that most of the robot was cleaned to Doctor Hudson's standards which meant it had to pass a white glove inspection.

Doctor Hudson spent time reading his emails and looking over some documents and didn't pay too close attention to what LR was doing.

"I'm ready to start working on its backside. I have some rope I'm going to tie to one of its legs and arms so I can have it suspended on its side." LR noted.

LR got a ladder and set it up to where he knew he could feed through what appeared to be lifting pads screwed into the steel framework in the overhead. Just like clockwork the robot was tied up on its side and LR went to work scrubbing away cleaning up the least bit of residual ocean debris.

The blower did a good job of sucking the chemicals out of the LAB and the chemicals were very fast drying.

The spacesuit the robot wore was removed on the divers' barge and placed in a bag that was left in the wooden crate. Doctor Hudson grabbed the bag and looked at it and asked, "Can you do me a favor?"

"Sure?"

"Take these clothes home with you and wash them. I want to put them back on the robot especially if we are lucky enough to restore it."

"Sure, no problem."

"Put all those clothes in my leather satchel and I'll walk you out of the lab carrying it, so you don't have to worry about a property pass or getting into trouble. I'll help you carry it to your car."

"Thanks, I appreciate that."

LR looked at the wall clock and saw it was already 8:00 P.M. but he knew Doctor Hudson sometimes stayed to midnight or later. He was a driven man.

"What do you want to do now?"

"The floor is all ESD neutralized?"

"Yes, and I check it every day. We have a humidifier and ESD neutralizer running all the time. The mat covering the floor has a wire mesh in it grounded."

"Okay, then it should be safe to open it up. The Cart has steel wheels so it should be making contact."

"Let me check it with my meter."

Using a digital meter, LR checked resistance from his work

bench ground to the cart and the floor and they all read zero ohms.

"We are good, everything is ground potential."

"Did you see any access panels when you cleaned it?

"Yes, it looks like its entire chest plate is an access panel."

"Okay us open it up."

LR walked over to his workbench got his electric screwdriver and an assortment of screw blades and plastic medicine bottles to put the screws in to make sure none got lost. Zip-zip-zip, the fifty-four screws were removed and after a little mechanical agitation with a flat blade screwdriver, the breast plate came open.

LR took off the robot's breast plate and sat it down on the lower platform of the cart which was nice and handy storage.

"You know most people do not believe aliens exist."

"Nor would they believe they have robots and circuitry like this."

"It's amazing, its all pristine inside here, this cavity didn't leak."

"Those four switches look like power breakers. They have heavy wires going to them?"

"If this is dry, I wonder what tripped the breakers?"

"Its hard saying. In some applications we have breaker trip devices to protect circuitry from over heating based on temperature. This could be a similar situation."

"You mean the robot tripped its own breakers to do an emergency shutdown to protect the circuitry."

"Sure."

"But how would it know it would ever get picked up off the bottom of the ocean?"

"I can certainly think of one way."

"Such as?'

"Intuition. It had on a space suit just like the beings in the space craft. It was probably their equal if not more so. It might have assumed there would be a good chance our curiosity would drive us to retrieve it and restore it."

"Very interesting theory."

"One thing I'll say is it's a good thing those other aliens shot it down and not us. Hopefully it has no hostile intentions when we wake it up."

"I hope so to."

"Us leave the breast plate off for now if the power modules are in this cavity, the power might still be there to operate it for a while. But for now, we need to attempt inspections of the rest of the body to see if there is any saltwater intrusion in the rest of it."

"We don't have much left to check, the head, arms and legs."

"Us start with the head. That's probably critical if it's flooded that could be a serious problem."

"I have a question."

"How would we know there was a robot on this space craft?"

"Damn good question. Someone some how sure as hell knew."

"I think there is a lot more to the story than we realize."

"Us don't even go there. Some things are not worth knowing."

"Aright let me see if there is some way to get the head apart."

LR looked and looked and felt and nothing seemed obvious. Doctor Hudson looked and said, "Maybe it's a sealed unit like the chest cavity?"

The robots' eyes were closed, LR lifted one of the eye lids and said, "It looks like a normal eye to me."

"Us check out the arms and legs."

After exhaustive checking LR said, "I see no entry to the arms, legs, neck, head. It's a sealed unit."

"It sure appears that way."

"Doctor Hudson, I know in the past when we ran into a situation like this before, I suggested us just turn the damn thing on and see if it works. You were dead set against it because it wasn't logical to you."

"That's because there is always a logical way to power up a system to make sure you do not damage it in the process."

But this is a case of a lot of unknowns. I know your boss wants you to cut it open and find out how it works, but I think its way over our heads, and we should just try to turn it on."

"This is one time I may have to agree with you, because I'm sure there are no alternatives."

"I like the theory it did an emergency shutdown and saved itself. How we came to find out about it will be a mystery and how we restored it will be a bigger mystery."

"Any other time I would say you are dead wrong, and we must explore all other possibilities first but the fact its chest is dry tells me there may be some hope of restoring it by reapplying the power."

"I agree, we got nothing to lose."

"If it doesn't power up then we will slice and dice and cut to pieces to see what makes it tick."

"Any suggestion as to breaker order?"

"Logically I would think from one side to the other. Can you see any marking on the switches that might indicate order?"

"There are markings, but they are all alien script of some sort."

"I guess you'll just have to flip them and hope we get lucky."

"One of them looks like a Chinese number four - Sì [四]on the far-right switch."

"Dr. Hudson always ready for a good one liner said, "Alright, pick the breaker on the other end and start turning them on, but if in doubt pick C."

"How do you know that's how I passed all my college entrance exams?"

"Good guess on my part."

"Here we go. Hopefully it doesn't wake up and start killing us."

"What's the worst that can happen to us? We die and I'm old already."

LR turned on the first switch, not much happened, then he turned on the second breaker and there were suddenly a few flashing lights on what appeared to be a module. Then he continued flipping the switches on and after all four breakers were turned on there was no noise but lots of blinking lights on the modules.

"Seems to be a lot of activity," Doctor Hudson said.

"Don't know what it means," LR stated.

Doctor Hudson wearing his white lab coat with his name tag stood back taking it all in, wondering how this amazing event was able to come about was watching the robot for any movement then suddenly saw the eyelid of one of the eyes open, then the other eye lid. The eyes blinked a couple of times then suddenly, the robot moved his upper torso upwards and then looked around the room and focused on Doctor Hudson's name tag.

CHAPTER SEVENTEEN
TIĀNCÁI

The robot sat there staring at Doctor Hudson and asked, "Are you doctor Hudson?"

"Yes I am."

"Doctor Hudson, I'm Tiāncái."

"Tiāncái this is my lab assistant I call Lab Rat, nick named LR. His real name is Paul."

"Hello Paul."

Tiāncái looked down and said, "I notice you have my breast plate removed."

"We took you apart as much as we could to see if we could restore you."

"It looks like you restored me. Would you mind putting my breast plate back on?"

"Sure, would you mind laying back down, it will make it easier for me," LR replied.

Tiāncái responded, "Yes I understand that would be easier for you." He then laid back down and LR commenced to put the breast plate back on.

"I don't know what the torc specs of your screws are, but I'm putting on 25-inch pounds of that's okay?"

"Twenty-Five-inch pounds would be more than sufficient."

LR slowly put the 54 machine screws back into Tiāncái's torso and soon the breast plate was back in place.

Doctor Hudson then said, Tiāncái, your uniform needs cleaned. LR is going to take it home and launder it for you tonight."

"Thank you. On the space craft or back at my home world I always had fresh uniforms available."

"Tiāncái, do you know what happened to your space craft?"

"Yes, we were shot down. Where did you find me?"

"You were at the bottom of the ocean inside the space craft."

"Were there other bodies in the spacecraft?"

"From what I understand according to reports I read; the crew was sitting in their chairs in front of consoles strapped in. Strangely there was no damage to inside the cabin of the spacecraft. All the damage appeared to be on the outside."

"Doctor Hudson, do you believe in reincarnation?"

"Tiāncái, on this planet we have a religion that has a document called the Bhagavad Gita. The people who follow this indoctrination or Krsna Science as they call it believe in reincarnation. I've read that document."

"What do you think of reincarnation?" Tiāncái asked.

"I really do not know if it happens or not. I have no way of knowing."

"This document Bhagavad Gita, can you provide me a copy."

"Certainly, but it will have to be tomorrow during the day

because its late at night and all the bookstores are closed."

"That will be soon enough."

"Tiāncái, nobody knows we have restored you. I have no idea what they have in mind for you, but they have given me a lot of time to restore you. If we tell them you are restored, they will take you away and I have no idea what their plans are. I recommend that when we leave tonight, you play dead so that nobody knows you have been restored and that will give me some time to figure out what's going on."

"Not a problem Doctor Hudson. I want to read Bhagavad Gita before I leave here."

"Tiāncái, may I ask you a question?"

"Sure Doctor Hudson."

"Before I ask the question, I want to say Tiāncái, your English is excellent and I'm very happy you can communicate with us."

"Thank you, Doctor Hudson, I'm happy I can effectively communicate with you."

"Tiāncái, I'm curious as to why you are interested in reincarnation?"

"Doctor Hudson, two of the crewmembers on our ship thought they knew each other in prior lives and were reincarnated."

"That's very interesting. What made them think they were reincarnated?"

"They had similar dreams. They were very close and in fact I know they became lovers."

"I see. And by these dreams they thought they were reincarnated?"

"Yes, as they described their dreams to each other they became convinced they knew each other in prior lives."

"Does the planet they came from believe in reincarnation?"

"No. The concept is very alien to them."

"Then how did they determine they were reincarnated if its not studied on your planet?"

"We were here studying earth for a while. We downloaded tremendous amount of information on multiple missions here and in some of the data acquisition that pertained to religions and culture, they became aware of reincarnation and started to believe their dreams must have come from that."

"Tiāncái, it's getting late, and we need to leave soon go home eat and get some sleep, plus LR needs to wash your space suit. I would like you to lay down and play dead until we return in the morning. I would like to hear more about this couple if you don't mind."

"Doctor Hudson I will do as you requested and I'm looking forward to reading the Bhagavad Gita."

"Thank you Tiāncái, this room is very secure, very few people are allowed in and there is a guard outside the door who will not let anyone in who's not on the access list which is a very short one."

"What time will you be back, Doctor Hudson?"

"I figure about eight hours from now."

"All right Doctor Hudson, I will see you then."

Tiāncái laid back, closed his eyes and nobody would know he was alive.

Doctor Hudson and LR left for the night with Doctor Hudson carrying his leather satchel with Tiāncái's uniform.

LR went home, put the uniform that felt like delicate fabric in the washing machine and set it to cold wash and put a reasonable amount of detergent in and started the cycle. After throwing some food in the microwave, LR poured himself a nice glass of Cabernet Sauvignon and sat down at his recliner in front of the TV and was watching the news and eventually heard the washing machine alarm announce the uniform was washed. He then put it in the dryer and selected a warm setting as he didn't want to shrink the fabric. In 45 minutes, it would be dry and ready to press if required.

LR sat back down in his recliner, ate his meal, polished off that nice glass of wine to wash it down and surfed the TV channels looking for something interesting to watch and observed a few things for a few minutes, he looked at the clock on the wall and after what he thought was about 35 minutes, went to the dryer and pulled out the clothes. They were dry and not wrinkled and held their press just like they had come from the dry cleaners.

This is interesting.

LR folded the clothes, put them into Doctor Hudson's leather satchel and set it by the garage door so he would not forget it in the morning. He then polished off a second glass of wine and went to bed.

Tiāncái's eyes were shut but he was fully operational. Tiāncái had a wireless capability and had hacked into Earth computers before. He still had all his memories which included everything he did since coming off the assembly line.

Tiāncái knew his final moments with the crew and their demise from evil *Rusnarian* Aliens who were an existential threat to planet Earth. If he ever made it back to the Empire, he would make a full report on the incident and the evil *Rusnarians* would have to be dealt with. They were not only a threat to planet Earth, but they were now a growing threat to a lot of other areas of the galaxy. The showdown would have to happen. However, his first problem was getting off the planet. At the present time there seemed to be no way home.

In the morning Doctor Hudson and LR met in the parking lot and LR handed Doctor Hudson his leather satchel. They were like permanent fixtures in the LAB. Nobody spent as much time in the LAB as these two guys and most of the time nobody else knew what they were doing because they were always given incredible missions to perform with very little time to accomplish it.

They didn't realize it, Tiāncái had extremely good hearing and he could tell simply by the footsteps who it was coming up to the door. In complying with Doctor Hudson's request, he remained laying down with his eyes closed even though in the middle of the night he sat up looked at the electrical adapter on the workbench, opened a secret compartment they missed identifying thanks to the way the chest plate was designed creating a crack long the conformal design.

He pulled out his power cord which could easily be adapted and was currently arranged for Earth power in case he needed it and plugged himself in for a trickle charge and went back to exploring the Internet downloading numerous files and found a Bhagavad Gita eBook and downloaded it and quickly scanned it. This was a huge revelation to Tiāncái as it spelled out this religion's views on reincarnation. He knew his friends Marla and Beryl had studied sources of it when they were searching for answers about their past lives, they thought they lived.

Tiāncái could multi-process. After the download of Bhagavad Gita from the internet he was analyzing its content throughout and in the process was learning all the Sanskrit phrases as a good robot would want to know absolutely everything contained in the book. His first level of analysis produced a summary the writers and editors were well equipped with language skills that were uncommon, robust, and on a much higher level of intellect compared to most literature found on planet Earth.

By the time Doctor Hudson and LR showed up, his power pack was fully charged and good for several more days. He was continuing his analysis of Bhagavad Gita even when the men walked into the LAB because dealing with them was actually a low bandwidth requirement.

With the door shut and the curtain wrapped around so that nobody could accidently walk in and see Tiāncái, Doctor Hudson assuming Tiāncái was fully alert said, "Tiāncái we are back you can sit up now."

Tiāncái sat up then swiveled his body around where his legs were sticking down the side of the cart.

LR handed Tiāncái his space uniform and said, "Your uniform is now clean, you can put it on."

"Thank you, Paul, I like wearing a uniform, as it makes me feel a better part of the crew and makes them feel better having me around."

Tiāncái had his uniform on in a minute when LR noticed he was barefoot.

"I didn't realize you didn't have shoes on. They must have removed them on the Divers Barge."

"We wear space shoes, which have sure-grips on the bottom to make sure we do not slip."

Doctor Hudson said, "The bookstores do not open for a couple hours, when I go get you a copy of Bhagavad Gita, I will pick up some shoes and socks for you to make you appear like you wear them. Is there any type you prefer?"

"Just a minute Doctor Hudson, let me check a few of my records."

"In about thirty seconds Tiāncái said, I've located the type I would prefer. May I use your computer to show you on the Internet?"

"You know how to use the Internet?"

"Absolutely, I copied 50 terabytes of your internet in the past. I currently have 25 terabytes stored in my memory of past downloads."

Tiāncái stood up and walked over to the computer terminal on the desk next to LR's work bench.

He then moved the mouse around to bring up the screen as the computer was never turned off and turned around at LR and asked, "What's your password to logon?"

"Magic."

"Really?"

"Sure, who would think of trying that password?"

"You need to change your password to make it stronger, so you don't get hacked."

I have no problems remembering Magic."

"If that's the case change it to Magic#1Magic#2magic#3Magic#4 and the hackers will have a hard time breaking in."

"Alright after you finish, I'll change it. That's actually a good idea."

Doctor Hudson looked at Tiāncái and asked, "How do you

know about hackers?"

Doctor Hudson, we hack hackers all the time because they are an easy source for passwords, so we don't have to waste our time."

"Have you hacked computers on Earth?"

"Yes, how do you think I obtained 50 Terabytes?"

"Our computer security is that bad?"

"Your computer security and your crypto are easy to break."

"Would you be willing to help us fix that problem?"

"Would you be willing to help me get home to the Empire?"

"If I knew how I would."

"I can teach you how."

"I seriously doubt you can teach an old dog new tricks."

"Doctor Hudson, I know I can teach you. Do no be scared or fear because I know what I'm capable of and all you must do is cooperate and together we can do a lot of things this planet thinks is impossible."

"Tiāncái, I'm not sure we have a lot of time to do anything. My masters will soon be demanding results and eventually LR and I will be removed out of the picture if I do not provide results. Plus, I'm sure as soon as I tell them I've restored you, they will have their own ideas of what to do with you."

"Doctor Hudson if you are willing to trust me, I can break out of here and secretly work with you. Together there is much we can do."

"All right, Tiāncái, I will help you as much as I can, and I sense that if I get you back to your Empire it will be the best thing for planet Earth."

"Paul, are you dedicated to Doctor Hudson? Will you betray him?"

"Tiāncái, Doctor Hudson knows he can count on me. I will do whatever he asks of me."

"What if it gets you into trouble?"

"I am not concerned about trouble as long as Doctor Hudson approves of my actions."

"Alright Paul or would you rather me call you LR?"

"I like LR because I'm used to it and feel comfortable."

"Alright LR, that will be the case."

Tiāncái didn't need to ask how long Doctor Hudson thought he had before other players would enter the picture because thanks to LR's back door he was already hacking Doctor Hudson's accounts and soon broke in. He now knew everything the establishment had to say via the Internet to Doctor Hudson. In about thirty minutes Tiāncái had broken into the accounts of everyone associated with the downed space craft. He knew every player and every move they made. He now knew exactly how much time he had and how soon it would before he needed to escape and take on a new identity.

The next three days were quite interesting because Tiāncái populated ops-brief with a brazen report and recommendation to raise the spacecraft to re-engineer it and it wasn't attributed to any particular contributor. That created quite a controversy and investigation as to who did it. Nevertheless, it put the idea in a few people's heads which was Tiāncái's plan and very quickly that moved ahead as powerful people got behind the project of raising the spacecraft.

Tiāncái knew the best way to raise the craft. It did not weigh a lot. Most of its weight was salt water that would drain out as they got it up to the surface to raise it on a barge. Tiāncái again sent out an unattributed entry to the ops-brief that laid out the plan to easily raise the space craft. There were multiple emergency access hatches, and the idea was once it got near the surface, they would open those other hatches to drain the space craft as they loaded it onto a barge.

Per the recommendation from an anonymous person who wished to not be identified, the simple solution was to raise it very slowly to not put a lot of stress on the rig raising it and as they opened the other emergency hatches that could be done in shallow water it would lesson the load on two cranes necessary to lift it. Once they got it in the air when it would be considerably lighter, a tug would push a barge under the space craft to lower it on and a tarp would immediately be placed over the space craft to keep its existence away from the public.

The raising of the spaceship took on a life of its own and helped to eliminate a lot of interest in the robot for the time being.

Tiāncái knew it was a matter of time before they would shift their focus back to him and he already laid the groundwork with Doctor Hudson.

By the time they shifted their focus back to the robot, the spacecraft was on a barge on its way to a facility that had a major Naval Air Base on the waterfront. This facility had a top-secret hanger for special projects and was fully secured. Tiāncái would then assert himself to help them repair it and make it flight ready.

What was unique about this Navy Hanger is after they repaired the space craft, they could put the spacecraft back on a barge and take it up to Vandenburg and launch it out into space from there. The space craft could not leave the planet fueled up. It would be too heavy and have undue stress on the hull. Once out in space they could fuel it up with liquid hydrogen from a few shuttle missions.

CHAPTER EIGHTEEN
WHERE'S THE ROBOT?

Once the space craft was inside the hanger barely fitting the interest in the robot came back and soon the director showed up with a couple professors from MIT that were going to take over from Doctor Hudson and haul the robot back to Massachusetts where proper engineering analysis could be done.

Doctor Hudson knew they were coming for the turnover and Tiāncái said, "Let me handle this, Doctor Hudson."

"What do I have to lose?"

"Nothing. Just watch and observe."

The director led the two MIT Prima Donna's into the Lab thinking they would find a dead robot.

Tiāncái was behind the curtain. They didn't know Tiāncái's status.

"Dr. Hudson, this is Dr. King and Dr. McMahon here to take custody of the robot and they will be taking it to MIT so they can figure out how to make it operational."

"Director, have you really lost faith in me?"

"You certainly had a lot of time to do your magic, and these men have assured me they can quickly analyze his circuitry and make sense of it all."

"What if the robot doesn't want to go?"

"What the hell are you talking about?"

"Why don't you ask him yourself."

Doctor Hudson was so upset at these wantabee's King and McMahon, he wanted to flame their assess and prove to them a point.

The director was pissed and asked, "What the hell are you talking about Doctor Hudson?"

Doctor Hudson nodded to LR who then pulled the curtain back and there was the robot standing with his immaculate clean space uniform on.

"Hello gentlemen. It appears you didn't have adaquate faith in Doctor Hudson why is that?"

All three were standing there stunned.

Finally, the director had the nerve to ask, "Is this the real robot?"

"Why don't you go outside and check the security guy's logs and see who else has entered this room besides the three of you and Paul and I."

Tiāncái now did his part that had a mysterious effect on the director.

"Director, I really don't like you, I'm upset what you have done to Doctor Hudson over the years. I'm going to show you something."

The robot walked over to the director and picked him up by his shirt and lifted him up in the air with one hand and walked over to the MIT guys and said, "I will only communicate through Doctor Hudson. Would you like to see me kill the director?"

"No, please let him down."

When the robot let the director down, he was already unconscious thinking he was dying. The robot wasn't going to kill him, but he wanted to send a message.

"You guys can stay here and work with Doctor Hudson, but I'm not going to MIT, understand?"

"Yes, we understand."

"Good. You will benefit greatly by your cooperation. I suggest you grab a couple chairs, and we'll have a little talk."

"What about him?" One of the researchers asked fearing the robot might have killed him.

"I have excellent sensors. He's unconscious but he will come to in a few minutes and may run the hell out of here like a scared rat."

The two MIT scientists were so scared they didn't budge so LR grabbed a couple chairs and put them next to the scientists and said, "Please relax and just sit down and us see what Tiāncái has to say."

The two scientists sat down and LR provided Tiāncái a chair so that he could face them direct.

"Gentlemen, I've been coherent since the day I arrived. That night Doctor Hudson and LR revived me. They took a sophisticated approach and figured out what they needed to do, and it worked. I'm fully operational now and have been for over a week. You will probably recall the two of you received emails from *anonymous*. That was me."

"I suppose you are full of all kinds of questions you don't

quite yet know to ask. I've predicted them and will help you out. Your nagging question is how I came here and how my spaceship ended up at the bottom of the ocean?"

The scientists were still too shocked to think for themselves and soon responded, "Yes we would like to know."

Tiāncái then laid it on them. "Earth is in a real serious situation now. Unless I can get back to the Empire to inform them what happened with the Rusnarians here, there may not be much hope for Earth."

"How could we possibly get you back to your empire?"

"If you work with me, we can repair the spaceship I arrived in and then I can get back and make all the appropriate reports. I have the entire confrontation in my non-destructive memory banks. Once the Empire is notified, they will come here and the Rusnarians will be shoved back so far away, you will not have to worry about them in your future timelines for at least 1000 years."

Soon the MIT guys started relaxing and there was a lot of Q and A going on. MIT Scientists soon understood this world had insufficient means to protect itself.

The special projects director slowly came to and for a while was in a semi-conscious state hearing the discussion going on. By the time he fully became alert, being a smart man that he was knew he should be in the listen mode for a while as some interesting scenarios were now unfolding.

About the time the director started to chime in, the Tiāncái said, "If you want to be able to get that space craft flying in the shortest period of time which may result in saving Earth from destruction, it would be best if I was taken there and help bring the systems back online so we can do a survey of what is in critical need of repair."

The director said, "First thing we will have to do is give you a change of clothes, you can't go into the facility with an Alien Space Suit on."

"Not a problem. I can wear whatever I need, and you think appropriate."

"I have an idea," LR said.

"And what is that?" the director asked.

"The robot is about my size. I'll swap clothes with him now and I'll wear his space suit when we leave, and I'll go home and change."

"I would like the space suit back when I fly back to the empire," the robot responded.

"Not a problem. I'll bring it to you after I change clothes at home."

"Thank you."

"When do we go?" Doctor Hudson asked.

"With the big challenges we face, we need to go right now," the director said, knowing this would advance the timeline at breakneck speeds and impress his superiors.

LR looked at the robot and said, "Come over by my work bench we can swap clothes there."

In a few minutes after the change of clothes the group departed the LAB and the security guard logged in six people leaving. When the logs were reviewed, there would be an investigation into how the numbers didn't match in the number of entries and departures.

"How is everyone going to get to the base?" one of the MIT researchers asked.

"For today, I'll take you two guys. Doctor Hudson, can I trust you to get the robot to the base?"

"Absolutely sir. But which building?"

"You can't miss it. Building 28, one of the two large circular buildings build back in the 1930's for the Navy's dirigibles USS Akron (ZRS-4) and USS Macon (ZRS-5)."

"Which one of the two?"

"The one with all the doors closed and armed guards outside."

"Where do I park my car?"

"In front of the building is a side street. We'll have a reserved parking sign with your name put up on it."

"Alright LR and Tiāncái, us get going. Tiāncái, you get in my car, and we'll follow LR home so he can change his clothes. LR after you change, put the space suit in a shopping bag and bring it with you."

"Alright Doctor Hudson."

"LR one other thing."

"Yes Doctor Hudson?"

"On the way to your home drive a little more conservatively and not like a bat out of hell."

"Understand all Doctor Hudson."

In twenty minutes, they were parked in front of LR's home with his car parked in the driveway. His wife was a little surprised when he came home wearing a space uniform with Alien markings and insignias on it and asked:

"What the hell have you been up to?"

"I'm sorry dear, its part of that secret project I can't tell you about."

LR's wife thought she had seen it all!

LR quickly changed into one of his Lab Rat outfits and grabbed an extra shopping bag they had from shopping they often utilized to put recyclables in the blue container for weekly pickups.

The men then left LR's home. It took about twenty minutes to get from LR's home to North Island with Doctor Hudson driving. Doctor Hudson the absent-minded professor often needed a wing man to guide him to his destinations.

Doctor Hudson didn't like back seat drivers. LR knew to avoid it, but sometimes he couldn't help it. Doctor Hudson missed his turns quite often. Perhaps when he was alone, he did better?

As an example, they were going down to Mission Valley one time and LR tried to help Doctor Hudson and he said, "You should get in the right lane, so we don't miss our turn."

"I really do not need your help with my driving!"

LR bit his lip but Doctor Hudson failed to get over to exit Rosecrans Exit as they were coming back from Industrial Liquidators on Convoy getting a few computer parts for assembly of some electronic gadgets. Since they missed the turn and were soon approaching the Clairemont exit, LR asked, "Is there any reason why we are going to Los Angeles?"

Doctor Hudson was immediately embarrassed and upset. So LR initiated some guidance and got them turned around and soon heading down Rosecrans where Doctor Hudson wanted to go to his favorite restaurant for lunch: *Denny's*.

The mere thought of Doctor Hudson driving them over the

Coronado Bay Bridge sent shivers through LR. But held his comments and said a few prayers.

Tiāncái was sitting up front with Doctor Hudson looking at everything and exploring the internet on several simultaneous wireless links in parallel studying everything about the areas they traveled and the military base they were soon approaching.

Doctor Hudson who had to drive on military bases frequently had a military sticker on his car even though recently they had been discontinued due to cost and realization terrorists would simply kill a person take their I.D. and car and drive it on the base.

The former car sticker business was a boondoggle and created administrative delays and headaches because people were not aware the sticker date expired until the gate guard would not let them enter. And if they didn't have up to date insurance and car registration papers with them, they would have to drive home and get them, usually wasting most of their morning.

Whoever determined to get rid of the car stickers deserves a medal because they have already saved the government millions upon millions worth of money not wasted on such foolish policies. No doubt some dysfunctional DOD person would one day come up with a great idea to put stickers back on people's cars and they would be wasting money again. But hey, it was another one of those great jobs programs the government liked to help employ people despite the waste and institutionalized functional delay.

LR felt grateful that Doctor Hudson didn't get them killed going over the bridge. The next obstacle would be finding the parking spot and the hanger.

Thanks to Tiāncái's internet access pulling up google maps,

he guided Doctor Hudson to his reserved parking spot. For some strange reason Doctor Hudson didn't mind having the robot directing him. *Maybe it was the novelty of it,* LR wondered.

Aside from the reserved parking spot they easily found there was a person in a Uniform there partly guarding it because this was one of the two hangars helicopter squadrons utilized and full bird Captains part of their squadrons had the tendency to park anywhere, they wanted.

The young sailor in his dress uniform had already informed three full bird captains they couldn't park there and being talked to by a junior enlisted person that way made them angry and one of them even had the audacity to tell the young man *to shove it, he was parking there anyway, and he could give a damn who Doctor Hudson is.*

"Sir with all due respect, the base CO has given me his number to give to you so he can explain to you why he'll be sending the tow truck to tow your car away and impound it until you go to traffic court."

The young, enlisted man loved having leverage over an asshole Navy Captain who suddenly wasn't having a good day as he spotted the sailor also had a walkie-talkie on his being. Therefore, on the better part of valor the Navy Captain already late for his meeting drove off desperately looking for a parking spot and dreaded he might have to drive all the way down to a sandwich shop that had a few parking spots that intermittently opened as people went in to buy food.

Thanks to Tiāncái's web surfing, they knew exactly where the entrance was to go in. One of the hangers had a lot of activity with air crews coming and going, the other one appeared totally locked down with a couple enlisted men in their green camouflaged working uniforms at the secured entrance.

As the three men approached the enlisted man with a senior

rating indication asked, "Sir are you, Doctor Hudson?"

"Yes. They are expecting the three of us."

"Sir, this petty officer will escort you inside, the senior enlisted said."

"Thank you."

Going inside the building, Doctor Hudson an inquisitive man looked at the insides of the building and noted the engineering marvel. Its huge concrete beams were no doubt build to withstand bomb blasts and protect whatever was inside at the time, a byproduct of the lead up to WW2 when the base went through drastic changes.

After whimsically looking over the building, Doctor Hudson looked forward at the object sitting in the middle of the hanger with very few people around it.

Doctor Hudson then said, "Tiāncái is this how you made it to Earth?"

"It sure is but I didn't arrive in the manner I wished I had."

Off to the sides they noticed some coffins and were quickly greeted by the project director and the two MIT professors.

Tiāncái asked, "What are those things," pointing to the ornately fashioned coffins the government spent a lot of money on because of the rush.

"Those are coffins we put the deceased in and will load them up and take them to a cemetery for burial."

"Would it be possible to preserve the bodies in refrigerated units so that I can take them home for proper ceremonies at their home planet?"

"I suppose we could work something out like that if you help us restore this space craft and show us how to use it."

"It will be my pleasure."

The director turned towards another civilian now walking up to him, who was obviously his assistant and said, "Mike we have a change of plans. Rent a refrigerated truck and store the bodies in them for now."

"It may take us a day to set up the rental and the bodies are already starting to stink really bad."

Tiāncái who had already surfed the internet for solutions responded, "May I make a suggestion you send someone for dry ice and pack it in those containers until your refrigerated units arrive?"

"Good idea," the director said.

"Mike, get someone to pick up some dry ice right away."

"No problem, that's a lot quicker than renting truck trailers."

Doctor Hudson noticed the spacecraft was covered up with large tarps attached to staging materials that created a temporary building within side the building. And the obvious entrance had someone sitting at a temporary desk with an access binder, laptop with a power cord running over to a power outlet on one of the support columns of the roof and an old-style telephone.

"The project director said, shall we go inside and take a look?"

"Sure, why not," Doctor Hudson responded.

The delegation then walked past the guard at the desk who knew these men were expected and had looked at all their faces on his laptop moments before they passed by.

There was a curtain at the entrance to this temporary staging structure with lots of tarps hiding the spacecraft.

And there it was an incredible sight. A black triangular shaped space craft with a couple angled dorsal near its rear.

Tiāncái asked, "Can we walk to the rear of the aircraft, that's where I think the damage was."

"Sure, go ahead."

Tiāncái led the group to the back. The project director was quite curious as to the functionality of the equipment back there. Tiāncái scouted the damage and was immediately relieved the nuclear thruster engines were both intact. All that was wrong was some of the piping and control cables going to the port thruster engine were damaged.

"That's why we lost power and control of the ship and only had the ability to crash land in the ocean," Tiāncái said.

"What do you think?"

"I think I can work with your machinists and engineers, and this can be repaired and can fly again."

Tiāncái was pleased thus far from what he found. He then said, I want to do a cursory inspection of the hull to make sure it isn't damaged that would make it dangerous to attempt hyperspace velocities.

The men followed Tiāncái as he walked around the hull of the space craft and was pleased the Earth people had sat the craft down on conformal blocks they created as to not stress the hull when they transported it on the barge. In the middle of the night when they took the space craft from the nearby dock to the hanger it was suspended by lifting rig and then sat back down on the conformal blocs.

The hull was an exotic design. The ribs were a thicker amount of material than what went on the hull that had carbon nano tubes, graphene, titanium, aluminum, and copper sheets in numerous thin layers that created an extremely strong and resilient hull that could handle the light speed transition into hyperspace velocities required to go long distances in the galaxy. If these Earth people knew how far away the Plastradavious Empire was from Earth, they would not believe it possible to go the distance.

The way the hull physics worked and Tiāncái knew this all too well: if there were any cracks at all it was finished. It could not be repaired. He was able to see most of the hull at the bottom except where the conformal blocks were. When cracks developed due to mechanical failure induced by space weapons, they usually went longitudinal around the spacecraft so if there was a crack it would not be just under the blocks but in a lot of other areas. The inspection was reassuring in that now all was needed was a careful look above centerline to see how the hull looked there.

Tiāncái noticed several ladders and asked, "May I use one of those ladders to look at the upper structure?"

"Sure." The director responded.

Tiāncái moved one of the ladders to where he would have a commanding view of a lot of the upper structure and was soon relieved to note there was no apparent damage in the most critical part of the spacecraft that had the greatest amount of stress during the light speed transition which created far more shockwaves than breaking the sound barriers creating sonic booms.

The humans watched Tiāncái with great interest as he moved the ladder around systematically for a couple hours closely observing everything making a complete trip around the spacecraft and when the ladder was back almost where he started, he said, "One of the design specifications of this spacecraft was to do a waterborne landing like we did. But with enemy spacecraft chasing us down to the surface of the water, we could not do the normal method and my captain told me to submerge it to make sure the enemy couldn't destroy us."

"Because of our thruster failure once we were submerged and going deeper, we were not able to reorientate the spacecraft, so it continued to the bottom of the ocean where a couple items leaked and started filling it with sea water. The people who are in those coffins didn't live long as the sea pressure soon killed them. Knowing the ship would quickly fill full of sea water, I shut down the ships computers and electronics to make sure they survived and possibly be brought back online if for some reason the craft was ever raised. Then I deactivated myself by tripping all my power breakers."

"Shall we go inside the spacecraft and take a look the director asked?"

"Yes, I would like that," Tiāncái said.

The group walked up the stairs put in with the staging and across a level area that was put there in case they needed to do crane work.

There were temporary lights strung through the space craft. The Cash in Advance Boys had been in doing a lot of photography and were escorted out of the building while the guests were in the hangar.

"I'm surprised it looks so clean," Tiāncái said.

"We brought in a cleaning crew with soapy water and cleaned it up quite a bit. There was a lot of ocean debris in the ship when we lifted it off the bottom of the ocean."

"I would not doubt that Tiāncái said."

"Obviously there is a lot of cleaning left to do. Perhaps you can guide us, so we don't damage anything."

"Sure, that will not be a problem," Tiāncái said and walked around the control room."

"Will you tell us what all these things do?" the director asked.

"I'll need to get it operational first so I can show you. Otherwise, you will not understand much of it."

"Yes, we realize that. How soon can you start that process?"

"As soon as we get it all cleaned up, then it will be time to start."

"All right, after we leave the cleaning crews will come back and do as much as they can."

"I'm not leaving. I will help the cleaning crews. I will also give them some information on what they need to bring to clean it more effectively."

"Sure, if that's what you want. How long will it take?"

"If you give me around the clock cleaning crews, perhaps a couple days."

The director was now in the surprise of his life. One of the MIT professors said, "We will assist in the cleaning with the robot."

"You don't need to do that professor."

"This will give us some quality time with the robot. That's why we are here and if we can assist him, I'm sure he will be willing to talk with us."

"That I will," Tiāncái responded before the director could get any words out."

Doctor Hudson then said, "LR and I will spend our days here with Tiāncái and help as well."

"That's not necessary Doctor Hudson," Tiāncái responded.

"Oh, but I insist. It will give me some time to enjoy with you. This is a rare opportunity."

"If you insist Doctor Hudson, I will be very proud to be in your company."

"Likewise, Tiāncái."

Tiāncái turned and looked at the director and said, "I just emailed you a list of cleaning supplies we need immediately."

The director turned blue and asked, "How do you know my email address."

"Director, your Earth communications, and cryptology are very inferior. You don't stand a chance against galactic capable Aliens like the Rusnarians. When you get a chance, check your inbox."

The director stood there stunned. Not only did the robot almost kill him, but he had also just given him the grimmest news he ever received in his lifetime. He also knew by the tenor in the robot's voice that email would be sitting in his in basket.

"Alright you guys keep looking, I need to go down to the security checkpoint where there's a laptop, I can check my email."

Tiāncái led the group through the well-lighted spaceship and explained what everything was.

The Director went to the security guy at the entrance to the staging area and said, "I need to use the laptop for a minute." He then went to the internet where he brought up a mobile APP and soon was into his email account and there it was, an email from Tiāncái@gmail.com. The director was stunned. He immediately forwarded the email to Mike and directed him,

"Get all these supplies and bring them to the compound at N.I. (North Island) as soon as you can."

He then went back to the spacecraft and approached the men and the discussions they were having with Tiāncái.

One of the MIT professors asked, "How far did you travel to get here?"

"The best way to describe the distance is about one third the diameter of this galaxy you call the Milky Way."

"How long did it take you to get here?"

"Three weeks based on your time and calendar."

"Can you tell us about the crew?"

"Certainly, and sadly out there amongst those caskets are two of my very close friends. It may seem illogical to you that a robot can have friends. But we do."

"I do not see why not," Doctor Hudson responded.

"Marla and Beryl were very close. Soul mates as you people on Earth would say. They traveled through space together on multiple missions. At first, they were just crew members, not only on this ship but others. Through quarks of nature and unknown reasons they were repeatedly assigned to the same spacecraft over and over and eventually developed more than a friendship."

Doctor Hudson asked, "Tiāncái, were Marla and Beryl going to spend the rest of their lives traveling in space on missions?"

"It's interesting that you asked that question Doctor Hudson. This was to be their last mission. They had put in their retirement papers and were going to spend the rest of their lives looking into reincarnation because they felt they were former lovers traveling from reincarnation to another."

"What led them to believe that?"

"They had vivid memories of vivid dreams of each other from multiple lifes that clearly intersected and reinforced the notion. That's why I wanted to read the Bhagavad Gita to better understand the concept."

"Did you finish the copy I obtained for you."

"Thank you, Doctor Hudson, for delivering that book too me. Since I have 100% photographic memory because I'm a robot, I only had to read it once to encode it into my computer memory, but I have analyzed the entire content over five hundred times, carefully paying attention to every word and every phrase. There is no way I can validate the conjecture of the thesis of that book, but if Marla and Beryl died believing it is true then I'm happy because when they died, they were not frightened and scared and as I looked at them in their final moment as they were dying and there was nothing I could do to save them, I was comforted by the notion, they thought they would soon meet in another life."

"I'm sure it's a tragic sight to watch two lovely people die."

"Doctor Hudson, you might think of me as merely a robot, a mechanical man but I can assure you that my extensive subroutines and macros are designed with an element of empathy to make us feel more human like. I understood the significance of Marla and Beryl's passing and there was nothing we could do about it. We were trapped in the circumstance at the time. That is one of the motivating factors for me to get back to the Plastradavious Empire and alert them how the Rusnarians are on the imperialistic movement to conquer and spread their illegitimate grip over more of the galaxy including the potential to lay waste to your planet Earth."

In an hour a working party showed up delivering cleaning supplies to the entrance to the staging and covered area but were not allowed inside and had no idea what it was, but their curiosity was of course magnified by the canvas covering. One of the guys working said,

"They are probably hiding a TR-3B."

"Or the new SR-74?"

Soon there were 10 palets of cleaning supplies and the stevedores all left the hanger under escort knowing something really cool was behind all the canvas. Some of them figured, *it was likely a crashed Alien UFO they picked off the bottom of the ocean and were cleaning it up for more discovery.*

After the Hanger was cleared of people without the need to know the group was encouraged by Doctor Hudson to go down and grab a bunch of cleaning supplies and start to work.

Luckily for the spaceship, most of the electronics were installed with hermetically sealed structures and only had fiber or power cables attached on waterproof connectors. That wasn't done for any thoughts of water damage, there were other things in the galaxy just as bad as water for electronics and thus was built conservatively.

The men started cleaning including the director wearing a tie he soon took off and put into one of his pockets.

"This is less than ten percent of what we already removed," one of the cleared workers said now assisting.

Around 10:00 P.M. Doctor Hudson said, "I think we did enough for the day, us all go home get cleaned up and take a break."

"Sounds good to me," LR responded.

Nobody else had anything else to say about leaving.

To all their surprise Tiāncái said, "I know you guys need a

break. I'm a robot and do not desire or require a break, I will continue cleaning thought the night if you do not mind."

They were all too tired to argue and left carrying with them a few aches and pains as most of them were not accustomed to physical labor of this magnitude.

They all took bags of trash, mainly filth-soaked handy wipes with them when they left the space craft and sat them down on the floor of the hangar in a nice pile.

Tiāncái could now clean more effectively since he didn't have the neophytes in his way, and he got busy with robot efficiency and just piled the dirty handwipes up in the middle of the floor in each compartment he worked starting from the bow working his way aft.

The mattress like devices in the bunk rooms were too damaged to be saved. They ended up piled up in the middle of the control room with all the other garbage. By 6:00 A.M. Tiāncái had completed an amazing amount of cleaning. Thanks to the design of the ship, there were not many bilge areas. The lower portion of the ship was sealed tanks for water and fuel and sewage for the recyclers. Everywhere visible on the main level was essentially all they really needed cleaned. Other than a film on the ceiling, no deposits of significance was left and easy to clean with some of the commercial solutions delivered. Since Tiāncái didn't have to worry about breathing since he's a robot, he could saturate the area in a very quick manner for more effective cleaning starting on the top and working down. The change was astonishing. He then started bagging all the debris and dirty handy wipes into trash bags creating impressive piles.

By 7:00 A.M. the security guy heard the noise of someone coming across the scaffolding and looked up and saw the robot carrying trash bags. He of course didn't know it was a robot and it scared him as he realized he had spent the night there thinking he was all alone. The robot carried four filled trash bags down the stairs and deposited them in the hangar at the location where the other guys had left trash bags and went back up on the scaffolding and across into the spaceship and came out with another four bags of trash. Tiāncái then walked over and started building a pile and continued making the trips. The security guard was mesmerized. The dude was doing massive amount of work and not a single drop of sweat. The trips continued for a solid hour as Tiāncái completely de-trashed the spaceship.

Chapter Nineteen
Light Off

At around 8:00 A.M. the trash was all empty from the spaceship onto the big pile and only a small section of the floor needed cleaned which took Tiāncái another fifteen minutes to complete filling up another trash bag he hauled down to the large pile of trash about the time Doctor Hudson and LR came into the hanger.

Previous workers had left fans on the ship to move the air out of the spacecraft that didn't smell so great in the beginning with the rotting corpses and Tiāncái had a few of the fans now running and positioned in a way to quickly evacuate the chemicals out of the air in the ship now dumping and dispersing into the large hanger.

"Doctor Hudson, you arrived at a good time. I'm ventilating the spacecraft now because I used a lot of chemicals after you left last night. I would like you to wait about 15 minutes before we go up there," Tiāncái stated.

"What's in store for today?" Doctor Hudson asked.

"The air in the spaceship should be clearing out shortly and we can start doing some internal checks."

"How will you know the air is safe?"

"I have sensors built in I can check the air quality to make sure it will be safe for you then."

"Sure, that sounds good to me. I want to finish my coffee anyway."

Tiāncái noticed the two had Starbucks coffee cups LR and Doctor Hudson obtained when they drove onto the base that had several commercial fast-food places to make the sailors happy.

"Did you sleep well Doctor Hudson?"

"Yes, I went home had a snack, a nice stiff drink, took a shower and some sleeping pills and went out like a lamp. Woke up this morning without the need for an alarm clock."

"How about you LR?"

"Well after I spent an hour trying to convince my wife I wasn't nuts for wearing an Alien Space Uniform home, everything was about normal except we went to bed later than we usually do."

"Why so late?"

"Because she likes to argue and wanted to argue about the space uniform until I gave her a wild story that she believed and backed off."

"What was the wild story?"

"I said I wasn't allowed on the Alien Space Craft if I didn't wear the Uniform. And when she asked what happened to my clothes I said, the Aliens wanted to keep them."

"How did that work out for you?"

"I'll probably be sleeping in the guest room for a few weeks."

Tiāncái had 300 built in hardware timers he could use for anything. He also could employ software timers, but the hardware timers were more exact by nanoseconds. At the fifteen-minute mark that he set for the final ventilation of the spaceship, the timer alerted him, and he said, "I'm going up into the spaceship now to do an air sample, I'll give you a thumbs up if its safe to come up. Also ask this person to arrange to have the trash removed since a lot of it contains chemicals that will saturate the hangar if not disposed of."

The security guy said, "No problem, I'll make that call now." He had a special number to call to report any incident or make requests for the group working on the spaceship.

The men were soon walking up into the spaceship after Tiāncái gave them a thumbs up. To say they were not the least bit dazzled was an understatement. The night and day difference were astonishing. They now had an idea about cleaning with robot efficiency.

"It looks brand new inside here." LR said.

"This is how we would normally expect it to look," Tiāncái responded.

Tiāncái then went over to a section of the wall and pressed a couple of times. He was pressing on a hermetically sealed switch.

Doctor Hudson and LR then herd some strange noise and suddenly the wall opened revealing a hidden cavity that had clear sealed boxes with red circles that could be seen through the transparent material. Tiāncái slowly hit all ten red circles and as he hit each one of them a strange sound started.

He then stood back, and the wall closed again.

"What was that all about?"

"I just turned on the nuclear reactor that provides all the power and initiated a startup of an executive computer that will now enable me to power up the rest of the ship or portions I wish to power up."

Even though the temporary lighting provided by the Navy in the hanger was still lit, the normal ship's lighting started turning on in a more pleasant wavelength. The temporary lighting seemed harsher in comparison.

Tiāncái said, if you do not mind, I would like the temporary lights turned off. I prefer our normal lighting which you will also soon feel is more pleasing."

"Sure, it looks like all we need to do is disconnect the string of lights from this power cord which looks like it also has a switch on it. Let me see if I can just turn it off."

LR hit the temporary lighting main switch and all the lights in the string turned off. And just like Tiāncái said, the actual ship's lighting was far more pleasing.

LR and Doctor Hudson were looking on in complete amazement. With the executive processor operational, Tiāncái could communicate to it with his wireless capability. The non-destructible memory within the executive processor had the history of what happened including the shutdown and crash into the ocean. The executive processor had some astonishing capabilities and soon learned from Tiāncái everything that happened to Tiāncái since arrival in about five seconds thanks to their high bandwidth wireless. Tiāncái directed the executive processor to start turning on the ships computers and circuitry and perform diagnostics on all of it to determine what was damaged.

The quadruple redundancy ship's computers allowed for a lot of combat damage and keep working. The executive processor turned on the first ship's computer and had it start doing self-diagnostics then sequenced through the other three who were soon doing similar tasks.

Tiāncái was soon given a good report that none of the computational or communications equipment had defects.

During the crash into the ocean, Tiāncái got everything shut down in time to prevent damage from possible saltwater intrusion or any other casualty the submergence might have triggered. Tiāncái didn't need any of the display technology but knew the Earth people did and realized now would be a good time to show them a little of his world using some of the holographic capabilities.

I've directed the computer to perform diagnostics and display English translations on the screen with diagnostic status so that you Doctor Hudson and LR can see what's going on.

The intricate diagnostics and system status graphics were quite impressive. And then the holograph started playing. The control room lights dimmed to about half power and the holograph also given in English translation started showing the Plastradavious Empire home worlds. Tall buildings, three dimensional Skycar air freeways, and amazing structures soon enthralled Doctor Hudson and LR.

Then they saw another holograph showing a star field.

"What you are looking at is one third the distance of the diameter of the galaxy from this location."

"That's amazing."

Meanwhile the diagnostics continued checking out the entire ship. The non-destructible memory in the computers already had the failed propulsion unit disabled for safety concerns. The starboard powerplant received satisfactory checks up to actual light off and test.

The last major check now would be a critical one especially if human passengers were taken aboard: the antigravity machine.

As LR and Doctor Hudson continued watching the

holograph, Tiāncái announced, "I'm going to test the anti-gravity now. You will feel lighter and can jump higher. If you attempt to jump, be careful you could bang your head on the ceiling."

The anti-gravity machine did its trick and even with just a small percentage of antigravity they all felt lighter. It was quite a surprising feeling.

As soon as the video ended, Tiāncái said, "I have a complete status of the spacecraft. I'm very lucky we didn't sustain terrible damage plunging into the ocean."

"How about the spots, where the ocean leaked into the space craft?"

"While I was cleaning last night, I went to those locations which I had in my memory banks and was able to do the repairs necessary to make the spaceship airtight to return home. All I need to do is fix the propulsion system and I can leave."

"What about taking you up to Vandenburg to launch you into space?"

"I did some calculations and since I'll be lifting off the planet without a crew and do not need any food and water, I can offload all that, I can return home by taking on two thirds a normal full tank and with the lightened ship get out into space and return."

"What about the Rusnarians? Are you not worried about them shooting you down when you attempt to leave this solar system?"

"I was hampered with two things. First, we were a scientific expedition ship with no defensive weapons on board. Secondly, I could not radically maneuver the ship with the anti-gravity machine turned on and humanoids on board.

They could not withstand the G-Forces I can. With reduced weight from no passengers and reduced fuel load, I will be able to maneuver even more radical which will prevent them from targeting me. When I transition above light speed, I do not have to do it slowly to preserve human's lives. I can do an instantaneous jump. They will not even see me leave I will be gone so quickly."

"It seems to me once we get that Port propulsion unit fixed you will be able to leave."

"Yes, Doctor Hudson and thanks to your help, I've emailed you some documents that you can chose to do what you want with them. Earth has no idea what they contain, but thanks to your help, I will be able to go home and report what happened and bring justice to my friends Marla and Beryl. But there is one additional Item I will need."

"And that is?"

"I'm lucky to have about one half fuel load of hydrogen. I would like to leave here with at least two thirds or more. I want you to arrange for that loadout."

"I'll probably be able to do that, but we'll have to come up with a story."

"Certainly. Tell them I want the Hydrogen so that I can go to Area 51 and demonstrate my ship. I'll fly there to show scientists at area-51 the ship and give a few people a test drive, drop them off then depart."

"Sounds like a plan. Now us get to work on your propulsion unit."

Tiāncái was lucky his space craft was in a hanger at North Island. Often tied up at N.I. were two nuclear carriers that required a lot of shipyard work done in their engineering spaces. Replacing pumps, bearings, hydraulic actuators, and a variety of other industrial processes created the need for some especially good welders, machinists, and electricians who worked in Nuclear Areas. Navy Nuclear Welders were the finest on the planet. Their certifications and proficiency were always top notch.

With a lit-up spacecraft now the Cash in Advance boys were even more interested in the project. They soon were visiting the spacecraft at odd hours. Tiāncái refused to leave and said he would remain until he flew it up to Area 51 for the demonstration.

The Cash in Advance boys showed up just as Doctor Hudson was getting ready to leave for the day with LR. Then four suits walked in and when the security guy tried to stop them, the 4 Star Air Force General Kenney, they brought along to see the eye Candy said, "These Gentlemen are with the CIA and cleared to see anything here and on the base. Stand aside and do not impede their access."

"But sir, I have my orders."

"See these stars son? Those are giving you new orders and I out rank your base CO and can relieve him then I will be your boss. Is that what you want me to do?"

"No sir, I do not wish to see my CO relieved. I like him."

"Then you know what you must do to protect his career. If you want, you can call him and ask him to meet *General Kenney* on the spacecraft where we can have a friendly discussion and plan our golf game tomorrow."

"Yes sir, I'm sure he would want to meet a 4-star Air Force General."

"With the Joint Chiefs of Course."

"Yes sir, I'm sure he will want to come right away, go aboard and let me call him."

General Kenney led the Cash in Advance boys aboard the space craft, meanwhile the poor subdued security guy called the Base Duty Officer and said, "Captain, I'm Bledsoe with security. Could you locate the Base CO and have him call me back immediately, "Let him know this is an emergency."

"What's the issue Bledsoe?"

"When you inform the CO, it has to do with a 4-Star Air Force General now inside building 28, he will want to call me quick."

The duty officer called the Base CO and explained the conversation he just had with Bledsoe.

"Come by my home and pick me up with the duty van and drive me there ASAP."

When the CIA Gulfstream G700 landed at North Island which they do now and then incognito, they usually announce if they have senior military aboard to make accommodations and arrangements for them. On this trip no such advisory was given out because the Cash in Advance boys had their own driver there to pick up the group and drive them directly to building 28.

The two guards outside the building were not going to tell a 4-Star General "No." when he easily got access to inside the building.

In 15 minutes, the Base CO and the duty officer pulled up to building 28 and the two guards were obviously frazzled.

"Is General Kenney inside the Building?"

"Yes sir, he's with some CIA guys."

The Base CO and duty officer walked into the building

and approached Mr. Bledsoe a security specialist who was definitely in over his head because of Beltway Power Plays.

"Is the General Kenney up in the space craft?"

"Yes sir."

The Base CO turned around and said, "Lt. Smith, forget you ever saw what you are going to see in a few minutes. You will sign a non-disclosure in my office tomorrow morning before you are relieved of duty."

"Yes sir."

The two men in uniform walked up into the spacecraft via the stairs and the staging walkway and were soon seeing the skin of the spacecraft and then walked inside the technological marvel.

Doctor Hudson and LR had already had a discussion with the CIA men who also had a few words with Tiāncái.

The CIA and Air Force General Kenney had their own agenda, but when Doctor Hudson said, "General Kenney, if you can use your influence to get some workers to help get this thing repaired, Tiāncái wants to fly it up to Area 51, give the guys up there a demonstration, and discuss ways he thinks he can help us."

"Why would he want to help us."

"General it's a very long story and it's getting late can we have that discussion in the morning. It will become crystal clear then and I'm sure at that time you will be very favorable to his recommendations."

"Alright, assuming we like what he's offering, what do we need to do to get the craft operational?"

"There is some damage to the Port Propulsion system that

Tiāncái believes our work force can repair with his guidance."

"Can you show us the damage?"

"Absolutely, follow us General we need to go down the stairs and to the rear of the spacecraft."

"Lead the way."

General Kenney looked at the Navy Captain who looked like he was about to have the worst day of his life. "Captain, come with us, we might need your assistance."

"Yes sir, General."

The group went down the stairs and walked around to the back of the spacecraft where Tiāncái pointed out everything that needed repaired.

Air Force General Kenney being rather sophisticated in aircraft knew this base overhauled not only Navy Jets but Airforce Jets as well and had a bunch of Navy Engineers who worked on Carriers thus there was plenty of talent to grab.

Tiāncái explained the pipe and the cables that needed repaired and the simple patch job they could do to restore operations.

"I realize you do not have all the metals on earth for that pipe, but if we simply cut out about a foot and install a thicker piece of steel pipe, I know it will weld to this metal."

"What kind of metal is it?"

"This metal does not exist on Earth; we call it Crestron-400. You can weld it to steel. The reason why we use it is it's much lighter than steel to reduce weight of the craft. If you can put a steel sleeve over, it that can handle 4,000 PSI it will be more than sufficient.

We have pipe that will fit over those pipes as a sleeve that can handle 5,000 PSI easily the captain who was a former nuclear engineer stated.

"What about the cables?" General Kenney asked.

"They can be fixed splicing in 14-gauge wire. I can identify the wires for the electrician. After the cable is spliced, I have some emergency stretch wrap material to put over it to protect it and fasten it back into the wireways."

"That doesn't look like it would take a lot of time to accomplish," General Kenney stated. He then asked, "How soon could you fly it up to Area 51?"

"As soon as I can load about four thousand gallons of Liquid Hydrogen?"

"Do you think all of this can be ready in three days?"

"Get me the hydrogen, the welder, and an electrician, most certainly."

"Captain, do you have sources of liquid hydrogen on this base?"

"No sir."

General Kenney turned to his CIA guys and said, "I want you to contact Andy, and have him load up 4,000 gallons of Liquid Hydrogen on a C17 at Vandenburg and fly it down here ASAP."

"Yes sir."

General Kenney then said, "Captain, I know you are not going to like this, but we have to refuel the space craft in here because when we move it out of the building, we need it to be gone, preferably flown out of here at night."

The Navy Captain asked, "How will we move it out of the building?"

Tiāncái then surprised them all. "After we load the Hydrogen, I can simply slowly fly it out of the building since I have an antigravity machine."

"Any chance you will simply take off and vanish?" One of the CIA men asked.

"Sir, this is what I would like to do," Tiāncái said as he looked directly at the CIA man, I would prefer you, Doctor Hudson, and LR fly up to Area 51 with me. For all that Doctor Hudson has done for me and his associate LR, it would be an honor for me if they fly up there with me."

"Why do you want me to go with you?"

"Well, think about it. If I were to be running away with my space craft, I would at least one to take you on a joy ride first."

"Is this some kind of joke?"

"I've studied you earth people, some of you have a sense of humor, evidently you don't."

Air Force General Kenney busted out laughing and said, "You have to admit that is funniest god damn thing you ever heard."

"It didn't seem funny to me at the time," The CIA guy responded feeling denigrated a notch or two.

"You earned a free ride on an Alien UFO. Think about how many of your Cash in Advance boys would like to be on that flight."

"I see your point sir."

"All right, we know what we need to do. The captain is going to get us a couple welders and electricians and get the repairs done. I'll make sure you get some hydrogen to fly up to Area 51. In the morning I'll be back for you to give me a briefing on what all happened and why you are willing to help us."

"It will be my distinct pleasure General Kenney."

"See you guys tomorrow."

The duty officer and the captain waited until everyone left and Tiāncái went back up into the space craft and looked over more system status reports.

The captain walked up to Mr. Bledsoe and said, "You handled this matter quite well. I want to thank you for all you've done."

"No problem Captain."

"Have a good night Mr. Bledsoe."

"Thank you, sir."

Tiāncái continued with his planning and preparations.

Mr. Bledsoe didn't have much to do now but surf the web because all was quiet. He was suddenly shocked on his laptop, he received a message and a picture from Tiāncái that popped up, "Mr. Bledsoe, this is Tiāncái, come up into the spaceship for a few minutes. I can tell you if anyone is coming, I have good sensors, I want to show you a few things."

Bledsoe looked around and walked up into the spaceship and Tiāncái said, "Have a seat Mr. Bledsoe, you earned a view of this. Don't worry about security, I'll be watching it for you."

He then played Bledsoe a two-hour holograph of his alien world. Bledsoe who struggled in the past to stay awake and drink several energy drinks was fully alert tonight. At the end of it he said, "I want to thank you for showing that to me. It means a lot to me."

"Mr. Bledsoe you probably think I'm a person, right?"

"Of course."

"I'm not."

"What do you mean by that?"

"I'm a robot."

"A robot?"

"Yes."

"You look like a person."

"Bang on my chest plate. It's harder than steel."

Bledsoe didn't know why he did it, but he banged on Tiāncái's chest and felt the medal.

"So, you are a robot?"

"Exactly."

"That explains why you are not in one of those coffins full of dry ice."

"I shut my power down and the ship after we crashed into the ocean. I knew we were finished. That allowed me to be resuscitated."

"What about the ship?"

Once I knew we were going to submerge I notified the computer and started shutting everything down. Most of the systems are in sealed containers that could easily survive seawater pressures. As well as my hermetically sealed robotic body."

"Will this ship fly again."

"Mr. Bledsoe, I will tell you something, but you must swear on your personal honor you will never reveal what I'm about to inform you about."

"Sure, I'm in the security business, I understand confidentiality."

"If your base Commanding Officer arranges to get the workmen he promised and some minor amount of materials, this ship will fly within a week."

"Where will you fly too?"

"The first place will be Area-51."

"Do you know what goes on at Area-51?"

"Yes, we know about all your secret aircraft and have routinely monitored your progress in the past."

"Why are you going to Area-51?"

"I will demonstrate the spaceship, then offer your government some assistance?"

"What kind of assistance?"

"If your government refuses to accept my help, this planet will likely be invaded by Aliens and destroyed in a few more years."

"Just like in some of the recent movies?"

"Yes, just like that."

"So, getting this spacecraft repaired really is essential?"

"Yes. Human survival on your planet depends on me going back to the Plastradavious Empire to get help."

"What kind of help?"

"We'll have to bring an entire battle fleet here to repel the Imperialist Rusnarians who plan to make this planet part of their portfolio."

"Which means what?"

"An Alien colony."

"Which means we'll have new masters?"

"If they operate like they have in the past, they will reduce the population of this planet down to less than ten percent of who lives here now.

"For the sake of this planet, I hope you are successful at getting back to your home planet."

"In a week from now I'll be on my way."

"How long will it take?"

"Three weeks."

The rest of the night was uneventful.

Bledsoe went back to his desk and had a lot to think about. Just the robot alone had a huge impact on his bearing. Being in security and a former spook for the NSA, Bledsoe had seen a lot of toys, especially with submarines and experimental craft such as the Sea Shadow. And now even with the latest Deep Shadow, it was apparent Earth had nothing comparable to the Aliens.

The following morning the sailor guarding two spots reserved for General Kenney and Doctor Hudson's had already had a few words with a couple commanders and a full bird Captain. Because of security, they could not put General Kenney's name on the parking sign. It merely said Mr. Kenney. The irate Navy Captain *Airdale* who pulled in ignoring the sign wasn't going to move his car until the junior enlisted man said, "Sir, I've been ordered to call the base CO immediately if anyone parks in General Kenney's reserved parking space. We have a tow truck standing by up the road about 50 yards if you would care to take a look."

The Navy Captain elucidated a few nautical terms laced with French F bombs and backed out and went looking for a parking spot. He knew it was his own damn fault for enjoying that Navy Lieutenant earlier in the morning that was bucking for a promotion. Since she wasn't in his chain of command, he could not be accused of fraternization or tailgate issues, he thought. God help him if she got transferred to his squadron.

General Kenney and his four-man Cash in Advance crew showed up at 8:00 sharp after having a nice breakfast at a local favorite, Golden Yoke Restaurant. Things were moving along smoothly and the boys up in Area 51 were all getting excited about the eye candy and wondered how they could get control of the space craft since the likelihood ship's computers and the robot were integral part of operating it.

The captain walked by the parking spot as the General pulled in and the captain saw 4 stars and realized the young sailor probably saved his dumb ass as he saw reality in the situation unfold.

As they all gathered in the spaceship, Tiāncái surprised all of them and said, "General Kenney, I would like to have a moment alone with you to discuss a few things I'm not sure the others need to know about."

Tiāncái didn't realize the Cash in Advance boys were virtually above the General in rank because they were a lot closer to the president. General Kenney nodded at the lead CIA guy who understood they would all know about it later anyway said, "We'll step out and let you guys have a little chat. We're going down to look at the damaged propulsion equipment."

Everyone left and soon Tiāncái was there alone with the

General.

"What's on your mind?"

"I want you to clearly understand what's going on and why it's important I get back to the Plastradavious Empire."

Tiāncái then explained the situation to the General who had some inclination something like this was going on, especially since their KH-14 took live video of the space battle.

"Also, it's important that I bring back Plastradavious Empire forces to avenge the deaths of the crew of this exploratory defenseless ship."

"I can understand how someone might feel about this."

"During operations the control room video and sound is recorded as well as all sensor data. I'm going to show you a video of the final moments before they all died from the savagery imposed by the Rusnarians."

"Sure, I would like to see it."

A replay of the final moments had a chilling effect on the general as the video of the control room and the frantic activity unfolded. To give quite a psychological emphasis the sensor data that included infrared, radar, and photonics showed on half the holograph. A sophisticated air force pilot like General Kenney who saw live combat in the early part of his career could intuitively see the big picture. He also could observe Marla and Beryl in their final moments. In a way it was gut-wrenching watching the two lovers perish together. At their very end because of their language that was displayed as subtitles superimposed that Tiāncái orchestrated, created a somber moment. It's rare for anyone to see two lovers die together. General Kenney was clearly touched, and it had far reaching impact on his own emotions and had a bearing on his future actions.

General Kenney was a wise person and had social engineering skills to get along with the likes of these four tough CIA bastards that would cut out a grandmother's heart if they had too, just to accomplish a mission. But he also understood America could not send boy scouts out to deal with savory characters they often faced, whether it be drug cartel or Castro associates operating in Venezuela and Nicaragua. KGB (FSB) and MSS operatives were certainly not boy scouts either and in places in the Middle East and North Africa had been a major challenge.

General Kenney had supported many CIA missions and knew vividly the type of action they often incurred. The GS700 they flew in was a testament to such action because the GS650 it replaced now lay broken into pieces in the bottom of the largest lake in Latin America, Lake Nicaragua with the bodies of CIA personnel harvested by the ferocious *Tigrones* as scientists have maintained that Lake Nicaragua is the only freshwater lake in the world with sharks and the scent of blood from the wreckage of the aircraft acted as a beacon to every hungry animal in the lake.

Since none of the spooks carried valid identity with them, and knowing how long flesh would last in Lake Nicaragua, there was no point in attempting rescuing the bodies since the chances of survival of that downed aircraft were minimal.

Since the Alien Robot had filled in a few blanks NORAD and NRO lacked, General Kenney would soon be sending one of the four CIA men back to Washington to brief the Joint Chiefs who would then send a representative with the DCI to the White House and explain the situation as they knew it along with the planned demonstration at Area 51 and subsequent events they expected. Earth was simply low hanging fruit with no means of intervening.

"Thank you for the special briefing," General Kenney said. I want to go down and see if workers have showed up to assist in the repairs you need done."

"I will go with you."

By the time General Kenney and Tiāncái arrived at the Port Propulsion Unit, the CIA men had taken over one hundred photographs with the special camera's built into their CIA cell phones that Apple would build into them in another five years for the public.

The CIA men were a little perplexed and asked Tiāncái, "How did the pipe and cable sustain damage, but the hull of the aircraft seems intact?"

The Rusnarians hit us with Kinetic Weapons because they didn't want to blow up the ship with lasers or beam weapons as they thought, they could capture us. They didn't realize we would do everything possible to evade capture. Those conformal hull sections temporarily sprang inwards rapidly with the Kinetic weapon strikes, that did the damage which disabled the propulsion unit that was shut down as a safety measure. Our only hope for evasion was to submerge but they were so close upon us we could not do the conservative plunge and because of the velocity and the steep angle we dove deeply in the water which immediately shut down the second propulsion unit not allowing us any way to maneuver but to ride the ship down to the bottom of the ocean. We might have been able to dislodge ourselves from the bottom of the ocean with the anti-gravity machine, but the craft had already started leaking with pressure building up rapidly to the point it was extinguishing the lives of the crew members. There wasn't anything I could do but shut down the ship's computers then myself to preserve us, hoping one day someone would find us."

Towards the end of the discussion there was some noise in the hanger as a group of shipyard people and Navy Officers arrived.

Bledsoe who was just about to turn over to his relief escorted the men back to the area they were going to work. All these men had been briefed and signed non-disclosures and were now in a different world of thought as all this unfolded in utter amazement.

The pipefitter brought along a half dozen different pieces of pipe since he didn't know the exact size he needed. They brought along with them a lot of equipment such as a welding rig, and pneumatic tools. The hanger had compressed air they could tap into to run their grinding wheels or anything else they needed to operate.

Tiāncái explained the repair to the pipe he needed and having studied via the internet welding specifications informed the welder the material would weld just like steel pipe and produce a good bond. After cutting out the damaged section of pipe, one of the short pieces of pipe he brought with him fitted over the top of the existing piper very nicely. After making some marks with a Sharpie pen after fitment was almost ready to weld after he took the grinder to clean off the ends of the pipe that was left after the damaged section was cut out. With a special brush vacuum the pipe was cleaned out in each end to make sure no debris was remaining. The new pipe as slid over the existing pipe then moved to cover both sections and aligned with the Sharpie markings. The welder then said. "You guys need to turn away and do not look at the welding or your eyes will receive damage."

The nuclear welder knew his business. He carefully welded that heavy pipe over the top of the existing pipe that he soon discovered had some real interesting properties. Because of the quality checks and careful welding, even though it seemed it would be a simple job, essentially took several hours. They would not be able to hydro this weld. The actual test would be an operational test. If the weld failed the propulsion would not work and would be shut down for safety reasons. Some repairs to ships and submarines ended up like that and in the case of a submarine might require a trip to test depth to verify the repair. The test equivalent to test dept for the space craft would be the transition above light speed where Max-Q occurred.

Utilizing drawings and some sophisticated equipment, Tiāncái had all the wires requiring splicing identified. He also found in the plans identical wire in the spaceship's food processors. Since there would be no living crew member Traveling three weeks back to the Plastradavious Empire with him, the food processor was disassembled and internal gold/copper hybrid wire was obtained for the splice he had coiled up and handed it to the electricians and said, "This is identical wire you can splice the cable with."

The electrician looked at the wire bundle and said, "Nice job on identifying the wires. It will make it easy for me to splice the cable."

The electrician had done gold soldering before. In some high-end electronics, all the joints had to be gold plated and gold/copper wire used. The copper in the material added to the physical strength, but the gold created the conductivity. He had been advised from an email he received from his supervisor he would be doing gold/copper wire splices and would have to do the gold soldering.

The electrician took a lot more time than the pipe fitter because he could not use a standard soldering iron. His gold soldering tool was something like a welder's torch to get the gold/copper hot enough. Because of the temperatures, shrink tubing could not be placed over the wire to slide in place because it would shrink long before it was slid in place. Tiāncái had a solution. After each wire was spliced one at a time, Tiāncái wrapped the wire with a stretch adhesive that with a minimum of heat applied locked it in place as if it were a solid tube like shrink tubing. It took the electrician the rest of the day and half of the next to finish the splices. Before Tiāncái did the final wrap and secured the cable back in the wire run, he went up into the spaceship and performed diagnostics that soon notified him the propulsion unit was safe to bring online. All essential repairs were now complete. Any other repair could wait until return to the Plastradavious Empire.

Timing was good because the C17 with five thousand gallons of liquid Hydrogen just arrived.

The C17 was towed into an area that had a dozen helicopters parked the day before. One of the captains involved in the parking fiasco the day before wasn't happy when he was ordered to have all those Helicopters moved out of the way because they didn't want to offload the hydrogen tank off the aircraft. They had a special hose that would easily reach through the hanger door opened a foot or so up to the Spacecraft that had an adapter they discovered they could attach to their special hose. Otherwise, they would have had to have a transition piece machined losing another day.

Within an hour of pulling the aircraft up to the hanger door they were moving hydrogen fuel and the building was cleared out except for Tiāncái who remained in the spacecraft monitoring the filling.

It was 8:00 P.M. before the hydrogen transfer was complete. Tiāncái was happy he had more than enough fuel to make it back to the Plastradavious Empire after a trip up to Area 51 to demonstrate the spacecraft.

The C17 was towed over to a parking spot near the deep submergence divers' buildings across the base and would fly back to Vandenburg in the morning with a nitrogen purged empty hydrogen tank.

The CIA guys all thought they would be given a ride on the spaceship and when they noticed all the alien mattresses had to be discarded because of the saltwater saturation, one of them a former bubblehead (submariner) said, "We can get some mattresses from the submarine base and have a place to sleep if we go on a long trip."

By midnight with bunks in place the staging removal was almost complete, with only the ladder and the entrance planks left it was almost time to move the craft out of the building and head to Area 51 where a variety of scientists were waiting to meet them.

Based on last minute haggling, the passenger list included LR, Doctor Hudson, General Kenney, and three of the CIA men. With the extra thousand gallons of Hydrogen Tiāncái wasn't expecting, that gave him sufficient fuel to carry the extra men to Area 51. At that time Tiāncái informed General Kenney who seemed to be in charge:

"Have them remove the planks out of the access, open the hanger doors and we can depart."

Within moments those two-inch-thick planks were removed off the staging left, and the temporary stairs moved away from the space craft. Tiāncái shut and locked the door to the space craft.

The CIA men and General Kenney were waiting for Tiāncái to start pressing buttons and manipulating controls. They suddenly felt lighter.

Tiāncái said, "Artificial gravity is now operating, you will fill lighter. I suggest all of you take a seat and attach your straps just like you do in your automobiles."

Nobody was at the controls of the ship. There was a twenty-foot viewer screen they could all see what was happening around them. Evidently the spacecraft was loaded with cameras.

"Who is going to fly the spacecraft?" General Kenney said with due curiosity.

"The spacecraft will fly itself. It knows where its going and how to get there."

General Kenney wasn't the least bit surprised as he understood these aliens had advanced capabilities they had yet learned about.

They could see on the viewer screen images of the hangar and areas of it they were passing and soon were outside the doors and slowly rising in altitude with a full panoramic view of San Diego in front of them as they slowly turned towards the northwest with no indication of noise.

Doctor Hudson wished he had some popcorn to eat while he was watching the viewer screen. The ship slowly continued to rise and in a few minutes Lindberg Field Air Traffic controllers were calling over at North Island asking, "WTF Over."

As the antigravity grew stronger the ship floated into the air at an increased velocity accelerating at 32 feet per second squared. The Lindberg Field Air Traffic controllers saw it and didn't believe it. An object was rising directly above North Island going straight up into the air gaining speed as if it were dropped from an airplane going in the opposite direction.

The moment of truth hadn't happened yet. They would soon realize the success of the repairs if they worked properly.

Tiāncái always in direct wireless communication with the ship's computer was notified in a while, "We are now at 50,000 feet ready to test the propulsion units."

The passengers looking at the viewer screen could see they were way up high and soon could feel some vibration they never felt before and soon it was obvious they were moving horizontally speeding up rather abruptly but was not feeling any G forces thanks to the anti-gravity machine that could compensate up to about 15 G's.

In a bit they could see the craft was banking as if it were in a turn and continued to accelerate out over the dark Pacific Ocean. The speed continued to build, and they instinctively knew they were going very fast as it appeared they could see the moon move which was on the far-left side of the viewer screen. In fifteen minutes, the craft slowed and pointed downwards and seemed go be heading to the ocean for a good five minutes then the craft leveled and banked and made a large course change and soon off the distance they could see a lot of lights and it was apparent they were only a few hundred feet above the water.

"General do you recognize the city in front of you?"

"I'm not sure."

In a few more minutes as they got closer it started getting more obvious, they could see an airport and a metropolis and hotels on a beach and the General knew instantly where he was."

"I'll be damned, that's Waikiki directly ahead."

"It sure is."

They slowed and flew silently over Waikiki then banked and flew over Diamond Head. The craft then pitched upwards pointing the stars and sped up. In a few minutes the thrusters kicked in which resulted in some people calling the National UFO Reporting Center with dozens of reports.

On the right half of the twenty-foot viewer screen a graphic popped up and Tiāncái said, "Those graphs are all the aircraft we passed coming to Hawaii and their flight numbers associated with their FAA flight plan."

The viewer screen went back to the panoramic section of space they now pointed.

The spacecraft appeared higher this time as they could see the curvature of the planet that was lit up to the north thanks to the Aurora Borealis.

"I can look in any direction or elevation at any time," Tiāncái said. Then he panned the image around and there it was for them all to see with utter amazement.

"I give you the Milky Way."

"Anyone who had filmed the Milky Way from Death Valley would appreciate this image," General Kenney said.

It seemed like they were only in the air fifteen minutes then Tiāncái moved the center viewpoint straight ahead where the craft was heading, and the ship pitched downwards obviously going faster than any of them had experienced in their lifetimes including a mach 2 super jet.

It was no doubt the West Coast and in particular happened to be the San Francisco Bay Area they quickly zoomed past as they went lower in altitude seemingly not slowing. The landscape was dark but moonlit they seemed to pass over quickly including lights from farmhouses and in a short while they were approaching a facility with lots of lights on it and were coming in very quickly and as if magic abruptly slowed down without feeling it.

People who were alerted they would arrive at this time were scanning the heavens with infrared and radar and suddenly this thing popped in and slowly approached an area in front of a Hanger they would be directed to, but Tiāncái already knew his destination.

Since the ship was fully operational and test flight completed with no diagnostic hits, Tiāncái now knew it was safe to transit back to the Plastradavious Empire.

Tiāncái said, "General, I know I'm going to disappoint a lot of your scientists waiting to meet me, but due to the urgency of the situation, I can't remain here much longer. I've already sent off a deep space message to the Empire, but they will not receive it for probably a year. I can get there in three weeks. One of the reasons why I went so high in the flight was to do some ISR as you guys' term it in your Air Force. I've determined the situation here is far more precarious and we do not have much time."

"What does that mean."

"General I'm going to let you and all the Earth people off the ship now and I will leave. I will be coming back if I make it there alive. Say some prayers as you may need then because I think the Rusnarians are getting ready to make their move. Hopefully I'll be back with the Plastradavious Empire Fleet before they do too much damage."

"Alright, I'll say a few prayers but I'm not going to warn a lot of people because I do not want to be the source of a large panic."

"Inform your government I will be back with help. You will not be on your own in this battle. LR and Doctor Hudson have earned my help because they restored me and made it possible for me to take the bodies of my friends back for proper burial."

"Alright Tiāncái, I'm looking forward to seeing you when you get back."

The General stood and said, "Gentlemen we will all be leaving the spacecraft now. Doctor Hudson and LR, I will take you back to San Diego tonight on my GS700."

"Thank you General."

Tiāncái walked over and pressed a button by the door, and it opened, and a ladder deployed from the spaceship down to the tarmac. The crowd was back behind a police line. As soon as all the passengers were off the plane. The ladder went back into the body of the spacecraft and the door shut.

The space craft silently lifted off the planet and went up a few hundred feet, spun around and started moving away from the crowd increasing speed and when it was about a mile away already doing several hundred miles per hour two bright spots lit up on the tail of the space craft which then pivoted upwards and let off a loud blast and soon a shockwave and disappeared.

The Rusnarian scouts that had shot down the spacecraft was on the far side of the planet and the last thing they thought was an operational Plastradavious Empire spaceship was anywhere near planet Earth.

Tiāncái had the advantage now. A super light craft not carrying people or food, just the ashes of his fallen comrades that went through the crematorium since their bodies had disintegrated to badly to preserve properly for a physical burying ceremony. The sum total of their ashes in protective plastic containers was five pounds. Also, since he didn't need the anti-gravity machine and had himself strapped in his seat with his special web, 25 Gs would not be a problem.

Eventually the first Rusnarian scout observed the Plastradavious research vessel spacecraft. And just like before they came after the spacecraft knowing it would be an easy conquest. Because of the angle they closed the range and got within weapons range and once again attempted their Kinetic weapons. The early warning receiver showed the Kinetic weapons coming and Tiāncái smiled as he did some random maneuvers making even a spread impossible to hit him and continued accelerating at max speed quickly approaching the light speed transition.

The Rusnarian expected the Plastradavious research vessel space craft to slow as to not face max Q and possibly kill the passengers. Since there were no passengers on board, max Q didn't really matter and Tiāncái had faith in his space craft since it proved it was strong when it dove into the ocean at high speed.

After a few more futile attempts to nail the Plastradavious Spacecraft the decision was made to go ahead and destroy it with laser and beam weapons.

The Rusnarians were maneuvering to get within range and knew the Plastradavious Spacecraft would have to stop accelerating as they were quickly reaching max Q allowing them to set up for the kill shot.

Instead, the Plastradavious Spacecraft kept accelerating and transitioned to light speed and continued accelerating. Any hope of killing the ship now was soon lost because it would take them at least thirty minutes to transition to light speed and by then the Plastradavious would be long gone.

In failure to shoot down the ship, they realized they may have just bought themselves a real war. The pushover planet was no longer their concern. Reports would soon be reaching the Plastradavious Empire that Rusnarians had shot down one of their unarmed ships killing the crew. *Where the hell this other ship came from was a huge mystery.*

The Rusnarians were days away from invading Earth. The task force commander refused to launch the invasion on the grounds he didn't want half his transports either on planet earth or going to and from while having to confront a major galactic force that could show up during such critical moments. Realizing planet Earth could put up some defense, though would lose in the end would severely complicate extracting the force if they were forced to retreat out of the area should the space battle turn negative.

This fear delayed the invasion by a month, then clearer heads prevailed, and the invasion planning, and preparations was now restarted.

The Rusnarians had wasted a month in doing ISR and other critical scouting functions to determine which critical Earth military infrastructure they had to take out. Hence the ISR missions began in earnest and suddenly there were many UFO reports coming in to the military and civilian reporting centers.

The Joint Chiefs already had their heads up thanks to Tiāncái and orders were given to seek out and attack and shoot down any UFO any large space craft approaching the planet would be hit with space deployed Hydrogen Bombs. Earth didn't have many options. For the first time in almost a hundred years, Russia, China, and America were allies again. They had no choice. Cooperate or die together.

The Alien ISR craft thought it would be business as usual that planetary forces would just observe them and wonder who they were. Suddenly it was a new ball game. Even though the kill ratio was four to one Alien shot down, the fact was the tenacious humans were killing enough ISR scouts, they were not getting a good enough macro picture on where to strike.

The Rusnarians were aware if they didn't prepare the battleground those Earth launched hydrogen bombs could take out their transports and kill tens of thousands of their soldiers.

By the time the Rusnarians had enough ISR missions complete to create a macro picture to know where and how to sit their transports down, deep space scouts sent out urgent messages to the Fleet. A massive enemy force was approaching!

The task force commander had no choice he had to protect the transports. He had to move them out of the solar system because he no other way to protect them but distance especially if a strong fighter bomber force penetrated his screen. By the time the Plastradavious Empire Fleet arrived, the transports were already to Alpha Centauri and hiding and awaiting recall, thinking they were safe. Unfortunately for them the person the Rusnarians hurt the most by killing his friends Marla and Beryl was back in his space craft but this time he was armed.

Tiāncái had developed a plan of his own the Plastradavious forces didn't know. He got way out in front of the fleet to do his own ISR and followed the transports and their few meager escorts to Alpha Centauri. Now with eighty percent of the fuels, he topped off upon returning to base and equipped with offensive weapons he was a dangerous opponent. Since the escorts were stretched thin, they could not protect all the transports and Tiāncái knew where each and every one of them were as he observed their transits and anchorages.

The transports thought they were far from the battlefield and their vigilance was thus impaired by irrational thinking.

Tiāncái's research vessel had four torpedo tubes designed to launch probes for study purposes. They were currently loaded with weapons that would fly almost harmlessly to their target and during terminal flight the rocket engines would kick on giving them huge thrust where an enemy had very little reaction time if he was not manning battle stations and ready to counterattack.

Right in front of Tiāncái was two easy targets. Two of the largest transports with 10,000 space marines on each one of them.

These were well-trained battle-hardened space marines. Earthmen had never fought the tenacity of these Rusnarian space marines.

Taking out 20,000 of them would probably make the Earth invasion untenable.

The maneuver was very tricky. Only a robot like Tiāncái could pull off something like this. At maximum range to hide the thrusters, Tiāncái accelerated above light speed. He had the coordinates of the two transports and the weapons launched above light speed would kick on at the tripwire range and aim for the center of the large target.

The kinetic force of the space torpedo by itself would do a lot of damage, but the time delayed warhead would be devastating after it entered the internal area of the transports, especially in their transportation decks with fully fueled and weapons loaded VTOL aircraft and fighter bombers.

The four evil space torpedoes were on their way. Tiāncái maneuvered at 25 G turn attempting to put space between him and the transports zipping along at such an incredible speed they could hardly detect or track him. The few hits they received by their radars and optics obscured the real danger approaching them.

The first two space torpedoes crushed through the armor plate of the first transport buckling the deck and ripping a hole in the side causing a rapid loss of atmosphere instantly asphyxiating many crew members, then the warheads went of BOOM-BOOM! The explosion was massive as it set off all the fuel and weapons loaded. There was enough oxygen in these massive assault transports to create the explosive oxidation that made the warheads even more potentially devastating.

The second transport a good distance away observed the explosion that diverted their attention and didn't see the fish come in for them. The first fish did not explode, but it produced a gaping hole in the side of the ship but the second one hit a beam and detonated which shoved the beam into the protective magnetic aperture of the antimatter reactor causing antimatter mixture with oxygenated air and a fierce very hot explosion, like phosphor going off that immediately cooked off all the weapons and fuel loaded in the VTOL's and fighter bombers. In two seconds after the gigantic fireball there was no trace of a ship ever existed.

The escorts a long distance away frantically tried to contact the two ships that no longer existed and then rushed to their aid leaving behind several more transports. During this time Tiāncái reduced the artificial gravity, had on his mag grip shoes, and reloaded the four torpedo tubes with weapons that were powered up and would be armed as soon as he launched them via remote control. Tiāncái then maneuvered at light speed to get in a path to launch at a group of transports that had now maneuvered near each other for mutual defense.

All four space torpedoes were set to detonate via proximity fuses. He might not destroy them all but would damage them enough to where they would be rendered useless to launch a landing force. That way he stood the chance of depleting more potential transports available. With the loss of 20,000 space marines a short time before, if the task force commander lost another 20,000, he would have no choice but to abandon the invasion and leave the area with the idea, this area would be under surveillance and if he ventured back here again any time soon, he might put his fleet at risk.

The Rusnarian task force commander believed he could adequately deal with the oncoming fleet now that he didn't have to worry about protecting his transports. Then suddenly he was getting deep space neutrino calls for help. The transports were under attack!

Just when he was ready to meet the oncoming fleet in a very wise space battle strategy designed to damage a lot of them to equal the playing field, he had no choice but to start sending assets away to go render help to the transports.

One robot on one ship turned out to be a force multiplier.

The Rusnarian task force commander getting reports that two transports had already been destroyed led him to believe there was a second force out there hitting him from his rears. It was the absolute worst position to be in and he had no choice but to do an emergency evasive maneuver to get back and save the transports. He would have to fight this second force chasing them which is one of the weakest defense postures he could place himself in since his eyes and ears would mainly be pointing in the wrong direction. Hence, he was forced to make the most cruel and unjust decision of his entire career and start sacrificing ships, turning them around to get battlefield reports to know where his enemy was and exactly what they were doing in his rears.

They had to jump above light speed to get to Alpha Centauri and he knew the enemy would do the same at the same time and while traveling above light speed they would be able to monitor him and know when he slowed and maneuvered.

The Rusnarians again had to sacrifice a few more ships to slow them and turn them and face the enemy. They were simply wasted because the oncoming force knew exactly where they were how they were maneuvering and could put weapons on them a lot quicker than if they were traveling in the opposite direction.

When Tiāncái's space-torpedoes did their work on the group of clustered transports, the Rusnarian assumed he was traveling towards a much stronger force who was wiping out his transports. It was no longer important for him to worry about what was behind him as he desperately needed to find out what was in front of him. And to his amazement, sensors were not detecting a fleet at all.

"The enemy must have cloaking devices," his tactics officer said.

"Nobody has yet been able to demonstrate cloaking devices."

"Those ships are not blowing themselves up, something is hitting them."

As the were approaching the only group of unaffected transports hidden the furthest, Tiāncái expended his last torpedo and quickly accelerated away from the battlefield. By the time he was out of range for the Rusnarians, the last torpedo hit another transport loaded with over 10,000 space marines. Effectively the invasion force was wrecked. The task force commander then ordered the bug out which meant *everyone to themselves and get out of here fast and head for home the best way you can.*

All the Rusnarian spacecraft accelerated to light speed in random courses. Their navigation systems plugged in random courses towards friendly space and no two ships would travel together. Once they got near one of their planets that had space defense capabilities they would start forming up and reassess the situation.

The Plastradavious Empire fleet INTEL was able to ascertain which ship had the task force commander on. They all converged on him. He would either surrender his ship or die. Either way, he knew his life was ruined and even though he advised not to invade Earth, he was forced to by his government who didn't think there could be serious repercussions.

Taking in consideration what he now faced, it was a terrible loss and didn't like the idea of handing over their secrets and technology to an enemy, he ordered a course reversal and attack head-on the chasers. The task force commander soon received withering fire from the flanks and head on attacks. Within a minute after the course change and refusal to surrender, his ship blew up into a great cloud of sparkling debris.

The battle was over.

The Plastradavious Empire did not come to rescue Earth. This planet was too far away to be of concern for them. They only came to teach the Rusnarians a painful lesson, "Don't ever fire on our ships again."

The Plastradavious Supreme Commander wanted to get to the bottom of the strange battle. Plastradavious INTEL had recordings at long distance of the Transports being attacked and destroyed.

And as they checked and rechecked the fleet and their navigation history, it was clear none of them had anything to do with it. But, the research ship, with the robot, was unaccounted for during most of the battle.

Plastradavious Supreme Commander contacted Tiāncái via a secure communication and asked, "Did you have something to do with those transports?"

"Sir, I think it would be best for our security, that actions in and around the transports are not further investigated in the event we need to do something like that again."

"When we get back to the Plastradavious Empire I would like to have a private conversation with you."

"I will be at your disposal, but with your permission I would like to go back to planet earth one more time. I promised them I would come back, and I would like to inform them, the Rusnarians are no longer a threat to them."

"Go to planet Earth, don't spend a lot of time there, come back to the Plastradavious Empire so we can have that private discussion. I will end the investigation, but there are a few details I would like you to give me."

"Yes, sir I will be heading there soon after I take care of this last matter."

"See you then."

"Bye sir."

CHAPTER TWENTY
BATTLE OF ALPHA CENTAURI

It was almost a miracle the Webb Space telescope was pointing in the direction near Alpha Centauri when the first Rusnarians Transport blew up. The explosion which was rather remarkable was soon shared among a lot of space and science interests. One explosion by itself does not trigger a lot of interest because explosions do occur in the universe for unknown reasons usually attributed to a super nova or some cataclysmic event. But when two or more explosions happen in close time and space, it suddenly creates a great amount of interest.

General Kenney had already briefed the Joint Chiefs and the DCI and had fifteen minutes with the President over the alien issues. Only a few knew about the possibility of a nearby space war and when the explosions started, fear struck General Kenney because of his private discussions with Tiāncái. And now it was happening. In his briefings he had warned about the possibility of a space war which led to reengagement with the Russians and the Chinese who had recently slowly eroded relations with the USA over a variety of issues brought on with COVID-19 and Ukraine.

When the leader of Russia is suddenly getting the kind of communications from the USA like he never expected he immediately sent the FSB (KGB) looking through his moles in the Pentagon, State Department, and Congress to get the essence of what really was going on. And suddenly when Ukraine was no longer anything they were concerned about because of this new space threat, they then took to heart Americans were serious about a nearby Alien Space War. Thanks to the Saratov Observatory, the Russians soon also witnessed the beginning of the Space war that seemed quite far off around Alpha Centauri.

China's MSS was also digging deep. Their California Senator they had milked for years on juicy intel was still sympathetic especially because of her political campaign contributions through Buddhist and Confucius organizations that from the periphery looked quite innocent, but in fact received direct payments from China's PLAN.

The sudden change in America was quite shocking to the MSS who at first thought it was diversion for some nefarious reason. However, some MSS assets not only love China they also love America. They are proponents of both China and America and want closer cooperation and understanding. The Confucius Society was chief among them and felt their efforts in America had achieved significant change in American stereotypes and attitudes to the point they felt flattered by some of their observations.

When Chinese observed the love displayed for Yuja Wang, Lang Lang, and Yo Yo Ma they knew the truth that was hidden in a lot of American hearts. Love and attachment existed for China in America. For the Confucius Society outlook, America had crossed a threshold that eclipsed a lot of the rest of the world in international relations because their great affection for artists and many of the wonderful talent flowing out of China. And when Americans visited China, the affection was real and apparent, how could you not love these Americans that loved China? Love is infectious.

Some of these Confucius spies very close to the centers of power of China and very close to high-ranking members of the MSS were actually the dependable canary in the coal mine. These MSS Intel Experts viewed the world through a very educated clear lens. It was through the Confucius network that MSS learned vividly a space battle really was happening and America's reach out to them was genuine and quite compelling.

Thanks to the Confucius spies, the leader of China was convinced very abruptly about the galactic situation and directed the PLAN to cooperate with the Americans at the greatest extent possible. Cooperation tends to expand cooperation in ways they would be fearful of doing in just the week before. The Alien threat was real, and the Chinese really had to deal with it and join their forces to protect each other or die independently when the Aliens came down to pick the low hanging fruit.

The series of explosion that now ripped though large areas of space around Alpha Centauri when huge transports full of fuel and bombs blew up, gave some military planners on Earth a sense they had some breathing room to work out contingencies and shuffle assets around. Bases soon had Russian, American, and Chinese soldiers working side by side in great fear the world may be destroyed from space. For Christian soldiers it was Revelations and End Times.

The greatest period of fear occurred within their own solar system as two great alien fleets converged and soon explosions of huge magnitudes occurred right in this solar system at distances no further away than Jupiter or Saturn. Even clumsy telescopes on Earth were more than adaquate to film these impressive observations of explosions when spacecraft disintegrated into large clouds of sparkling debris.

The fear started declining as it appeared the space battle

was receding and moving towards Alpha Centauri and then beyond it as it appears the velocities of the fleets hit impressive speeds to the point they could no longer be tracked very well.

Eventually it all disappeared, and all explosions ceased. To many it was felt the decision had been made and whoever it was in that space war had left the area. After a few days the military started to slowly stand down as there was not a single indication of Aliens. Any of the intermittent Alien UFO observations reported weekly or monthly completely ended. Other Aliens who might have been visiting Earth cleared out and apparently were long gone and not coming back any time soon.

Tiāncái suspected Earth had a wakeup call and approaching the planet might be problematic. As soon as he got within range of a communication satellite Elon Musk put up, he hacked into it and contacted General Kenney.

General Kenney noticed the call from an unknown number but answered.

"Hello how can I help you."

"General Kenney, this is Tiāncái from Plastradavious, I hope you remember my voice."

General Kenney was stunned. "Are you back now?"

"I'm actually in space approaching the planet and want to come down to Area 51 so I can brief you on all what happened."

"Sure, we would like you to fill in a lot of blanks."

"Alright, make the calls to arrange for me to have a safe landing and call back this number, I can receive you call even though I'm in space."

"I'll right, give me about half an hour I have a few people to contact."

Soon NORAD was called giving them the details that an Alien Ship would soon be landing at Area 51 and to advise the North American Air Defense System to not get trigger happy.

A call to the DCI and a quick meeting with the joint chiefs and General Kenney called Tiāncái back.

"Hello, General Kenney?"

"Yes Tiāncái. We put out an advisory you will be landing at Area 51 and will have a welcoming party."

"General Kenney, could you do me a favor?"

"What do you need?"

"Would it be possible to bring Doctor Hudson and LR to Area 51, I would like to see them again."

"That should not be a problem."

"Thank you."

"You are most welcome. How soon do you think you will be landing?"

"I think in about two hours, and I will approach Area 51 from directly overhead from 200,000 miles."

"Alright, we will be expecting you then."

The men hung up and Tiāncái did a light speed jump to 200,000 miles directly over the projected location above Area 51. When the ship changed course to Area 51, a radio strobe from Area 51 would do directly to the spaceship had one been sent. Doctor Hudson and LR were in the LAB doing some minor work getting ready to do another project.

LR's phone rang, and he picked it up.

"LR?"

"Yes, what can I do for you?"

"Is Doctor Hudson there with you?"

"Yes, he is?"

"Let him know an SUV will be pulling up in front of your building in five minutes to take you guys to the airport. A GS700 will be arriving there soon out of Burbank to take you both up to Area 51. Apparently, you have a special visitor coming there and your presence has been requested from high ups."

"I'm sure Doctor Hudson will be happy to go."

"Thank you get ready; they will be there shortly."

LR hung up the phone and said, "Doctor Hudson, we have a ride coming to pick us up in five minutes. We are heading back to Area 51."

Doctor Hudson started smiling and said, "Something told me he would be back about now."

The men grabbed their jackets with company logos on them and left the lab which no longer had their personal security guard and walked out to the front entrance and as promised in a few minutes the SUV pulled up and a guy in a suit got out of the front passenger side door and opened the back door for the two passengers.

The ride to the airport was quick, and they went to a private terminal where owners of private jets came in and out of. There was just a trickle of individuals.

"Security check here is a lot more humane," Doctor Hudson noted.

"I'm starting to get spoiled on these private jet rides. Not sure I can ever handle the airline cattle cars again," LR responded.

Soon they were on the plane heading up to 40,000 feet and the ride was less than an hour with the pilot going really fast all the way almost to the 17,000-foot-long runway they were directed to land on because the 7,000-foot runway was getting maintenance done on it.

The pilot taxied over to a hanger with doors now shutting. LR got to see a little inside before the doors were closed enough and could make out an exotic looking airframe. Also, to his astonishment, the floor was sinking. It was an elevator!

Tiāncái came straight down to area 51 and at about 5000 feet reorientated the craft radically slowing in the process. To the casual observer the spacecraft just popped in there from nowhere. NORAD measured the incoming going from almost 300,000 feet in a minute and half.

Tiāncái saw a roped off area and a dozen people behind it and the GS700 Jet and knew that's approximately where they wanted him to park his spacecraft which he did and after it was on the ground, the air traffic controllers started telling him where to land the spacecraft and he reported back, "I'm sitting on the ground there now."

It was merely coincidental that Doctor Hudson was stepping down the ladder from the GS700 behind LR at the same time Tiāncái stepped down from the space craft wearing his very distinguished space uniform.

The men approached the robot acting no different than if he were one of their human friends.

"Hello Tiāncái, good to see you again," Doctor Hudson stated.

"Doctor Hudson, and LR, my good friends, its an honor to see you again."

"We think its an honor for us Tiāncái," LR responded.

"I see you made it home and back," Doctor Hudson commented.

"Yes, timing is everything they say."

"How did things work out for you?"

"When I got back to the Plastradavious Empire they did a quick repair on my ship and fixed everything damaged that had jury rigged parts and reloaded all the standard features and got rid of the submariners' mattresses."

"Those were perfectly good mattresses, why did they get rid of them?"

"Workers said they smelled like diesel fuel."

"I'm sure that's not the only smell they had."

"After I was retrofitted, I joined the fleet heading this way."

"Did you encounter the Rusnarians when you came back?"

"Yes, and I'd say the Rusnarian task force commander paid dearly for taking the lives of Marla and Beryl."

"You know what they call that?" Doctor Hudson asked.

"After reading and analyzing the Bhagavad Gita 144 times, I would say he earned some bad Karma, and I might have been tasked to be a Karma angel."

"Was there a space battle?"

"Yes, I filmed a lot of it, but I also received what I didn't film through my artificial intelligence friends on the command ship that had whatever I didn't record so you have the entire battle."

"Interesting"

"Doctor Hudson and LR, when you get back to your LAB,

you will see you received some emails. I converted gun camera three-dimensional holographic video to standard internet video so you can watch a lot of it."

"I'll definitely check it out," Doctor Hudson responded.

A junior Air Force Officer approached the three and said, "We have a van to take the three of you to a place where you can relax and have some food and drinks or snacks and visit. Also, General Kenney is flying in to see you, says he'll be here in about two hours."

"Yes, I would like to speak to General Kenney." Tiāncái said.

"This way please," as the junior officer led the men and the robot to the waiting SUV.

As the men approached the SUV, the ladder on the space craft went back into the hull and the door closed. Tiāncái had directed the ship's computer to secure the ship he would be gone for a while.

It was a short drive from the hanger area to another area under a camouflaged tent. From the air nobody would not know they were inside a very large tent covering up temporary trailers brought in by a contractor supporting a new project at Area-51 for the Air Force. Inside one of the trailers was a canteen operated by a big bossom southern gal named Sheri who definitely made you aware she was in charge. Looks are deceiving. Sheri wasn't some dumb bitch off the street slinging burgers. Sheri actually was a spook and part of the elaborate intel fabric of the base to be able to hear things and make reports.

Sheri was poised to discover situations such as a dude is going through an emotional roller coaster because of a nasty divorce or a honey pot scheme with the FSB (KGB) or MSS. Yes, in real life that all happens, and big brother uses every trick in the trade to plug leaks on spiral development of leading-edge technology and Sheri was just another cog in spooksville that helped keep an eye on everyone and pay attention to trivial things that others would overlook because they were just too damn busy with their own lives and their own problems.

The group was led into the canteen and the junior officer said, Sheri will get you whatever you need, and she will put it on my tab. The officer winked at Sheri who would soon be applying her southern charm and it didn't bother her one bit to use every trick in the trade to disarm unsuspecting neophytes including the exploitation of her breasts as she knew some men fantasized over her nice big ones. Sheri had practiced in front of mirrors doing various poses to emphasize them and capture someone's attention to disarm their otherwise doubtful minds.

Coffee or drinks gentlemen?

"I'll take a coffee little cream and sugar," Doctor Hudson said.

"A coke would be fine," LR stated.

"How about you sir?"

"No thank you I'm fine," Tiāncái responded.

Sheri soon had the coffee with cream and sugar on the side and the coke for the table. The rest of the canteen seemed empty. Dr. Hudson didn't see how it could pay for itself.

During some of the test flights of that glorious craft LR saw just before the hangar doors were closed all the way, the canteen would be full of scientists and engineers going on for several days at a time. Some of those engineers and scientists went two days without sleep and managed to march on smartly thanks to routine ingestion of coffee.

Unfortunately testing spiral development doesn't always

work out too well. The Air Force wished there wasn't all those spaceship videos still out there showing them blowing up on the launch pad in the late 1950's. When program managers push timelines harder than quality control can keep up that's what happens. The *fly in the ointment* for the Airforce: early manned space flight for the Mercury program went out into space on Army rockets.

"That's a cute uniform you got on there. Are you dressing up for a special occasion?" Sheri asked.

"It's my uniform."

"Are you a test pilot?"

"No, I'm a robot."

Sheri busted out laughing and said, "You know working around here we sometimes get some real nutjobs."

"Stress related probably," Doctor Hudson mentioned in a clever manner.

Sheri knew that young lieutenant well, he was a spook too and wondered what kind of BS he was pulling on her today?

"May I ask you why you are wearing that uniform? I've never seen one like that before."

"All the crew members on my spaceship wear these uniforms."

"You got a spaceship?"

"Yes, it's parked over at the hanger."

"You guys are something else. Did that dipshit lieutenant put you up to this?"

"No, he just provided us the transportation," Doctor Hudson said.

"Are you part of his spaceship thing?" Sheri asked.

"No, we are just good friends."

"What do you do then?"

LR spoke up and said, "This is Doctor Hudson, he's a research scientist."

"And what's your name?"

"LR."

"What the hell does LR stand for?"

"Lab Rat."

"What's a Lab Rat."

"A guy like me who hides out in research labs with guys like Doctor Hudson who lets me tinker with all the toys he designs."

"What's this other guy's name with the space uniform on?"

"His name is Tiāncái."

"That's quite a name, never heard one like that before."

"That's because it's not from this world," LR responded.

"And what world would that be?"

"I'm from the Plastradavious Empire," Tiāncái responded.

Sheri now knew she had some real pranksters going on and she would get even with that young Air Force spook who will learn the hard way to never mess with a barracuda.

Sheri noticed the Letters PFM on Tiāncái's uniform and said, "I suppose that PFM on your space uniform stands for pure fucking magic?"

Tiāncái didn't quite understand Sheri but Doctor Hudson and LR knew Sheri was just being sardonic.

"Actually, it stands for Plastradavious Federation Military."

"I kind of like what Sheri said," Doctor said sarcastically.

"So, what you are trying to tell me is Tiāncái is a robot serving in the Plastradavious Federation Military and has a space craft parked over by the hangers?"

LR decided to make a fun bet with Sheri and since she already dropped a French F Bomb with her southern accent, he would be safe to lay it out.

"What's your name, misses?"

"I'm Sheri, glad to meet you LR," Sheri responded in a way that sounded just like a southern bell in the movie *Gone with the Wind*.

"Sheri do you like taking bets?"

"Certainly."

"Okay Sheri, this is the bet if I lose, I will pay you $1,000.00 cash today if I lose the bet. But if you lose you must show Tiāncái, Doctor Hudson, and me your tits."

"What's the bet?"

"I bet Tiāncái is a robot that landed the space craft by the hangers and is a member of the PFM from the Plastradavious Empire."

Before Sheri could answer, Tiāncái said, "Sheri don't take that bet because you will lose."

"You know I watch guys like you who pull stunts like this. I'll take the bet because I want the Jerkoff's $1,000.00."

"Don't say I didn't warn you," Tiāncái said.

"Say, Tiāncái I have a good Idea." Doctor Hudson said.

"What's that Doctor Hudson?"

"When General Kenney gets here us tell him about the bet and we can take Sheri over to your ship and you can give her, the General, and us a ride around the moon, while she shows us her Tits."

"If the General wouldn't mind," Tiāncái thoughtfully said.

"I personally know General Kenney," Sheri said thinking these assholes were just name droppers.

Tiāncái, do you have General Kenny's phone number," Doctor Hudson asked.

"I do but he's on a Jet Flying in here and will be here in about an hour."

Tiāncái looked at Sheri and asked, "Would you like a trip around the moon if I take you?"

"You guys are something else," Sheri said.

Time passed and after a snack and some more coffee, Tiāncái announced, "General Kenney's plane just landed. He'll be here in fifteen minutes."

"How do you know that Tiāncái?" Doctor Hudson asked.

"My ship's computer is keeping me updated, air traffic control is talking to the plane directing his aircraft over by my spaceship."

Sheri laughed and said, you guys are something else. If General Kenney walks in the door in fifteen minutes, I'll show you my Tits then."

"I recommend you wait and do it on my spaceship going around the moon," Tiāncái said.

"All right wise guy, you are so full of shit its pathetic, but I'll tell you what if you got a spaceship that can take me around the moon and bring me back today, I'll show everyone on the ship my tits and if necessary, I'll show you my ass too!" Sheri then let out a howl.

In ten minutes, the junior Air Force Officer and General Kenney walked through the door and Sheri said, "Oh my god!"

"Hi Sherry!"

"General Kenney, it's really you!"

"It is I."

"General these tricksters were trying to play a joke on me."

"Oh, yea tell me about it."

"This character with the PFM space suit on was giving me a line he is a robot and has a spaceship parked by the hanger."

"Is that so."

"General, ask Sheri about our bet," LR said.

"General Kenney looked at Sheri and said, I hope you didn't bet these guys."

"Don't worry General, I know he can't deliver."

"What did he say he could deliver?"

"He said, he can fly me around the moon and have me back here today."

"Tiāncái would you really do that for her?"

"General, only to support my friend LR's bet."

General Kenney looked up at the young Lieutenant and asked, "Do you think we can all fit in that SUV?"

"It might be a little crowded but sure."

"Sheri can sit on my lap, if necessary," The General said then smiled. He then said, "Come along Sheri, you will be the first woman on the moon."

"I'm game I want to see what you jokers are really up to." She then looked at the cook Ralph and said, "You are in charge, I'll be back later, maybe."

They all got to the SUV, and it was kind of crowded and Sheri said, "I always wanted to sit on a generals lap and hopefully make him horny too."

"Well Sheri your dream came true."

They drove to the spaceship and got out. Sheri was in a state of shock. "Is this for real?"

Tiāncái directed the ships computer to lower the stairs and opened the door and he led them all inside. As General Kenney was by the stairs he directed the young officer, "Call the Tower and let them know we are going for a ride, we'll be taking off and going straight up."

"Yes sir."

General Kenney then followed the group up into the spaceship and there were sufficient chairs for all of them. Tiāncái was standing by the door and welcomed him aboard and the ladder retracted, and the door shut.

Tiāncái said, "Everyone please take a seat and fasten your seatbelts."

Once the ship's computer signaled interlocks closed on all

the seatbelts the spaceship started going up into the air and the twenty-foot viewer screen looked awesome.

Ralph back at the roach coach as they called it, was also a spook and notified his boss: "Sheri's went with General Kenney and do not exactly know what time she is coming back."

"If she left with General Kenney, that's alright. You'll have to run the place by yourself until she gets back and hopefully doesn't get herself into trouble."

"I would not be the first time with that southern accent."

"That's true. A Georgia Peach carrying a couple delicious melons around."

The spacecraft slowly pivoted upwards, and it didn't feel like they were moving much but the sky turned dark, and the stars started to seem a lot brighter. The spaceship slowly started reorientating itself and the starfield slowly shifted as they were turning and pitching and soon a gigantic white blob entered the center of this twenty-foot-wide viewer screen. It dimmed quite a bit and Tiāncái said, "I had to tone it down because it was too bright with the magnification

The size of the moon suddenly was cut in half. Tiāncái said, "I had to cut back on the magnification as we approach the moon."

Vivid detail like none of them had seen before was starting to appear and they could get a sense they were rapidly approaching because the detail was getting far better. And soon there were no further adjustments.

The craft slowly came down and appeared like it was hovering a few feet off the moon.

"The moon has a lot less gravity so our antigravity machine

works a lot better here than it does on Earth," Tiāncái explained as to why they could hover so effectively. He then panned the view around the moon. It was an amazing sight. He then said I'm going to go up higher in altitude now so you can see it from a different perspective.

After letting them see the moon for about fifteen minutes, Tiāncái said, "It's time to go back to earth now."

The space craft reorientated and soon planet Earth was in the middle of the view screen.

"This is an incredible sight," Sheri said.

As they watched the Earth on the viewer screen, they could see the distance to the planet was quickly decreasing with speed and soon the planet filled the entire view screen and Tiāncái reduced the size of magnification, and the Earth was once again half the screen, but more vivid detail was starting to show. They soon appeared to be coming down on the planet in the middle of a vast ocean and were soon sliding over onto land and a desert area and withing a few minutes they were coming down on Area 51 where they zipped into again, leveled off and softly sat down exactly where the spacecraft parked before.

"So, you really are a robot?"

"Yes, I am Sheri."

"I suppose you guys want to see my Tits now?"

LR said, "That will not be necessary Sheri, we took advantage of your ignorance about these strange things, and it would be impossible for you to know. Don't worry about it."

"You know I think I'm starting to like you guys," Sheri said.

"I like you Sheri," Tiāncái said.

"Thank you, hon, I like you too."

Tiāncái had the door open and the ladder back out so everyone could leave.

General Kenney asked, "Can I talk to you alone for a few minutes?"

"Sure, no problem," Tiāncái responded in an Earthly like manner.

After the rest were outside waiting, Tiāncái asked "What did you want to talk about General?"

"Can you tell me what all happened out there in space that caused all the explosions we photographed from this planet."

"General, let me shut the door to the spacecraft to improve the lighting for the holographic display and I'll show you it."

"Sure, I would like to see it."

Tiāncái said, "There is a lot of time lapsed photography because it would take several days to see it all."

"Sure, I understand, no problem."

"Tiāncái showed the general essentially the video of the entire battle from multiple ship perspectives. It was like being at the movies seeing incredible cinematography.

Tiāncái didn't need to look at the video, he had it all memorized, he was more curious as to how General Kenney would respond to it.

The powerful imagery had a profound impact on the psyche of General Kenney who watched very patiently and saw it all.

"Is there anyway I can get some of this video so I can give a briefing to my chain of command?"

"If you ask Doctor Hudson and LR nicely, I'm sure they can help you out, I sent them copies of this video."

"Tell me Tiāncái what is your plans."

"General, I was given permission to visit, but they do not want me to stay here long. I'm soon going to depart."

"Will you be coming back this way?"

"In conversations with the Plastradavious Empire Task Force Commander who led the fleet here, we exist at such a distance that its unlikely we would be coming back this way any time soon. We are almost one third the distance of the galaxy away from here. So, it would serve no useful purpose."

"But you came here, and your ship was damaged?"

"We were here specifically for scientific survey purposes. We wanted to know what kind of beings lived here and what your diversity of life was like. We know all that so there is nothing more to gain by coming back.

"You could certainly help us develop."

"General, we have a general policy that we do not want to influence other civilizations. We want you to develop on your own and on your own timeline. In due time you will develop and move off to the stars. When you do go, try not to be imperialist like the Rusnarians attempted because that creates grief to other civilizations."

"I understand that, but I can't speak for future generations."

"Now you know through lessons learned there are good aliens and bad aliens. You need to be careful you do not reach out to the bad Aliens because if you do, you will discover they might be like the Rusnarians who demonstrated what EVIL does."

"Naturally, I would hope in the future that future generations are careful as they explore the universe."

"You need to develop space travel and slowly survey the area round your solar system and branch out from there."

"I assume that's how we will advance."

"By doing it all on your own timeline, you do not have to worry about the time implications that would be imposed if you developed with other civilizations."

"Something tells me you had a lot to do with this space battle."

"General, my own people are investigating it because they could not explain why and how certain things happened. If I was instrumental in some of the significant events, I was motivated to do so because my very close friends perished at the hands of the evil Rusnarians."

"I see."

"You know I'm just a robot, but my programming is very extensive. I had great affection for Marla and Beryl and when the Rusnarians destroyed their lives, my analysis came up with the obvious solution to make sure the Rusnarians did not spread their menace through the galaxy."

"What do you think contributed the most to their demise."

"They did not realize a robotic ship with a robot who had lost someone special could do what I did. They will never know how badly they were hurt by a small ship and a robot because they snuffed the life out of two wonderful people who I admired, Marla and Beryl."

Tiāncái had a lot of video and pictures of Marla and Beryl stored in the ship's computer and put a few pictures of them up for General Kenney.

"They were definitely a good-looking couple," General Kenny stated.

"Marla and Beryl raised me up from a primative robot to what I am today, I owe them my existence," Tiāncái stated.

"How is that?"

"General Kenny, I first met the couple when they were students in a robotic course at the PFM Academy. Back then I was a mere skeleton of what I am today."

"What kind of things did they do to expand your abilities?"

"Before they became space explorers, they were roboticists as that is what they majored in as cadets at PFM Academy. I was one of the experimental robots at the time and as lab partners they took custody of me and their robotic instructor, a Mr. Professor Dabbler Montovan encouraged them to expand my capabilities and develop me into a more advanced robot."

"What was the emphasis in doing that?"

"Our PFM was slowly embracing robotics as part of the military landscape. From drones to exoskeletons, to cyborgs, there was numerous studies and theories developed. As you know in warfare there is a lot of senseless killing of brave young men and women. The idea was to shift enough of the warfighting to robots and automated systems to reduce the number of PFM casualties. At the time Marla and Beryl were modifying me, the developmental mindset was that if professors had students that seemed to have a nackt for robotics, they were encouraged to develop those skillsets to the maximum extent possible."

"Professor Dabbler Montovan held conferences with Marla and Beryl and a few other promising and bright students, and they jointly laid out goals and areas of concentration for development."

"Do you have memory of those days and development?"

"Yes, there were a couple of decisions made that eventually had quite an extraordinary impact on my development."

"What was the nature of those decisions?"

"First of all, Marla and Beryl decided, they would preserve my memories even if my central processing unit was replaced."

"So, you have memories of your early years of existence?"

"Yes, I have memories that even precede Marla and Beryl."

"Were they complicated memories?"

"Some yes and some no. As an example, the results of a diagnostic scan for hardware that no longer exists in my body."

"Why would you keep such information if it's no longer applicable?"

"I purged a lot of that kind of information, but it was stored where my entire history has been recorded back at the Plastradavious Empire. If I want, I can go back at any time and sift through that information."

"Why would you do that if as an example it was diagnostic scans on hardware that no longer exists?"

"The only real purpose would be to provide information to a student to see how things evolved. In reality, it's part of robot history."

"How long did Marla and Beryl modify you?"

"One could say it was up to the minute they died."

"What were they doing to modify you? It seems they might have been overwhelmed with what was going on around them at the time."

"General Kenney, there are two ways robots get modified. They get modified with hardware changes, but we also get modified via the learning process. I was always in a state of learning while Marla and Beryl were living."

"What was the last thing you learned from Marla and Beryl?"

"Reincarnation and tragedy."

"What was reason?"

"I have some video recordings of Marla and Beryl when they were first working on me. I also have video of all the robot surgery they performed."

"Any of them that you think is a milestone."

"Yes, during my first processor changeout."

"How did that workout?"

"As you can imagine, Marla felt like she was killing me and was hesitant to do it."

"What convinced her to do it otherwise?"

"General Kenney, Beryl explained to her, just like the human body, it wasn't really anything without the memories and feelings. Beryl explained to her that all my memories would be retained, and my feelings provided by sensors and psychological subroutines would be almost unchanged, but with the modifications I would increase my sensor capabilities, hence could have more overall feelings."

"Did you have any awareness or analysis done after the modification that is meaningful?"

"Sure. First of all, I did not lose any data. Beryl was very sophisticated in the manner he backed up all my memories.

Secondly when I was ordered to do a diagnostic shutdown, my world went black. In a sense I must have felt like what humans feel when suddenly the world slowly becomes dark. And then after the hardware changes and my executive program rebooted all my strings and processor functions, I felt slightly better and noticed I could make decisions a lot faster. It did not take long to analyze my entire being felt better. My memory was expanded hence I could download, and store far more information than ever attempted."

"I imagine you spent a lot of time with Marla and Beryl?"

"While they were attending the PFM Academy, they spent all their extra time in the robot lab. I saw them frequently."

"And they were tinkering with you and working on you?"

"Yes. Professor Dabbler Montovan was always encouraging them to figure out how to make me waterproof. The fact I survived at the bottom of the ocean goes to show you how successful they were."

"What do you think led to making you so watertight you could withstand great sea pressure?"

"Each part of my body is self-contained. My arms and legs have their own pumps and actuators. The only connection between my arms, legs and head and the rest of the body, is fiber optic and power line in an integrated watertight cable that is molded and filled with a coagulating gel that turns into a soft solid upon curing."

"What is that gel compared to Earth products?"

"It has properties like your RTV used in electronics and many other functions in this world."

"You know a lot about my world?"

"Yes, when I left here to go back to the Plastradavious Empire to get help and retribution for the killing of Marla and Beryl, I took back Fifty Terabytes of information and stored it in PFM computer archives I would have access to later to study."

"Is there anything in there you find of value?"

"Of course, the Bhagavad Gita, Confucius Twenty Analects, Tibetan Buddhist Pathway to Enlightenment, the Torah, Quran, and the Bible."

"Have you studied any of them?"

"Yes, I encoded all of it and read it throughout and analyzed them all at least once, some twice or more."

"What is all that like compared to Plastradavious religions?"

"I think in some way they all address similar issues such as, is there life elsewhere in the Universe and what are the moral obligations for people to live and exist in ways as to not be savages."

"Having great exposure to humanity and a lot of other civilizations in the universe, how do you compare us Earth people?"

"Overall, you are *Noble Savages*."

"How do you come by giving us such an evaluation?"

"General Kenney, I am well versed on the lifestyles of civilizations on at least 500 planets. Some of them have no wars, others have no diseases, some of them have never experienced famine or hunger, some of them have no idea what snow and ice are. So, you see there is a degree of noble savages just within our own galaxy. You are not alone."

"Tell me how you eventually ended up on a spaceship with Marla and Beryl?"

"As Marla and Beryl advanced as robot designers they

created some very capable robots that were employed by the military and eventually space exploration. I was their guineapig. They took their improvements they did to me and put them on next generation robots. I went through a half dozen changes of arms, legs, and torso. Even my head was changed out a couple times to install more sensors."

"That must have been an interesting experience."

"It certainly was, and all of those engineering changes were filmed and archived to help train future robot designers."

"How did Marla and Beryl end up as space explorers?"

"Since they were designing robots to assist in space exploration, Marla and Beryl were sent out with some of their robot creations to monitor it and adjust as required to fit the task at hand. Sometimes they took me along because I did not require food and water or air to breath and Marla and Beryl knew there were a lot of tasks, they could give me to assist in their evaluation and report generation. Their unique ability to figure out tasking for robots on space exploration soon gave them an opportunity to go on long space missions to act as tech reps to keep the robots running in good order and adjust if necessary. This mission they died on was their fifteenth long distance exploration mission."

"Did you accompany them on some of those missions?"

"Yes, all of them."

"How did you get more involved with them, what was the catalyst if I may ask?"

"Certainly. In the early years they were experimenting on new ways of programming me. Marla concluded if she took me home, I would evolve by watching her actions and hanging out."

The lab at first was skeptical and fearful of allowing Marla walk out of the robot lab with such an expensive piece of advanced robotic development, but it was myself that quickly turned it around in favor of Marla's idea."

"And how did you do that?"

"I reminded Professor Dabbler Montovan I always had continuous wireless communication with the LAB and would report my location and any incident that occurred while there. Plus, they realized I had photographic surveillance capabilities and they would receive actual video of any predicament I found myself in."

"Did those capabilities come into play for any incidents?"

"Certainly. Parts of Plastradavious has areas that decayed due to corruption and criminal enterprise. On one occasion when Marla stopped at a store on the way home, we were accosted by a dozen individuals who were involved in nefarious activities that wanted to rob Marla who was well dressed and didn't know this was a bad area to avoid."

"I was dressed in non-assuming attire what you Earth people would say made me appear to look weak or nerdy, partly to hide the imperfections in my construction, including sunglasses to shield the imperfections in my eyes."

"The group surrounded us and pulled out weapons and threatened bodily harm unless Marla hand over her mall purse."

"What happened?"

"I advised the perpetrators I didn't want to hurt them and to back off, but they refused to take my warning and when they lunged at us, I quickly disabled half of them, and the other half ran away like scared rats."

"No harm came to Marla?"

"None whatsoever. The storekeeper who was often shaken down by this gang called the authorities when he saw trouble coming and the authorities quickly arrived and assessed the situation."

"I bet they got quite interested when they discovered you were a robot."

"That did create a bureaucratic nightmare since Marla and I both were technically PFM members, and the law enforcement had no legal jurisdiction over us. I injured a couple of the criminals quite badly and they wanted to arrest me until I explained to them that Marla and I did not fall under their jurisdiction and soon PFM military police who have jurisdiction over them arrived in good numbers and took over the case."

"What happened to the criminals?"

"Half of them went to a law enforcement hospital where prisoners are taken for medical treatment then faced justice. Thanks to my video recording they were able to identify all the gang members and when confronted with lengthy prison sentences they agreed to cooperate, so authorities were able to arrest the crime boss and shut down his syndicate. That impoverished area quickly sprang back to life thanks to all the criminal element removed.

"How did you staying with Marla help program you?"

"By observing her and everything she did I quickly discovered many things which were pointers to other things to evaluate. At that point in time my robot operating system called RBOS, allowed me multiprocessing. I had quadruple redundancy on my wireless connections and was able to go through lab computers on four separate channels to investigate and study things that Marla brought to my attention."

"Give me an example."

"Marla read a lot of books. Some were on tablet screens; others were on the wasteful practice of printing them on paper. She had a significant mixture of each type. While she was in her bedroom sleeping, I was always reading all her books and tablets, which gave me more pointers to things to investigate and check out."

"So, it was Marla who did most of your training, indirectly through this process?"

"No. Marla and Beryl were friends but not lovers at that time. Sometimes Marla had things to do, such as evenings with other men or women friends. When that happened, she arranged for Beryl to take custody of me, so I went to his home. There he had an equal amount of sources of information which I investigated. One day Beryl observed me reading a book and got the bright idea to take me to a library. On days with Beryl, we often went to the library together where I had huge access to information."

"A library has a huge amount of books and tablet books in it, how did you determine which books to read?"

"That was a simple process. I saw what Beryl was reading or other library goers and let them randomly lead me to the various sources. That random process quickly gave me a broad exposure which further helped me discover many more things to investigate."

"I suppose you were able to absorb vast amounts of information which then helped you evolve?"

"It did but I quickly ran into a problem I filled up my memory banks and storing information at the Lab computers to later recall wasted a lot of time and effort, so I determined I needed a bigger memory."

"What was done about that?"

"Unfortunately, I was operating with the maximum density memory they could install in me with the processor technology and memory technology available at the time."

"How did you handle it? Slow down and wait?"

"Since memory size was now a big issue for me, I cleared out a lot of memory space by uploading all unnecessary files to the Lab computer system giving me adaquate storage to study computer memory design. I found every article recently produced discussing advances in computer memory design and the issues of adapting a new memory or increasing the bandwidth of existing processors to benefit by having larger memories. I concluded a new architecture would be needed to increase bandwidth to a level where a processor would benefit from having a much larger memory. Taking in account all the information I gleaned from multiple reports and some rather unique suggestions by computer architects, a new topology that would give a processor far more robust connectivity and throughput."

"Can you give me any idea what that was like?"

"Actually, I was quite surprised here on planet Earth you have a scientist by the name of S. Y. Kung who taught at Princeton University who developed systolic arrays for your attempts to develop the Ronald Reagan Star Wars technology. A lot of the architecture I developed was a lot like Professor Kung's systolic arrays that allowed me to increase throughput by a massive amount."

"So, if I have my guys pull up systolic arrays, it might give us some ideas on how to increase memory throughput?"

"Most certainly."

"I take it that memory interface was built and you now, have it?"

"Yes. I put together a white paper and gave it to Beryl who took it to PARPA for consideration. PARPA looked at it and decided to attempt building a device which took a couple years, and I was eventually fitted with that new PARPA device constituting a much larger memory and segmented CPUs to do far more transactions quickly."

"What's PARPA?"

Plastradavious Advanced Research Projects Activity. They are the bureaucracy that choses and funds promising new technology development for the PFM.

"Do you operate with those PARPA computers now?"

"Yes, my RBOS runs on PARPA technology."

"How did Marla and Beryl become close?"

"They were always together and eventually decided they liked each other more than others. I might have helped seal the deal."

"How did you do that?"

"They would confide in me like a friend and ask me questions they knew I had vast resources in direct access that didn't require searches through computer networks. They both were vivid dreamers and in conversations with me they described their dreams, and each believed they must have had a past life. Eventually I got them talking about this and when they told each other their dreams they felt their dreams were almost identical in nature with the same characters and events. They eventually believed they were lovers in previous lives and had been reincarnated and brought to this life to be together again."

"That must have been a terrible sight sitting on the bottom

of the ocean with water coming into the space craft and the pressure rising to unbearable levels."

"They were not unhappy it seemed. They enjoyed their last minutes in each other's arms knowing they would be reincarnated and find each other again in the future."

Tiāncái did the most unbelievable action. General Kenney was completely captivated with what he saw. Up on the twenty foot viewer screen just like he was at a movie was the final scene with Marla and Beryl. They love each other to no ends. And when it was getting to the point they could no longer sustain, they departed together in a very romantic kiss that never ended. Their bodies were simply lifeless holding that pose as an endless message to all to behold. Tiāncái had captured the moment of love and death combining into something along the line of a Greek Tragedy. Soon the lights in the video recording were going out as Tiāncái was shutting down the ship at that time to protect it in hopes it might one day be salvaged. In the final moments the last remaining lit indicators on the ship's control consoles were extinguished. Tiāncái's own existence then went black as he too had shut down.

"Thank you for sharing all that with me. It gives me a lot to think about."

"General Kenney, you are a Noble Savage, but I have faith in that you will do good in the future."

"Thank you, I appreciate your comment."

"I would like to say goodbye to my friends LR and Doctor Hudson now. Just like I had to say goodbye to Marla and Beryl, this will be the last time I will see them."

"Sure, lets step down on the tarmac and find out where they are."

General Kenney led Tiāncái down the space craft ladder and back a few feet stood LR, Doctor Hudson, and Sheri who had great curiosity on their faces since the General had spent quite a long period of time alone with Tiāncái.

"Here they are," General Kenney said and approached them.

Tiāncái approached LR and Doctor Hudson and said, "Before I leave, I wanted to say goodbye to you and thank you for restoring me so that I could do what I needed to do."

"We are glad you were designed so well that we were able to do it," Doctor Hudson responded.

"Marla and Beryl were excellent robot designers and I owe all my ruggedness to their forethoughts in how they constructed me."

"What's your plans Tiāncái?"

"Life will not be the same or as enjoyable as it was with Marla and Beryl, but I have a few things to finish for them they did not complete prior to our mission."

"Sounds like you have something interesting to do?"

"Yes, I might even have offspring."

"What do you mean by that?"

"Successor Robots."

"I hope they are as good as you."

"With Marla and Beryl's innovations they might even be better."

Tiāncái held out his hand to LR and said, "Thank you LR for everything you did and be sure and take care of Doctor Hudson."

"I certainly will as long as he allows me to give him help when he's driving."

Tiāncái then turned to Doctor Hudson and said, "You have an excellent assistant here. You have time to train him to be your legacy."

"I'll give it my best shot."

Tiāncái did a Plastradavious deep bow, that seemed similar to some Earth cultures, then raised back up and turned around and walked back up into his spaceship. As soon as he was through the door, the latter pulled up into the hull and the door closed. A few seconds later the spacecraft started going up into the air twisting as it changed heading. The speed increased rapidly and as it was nearly a mile away, the rear end lit up as the propulsion motors came online and the craft then moved away very quickly and pitched upwards and shot up into the sky at an amazing velocity. In just a few seconds it was no longer visible.

Tiāncái now wondered, how did Marla and Beryl determine they were reincarnated lovers? It had to be the case since they never discussed any subtle memories of a time before they met. Was it possible there was a dimension skip that resulted in the loss of many possible memories until they reconnected? How any of the memories came to be, was also a profound mystery.

Chapter Twenty-One
Doctor Hudson

Doctor Hudson's days were numbered. His age crept up on him and soon the luster of coming to work was no longer there. Without fanfare or a retirement party he ceased coming to work.

LR was caught up in his own world and their former illustrious lab was no more and he was doing a variety of other tasks, getting by, and simply waiting for his own retirement.

Doctor Hudson was slowly starting to have physical problems and more and more difficulty in getting around. Soon it was a foregone conclusion his automobile, the tank was a hazard to the public and his doctor advised him to avoid driving it.

Doctor Hudson was slowly turning into a bitter man as life just no longer had its sweet moments, especially with the loss of mobility and no longer being gainfully employed doing interesting things. Worse yet he woke up one morning thinking about his situation and realized he had no authentic Metaphysical Consciousness as he thought about that lovely song by the performer Carly Paoli who sang: "If nothing is sacred, what are we fighting for?"

Doctor Hudson was about to call it quits, swallow a bunch of sleeping pills, sitting in his recliner watching cable TV News not being inspired at all and never receiving visitors.

Suddenly the doorbell rang.

"I wonder who the hell that is?"

Doctor Hudson looked through the security lenses on the door and could see a well-dressed young man with a suit on. It seemed safe to open the door so he opened it and asked, "What can I do for you?"

"Doctor Hudson?"

"Yes, that's me."

"Sir, may I have a word with you?"

"And who are you?"

"My name is Beryl."

"Do I know you from somewhere?"

"No, you knew my father."

"Who's your father?"

"Tiāncái."

Doctor Hudson stood there utterly stunned.

"Is this some kind of joke?"

"My father asked me to give this to you and I would like to tell you why I'm here." Beryl handed Doctor Hudson a very thin tablet, thinner than he ever seen before and as soon as the tablet scanners detected Doctor Hudson's face, with a few more wrinkles, it started a video for Doctor Hudson.

"Doctor Hudson, I'm sorry I'm not there with you. I have a lot of things I'm doing and can't take the time to visit, or I would have. I thought under the circumstances I would send my son to you and give you an update about myself and also if he can be assistance to you in any way, he's there to help."

Doctor Hudson knew very few people knew about Tiāncái and realized the enormity of this and looked up at Beryl and asked, "Are you a robot Beryl?"

"Doctor Hudson, yes I am."

"Alright, come in please and tell me all about it."

After a while, Beryl updated Doctor Hudson with all the events that shaped Tiāncái's future and what he was now doing at his own personal robot lab where he was working with Plastradavious PMF space exploration. Then the discussions turned to why Beryl was really visiting.

"You see Doctor Hudson, my father knew the day would come when it would be harder for you to get around and you would have challenges with life, whether it be personal security or mobility. I'm here to help you."

"What if something happens to you? I have no ability to take care of any issues that may arise with your robotics."

"Not to be concerned Doctor Hudson, my sister Marla will check up on us now and then in case I have any issues and report back to dad any concerns."

"Alright then. Do you think you can learn how to drive my car?"

"I'm sure that should not be an issue."

As days and weeks passed, Doctor Hudson was feeling better all the time. He even discovered Beryl was a world class chef and nutritionist and for some strange reason when he sent him to the store to buy things, he never needed cash.

Doctor Hudson's tank was slowly restored to mint condition and was no longer the eyesore on the block. Some of the neighbor's young teenage daughters started trying to establish friendships with young Beryl but he was so totally aloof. Doctor Hudson's final years were as good as they could be. Thanks to Beryl giving him back his mobility he got to do some of the finer things in life such as attending the symphony or get wheeled around the park and zoo. Doctor Hudson's time eventually came, and he was no more.

When Beryl knew he was gone, he had his sister pick him up and they notified the authorities about Doctor Hudson's demise.

Doctor Hudson had no local relatives and as the authorities dealt with his situation, eventually a distant relative was discovered and summoned to come take possession of all his personal items, real estate, and net holdings which Beryl had multiplied for him using advanced alien technology to quickly multiply his wealth, so the relative who wasn't thrilled when he first showed up was soon delighted to discover he was now worth a lot thanks to Doctor Hudson.

Doctor Hudson in his will and power of attorney left a nice gift to LR. Doctor Hudson knew in his final days he was expiring, and he too was interested in reincarnation and as part of his very nice gift to LR he wrote, "I'll see you in the next life."

"I am a dreamer,"

"Maybe I could comb the mountains
In the wind
Or sit upon this stoop and grieve.

I was not much of anything
But like a parasite I breathed
And thought of daffodils.

Maybe I could live again to gain
Something brilliant
Like the shining of the moon
Or a highway to Spain
Or anything unusual for me,
Like climbing up thorn trees.

Maybe I could sit awhile and see
Myself backward
Like the other people look at me
When all alone I take the sea
To twist into a poem.

Maybe maybe maybe

There is still a possibility

For such a dreamer me."

Poem by W. Edwin Ver Becke who passed in 1996.

San Diego California

May 1st 2022.

Paul D. Escudero

保罗·道格拉斯·埃斯库德罗

The reason why I also sign my name in Chinese is to show my love for Chinese culture.

GLOSSARY AND NAMES

Part 1

Chevolite forces on Arkadanstra
Chevolite government
Colonel Kollins (Jeff)
Cronstine base and flight school.
Graviton: operates off gravity waves
Harkey Albatross Varco Lindy Foster
Harkey's home planet Ergzlt
Lexi Marceau, a beautiful singer
Planet Beckcen
Praximus Gartuka enemy stronghold
Provincial city of Darvner
Spetznar Enemy troops.
Spetznar strong hold area of Planet Kattnoggar
Squadron Commander, Lieutenant Colonel Baxel
Swiftshire Hotel in Bazanga Metropolis
Tunneling Spatializers

Part 2

Amber Godot: Bradly's lover

Bradly: from the town of Nazara

Capmoc-Drysvinskle: a tactical space craft maneuver

Chakravotry Class Fast Attack Space Warship Drakon Laser System.

Collectivist Confederacy Peoples (CCP) *Sinrex* class space Warship

Dongar: Crew Member

Enemy Collectivist Confederacy Peoples (CCP) *Near Star* class space warship

from the dormant volcano Avon Mons

Lugar Perfecto Bajo El Sol: Location of training

Madam Ayumi's Bar on the space station

Pasagralgian Defense Directorate

Planet Nartone where weapon test occurred

Sandra Lane: girlfriend

Tachyon Differentiators and Neutrino Spatial Pinger's along with their wide spectrum Chirp Convoluters

William (Bill) Grady Rachel

Part 3

Camile: a beautiful female Vrackline alien researcher.

Camp Pùtàiyáng 曝太阳 Etarka Falls part of Emperor Clauvious retreat

Canaris Bartrum: Space Explorer HMY Xīwàng-Zhīxíng pilot

Her Majesty Yānjoyduī: HMY

Light blue skinned people Vracklines

Míngquè civilization 明确 (crystal clear)

Míngquè Emperor Clauvious

Míngquè General Raskutan,

Noriyogan 海苔 瑜 珈 Vracklines translator designer and chief research officer.

Planet Zharkon-Xestra [Canaris Bartrum's home planet]

Planet-X's actual name was Crysantralon (Vracklines)

Red Brick Head 红砖头 Hóngzhuāntóu second female researcher – also a Spy.

Space Explorer HMY Xīwàng-Zhīxīng HMY Hope-star 希望之星

Violet and Ralcody: Vrackline kidnapped slaves

Vracklines Standard Code for Information Interchange VSCII

Yānjoyduī Planetary Security Forces Yānduī 烟堆 smokestack

Zainia female robot.

Part 4

Bradly's planet: Nartone
Bret Chancellor: Assistant Director of Starfish Undersea Survey Solutions
Demonic propensities
Jamison: salvage expert
PITA: Pain in the Arse
Plastradavious Empire: Tiāncái's home worlds.
Professor Dabbler Montovan
Rusnarians the enemy
SDHNC: Stiff Dude has no conscious
Sea Snake: Tethered submersible video recording system
Sheri and Ralph security plants at canteen in area 51.

The research vessel *Galactopus* operates bottom scanners and *Sea Snake*
Tiāncái's friends Marla and Beryl crew members of the ill-fated spaceship
Torch of knowledge
We are all swallowed up by the Tigress of nescience.
When pure love is killed the angels weep.
Yīnhuā: 阴花 female flower

AUTHOR'S NOTE:

This is a work of fiction. There are no living persons in this book. In fact, none of the story takes place on Earth, until a small sequence near the end.

This is a story about reincarnation. Some religions believe in reincarnation. I've read the Bhagavad Gita once before and I'm now reading it again with clearer eyes. I've studied the Tibetan Monk's Pathway to enlightenment. I understand their views of reincarnation and Karma. Just like in the Christian and Muslim religions, you must have *faith* since there is no compelling evidence any of it's true. Back in the Roman and Greek times, they had their gods as well and you had to have *faith* since there were no real direct evidence to show these spiritualistic ideas were created by the supernatural. When more advanced aliens arrive and expose their religious ideas to us, will they be operating off *faith*?

The main reason why I read the Bhagavad Gita in its entirety was my fascination as to why J. Robert Oppenheimer the grandfather of our nuclear weapons program studied it on almost a daily basis and quoted it with his famous statement after the first hydrogen bomb blast: ‹Now I am become death, the destroyer of worlds›.

Oppenheimer quotes Bhagvad Gita "Destroyer of worlds" after atomic bomb test - Bing video

You can imagine how I felt when I read that statement in the Bhagavad Gita that Oppenheimer quoted.

I do not have *faith*, nor am I a skeptic. I simply do not know.

I call myself a Galacticist. That means my focus is to the stars and the heavens. Unlike many with *faith*, I lack enough information to decide.

In some of my books I've warned the public about the folly of advertising our presence to the galaxy before we discover who the good aliens are and who are the bad aliens.

And how would you know?

Just like the Japanese cut off themselves from the outside world for over 300 years to figure things out, we need to cut ourselves off from the galaxy for 300 years and avoid EXPOSURE. Take that time to figure it out.

We need to take the time to covertly study the galaxy and make the proper determinations of who we should be involved with. But sadly, it may be too late. Our exposure is already most likely to lead to a tragedy as one day some aliens during the course of dinner asks another, "How does that human meat taste like?"

"It tastes like chicken."

American Space Researchers are all now being swallowed up by the *Tigress of Nescience* by their silence over the recent U.S. Navy release of UFO (UAP) video; my comments are already too late.

The fact the Navy and the DOD will not say those

are extra terrestrial space craft proves they are *gutless wonders* and what I would call cowards, promotion seekers who will march along smartly like robots because their civilian bosses have not given them permission to say *what they really think the UAP's are.*

Hate to tell you great military minds the obvious:

The average Polar Bear knows those are Alien spacecraft.

Get over it already Pentagon, the public is not that stupid and just because you guys are cowards doesn't mean we are. Yea we are ready for disclosure, might as well get it over. If organized religions can't take it, then its too bad they painted themselves in a corner with *Faith.*

And if they think its bad now, just wait until the Aliens show up with their own *Faith* that is diametrically opposed to what our major religions on this planet peddle.

I'm not an atheist. I just do not know all the answers mainly because science and society doesn't know either and people who operate off *Faith* are fools.

This is how the Pentagon should be treating these UAP's if they are the brilliant planners, they think they are:

If one or more groups of aliens came to this planet to investigate, they were probably followed here by another alien curious to why they showed up here.

Eventually as the various aliens spread knowledge of our presence here throughout the galaxy, the bad aliens who like low hanging fruit just might show up.

In the early part of the book, the battle of Praximus Gartuka takes place where the enemy Spetznar forces plundered the world and turned it into a garrison to launch raids to other planets.

Are we prepared to see our planet Earth turned into a garrison for an alien entity because we remain low hanging fruit because cowards at the Pentagon and elsewhere are too scared to say the obvious, those UFOs are piloted by Alien extra-terrestrials?

In the story I mention Mozart's Requiem. This is perhaps one of the finest compositions ever created in the history of mankind. There is some intrigue surrounding this piece and was not completed until after Mozart's death by an opportunist. Information from Wikipedia:

The **Requiem** in D minor, K. 626, is a requiem mass by Wolfgang Amadeus Mozart (1756–1791). Mozart composed part of the Requiem in Vienna in late 1791, but it was unfinished at his death on 5 December the same year. A completed version dated 1792 by Franz Xaver Süssmayr was delivered to Count Franz von Walsegg, who commissioned the piece for a requiem service on 14 February 1792 to commemorate the first anniversary of the death of his wife Anna at the age of 20 on 14 February 1791.

The autograph manuscript shows the finished and orchestrated Introit in Mozart›s hand, and detailed drafts of the Kyrie and the sequence Dies irae as far as the first eight bars of the *Lacrymosa* movement, and the Offertory. It cannot be shown to what extent Süssmayr may have depended on now lost "scraps of paper" for the remainder; he later claimed the Sanctus and Benedictus and the Agnus Dei as his own.

Walsegg probably intended to pass the Requiem off

as his own composition, as he is known to have done with other works. This plan was frustrated by a public benefit performance for Mozart's widow <u>Constanze</u>. She was responsible for a number of stories surrounding the composition of the work, including the claims that Mozart received the commission from a mysterious messenger who did not reveal the commissioner's identity, and that Mozart came to believe that he was writing the requiem for his own funeral.

I suppose the audience is wondering why I would write a book that showcases the notion of reincarnation. First of all, I say I'm a galacticist. What that means is I view all the answers I seek are out there in the galaxy. We may never find the answers stuck on planet Earth, so the sooner we get out there the better.

I studied the Bhagavad Gita and the Tibetan Buddhist Pathway to Enlightenment. I've also delved into Confucius and his 20 Analects. I read the entire New Testament of the Christian Bible and a large portion of the first part of the Old Testament seeking the answers to many questions I had.

What is common in all those religions? If something is shared in all of them, that means it is seriously meaningful.

They all require you to have *Faith*. All the information is anecdotal and some of it is based on a single conversation with one person.

A Galacticist lacks information to make an informed opinions or beliefs. For a Galacticist which I view myself, I can't make a logical decision based on *Faith*.

Having exposure to the information like I have in no way gives me the logical conclusion to have *Faith* in that information. Greek and Roman religions were exact science as well until *Faith* broke down and were supplanted with new ideas. Confucius Analects are approximately 2700 years old; the Christian Bible is 2000 years or so from its genesis, the Torah and Jewish religion which contains major section of the Old Testament is quite a bit older. Some Jewish concepts go back 8,000 years or older. Some of the items discussed in the Bhagavad Gita are upwards to 6000 years old. I have a Bhagavad Gita paper copy, (third gave the other two away), but you can also read it online: Bhagavad-gita Online version(s) | Krishna.com

Buddhism is an Indian religion or philosophical tradition based on a series of original teachings attributed to Gautama Buddha. It originated in ancient India as a Sramana tradition sometime between the 6th and 4th centuries BCE, spreading through much of Asia. It is the world's fourth-largest religion. Buddhism took hold in Asia mainly because Korean women adopted it and greatly expanded it at a time Korea was a major power in Asia. The Bannermen Dynasty of China was Korean centric.

To really get a good understanding of the concepts of Reincarnation, Krishna Science and Buddhist Pathway to Enlightenment has very interesting discussions about it.

What do I think about Reincarnation? I can conceive Reincarnation as well as I can *time travel* which I recently published a book about. What that means is I understand what others say happens. I would not have the basic clue of how it really works (or if it works) even though I've read a lot of information about it.

It comes down to this. You must decide what you believe and what *Faith* you want to have. For me since I'm a Galacticist, I can't make an informed decision about it since I lack information. I can watch from the sidelines and observe others explore the mystery.

Just think how much more calm life would be if reincarnation was real and we knew it happened. Some Hindus would argue that point with me.

The idea of the soul and the super soul as discussed in the Bhagavad Gita, gives you something to ponder. As someone who's been around electronics all his life including government programs, I can see where the functionality of the soul and the super soul makes sense. If I knew it to be true for a fact, that would be very comforting to me.

Now you know why so many Hindus are comfortable. Their feelings about this eliminates a lot of thinking they might otherwise have to do. But at the same token people in India who bathe themselves in the Ganges River, curse reincarnation as they feel their current horrible lives are a result of Karma in their prior lives. Immersion in the Ganges River is thought to purify them of their sins and facilitate liberation from an eternal cycle of life and death (in other words, reincarnation). Those bathers want it to end, they do not want another life of possible misery.

What I did with this book is to put forth a simple concept of two lovers that had love so great that in their next life they were allowed to be together again. I told the story of how it all came about and the circumstances of what led to the heart-breaking death when the two were no where near the end of their lives when one of them was suddenly taken away from them. In this case it was futuristic science fiction space related combat scenarios that did it.

In the first three portions of the book where reincarnations happened, the action was live and apparent with those involved. But in the final section, the awareness of the couple who died in each other's arms was presented in the eyes of a smart robot. In the spirit of science fiction what better messenger could you have than a robot? For those who read the book, you are probably aware this may be the first science fiction book on reincarnation that has several robots in the stories and scenes at Area 51.

In my *book 51 Reasons to Ask 51 Questions*, the idea of the soul is presented in a science fiction manner. That book was written after I completed reading Bhagavad Gita and decided I wanted to discuss souls which is part of the drama.

Something created this magnificent universe. Would something (many refer to it as God) so fantastic to create all this also be able to time travel or facilitate reincarnation?

In one of the four stories presented in this book, the character at a young age had vivid memories of dive bombing a WW2 aircraft blowing up aircraft carriers. At a young age I had those same dreams. Was I reincarnated from a Pilot?

Since I love many things Chinese, my Chinese name:

保罗·道格拉斯·埃斯库德罗